PLAYBOY UNDER THE MISTLETOE

BY
JOANNA NEIL

MILLS & BOON

All the characters in this book have no existence outside the imagination of the author, and have no relation whatsoever to anyone bearing the same name or names. They are not even distantly inspired by any individual known or unknown to the author, and all the incidents are pure invention.

First published in Great Britain 2010
Harlequin Mills & Boon Limited,
Eton House, 18-24 Paradise Road, Richmond, Surrey TW9 1SR

© Joanna Neil 2010

ISBN: 978 0 263 87921 6

Harlequin Mills & Boon policy is to use papers that are natural, renewable and recyclable products and made from wood grown in sustainable forests. The logging and manufacturing process conform to the legal environmental regulations of the country of origin.

Printed and bound in Spain
by Litografia Rosés, S.A., Barcelona

'There's no problem that I can see, Jassie, my love. You only have to look up to see that.' Ben placed a curled finger lightly beneath her chin and tilted her head upwards.

A sprig of mistletoe hovered over them, the pale, translucent berries a stark contrast to the dark green leaves. 'You see?' he said, his voice a coaxing rumble against her cheek. 'Mistletoe is for lovers…and I'd love more than anything to fulfil its promise…to kiss you and make you mine, just for one delicious moment.'

Ben didn't wait for her to answer, and if the truth were known she couldn't have spoken at all right then. The mistletoe gleamed faintly above them, and she knew that what *she* wanted more than anything was for him to kiss her…a long, sweet and thorough kiss… And, as if he had read her mind, that was exactly what he did.

When **Joanna Neil** discovered Mills & Boon®, her life-long addiction to reading crystallised into an exciting new career writing Medical™ Romance. Her characters are probably the outcome of her varied lifestyle, which includes working as a clerk, typist, nurse and infant teacher. She enjoys dressmaking and cooking at her Leicestershire home. Her family includes a husband, son and daughter, an exuberant yellow Labrador and two slightly crazed cockatiels. She currently works with a team of tutors at her local education centre, to provide creative writing workshops for people interested in exploring their own writing ambitions.

Recent titles by the same author:

THE SECRET DOCTOR
HAWAIIAN SUNSET, DREAM PROPOSAL
NEW SURGEON AT ASHVALE A&E
POSH DOC, SOCIETY WEDDING

CHAPTER ONE

WHY on earth had she agreed to do this? Jasmine risked a glance down from the lofty platform of the metal fire tower and immediately regretted it. Just looking out from that height made her feel dizzy, and it didn't help that the eager crowd watching from below were way too far away for their faces to be seen clearly. At this rate, with nausea and vertigo both coming into play, she'd very soon be a patient for real, instead of simply acting the part.

'You'll be fine,' Mike had said, in cheerful mood after he had persuaded her to take part. 'You're used to walking the fells in the Lake District, aren't you? And I recall you said you had attempted to climb Scafell Pike and Helvellyn, so this should be no problem at all. We're demonstrating a crag rescue here, and you know how that goes. Forget that this looks like a scaffolding structure. Just imagine that you're stranded on Scafell Pike, and everything will drop into place.'

Jasmine winced at his choice of words. Right now, the notion of anything dropping anywhere was enough to make her stomach plunge all over again. Not that Mike had any qualms about this venture. He was a coordinator for the various mountain rescue teams in this part of the country, and of course he would have very few concerns about the exercise.

'It's not at all the same,' she had protested. 'I had time to prepare for those and they didn't present me with a sheer, vertical face...not the bits I attempted, anyway.' She had shuddered. 'I can't think why I let you talk me into it.'

Mike had chuckled. Determinedly optimistic, he had urged her towards the base of the tower and coaxed her up the ladder to begin the ascent, following close behind her.

Which was why she was stuck here now, alone on the topmost platform, pretending to be someone who was lying injured on a crag. Lying injured... The words struck a chord of memory, and she recalled what Mike had said. 'Flail your arms around a bit and cry out for help. The crowd will love that. Then sink to your knees and pretend to topple over. After that, all you have to do is lie still and let the rescue team do the rest.'

So that's what she would do...anything to get this over and done with. She would perform her heart out for the crowd of people who were watching the rescue demonstration from the safety of the fire station's courtyard.

She wrapped her arms around herself in an effort to keep warm. It was not the best of times to be carrying out this operation—a freezing cold December day, with a smattering of snow in the air and the wind buffeting her from all angles.

It was also the final day of her course, marking the end of her week-long stay at the luxurious nearby hotel, and maybe if she lay down and thought about the comforting lounge waiting back there, with its log-burning fire, and the delicious cocktails or the aromatic pot of hot coffee that the waitress would bring, it would take away some of the stress of her present situation.

With that in mind, she went into her act with a bit more enthusiasm. 'Help,' she shouted, waving her arms and pretending to stumble. 'Help me, someone, please, help me. My leg's broken.'

Then she sank to the floor of the platform and waited for her rescuer to arrive.

It wasn't long before she heard sounds of activity coming from the ground below, along with the clink of chains and pulleys, and then, finally, she felt the thud of movement as someone began climbing the tower.

The whole edifice seemed to judder as her rescuer approached, but perhaps it was her overwrought imagination playing tricks on her. The tower was solidly based, wasn't it? It would not topple.

Even so, a faint film of perspiration broke out on her brow. The nausea began to return in full force and she muttered a few curses that should have had Mike squirming in his boots if he'd been anywhere near.

'Whatever did Mike do to deserve all that vitriol?' a deep, male voice enquired, the tone threaded with a hint of amusement. 'Letting loose a plague on him is kind of overkill, don't you think?'

'You wouldn't say so if you were in my shoes,' she retorted, sucking in a sharp breath. 'I could have been watching all this from a safe distance if it weren't for him. I could even have slipped away out of the cold and gone back to the hotel to enjoy a glass of something laced with a warming dash of brandy.'

'You can still do that.' The man swung his legs over the metal rail and dropped down onto the platform beside her. He hauled a metal basket stretcher over the bar, and placed it down on the platform floor. Then he looked at her, taking in her pale features, and in an instant the smile on his face became transfixed, very much as though he had suddenly found himself locked in a time warp.

'Jasmine?' The word was a soft breath of sound. 'Is it really you?' His gaze was fastened on her, his eyes widening as though he couldn't believe what he was seeing.

She stared back at him. 'Ben?' All at once she couldn't breathe. What was he doing here? What did he have to do with the rescue services, and how was it that she should run into him again after all this time?

'How long has it been?' he asked, echoing her thoughts. 'Five years?'

'Something like that.' She frowned. Her jaw was locked in a spasm of disbelief and shock was beginning to set in. She had never imagined that she would ever see him again, but here he was, in the flesh, and even after all the years that had gone by, it was clear that he still had the ability to make her heart pound and cause the air in her lungs to be constricted.

He hadn't changed at all. He was as ruggedly handsome as ever, his black hair neatly cropped to outline his sculpted features, those blue eyes ever watchful and his mouth beautifully expressive, just as she remembered.

'You're down here to take part in one of the courses being run at the Royal Pennant Hotel, I take it? I've been speaking to a few of the people who were attending the medical seminars.' He had come out of his reverie and had snapped back into action in an instant, beginning to prepare the metal cradle to receive its patient.

It wasn't so easy for Jasmine to get back into the swing of things, but she made an effort. 'That's right. "Critical Care and The Role of the First Responder".' This last day was taken up with the activities of the emergency services, and although it wasn't an essential part of her course, she had stayed on to get a better idea of what was involved. It was already on the cards that one of these days her job with A and E might involve her going out on call. In fact, up until now the idea of doing that had been quite appealing.

'We'd better slide you onto this stretcher and get you strapped in,' Ben said, becoming businesslike. 'People will be wondering what's going on.'

How had he managed to return to his customary efficiency within a matter of minutes? She felt oddly disgruntled. It hadn't taken him long to get over his astonishment at seeing her again, had it? But, then, why should she expect him to be affected in any way by meeting up with her? He had made his final break with the village five years ago, leaving without so much as a backward glance, and why should it matter to him that he had left her nursing a bruised and battered heart?

He frowned, glancing at her briefly. 'Are you all right?'

'Yes, I'm fine.' She wasn't going to let him in on any of her thoughts. Far better that he should remain in blissful ignorance. Ben Radcliffe had the power to unsettle her without even trying, and she had discovered long ago that her only defence against him was to keep her feelings locked away inside her.

She shivered a little as soft flakes of snow began to drift around her, settling here and there on her jacket. 'Shouldn't there be someone else up here with you, doing this work?' she asked.

He shook his head. 'The powers that be planned this as a one-man rescue...for places where there is restricted access. So I'm on my own. But, no matter... I'll splint the broken leg and lift you into the cradle as gently as I can.' He gave a half-smile. 'It shouldn't be too difficult. If I remember correctly, you were always a slip of a girl. It doesn't look as if things have changed very much.'

She frowned. How could he tell? She was wearing a waterproof jacket over a warm woollen sweater and snug-fitting denim jeans. For extra warmth she had added an Angora scarf. She wished she could pull it up over her face so that she could hide away from him, very much like an infant who imagined that with her eyes covered she could not be seen. She didn't want him reading her thoughts and dragging her vulnerabilities out into the open after all this time.

'Are you still living at the cottage?' he asked, deftly strapping splints into place. For extra security, he bound both of her legs together.

'Yes, I am. I never left Woodsley Bridge. I suppose I was fortunate in that I was able to do most of my medical training at the local hospital.' That had been the perfect option for her, but it hadn't done for Ben, had it? He'd started his medical tuition at a prestigious teaching hospital in Carlisle, some eighty miles away from Woodsley, coming home whenever he'd had a few days off just to make sure that his grandmother was all right. Even after she'd died, he'd come back to Mill House once in a while to keep an eye on things, but in the end, when other opportunities had beckoned, he couldn't wait to leave the village behind once and for all.

He glanced at her briefly. 'You always did love being home and having your family close by, didn't you?' His mouth made a bleak downward turn, but it was there only for an instant, so fleeting that she might have imagined it. His good humour was restored almost at once. 'Let's get you onto the stretcher, shall we?'

'All right.'

He knelt down beside her and leaned closer. 'I'm going to put my arms around you and lift you onto it. You don't need to do anything except keep very still. Let me do all the work, okay? We have to do this for real, just in case anyone down there has a long-range camera lens zoomed in on us.'

She made a face. That possibility was more than likely. The press were out in force, along with a team from the regional TV studios, keen to film the day's activities. It wasn't just the people on the course who were interested in what was going on—visitors from all around had come to see the events being staged by the rescue services. The hotel was doing a roaring trade.

He slid his arms around her, cradling her for a moment as he tested her weight, and that was almost her undoing. How many times had she wondered how it would feel to have him hold her this way, only to shy away from that thought? But now it was happening for real, so that she felt the strength of those arms closing around her and became aware of his innate gentleness, and above all she absorbed the warmth of his body next to hers.

'Ready?' His cheek brushed hers as he moved to get a better grip, sending a ripple of flame to run through her veins. In the next moment she was being lifted and very carefully placed on the stretcher. 'Okay, now we need to swing your legs into position. Easy now… Let me take the weight… Remember you have a nasty fracture. As soon as we have you settled, I'll fasten the harness.'

She was glad when the manoeuvre was finished. Every time his hands touched her, to position her or adjust a strap, her body went into meltdown. She wasn't at all sure how much more of this she could handle before she ended up giving herself away. It wouldn't do to have him know how her fickle, treacherous body responded to having him near.

He was the man who'd had the girls back home burning up in a fever of excitement. He'd only had to look in their direction and they had queued up, vying for his attention, and she had vowed she wouldn't be one of them. Ben was never going to stay around long enough to have a long-lasting relationship with anyone, was he? He couldn't even manage to make a go of things with his father.

'Are you all set?' He gave her a fleeting glance. 'I'm going to climb back over the tower and give the signal to the men on the ground so that they can begin hauling on the ropes to lower you down.'

She nodded warily. 'Are you quite sure they're going to hold?' The stretcher rocked from side to side as he tugged on the ropes and raised it up a fraction. Perhaps if she just closed her eyes and imagined she was swinging in a hammock in her mother's garden, this whole nightmare would end.

Her unease must have shown in her expression, because he chuckled softly. 'I'll be with you all the way to steady the stretcher as you make the descent. My harness is attached to the line so that I'll be alongside you. My feet will be on the base rail of the stretcher. Don't worry about a thing. I'll take care of you. Trust me.'

She closed her eyes fleetingly. She had long ago given up on any idea that he would be there to take care of her, or that he would be by her side whenever she needed him. Those were dreams from fantasy-land, weren't they? As her brother's friend, he had always been around, coming to the house, teasing her playfully until warm colour had filled her cheeks…but that was where it had ended. She had always been stranded on the fringes of his circle, looking on from afar, watching him struggle with his own demons and being unable to do anything to help.

He gave the signal to the waiting rescue team and then supported the basket stretcher as it was lifted over the rail. Then he followed, true to his word, accompanying her every bit of the way, his feet resting on the base of the stretcher, his long body leaning over her, his hands guiding the rope that lowered them to the ground. It was strangely comforting having him watch over her that way.

It was all over in a matter of minutes. 'You're safe now,' Ben said, giving her a reassuring look as they reached ground level. 'Home and dry. No worries.'

The people assembled in the courtyard were clearly impressed with the smoothness of the operation, and there were smiles all around. Ben supervised Jasmine's transfer into the waiting ambulance, and then Mike appeared with steaming mugs of coffee. Once she was out of range of the onlookers, the patient miraculously recovered.

Freed from the restraints of the harness, she sat up and looked around at the interior of the ambulance. The windows were darkened and with the doors closed they were spared from prying eyes.

'That was a great show,' Mike said, looking from one to the other. 'A very smooth rescue mission…so you'll be able to go home now and relax.' He paused. 'Until next time.' He grinned at Jasmine's pained expression.

'I don't think you should be having any ideas on that score,' she told him, giving him a look from under her lashes and clasping her coffee mug with both hands so that the warmth seeped into her. 'I'm not likely to be volunteering again any time soon.'

Mike feigned disappointment. 'Are you quite sure about that? I had you pencilled in for at least ten more meetings.'

She frowned. There was no way.

Sitting across from her on the opposite stretcher bed, Ben gave a wry smile. 'Jassie copes well enough on mountain slopes where she can fend for herself,' he said, 'but this is not quite the same. She's never been one to rely on others, so putting herself in someone else's hands must have been quite an ordeal. She's always been an independent soul.'

Jasmine sipped her coffee. His comment startled her. He seemed very sure of himself, as though he knew these things for a fact, so could it be that in the past he had actually been aware of her presence when she had thought him oblivious? It was true they had belonged to a group that regularly climbed the fells, but she had always teamed up with a friend on those occasions, whilst he had been accompanied by his fellow medical students. She frowned. Had he really taken note of what she was doing back then?

'Well, she did a great job today…you both did,' Mike said. He stood up. 'I'll say goodbye, then. Drink up and get warm. I should go and see what the rest of the team are up to…so thanks for your help this afternoon, both of you. I'll look forward to meeting up with you again.'

They nodded and murmured their goodbyes, and Mike left the ambulance, closing the door behind him to keep out the cold wind.

'What will you be doing now?' Ben asked, looking at Jasmine. 'I'm guessing this is your last day, isn't it? Are you planning on going straight back to the hotel?'

She nodded. 'I need to pack up my things and start heading back to the Lake District. It's been a good week, but I'm looking forward to going home. I'm supposed to be helping my mother put up Christmas decorations this weekend, and once that's done I'll make a start on my own place.'

'Are you sure that it's wise to travel that distance in this weather? It's over sixty miles away, isn't it?' Ben was frowning. 'The snow doesn't seem to be clearing up, and if it thickens and starts to settle, the roads could soon be covered. Wouldn't you do better to stay over-night at the hotel?'

'And risk being stranded here?' She shook her head. 'The main roads should stay fairly clear, I imagine, if the gritters have been at work. My room is booked for the night, but I think I'd prefer to set off as soon as possible and take my chances.'

'Hmm.' He studied her thoughtfully. 'So you won't be staying to have dinner at the hotel before you leave? It had occurred to me that perhaps we might have a meal together and talk over old times.'

She hesitated a moment before answering. From the way he was talking, he must believe that everything that had gone before was simply water under the bridge. The fact that his thoughtless actions had ruined her brother's life hadn't made so much as a dent in his confidence, had it? Or perhaps he felt that enough time had passed, the situation had changed, and they could all go on as if nothing had happened. For her own part, she couldn't make up her mind whether he was entirely to blame for what had gone on. She was fiercely loyal to her brother, but sometimes life didn't turn out quite the way people wanted.

'That would have been something to look forward to,' she answered softly, 'but I daren't risk any delay. I just have to stop by the hotel to pick up a suitcase and some packages—I managed to do quite a bit of Christmas shopping while I've been staying here. It seemed like too good an opportunity to miss, looking around the shops in a different town.'

Still, the thought of sitting down to eat a hot meal before she set off was very tempting right now—she wasn't even going to think about how it would be to stay with Ben for a little while longer.

As an afterthought, she added, 'But perhaps I could ask room service to send up a light meal and we could talk while I do my packing? After all, it probably wouldn't be wise to start the journey on an empty stomach, would it?'

As soon as the words slipped out, she was regretting them. What had possessed her to suggest such a thing? Was she mad? He was her brother's sworn enemy, a heartbreaker with no conscience, and here she was, actively encouraging him to spend time with her...and in her hotel room, at that. Had she taken leave of her senses?

'I'd like that,' Ben said, a look of satisfaction settling on his features. 'I'll follow you back there, just as soon as you're ready to leave.'

'I'm ready now.' She'd already burnt her boats, so she may as well go where the tide led her. 'As you say, the weather's not good, so it would be as well not to delay too long.' She stood up, taking time to adjust her scarf before picking up her empty cup and heading towards the door of the vehicle. Ben responded swiftly, unfurling his long body from the seat and going after her.

They went to the car park, and from there they started the journey to the Royal Pennant Hotel. Ben followed her for some two miles along the Yorkshire roads until at last they turned into the hotel's wide forecourt. He drove carefully, she noticed, all the time mindful of the road conditions. The snow had turned to sleet, making the lanes slippery and treacherous.

She wasn't looking forward to the long drive home. Her small car was reliable, but it wasn't built for good manoeuvrability in snow and ice. His car, on the other hand, was an executive-style, midnight-blue saloon, built for power and road-holding capability.

It was a relief to arrive at the hotel, and the grand entrance hall was more than welcoming. It positively enveloped Jasmine with its warmth, reflected in the glow of polished mahogany timber, the sweep of luxurious carpet, and the orange and gold flames of the fire that crackled in the huge fireplace.

'My room's up on the first floor,' she told Ben. 'I'm lucky in that I have a small sitting room set apart from the sleeping area, so we'll be able to eat in comfort.'

'That sounds ideal.'

Once they were in the room, Jasmine waved him to a seat by the table, and then took off her scarf and jacket and laid them over the back of a chair to dry.

'This is a lovely room,' he commented, looking around. 'It's all very tastefully decorated.'

She nodded. The curtains and upholstery gave it an elegant but homely feel, and everything was pleasing on the eye.

Ben glanced beyond the sitting room to where part of the large double bed was visible, its counterpane matching the fabric of the curtains. 'It's good that they've separated the sleeping area from the living area with a narrow wall partition—it tends to give a notion that they are individual rooms and yet keeps the general feeling of spaciousness.'

'Yes, it does. I was really pleased when I first saw the room. I wouldn't have chosen to be away from home, but I've been comfortable here, and I have everything I might need, like a phone, desk and writing materials. I also brought my laptop with me so I've been able to sit here of an evening and type up my notes from the course.'

She ran a hand through her long, burnished chestnut hair, tossing her head slightly, allowing the waves to ripple freely. It was good to be uncluttered by her outer garments, and for the first time that day she took a deep, satisfying breath, content to be back in the cosy confines of her room.

'Perhaps you'd like to order room service for both of us,' she suggested, 'while I start on my packing?' She glanced at Ben as she went to place her suitcase on the bed, but something in his gaze made her stop what she was doing.

He was watching her closely, a glimmer of pure, male interest in his blue glance as it trailed over her, taking in the silky sweep of her hair and wandering down to trace a path over the gentle curve of her hips.

'I'd almost forgotten how beautiful you are,' he murmured, his gaze returning to settle on the soft curve of her mouth. 'Whenever I thought about you, I'd remember your smile, the way you had of looking at me with that guarded expression, as though you weren't quite sure what trouble I'd land myself in next. But it was always your hair that fascinated me. It's so glorious that I'd long to run my fingers through it, very much as you did just then.' He smiled. 'Only I would have lingered a while longer, I think.'

His gently seductive manner unsettled her, causing her to falter as she set the suitcase down on the bed. Had he really been thinking about her from time to time? She hadn't expected that. How was she to deal with this man from her past now that he had turned up, out of the blue, the one man she had kept at a distance all this time for fear of being hurt? He'd been a charmer, a man who'd known exactly how to wind women around his little finger, and it didn't seem as though much had changed.

She fumbled with the zip of the suitcase, encountering resistance, and within a second or two Ben was beside her, his hand resting briefly on hers. The fleeting contact caused a tide of heat to surge through her veins and brought a soft flush of colour to her cheeks.

'There you are,' he said. 'It's free now.'

'Thank you.' She tried breathing slowly and deeply for a while in an effort to calm herself down. She studied him, letting her gaze run over his features and trying to assess what really lay behind that calm, unruffled exterior. 'It's been a while since we last ran into one another,' she murmured, struggling to find her voice. 'I'm surprised that you thought about me at all.'

'It would be hard not to think about you,' he responded with a faint smile. 'After all, we both lived in the same village, and I watched you grow from a lively tomboy who landed in almost as many scrapes as I did into a lovely, serene and accomplished woman. It would have been very strange if I had forgotten you after that, just because we were separated by a few miles.'

She gave him a long, thoughtful look. Was he teasing her, trying to lead her along the same route that all those unsuspecting young women had travelled back home… like Anna, her brother's girlfriend? She had to be wary of him. He simply wasn't to be trusted.

'Like I said, maybe you should order some food for us…the menu is on the desk. I'll have a jacket potato with cheese, please. And a pot of coffee would be good. I've a feeling I'll need something to sustain me on the journey.'

He nodded, accepting her change of subject without comment. Glancing through the menu, he said, 'I think I'll go with the ham and cheese melt. Leave it with me.'

She nodded and turned back to her packing. Some fifteen minutes later, she had managed to cram most of her belongings into her case, and Ben lent a hand with zipping it up.

'All this for one week?' he murmured, lifting a questioning brow. 'How can any woman need so many changes of clothes in such a short space of time—unless, of course, you've been throwing yourself wholeheartedly into the night life? A few boisterous nights in the bar with the people on your course?' He was looking at her quizzically, and she shook her head, giving off an air of innocence. He lifted a dark brow.

'Well, maybe a couple,' she amended with a laugh. 'Though they weren't what you'd call boisterous…more of a lively and animated type of evening, I'd say, especially as the night wore on.'

His eyes took on a contemplative expression. 'No intimate dinners for two, then? Does that mean you're not involved in any serious relationship at the moment? Or maybe you've a boyfriend waiting for you back home?'

She frowned. Why did he want to know that? There was no way she was going to let him wheedle his way into her affections, was there, given his past history? Enough was enough, and she decided to sidestep his questions. Why should he learn every detail of her private life when she knew nothing of his? Simply guessing what he might have been up to was bad enough.

'It means,' she said, looking down at her overstuffed case, 'that I've packed my suitcase full of the Christmas presents I've bought for friends and family while I've been up here. Like I said, I couldn't resist the opportunity to explore the shops in a new town…and with Christmas just three weeks away, there was no time to lose, was there?'

His mouth curved. 'I guess not,' he said, accepting her avoidance tactics with good enough grace. Then he moved away from her as a waiter arrived with the food, setting it out on the table.

'I ordered a couple of desserts, too,' Ben told her when the man had gone. 'All this is my treat,' he said. 'I told the receptionist I would be paying for it.'

'Thank you…but you didn't need to do that.' She eyed up the mouth-watering fruit crumble topped with creamy custard and felt all her good intentions fade away. How had he known that was her favourite? 'That's my diet blown for the week,' she added mournfully.

He laughed. 'I don't believe that you've ever needed to diet in your life,' he said, looking her over. 'You've a perfect hourglass figure…'

She steeled herself not to rise to his bait. 'Perhaps you should sit down and eat before the food gets cold,' she suggested, doing her best to bat his comments to one side. 'And tell me how it is that you came to be working with the rescue services this afternoon. I thought you were working in A and E, the same as me.'

She pulled out a chair and sat down opposite him at the table. Glancing out of the window she could see that in the grey light of the afternoon the snow was beginning to thicken, fat white flakes coming down in a steady flow.

'I wanted to try something different,' he said, taking a bite out of his toasted sandwich. 'I used to enjoy climbing in the Lake District and thought I might volunteer my services for the mountain rescue team. Then one of the team members here fell sick, so Mike asked me to come and do today's stint. I suppose that's why you didn't see my name on the advertising bumph.'

She nodded. 'I wondered if it was something like that.' She scooped up a mound of potato. 'I expect you know most of your local team already, don't you? That will probably make things easier for you, won't it?'

He shook his head. 'I won't be working with my local team because I'm preparing to go back to Woodsley. I've served out my notice at the hospital where I've been these last few years.'

Jasmine put down her fork and stared at him. 'You're going home? After all this time?'

'That's right. I might not be too welcome back there, but five years has perhaps been long enough for me to stay away. There are things I need to deal with, and I think it's probably high time I started to put my life in order.'

She pressed her lips together. The news had come as a huge shock. How was she going to cope if Ben came back to the village? Woodsley Bridge was a relatively small place, and the chances of seeing him around and about were pretty great. There would be no escape.

Even so, she couldn't prevent the thrill of nervous excitement that shimmied along her spine at the thought of him coming home. But that was the unruly, wanton side of her body betraying her, wasn't it? Common sense told her that there would be nothing but trouble if Ben went back to the Lake District. How would his father react?

Worse still, how would her brother Callum deal with the wanderer's return? Once, he and Ben had been best friends, but all that had changed. He blamed Ben for taking Anna away from him, and that anger had not dissipated. It had continued to simmer throughout all those long years.

How was she going to deal with this? Was she destined to stand on the sidelines and watch the process of bitter condemnation start all over again?

CHAPTER TWO

JASMINE frowned, gripping the steering-wheel firmly and making a determined effort to concentrate on her driving. Starting out on the long journey home, she was still reeling from the bombshell that Ben had dropped just a short time ago.

Her mind was caught up in a fog of confusion. One minute she had been secure in her own sheltered world, and now, in an instant, everything had changed. Somehow, she couldn't come to terms with the fact that from now on he would be staying around. For her, life in her home village of Woodsley Bridge would never be quite the same again.

It was early evening now, already dark, and snow was falling in a gentle curtain, lending a picture-postcard atmosphere to the landscape. The branches of the trees were topped with thick ribbons of snow, the rooftops of isolated farmhouses had become a pristine white and all around snow spread like a glistening carpet over the fields. It was lovely to look at, but not so good when she had to drive in it.

She had already been on the road for half an hour, and there were still many miles left to go. She was keeping her fingers crossed that the steady downfall would ease off at some point and that at least the roads would stay clear.

Ben was following her on this first lap of the journey. 'My route follows yours for the first fifteen miles or so,' he had told her before they'd set off, and she had looked at him in surprise.

'But I thought you were living in St Helens, down in Cheshire,' she responded with a frown. Surely that was in the opposite direction?

Driving along, she recalled their conversation. 'I didn't realise you knew where I was living,' he had said, raising a brow.

She'd given a faint shrug. 'Information filters through from time to time about what you've been doing or where you are. People might have caught a glimpse of you, here and there, or maybe their friends and relatives have been further afield to a hospital for treatment…it really doesn't take much for word to get around.'

He'd smiled crookedly. 'Tongues will always wag, won't they? I expect rumours are rife about all my transgressions. The village folk could never quite get over my youthful misdemeanours, could they? *That Radcliffe boy's up to his tricks again* is about all I ever heard from them. Even when I was doing my medical training they were convinced I'd be thrown out for something or other.'

He wasn't far off the mark there, Jasmine acknowledged inwardly. His father had made it clear from the first that he wasn't expecting him to finish the course, and perhaps that was because his son had such a wide range of interests that he found it hard to stick to one in particular. Ben was a wild spirit, always game for anything, and even at medical school he had managed to raise brows. News of his exploits quickly found its way back home.

'Well, you did get into trouble for almost setting fire to the kitchen in your student residence,' she murmured. 'And then there was that time when you and your friends stayed out all night and turned up at your lecture next morning looking the worse for wear.'

He made a face. '*Almost* being the operative word about the fire,' he said. 'I only left the omelette cooking on the hob for a minute or two while I went to help a fellow student who had cut her hand…and the fact that the smoke alarm didn't go off was down to someone else removing the battery and forgetting to put it back. I think he was fed up with it going off every time he made toast.'

His brows drew together. 'And as to the night out, why should that have turned out to be a disciplinary offence? At least we turned up for the lecture on time next day. Some of these people on the boards of universities seem to have no recollection of what it's like to be a student. Yet I'll bet they had their moments, if the truth was known.'

'You make it sound as though it was all unfair,' she said with a wry smile. 'Anyway, I'm sure that's all in the past. I heard you'd done well for yourself in the last few years. There was a piece in the paper about you setting up a new emergency paediatric unit at the hospital in Cheshire…' She frowned. 'But that brings me back to what I was saying—if you're following the same route home as me, I'm guessing you must be living and working somewhere else at the moment.'

He nodded. 'I've been doing some locum work up in Lancashire, so it made sense to stay there for the last couple of months. And, of course, it meant I was able to come and do the stint with the rescue services today, since I'm based not too far away.'

It made sense to Jasmine. He had always been a restless soul, and from what he had just described of his travel arrangements, things didn't seem to have changed very much.

Now, though, she glanced in the rear-view mirror and saw that he was still following behind her, his beautiful car eating up the miles without the slightest hint of difficulty. She wasn't so lucky. Her own car had been throwing up problems along the way.

The outside temperature had dropped to below freezing, and it seemed that her tyres were not up to the job of gripping the slippery surface. She had to take extra care on the bends in the road, and as if that wasn't enough, the snow was still coming down thick and fast so that her windscreen wipers were struggling to clear it away.

The roads were becoming increasingly clogged with snow as drifts began to pile up along the hedgerows, and now she was worried that she might not be able to go on much further. Perhaps Ben had been right when he'd suggested she should stay overnight at the hotel.

Still, she wasn't the only one who had decided to venture out. A few drivers were following the same route, doggedly determined to get home.

She looked at the road ahead. The car in front of her was negotiating a bend, and as the road sloped downwards the driver seemed to have trouble maintaining a straight course. He swerved as the car in front of him suddenly drifted in an arc across the road, the unexpected action causing him to veer wildly. A second or two later, he rammed his vehicle sideways into a large oak tree. Still in a skid, the other car swivelled around, hitting his front end and coming to a halt halfway across the road.

Jasmine's stomach clenched and her pulse began to quicken. Her mouth went dry and she was uneasily aware of the thud of her heartbeat as it rose up into her throat. How was she going to avoid being part of the pile-up ahead? Both cars were taking up a good half of the road directly in front of her, and she wouldn't be able to stop in time to avoid them. She couldn't brake or she would go into a skid, too. She had no choice but to go on.

Her mind was racing. She was all too conscious of Ben not far behind her, and she didn't want to risk him being caught up in any collision. Her only hope was that, with any luck, he would have seen what was going on, and would be able to find some way of avoiding trouble.

She wasn't going fast, but now she changed to a lower gear, slowing the car and carefully steering through the only gap available between the cars and the hedgerow. Thankfully, no one was coming in the opposite direction. Then, as she tried to steer a course away from trouble, the camber of the road changed, throwing the car out of kilter in the bad conditions, and a moment later her vehicle slewed violently around, slamming her headlong into a snowdrift.

The car shuddered to a halt, tipping over at an angle, and she stared at the windscreen, seeing nothing in front of her but a blanket of white. Apprehension clutched at her insides. It seemed very much as though she had plunged part way into a ditch, and maybe the hedge-row had stopped her going any further. Her heart plummeted. Now it looked as though she was going to be stranded here, miles away from anywhere, in a dark, frozen void.

The engine had cut off. There was silence all around, and it seemed as though she was enclosed in a capsule, shut away from the outside world. It was eerie and scary at the same time, being trapped in this pale wasteland.

'Are you okay?' A moment or two later; Ben was pulling at the door of her car while she was still trying to take stock of everything that had happened.

Relief washed over her. Ben was safe and she wasn't alone. 'Yes,' she answered, struggling to keep her voice level. 'I'm okay.'

'You're quite sure that you're not hurt in any way?'

'I'm sure. I'm not hurt.' She blinked, looking around at the overwhelming mass of snow that covered three sides of her vehicle like a half-built tunnel. She tried to gather her thoughts. 'Did you manage to keep your car on the road?'

'It's fine. I've parked just along the road from you.' He hesitated. 'If you're positive that you're all right, I need to go and check on the other drivers. If we don't clear the road fast, there could be another accident before too long. We have two people keeping watch, so that they can try to alert people to the danger, but it isn't safe and I need to hurry.'

She nodded. 'I'll come with you.'

'There's no need.' As she tried to slide out of her seat, he laid his hands on her shoulders, lightly pressuring her to stay. 'You look as though you're in shock,' he said. 'You're trembling. Stay there and I'll be back as soon as I can.'

He was right, she realised after he had gone. Her body was still mourning the loss of his reassuring touch, but that was only because she was in a state of shock, as he'd said…wasn't it? She tried to move, but her legs let her down and her hands were shaking. Her car was slanted at an odd angle to the ground and she wasn't at all certain how she was going to get it back on the road.

For a minute or two, she sat very still, concentrating on breathing deeply in an effort to compose herself. No matter what he said, Ben most likely needed help. If they didn't move the other car to the side of the road, it would be a danger to oncoming drivers. It was also quite possible that one or both of the people involved in the accident might be injured. Sitting here wasn't an option, and somehow or other she had to pull herself together and try to help out. Bracing herself, she drew another shuddery breath of air into her lungs, and a moment later she slid out of her seat and went to find him.

He and another man were trying to steer the crumpled car to the side of the road, but the vehicle that had rammed into the tree was still in the same position as before. The driver was at the wheel, and she guessed that Ben must have already spoken to him. The man wasn't moving, but perhaps that was because he was traumatised by what had happened.

She went over to car and opened up the passenger door. 'Is there anything I can do to help you?' she asked. The man was in his fifties, she guessed, with a weathered complexion and streaks of grey in his hair. His expression was tense, as though he was hurt and was steeling himself against the pain. 'I can see that you're holding your arm,' she murmured. 'Is it giving you some problems?'

He nodded, his lips compressed. 'I wrenched it when I went into the tree. Help's on its way, though. The man from the BMW told me he's a doctor…he came to take a look at me and said I'd probably dislocated my shoulder. He had to go and shift the car out of the way, but he's coming back.'

'I'm sure he'll be able to help you.' She quickly tried to assess his condition. He was wearing a cotton shirt with a sleeveless fleece jacket over the top, and even in the darkness she could see that the shoulder was strangely distorted. 'He and I know one another, as it happens—we're both doctors.'

He managed a weak smile. 'I suppose I'm lucky, then, that this happened while you were around.'

'You could say that.' She hesitated. 'Is it all right if I switch on the interior light? Perhaps I could take a look at you and see what we're dealing with?'

He gave a slight nod, and once the light was on she examined his arm and his hand. 'Can you feel your fingers?'

'I don't think so. They're a funny colour, aren't they?' He frowned. 'That's not good, is it?'

'Well, it means we probably need to put the shoulder back in its socket sooner rather than later. Your circulation is being stopped or slowed down, and we have to sort it out fairly quickly.'

She glanced around and saw that there was a cushion on the rear seat. 'If we put the cushion between your arm and your chest it may help to make you feel more comfortable in the meantime.'

He nodded again, and she went to get the cushion, coming back to gently place it in position. A faint look of relief crossed his features.

'That feels a bit better,' he said, breathing hard and gritting his teeth. 'Thanks.'

'You're welcome.' She glanced at him. 'Are you hurting anywhere else? I noticed the driver's door is buckled…has that hurt you in any way?'

'I don't think it's done anything too bad. It feels as though I'll be bruised for a while, but basically I'm okay. It's just the shoulder. It hurts like the devil.'

'I can imagine it does.' She hesitated momentarily. 'Will you be all right for a minute or two while I go and get my medical bag from the car? We should be able to put your shoulder back in position for you—and we can at least give you something to relieve the pain.'

'That would be good.' He seized at the chance. 'Whatever you can do…'

'Okay.' She slid out of the car once more and trudged through the snow to her own vehicle, thankful that she was wearing strong leather boots.

'What are you doing?' Ben asked, coming over to her, his brows drawing together in a dark line as she retrieved her bag from the car. 'I thought I told you to stay where you were. At least you would have been warmer in there, and you know you shouldn't be wandering around when you've just been involved in an accident. You could be injured and not realise it.'

'I'm a doctor,' she said in a succinct tone, her green eyes homing in on him. 'I think I'd know if there was something wrong with me.'

'Not necessarily.' His gaze lanced into her. 'You should let me check you over.'

She raised both brows. 'We both know that's not going to happen.' Just the thought of him laying hands on her was enough to make colour sweep along her cheekbones. She just hoped he couldn't see her reaction, and to avert disaster she went on, 'It looks as though only one man was injured. Apparently, you said you'd go and help him.'

'That's right.' He studied her briefly, and clearly he must have decided not to pursue the point about her staying in the car.

'Well, it looks as though his circulation's compromised, so I think it would be best to try to put the shoulder back in place here and now, rather than wait.'

'Yes, that's pretty much the conclusion I came to.'

Jasmine was thinking out a plan of action. 'In that case, he'll need a sedative and a painkilling injection,' she added. 'I have the medication we need in my medical bag.'

'Good. You're right, it will probably be best to inject the joint, rather than set up an intravenous line and anaesthetise him. That way, he would be knocked out completely, but his recovery would take longer, and these aren't exactly the best of circumstances for him to be undergoing that kind of treatment.' His gaze ran over her once more. 'We could do it together, if you think you're up to it…?'

'I am. I'll be fine. I'll support him while you do the reduction.'

'Okay, then. Let's go and see how he's doing.'

The injured man, they discovered, was becoming paler by the minute, and his lips were beginning to take on a pinched appearance.

'Ian,' Ben said, slipping into the passenger seat beside him, 'we're going to give you something that will help you to stay calm and relaxed throughout the procedure, and then I'll inject a painkiller directly into the joint. The drugs will help to relax your muscles at the same time. All that means you shouldn't feel too much discomfort when I put the bone back into place. You should feel immediate relief from pain when that's done.'

Ian's lips moved in what they took for agreement. 'Anything,' he said. 'Please, just put it back so that I can start to think straight again.'

They worked together to give him the medication and prepare him for the manipulation. Then they manoeuvred him from the driver's seat to where they could work more comfortably. Jasmine positioned herself to one side, getting ready to stop any sudden, untoward movement as Ben popped the shoulder back into its socket.

As soon as it was over, Ian slumped back in his seat. 'Thanks,' he said. 'That was really painful until you two set to work.'

Jasmine was pleased to see that his fingers had started to regain their normal colour, which meant his circulation had been successfully restored. 'You need to keep the shoulder very still,' she told him. 'Any movement will cause more damage.'

Ben had been searching through his own medical bag and now he brought out a shoulder sling. 'This should help to immobilise the joint while it heals,' he said. 'The tissues around the shoulder will probably be inflamed and swollen for a few weeks, so I'll prescribe some anti-inflammatory tablets for you. I can give you some to be going on with, but you should get the shoulder checked out at a hospital as soon as possible. They'll probably do an X-ray to make sure that everything's okay…and they'll want to make sure that you have no other injuries.'

Ian nodded. 'Thanks. Though I don't know how I'm going to get to a hospital in this weather. I don't even know how I'm going to drive…or even if the car is capable of getting me anywhere.'

'Same here,' Jasmine said. 'Mine's halfway down a ditch. It seems we're both in the same boat.'

'Wretched weather.' Ian grimaced. 'I suppose I could call for a taxi…we could share, if you like. That's if anyone will come out in this weather, of course.'

'There's no need for that,' Ben put in. 'I can help out. My car's not damaged in any way, so I can drive both of you. Actually, there's a cottage hospital with a minor injuries unit not too far away from here. They have X-ray facilities, so they should be able to sort you out.' He looked at Ian. 'I'll drop you off there, if you like, and maybe you could call a relative to come and pick you up later?'

Ian thought things through. 'I expect my son will come once he finishes work. He's on the late shift, but he has a four-wheel drive, so I don't suppose he'll have too many problems with the road conditions.'

'What about you, Jasmine?' Ben's gaze rested on her. 'You're not going to be able to make it to Woodsley Bridge tonight, are you? I can put you up at my place overnight, if you want. At least you'll be warm and safe there, and we can make arrangements to have your car towed to a garage in the morning.'

A surge of relief flowed through her. 'Thanks,' she said, giving him a quick smile. 'I'd appreciate that, if you're sure you don't mind? It's getting late, and it's a weight off my mind, knowing that I won't have to start making all sorts of arrangements at this time of night.'

'Good. That's settled, then.' Once he had everyone's agreement, Ben was ready for action. 'We'll load your luggage into the boot of my car and get under way.'

He helped Ian into the BMW, making sure that he was secure and comfortable in the back seat. 'The hospital's a couple of miles down the road,' he said. 'We'll have you there in just a few minutes.'

Jasmine sat in the front passenger seat, absorbing the sheer luxury of Ben's car. Everything about it spelled comfort and opulence. The temperature was perfect, the seats were heated, and the upholstery gave off a rich scent of supple, new leather. There was even soft music playing in the background.

It all lulled her into a false sense of security, making her feel as though everything was right in her world and that it was perfectly normal for her to be sitting here next to Ben. She tried not to notice how his strong fingers closed around the wheel, or the fact that his long legs were just an inch or so away from her own. The material of his trousers pulled across his powerful thighs, drawing her attention, and she quickly looked away.

When they arrived at the hospital, they went with Ian into the casualty department and waited while a triage nurse took details of the accident and organised an immediate appointment for him in the X-ray department. Then Ian rang his son, and once they were confident that arrangements were in place for him to be picked up later that evening, they said goodbye to him and set off for Ben's house.

'It isn't too far away,' Ben said, as he turned the car into a country lane. 'We've had to make a bit of a detour, but we should be there soon. I'll rustle us up something to eat—it seems like an age since we had that snack back at the hotel.'

She gave a crooked smile. 'I know what you're thinking... I should have stayed there and agreed to have dinner with you. It would have saved all this trouble.'

He sent her a sideways glance. 'I wasn't going to say that...far be it from me to say I told you so.' He grinned. 'But sitting down to a relaxing dinner with you and taking time to catch up with all your news would have been good.'

She sighed. 'I know. But I did so want to get home.' He didn't need to know how wary she was of being in close proximity with him for any length of time. 'It's just that my mother will be putting up the Christmas tree tomorrow evening, and it's sort of a tradition that I help her with the baubles and decorations. I love this time of year. We always have Christmas carols playing in the background while we dress the tree, and my dad brings us hot liqueur coffees and warm mince pies, so that we really get into the festive spirit.'

She smiled. 'Of course, he complains that he's not really ready to celebrate three weeks early while he's still working, but as a GP he could be tending patients on Christmas morning, so we tend to ignore that and get on with it.'

Ben grinned. 'Your father has always been a solid, easygoing man, though, hasn't he? Nothing ever really fazes him. I suppose that comes from taking care of all the folk in the village for years on end and dealing with their quirks and foibles.'

'That's true.' She sent him an oblique glance. 'What about you? Will you be going back to the manor house to stay with your father?'

He shook his head and his expression became sombre. 'I don't think so. That wouldn't go down too well. My father and I have never seen eye to eye over anything very much.'

'But you'll be spending Christmas with him, won't you?' She frowned. 'Now that you're going home, surely he'll be glad of the chance to see you again after all this time? Perhaps you'll be able to forget what went on in the past and try to start over again.'

'It sounds good in theory,' Ben said. His mouth flattened. 'But, truthfully, I don't suppose he'll welcome me with open arms. He can be stubborn at the best of times.'

'I'm sorry. That's so sad.' Her green eyes clouded. 'It's such a shame to see a family torn apart at the seams when maybe a word or two could put matters right.'

His expression was cynical. 'Do you really imagine that I haven't tried?' He shook his head. 'I know you mean well, Jassie, but you should give up on trying to reconcile my father and me. I've come to the conclusion that it isn't going to work. I've written to him, tried to talk to him on the phone, but he's brusque and unco-operative, and I have the feeling that I'm wasting my time. It's not even as if I'm the one in the wrong…well, not totally, anyway… But it doesn't seem to make any difference to how he thinks and feels.'

His mouth made a flat line. 'Things were said, on both sides, that should have been left unsaid, and the damage has been done. The wounds they leave behind never truly heal.'

'I don't believe in giving up,' she murmured. 'Not where family is concerned, anyway. I'd always be look-ing for an opportunity to put things right.'

His expression softened. 'That's because you're a sweet, generous-natured woman who only ever looks for the good in people. I'm just afraid that before too long you'll find yourself disillusioned, and that would be a terrible shame.'

She absorbed that, subsiding back into her seat without comment. The only way she had ever been disillusioned had been in her dealings with Ben. Over the years, she'd watched him, wincing as he'd made his mistakes, biting her tongue when she'd wanted to speak out about his various entanglements, wondering if there would ever be a time when he would look at her with the light of love in his eyes.

But that had been asking for the impossible—how would he ever have done that when she'd constantly shielded herself from him for her own protection? Besides, she had long ago given up on that dream world. Life had thrown a spanner in the works when Ben had gone away with Anna.

She could never keep up with Ben. He had been like quicksilver, constantly on the move, rising to challenges as and when they'd arisen. All his youthful energies had been fuelled by rebellion against the hand life had dealt him…losing his mother at a very young age had been a raw deal, the worst, and who could blame him for his confusion and disenchantment with life? No wonder he'd run amok through the village in his tender years and stirred up a storm.

Knowing all that, maybe it was the reason why Jasmine had always looked beyond the vigorous, determined exterior to what lay beneath.

Her feelings for him had never changed. They just became more impossible to manage as time went on.

CHAPTER THREE

'This is it,' Ben announced after a while, turning the car into a snow-filled drive. 'My house—I usually think of it as my summer place, since I mostly use it for holiday breaks or those times when I need to get away from it all…but the title doesn't exactly fit at the moment. Still, I hope you'll like it.' He cut the engine and turned to face Jasmine. 'Let's get you inside and into the warm.'

'Your summer place—does that mean you're not renting short term, that this is actually your own house?' She was puzzled. 'After all, you must have a house in Cheshire as well, if that's where you've been living for the last few years.'

'That's right. I bought this as a run-down property some time ago and spent a year or so doing it up.'

'So renovating properties is one of those interests that you kept up? Working on Mill House back in Woodsley Bridge was just a start?'

'That's true. I've always been enthusiastic about restoring houses…ones that particularly interest me, that is.'

She frowned. 'I wasn't sure whether your father would have put you off. He didn't go along with any of it, did he?'

He made a wry face. 'Unfortunately, my father and I don't see eye to eye on a number of matters. With Mill House he was convinced I was wasting my time… and money…and he did everything he could to put me off starting the work. Even though it was a successful restoration in the end, he maintained it was money that could have been spent on more solid investments.'

She nodded. 'He couldn't understand why you went to all that effort, could he?'

'No. But, then, sentiment never came into his calculations.'

Jasmine understood Ben's difficulty. Stuart Radcliffe never had time for such creative projects. He was an old-fashioned man, putting his faith in good bookkeeping and heavily involved with upper-crust institutions. Ben's ideas were very different, stemming from the heart, and Stuart could not go along with that. To him they were risky, pointless ventures, whereas he was all about safety and security.

Ben held open the door for her and she slid out of the car, looking around at the broad sweep of the drive and the sprawling white-painted house. It was set in open countryside, and as the moon cast its light over the snow-laden fields, she caught a glimpse of hills and dales and gently forested slopes all around.

She looked closely at the house. She could see why Ben would want to work on this lovely old property. Clearly, it had stood the test of time, and now, with a fresh coat of paint and what she guessed were renovated windows and roofing, this was a splendid example of what could be achieved.

'Of course, you're not seeing it at its best in this weather,' he commented as he went to retrieve her case from the boot. 'If you were to come here in the summer you would see it in its full glory.'

'I think it's lovely.' She dragged her gaze back from the scenery to the front of the house. A lantern glowed in the wide porch, welcoming them with its golden light, and to either side there were hanging baskets, filled to the brim with winter flowers. There were pansies, big, bright blooms of deep violet, azure blue, burgundy and stunning orange. Mixed in with those were purple-leaved sage and long stems of trailing ivy. It was a glorious explosion of colour that said no matter that it was winter, plant life was exuberant and thriving.

He put his key in the lock and opened the front door, ushering her inside and placing her case on the floor by a decorative plant stand. Ferns filled the shelves, their vibrant green a charming contrast to the mellow wood. The hallway was large and inviting, with a deep-piled carpet and walls that were covered with delicately textured paper that was pleasing on the eye. To one side there was a Georgian satinwood table, beautifully inlaid and elegant with delicately curved legs. A bowl of vivid red cyclamen provided a splash of rich colour that was reflected in a large, gilt-framed mirror that hung on the wall.

'I'll show you to the living room,' Ben said. 'I've laid a fire in the hearth, so once I light it the place will be much more welcoming. The central heating's on, so we'll be warm enough.'

'I'm toasty already,' she said. 'The heat enveloped me as soon as I walked through the door.' She was still looking around, trying to take everything in. 'This house

must be…what…seventeenth century?' There were
exposed oak beams all around, and an oak staircase
led to a mezzanine floor that could be seen from the
hallway. Even from where she was standing, she could
see through the wooden rails of the elevated balustrade
that the upper level had been tastefully furnished with
comfortable chairs and an antique desk. All around, the
lighting was subdued but warm, throwing out soft pools
of light here and there.

He nodded. 'It is…late seventeenth.' He showed her
into the living room, where the centrepiece was a huge
fireplace, made of beautifully polished wood topped
with an intricately carved cornice. 'I tried to restore it
carefully, keeping the original features intact wherever
possible.' He bent to light the log fire and stood back
after a minute or two, waiting as the flames took hold.
The logs began to crackle and throw up orange and
gold sparks, sending a pool of light into the room. 'That
should soon make things more cheerful,' he said.

'This is so wonderful,' she told him, looking around
in awe. There was a richly upholstered sofa close by the
hearth, along with matching armchairs, and it was easy
to see that Ben's flawless taste in furnishings was innate
and impeccable. There was an elegant bookcase to one
side of the room, complemented by a glazed Georgian
display cabinet and a small occasional table.

'It's such a treat to see a place like this,' she said, full
of admiration for what he had achieved. 'You must have
worked so hard to make it look this good.'

'It took a fair bit of time and effort,' he agreed, smiling. 'Let me take your jacket and then you should make
yourself comfortable on the sofa while I start supper.
I'll show you around after we've eaten, if you like.'

'I would love that, thanks…but perhaps I could help with the food? There must be some way I can make myself useful.'

He mulled it over. 'Perhaps you'd like to do the salad? The ingredients are mostly ready prepared, so they just need to be tossed together in a bowl with some dressing. Just give me a minute while I take your case upstairs and put the car in the garage.'

'Okay.'

The kitchen, she discovered, was another perfect combination of golden oak units, granite worktops and a quarry-tiled floor. It should perhaps have been cold, given the type of floor covering, but under-floor heating meant that it was warm and inviting.

'I thought we might have a couple of grilled steaks along with pan-fried potatoes,' Ben said, a slight frown indenting his brow. 'Does that sound all right to you? You haven't gone vegetarian on me in the last few years, have you?'

'Not yet,' she murmured. She rolled her eyes. 'Steak sounds like heaven to me. I'm starving.'

'Good. Then we'll get started.' He switched on the grill and fetched steaks from the fridge, and within a very short time they were ready to sit down to a feast. The steaks were cooked to perfection, and he added mushrooms and tomatoes so that the whole meal was mouth-wateringly delicious. Jasmine's salad was a crisp mix of lettuce leaves, bright peppers, radish and coleslaw.

'We could eat in the dining room, if you like, but sometimes the kitchen has a much cosier feel,' Ben said. 'What would you prefer?'

'This is just fine by me,' she murmured, looking around. There was a small square table to one end of the kitchen, with stylish, high-backed oak chairs that lent a touch of distinction to the breakfast area. This quiet, uncluttered area exuded an atmosphere of comfort and relaxation, and she could imagine Ben sitting here of a morning, eating his breakfast and reading the newspaper.

'So, tell me what you've been doing with yourself these last five years,' Ben said, waving her to a seat and setting out the plates of food. 'You've mentioned you were working in A and E, and obviously you're interested in furthering your career, as you were doing the course in critical care.'

'That's right.' She added a helping of salad to her plate. 'I'm working as a senior house officer at Wellbeck Hospital. I've been there for a number of years now, so it's almost like home to me, and I get on well with everyone there. I've never particularly wanted to work anywhere else.'

'Does the fact that you attended the course mean you're thinking of branching out?' He sliced off a piece of steak and started to eat. 'I mean, were you thinking of going out with the rescue services?'

'Maybe. I've been giving it some thought. Only perhaps I'll go as a volunteer to begin with. I know the local team could do with extra hands, especially people who are medically qualified. They used to have a doctor on call, but he recently retired, so they're looking for someone to take his place.'

'Yes, I heard about that.' He poured wine for both of them. 'Actually, they've already found his replacement.' He looked at her intently, and there was almost an expectant quality about his expression.

She returned the look, frowning, and then her eyes widened. 'Are you telling me that you're going to do the job?'

He nodded. 'It's really only an extension of what I've already been doing in Cheshire. I'll be on call with the local team, as well as acting as a first responder in cases where the emergency services need a doctor to arrive on the scene fast. The rest of the time I'll be based at Wellbeck.'

'Wellbeck?' Jasmine gasped. She couldn't stop that small explosion of sound. 'You mean we'll be working together?' She laid down her fork and stared at him, trying to take it in. A pulse began to throb heavily in her throat. 'What kind of role will you be taking on there? Is it a permanent post?'

'It's temporary. It's just a short-term contract, for a couple of months, filling in for the specialist registrar in A and E while he's over in the States.'

Slowly, her heart rate began to return to normal. It was such a shock, learning that they were to work together. It was one thing to know that he would be living near her, but to be seeing him every day at the hospital where she was based was altogether a different thing.

She picked up her fork and let it hover over the mushrooms on her plate.

'Don't tell me I've managed to put you off your food?' Ben queried lightly. He was watching her, his gaze moving over her as though he could read and understand every detail of her expression. 'You and I will manage to get along well enough, won't we?'

'Of course. I mean… I… It was so unexpected. I'm not sure what I thought you would be doing back at Woodsley, but for some reason it didn't occur to me that you would be coming to the local hospital. One of the hospitals where you did your training, perhaps, in Carlisle or Edinburgh, but Wellbeck was never top of your list of preferences before, was it?'

'Times change, people change,' he said with a negligent shrug. 'The opportunity arose and I decided to grab it.'

'But why now, after all this time?' She swallowed some of the wine, aiming for Dutch courage and feeling it warm her all the way to her toes. Or perhaps the warmth was merely as a result of the fact that he was sitting opposite her and she had no way of escaping that penetrating stare. He knew how she felt about having him around. He had picked up on her guarded responses, and he knew full well that her alarm systems were on full, chaotic alert.

'I heard that my father was ill.' He said it simply, in a matter-of-fact tone. 'He wouldn't have told me himself, of course, but word filtered back to me via friends in the know.'

'I hadn't heard anything about that.' Jasmine frowned. 'My father's his GP, but of course he wouldn't have said anything to anyone. I've seen your father out and about from time to time, but I didn't realise that he was sick.' She looked at him, her gaze troubled. 'Is it serious?'

'I'm not sure. All I know is that he's seeing a specialist about problems with high blood pressure. It's possible that hypertension could have affected his kidneys, but I don't know anything for certain.' He pressed his lips together. 'I'm not surprised…he was always uptight and on edge, not the best recipe for good health.'

'I'm so sorry. You must be very worried about him. What are you going to do?'

He shrugged. 'I don't know. Somehow I'll have to find a way of keeping an eye on him. Blood is blood, after all, and there's no denying the fact that he's my father. I shan't rest easy unless I know I've done everything in my power to make sure he's all right, whether he wants my help or not.'

She reached for him, laying her hand on his. 'It must be so difficult for you…he's never been an easy man to get along with, and now you're disrupting your life so that you can do the right thing. I hope you can make him see sense and put all the bad feeling behind you for once and for all.'

'So do I.' He gently squeezed her hand, drawing her fingers into his palm. He was warm and vibrant, his inner strength transmitted to her as if a special bond had been created between them. It was as though he had drawn her into his embrace and wrapped her in his powerful masculine presence.

Then he reluctantly broke the link between them, and Jasmine struggled to bring her thoughts back to some kind of order. It suddenly came home to her that she was here, in his house, dining with him, and in all the years she had known him she would never have dreamed of sharing this precious moment of intimacy with him.

She would even be sleeping under the same roof as him, and only now did it occur to her that she needed to keep an especially tight watch on her feelings. It would be all too easy to fall for Ben. Even after all these years, when the folly of a youthful infatuation had passed, there was still a lingering pool of yearning, a soft tugging at her heart that told her she could come away from all this with her emotions in tatters.

He moved away from the table a short time later, clearing away the plates and stacking them in the dishwasher. 'I can offer you fruit salad for dessert, along with cream or ice cream, or perhaps you'd prefer something more substantial, like treacle sponge and custard?' He lifted a brow in query.

'Fruit salad would be lovely, thanks...with ice cream.' Her mouth made a crooked shape. 'It seems the wrong season to be wanting that, but I could eat it all year round.' She sighed. 'I wonder if the snow is easing off at all? I rang the garage to ask if they would pick up my car for me, and they said they would try to do it tomorrow. I've no idea what damage might have been done—but at least the insurance company will offer me a hire car while it's being repaired. I'm just wondering if I'll still be able to make it home tomorrow.'

He lifted the blind at the window and peered outside. 'There are just feathery flakes coming down now. I expect the snowploughs will be hard at work tonight, and if the worst comes to the worst and you don't want to drive, I could take you home. I could do that anyway, if you like. I have to be back here on Monday, because my locum job finishes and I need to hand over to my successor, but I can't see any problem. Either way, we'll make sure that you get home.'

Her mouth curved upwards. 'Thank you for that. I owe you. I'm beginning to be really glad that I met up with you today.'

'Even though it stirred up a few demons?' His blue gaze glittered as he placed the dessert in front of her. 'I would always look out for you, Jassie. You have to know that. You were the only one who never condemned me, whatever I did...apart from my grandmother, of course.

She was always on my side…a real treasure, a gem of a woman with a heart of gold. She had lots to say about what I should do and how I should conduct myself, but she never forced her opinions on me or berated me when I made the wrong choices. I think she had faith in me that if I followed my own instincts, things would generally turn out all right.'

He sat down once more and began to eat his own fruit salad. 'And mostly they did, except where my father was concerned.'

'I liked your grandmother.' Jasmine remembered the dear old lady who had lived close by her father's surgery. She had been Ben's maternal grandmother, a cheerful, lively woman who had always been busy making jam or doing craftwork for the village fete. 'We used to talk sometimes, whenever I went by Mill House, or we would meet up in the village sometimes. She was thoughtful and kind…and she always had time for people.'

'She had a lot of time for you.' His face was sad and his eyes clouded with memories. 'She used to call me when I was away at medical school and tell me about the things you'd been up to. I heard all about it when you decided to train as a doctor, when you passed your finals and bought your cottage, even about the various young men you dated from time to time.'

Jasmine blushed. 'She didn't! Why would she even mention that to you?'

'Perhaps because she knew I'd be interested.' His gaze slanted over her, taking in the silky swathe of her hair and the clear green of her eyes. 'You always steered clear of me, and I can't say that I blamed you, but I was definitely keen to know what type of man caught your attention. I can't say I approved of some—I was pretty sure their intentions were none too good—but then my grandmother pointed out that people in glass houses shouldn't throw stones.' He smiled. 'She was a shrewd woman, my gran.'

'She was, but you obviously didn't take her up on any of her advice.' She had recovered herself by now, and was ready to fend off any more comments he might throw her way. He knew she was vulnerable, and he would play on that. Ben was a master of the art of winding women around his little finger. He would find a way of creeping under her guard without her even realising what he was doing.

They finished off the meal in the living room drinking coffee by the open fire, and she asked him about his work in the A and E unit in Cheshire and how he had come to set up the new paediatric unit.

'One of my specialties was working with children,' he said. 'It wasn't very satisfactory, treating them alongside adults who were injured, so we thought of ways we could partition off a separate area for them. We had child-friendly murals painted on the walls and provided play activities for those with minor injuries. The most important thing was that we recruited staff who were trained in paediatrics. In the end, the management was so impressed with what we'd done and with how smoothly it worked that they arranged funding for a permanent children's A and E department.'

'That must have given you a lot of satisfaction,' she acknowledged. 'We're lucky at Wellbeck, because we have good facilities there for both adults and children.' She hesitated, dipping her spoon into the chilled mix of pineapple, grapes and peaches. 'I would never have expected you to choose to work with children.'

She had no real idea how Ben would interact with the little ones in his care. His skills as a doctor weren't in doubt, but looking after sick and injured children was difficult for the best of the medical profession, let alone someone who had no real experience of how youngsters behaved or reasoned. After all, Ben was an only child who'd lost his mother when he had been five years old… and he had no young nephews or nieces to show him the way. And yet, against all the odds, he seemed to have succeeded in what he'd set out to do.

'I find it exhilarating sometimes,' he said. 'Children have no artifice. They say it as it is, and you always know exactly where you are with them. And when they recover from whatever ails them, they bounce back at full steam, ready to get on with whatever takes their fancy. It can be truly rewarding, working with them.'

'I can imagine. I just never thought I would see you in that role.'

They talked for a while longer, and then he said on a questioning note, 'Would you like to see the rest of the house?'

She nodded. 'Yes, please. Actually, after that I'd be quite happy to settle for a good night's sleep. It seems to have been an unusually long day.'

'It's certainly been eventful.' He smiled. 'I'll show you to your room.' He stood up and started to walk towards the hallway, commenting lightly, 'There aren't a lot of rooms, as you've probably already gathered. Downstairs there is the living room, kitchen, dining room and a bathroom, and of course you've seen the mezzanine floor. That's what I think of as my study— I have my desk and computer up there, and there's a bookcase so that mostly everything I need is to hand.'

'I noticed it as soon as we arrived. It looks so peaceful up there, and all that golden oak adds to the feeling of comfort and well-being.'

'I think so, too. I enjoy knowing that a good deal of the house is made up of natural materials. I tried to keep true to that theme upstairs, with the same exposed beams and oak floors for the hall areas. There are three bedrooms, one with an en suite bathroom, and there's a separate bathroom between the other two.'

He led the way up the stairs, and she was truly impressed by the love and care that had gone into making this house a home. The master suite was decorated in gentle tones of blue and grey, with small items of exquisite antique furniture providing storage or seating.

'I thought you might like the larger of the two guest bedrooms,' he said, showing her into the room. 'It faces out onto the garden, so you have the sun in here a good deal of the time.' He watched her expression as she gazed around. 'Will you be all right in here, do you think? There's mostly everything you might need, and you'll find a washbasin and toilet set into the recess. There wasn't room for a proper bathroom, but you can always use the one next door if you prefer. Either way, I've put out soap, towels, shampoo and so on. Just give me a shout if there's anything I haven't thought of.'

'It's absolutely perfect,' she told him. 'I love the soft cream and gold colours in here. It's a lovely room.' There was even a small escritoire where she could sit and write if she wanted…not that she had any intention of doing that, but it was a delightful addition to the room.

'I'm glad you like it.' He came to stand beside her, sliding an arm around her shoulders. 'Of course, if you should change your mind…if you decide at any time that you'd rather come and share with me, you're more than welcome. There's actually nothing I'd like better.'

His comment took her breath away…quite literally. Not only that, he was standing so close to her, not pressuring her in any way but so near to her that she felt the brush of his thigh against hers, and her soft, feminine curves were gently crushed against his long body. She loved the way he was holding her, but her nervous system was already signalling danger, clamouring a warning, while all the time her foolish body was firing up in feverish response.

Slowly, with infinite care, he drew her closer, his hand coming to rest on the gentle curve of her hip. He lowered his head and sought out her lips, and in the next moment he was kissing her, a tender, sweet exploration that rocked her to the core of her being. His hands stroked along her spine, urging her even nearer to him, and as her breasts softened against his chest and her thighs brushed against his, she knew that she was standing on a virtual precipice.

Her heart was pounding, her whole body overwhelmed by a hot tide of longing. She wanted, more than anything, to take up his gentle invitation, but after years of watching him from afar she knew all too well that this could be her undoing.

'Ben…' She mumbled the words against his lips, and ran her hand shakily over his hard rib cage. 'Ben, I can't do this…' Even now, her traitorous body was trying to cling to him, desperate for one last moment of exquisite fulfilment, and perhaps he recognised that because he kissed her again, trailing his lips over hers and scorching a path along the slender curve of her throat.

'But you want me...' he said, his voice roughened with the edge of desire. 'I feel it with every heartbeat, with the way your body softens against mine. Take a chance, Jassie...just this once, let your heart rule your head. I won't let you down, I promise you. I'll take care of you. I'll make sure that you're all right. I'll keep you safe.'

If only she could believe him. If only she could let go of all the bonds that held her back. Would it be so wrong to spend this night with him, to taste for once the joy of being with him in the one way that really mattered?

But how could she trust his promises? Hadn't he said those same things to Anna years ago? And where was she now?

How would Callum feel if he knew that his own sister had betrayed him with the one man who had destroyed his dreams? She couldn't do it. Her peace of mind would be destroyed for ever and there would be no going back.

She laid her hand, palm flat, on his chest. 'I'm sorry,' she whispered. 'It just wouldn't be right. You and I could never be together.'

For a moment or two, he stayed very still. Then he seemed to pull himself up, as though willing himself to move away from her. He rested his cheek against hers, his breathing ragged as he registered what she was saying.

Then he reluctantly eased himself away from her. 'It's okay,' he said, his gaze meshing with her troubled green eyes. 'Don't worry about it. I should have known better.' His mouth made a crooked downturn. 'It's just that I've waited such a long time to see you again, Jassie, and you're exactly as I remembered…such a beautiful woman, so gorgeous I couldn't believe you were actually here with me. I couldn't help myself.'

He held her at arm's length. 'But I'll behave myself from now on, I promise…or at least, I'll try my very best,' he amended hastily, a slight frown knotting his brow. 'Perhaps you'll have to forgive me one or two minor lapses. I'm not—'

'I think perhaps you should stop right there,' she murmured, sending him a shrewd glance. 'You're digging yourself into a hole.'

He gave a husky laugh. 'I am, aren't I?' He studied her fleetingly as though trying to imprint her features on his mind for one last time. 'Try to get a good night's sleep, Jassie.' He frowned. 'For myself, I doubt I'll manage it. I think I'll probably be taking a long, cold shower.'

CHAPTER FOUR

'BREAKFAST should be ready in about twenty minutes,' Ben called, knocking on the bathroom door just as Jasmine stepped out of the shower. 'Is that okay with you?'

'That's fine, thanks,' she answered, wrapping herself in a towelling robe. Her long hair fell in damp waves below her shoulders, and she wondered belatedly how she was going to get it dry as there was no hairdrier in her room.

'Do you have everything you need?' Ben asked, and she was just about to mention the hairdrier when he added on a thoughtful note, 'Could you do with someone to wash your back, perhaps…or maybe you could use some fresh towels? I'm sure I could find some and bring them to you. It's no trouble at all…I'm only too happy to help out in any way I can.' His voice was huskily coaxing, deep and intensely masculine, stirring up all kinds of wild imaginings in her and sending fiery signals darting along her nerve endings. She was all too conscious that there was only a thin door separating them.

'I can see that your good intentions didn't last long,' she said, a hint of amusement in her tone. 'Obviously the cold shower didn't work.'

'That's because I kept imagining you in there with me, and before too long, the water turned to steam,' he said mournfully, but his words took on a tinge of hopeful expectation as he added, 'Are you absolutely sure you don't need any help in there?'

'I'm quite sure, thanks.'

'That's a shame…' He gave an exaggerated sigh. 'Still, nothing ventured, as they say.'

She wrapped her hair in a towel and smiled to herself at his persistence. 'But I could use a hairdrier if you have one,' she told him. 'Otherwise I'll let my hair dry naturally.'

'Hmm.' He seemed to be giving it some thought. 'There's definitely one up here somewhere. Have a look in the second guest room. That's most likely where it is. I'd find it for you, but the bacon's cooking downstairs, and I'd better not risk a repeat of the omelette fiasco.'

'Of course you shouldn't. That would never do, would it? You've spent too long working on this house to have it go up in flames.'

'Too right,' he said. A moment or two later, as she heard him padding down the stairs, she began to quickly dress, pulling on fresh jeans and a cotton top that clung to her curves.

Then she tidied up the bathroom and went into the guest bedroom to look for the hairdrier.

She'd seen the room briefly when Ben had shown her around yesterday evening, but now she took a moment to look at it more carefully. This room was only a little smaller than the one she was using, but it was partitioned into a main bedroom and what appeared to be a smaller dressing room. It wasn't being used as such, from the looks of things when she went to investigate, because there was a small, single bed in there, almost like a child's bed.

The décor throughout both rooms was exquisite, with pale gold fabrics offset with sparing touches of dark red and the palest of greens. The carpet was the colour of sand, and the furniture was the same oak that had been used everywhere else in the house.

There was a dresser by the window, and Jasmine went there first of all to look for the hairdrier. She didn't see it among the collection of fragrance bottles and hand lotions on the tabletop, but it was always possible that it might be in one of the drawers.

She opened the uppermost drawer and straight away found what she was looking for. Smiling, she lifted the hairdrier out, and then glanced at the various bits and pieces that lay beside it. There was a hairbrush and comb, some ornamental hair clips and a small jewellery box containing a couple of bead necklaces and a set of earrings.

She closed the lid of the box, a small frown starting up on her brow. Next to the box there were a couple of picture books, the sort that might be read by a young child with his mother.

It was all very odd. Were these mementos of Ben's own mother, and relics from his childhood? Somehow, she didn't think so. The books were reasonably modern, and the jewellery was the sort that you could probably buy on the high street these days.

A more likely explanation was that Ben had a girl-friend who stayed here from time to time…Anna, per-haps? After all, his relationship with Callum's girlfriend must have been serious enough for him to risk alienating Jasmine's brother and at the same time cause more bad feeling between him and his father.

It was common knowledge that Stuart Radcliffe had not been pleased when his son had decided to go off and…in all likelihood…set up house with a young woman from the village. He didn't go along with a lot of the ways of the twenty-first century. He was a man of high moral standards and his son's behaviour went against the grain.

But Anna wasn't living with Ben now, was she… unless she was back at his house in Cheshire?

It was all too much for Jasmine. She was getting a headache just thinking about it, and she closed the drawer and went back to her own room to finish getting ready.

'You made it,' Ben said as she went into the kitchen a few minutes later. He looked her over, his blue eyes lighting with approval. 'You look fantastic. A man's dream come true, all lissom and lovely—and I can see that you found the hairdrier. It looks as though your hair's made of pure silk. It's beautiful.'

'You never lost the art of charming your way around women, did you, Ben?' She gave him a wry, speculative glance. Did he imagine she would fall for his easygoing, seductive manner? Anything was possible, of course, but she had just had a nasty reminder about why she should steer clear of getting too deeply involved with him. He was a man who was constantly on the move, flitting between people and places with reckless abandon.

His expression became thoughtful. 'You don't seem to be in too good a mood, all of a sudden. Are you worrying about your car, or about getting home, maybe?'

She shook her head. 'No. I'm sure that will all be sorted eventually.'

'That's right. I thought it might be best if I take you home, as the snow's still lying about. I expect you'll be able to pick up your car in a day or two, won't you?'

She nodded. 'Yes, my father will probably bring me back here to collect it.'

She glanced around, seeing that he had laid the table for breakfast and that the food was ready to be set out on the plates that were warming under the grill. 'I feel guilty that you've done all this… I meant to get up early and help with everything, but that mattress was so soft I curled up like a baby and just didn't want to wake up. I'm annoyed with myself.'

He laughed. 'If you slept overlong, then you probably needed it. Come and sit down at the table and I'll serve up. We've bacon, eggs, tomatoes…and there were some fresh mushrooms left from yesterday, so I've cooked them, too.'

'It sounds wonderful…smells wonderful, too.' She sat down and saw that he had made toast and set out marmalade and apricot preserve. There was also a pot of coffee, giving off a satisfying aroma that mingled with the appetising smell of cooked bacon.

'Shall I pour coffee for you?' she asked. She could do with a reviving cup. It might help to sweeten her sour mood. He had been right when he had picked up on her unhappy frame of mind, but she didn't even understand herself why she was out of sorts. Why should the ins and outs of his private life bother her? He had never hidden anything from her. Relatively speaking, his life was an open book.

'Thanks.' He put a plate down in front of her and then went to take a seat opposite her. He started to eat, and then asked softly, 'So if it isn't the travel arrangements that are bothering you, what else is giving you grief?'

She passed the coffee across the table to him. 'Nothing at all. If anything, I'm just reflecting on things, that's all.' Her gaze met his. 'I found the hairdrier in a drawer with all sorts of bits and pieces—some jewellery, a hairbrush... Of course, it's perfectly natural that you should have people to stay with you, or even live with you, but I couldn't help wondering if those things belonged to Anna.'

He nodded. 'Yes, you guessed right. She stays here from time to time and uses the place for holidays, short breaks and so on.'

So he did still keep in contact with her. Jasmine slowly absorbed that piece of information, a small frown indenting her brow. 'And the books?'

He seemed puzzled. 'Books?'

'Children's picture books. They were in the drawer alongside the other bits and pieces. Does Anna have a child? Is that why there's a single bed in the dressing room?'

'Ah, yes. They would be Kyle's storybooks. I didn't realise that she had left them behind.' Ben paused awkwardly for a moment. 'He's four years old, a great little boy but a whirlwind of activity. It's hard to keep up with him sometimes.' He swallowed some of his coffee and then replaced his cup on its saucer. 'I have a photo of him. Would you like to see it?'

She nodded slowly. All at once her appetite had disappeared and the food began to taste like cardboard in her mouth.

His jacket was draped over the back of a chair, and now he went to forage in the pocket, drawing out a leather wallet. 'There he is,' he told her, handing her a small photograph showing an impish young boy laughing into the camera. He had the same black hair and blue eyes as Ben, and as she carefully studied his picture, Jasmine felt as though a little piece of her had died.

'He looks like a lively youngster...a happy-go-lucky kind of boy,' she murmured huskily. She studied the photograph a moment longer before handing it back to him. 'Is he your son?'

He appeared to be taken aback by her question, hesitating a moment before asking, 'What makes you say that?'

'Isn't it obvious? He looks a lot like you. You and Anna were an item...still are from the sounds of things. So it doesn't take much to draw conclusions from that, does it?'

'No, apparently not. Though I wouldn't say that Anna and I are still involved in the way you imagine. I look out for her and obviously for Kyle, too. She doesn't have any parents or any family to turn to, and so I feel it's up to me to make sure that they're both all right. I do what I can for them.'

She noticed that he hadn't answered her question, but for the moment she left that to one side. Perhaps, for some reason, he was reluctant to acknowledge his role in Anna's life, and given the recriminations that had followed the pair, she couldn't really blame him for that. 'You always looked out for her. Isn't that why you gave her the job at the Mill House Bakery once it was restored?'

He shrugged. 'She seemed the ideal person to take charge there. She was young, certainly, but she loved baking and was very good at producing wholesome food. She was also good with people and had a way of charming the customers.'

He picked a slice of toast from the rack and began to butter it. 'My gran thought she would be the perfect person to run the place. Of course, Anna always looked in on Gran at Mill House and made sure that she was all right, so they got on really well. She had a homely way about her, Gran said, and she knew how to pretty up the tea shop and make it welcoming.' He smiled. 'Besides, Gran had a yen for Anna's oatcakes. She said they were delicious served with cheese or pâté.'

'That was true. I tasted them myself. And as to your grandmother's advice, she was a wise lady and above all she was a good judge of character.' She started to eat once again, pricking the egg with her fork so that the yolk spilled out. 'So what is Anna doing now? After all, she left all that behind her when she went to Cheshire with you.' He had put someone else in place to keep the business going, a middle-aged woman with a flair for patisserie, and the enterprise was still thriving.

'Anna runs her own catering business from home, supplying specialty cakes, biscuits, gingerbread men, and so on. It works well for her, because it means that she can keep an eye on Kyle while she's baking. He's just started school, though, so I suppose she'll have more time to herself from now on.' He frowned, spearing mushrooms with his fork. 'That's perhaps a good thing, because she's been finding it difficult to cope lately. She's not well…in fact, she hasn't been well for a long time.'

Jasmine felt a rush of concern. Whatever she thought about the triangle of Ben, Anna and her brother, she had always liked the girl that Callum had brought home. He had said that she was the one for him, and she and her parents had welcomed her to the fold.

'What's wrong with her? Is it something that she's talked about? I noticed that she often tired easily, and maybe she was a little breathless sometimes, but she never complained and I thought perhaps it was just that she'd been overdoing things, working late in the bakery. She was always looking for ways to improve the layout of the tea shop or add new products to the menu.'

He hesitated before answering. 'She has a congenital heart problem...though she won't thank me for telling you that, and I hope you'll keep it to yourself.'

She gave a soft gasp. Then she nodded. 'I will, of course.' She frowned. 'Is she having treatment for it?'

'Some medication to regulate the heartbeat. The condition was diagnosed some years back, and I think the feeling was to wait and hope that it wouldn't be too problematic. Unfortunately that turned out to be a false hope. She's been seeing her original consultant back at Wellbeck on a regular basis, and he's of the opinion that she's going to need surgery fairly soon.'

'I'm so sorry. I had no idea.' The news was troubling, and she was sad, imagining what Anna must have had to contend with over the years, more so now that she had a young child to bring up. It was very likely that being pregnant and giving birth would have put an added strain on her heart. 'I can't think why she didn't want anyone to know what she was going through.'

His lips made a flat line. 'Anna is a very private person. There was a good deal of bad feeling when she left Woodsley Bridge, and she was concerned that she had hurt Callum deeply. Personally, I think that concern was misplaced. He had it in his power to win her back, but instead he chose to let her go.'

Jasmine pulled a face. 'I'm not sure that he could have competed with you. Everyone knew you only had to click your fingers and the girls would come running.'

His mouth twisted. 'You're exaggerating. Like most people in the village, you're looking at the surface picture and not delving into what really goes on.'

'Am I? Maybe.' She gave a dismissive shrug. 'Is Anna's need for privacy the same reason why you won't admit to being Kyle's father? Does Anna want you to keep it to yourself? I don't understand why either of you would need to do that.'

He swallowed more coffee. 'That's just the way it is,' he said, his face becoming serious. 'I'll abide by Anna's wishes. What matters is that I knew that I could take care of her, and I promised her that I wouldn't let her down.'

'But you didn't marry her?' Perhaps that was why he didn't want to acknowledge the child was his. Surely any decent man would want to provide for his child, and it would be shameful for him to admit that he had been unwilling to make a proper commitment to Anna?

His gaze met hers. 'No, I didn't. Anna wanted her independence, and I can understand that. She lost her parents at an early age and was brought up in foster-care. Perhaps that's why we get along so well together. It seemed that we had something in common, with me losing my mother and my father being so distant…and I could understand how she felt when she was striving to rise above her background. She wanted to find her own way in life, but she was vulnerable and she needed a helping hand to get there. I was happy enough to provide that helping hand.'

Hadn't he sidestepped the question once more? Jasmine frowned. Perhaps she was right in her summing-up. He wouldn't own up to being the father because he hadn't been prepared to make a proper commitment to the child's mother. How would that information go down in a small village like Woodsley Bridge…and, furthermore, how would his father react? It would be one more blow to any chance of recovering that relationship.

Whatever the ins and outs of the situation, it was clear that Ben still cared very deeply for Anna. He was still concerned about her five years after they'd left Woodsley together, and he kept a picture of the little boy in his wallet. How much more did she need to know?

'I'm sure she must be thankful for all that you've done for her,' she said, straightening up, 'just as I appreciate all that you've done for me. Are you sure it won't put you out, taking me home?'

He shook his head. 'Not at all. I want to take a look at Mill House and make sure everything's ready for me to move in. I've been leasing it out for the last few years, but the tenants moved out a month ago. I thought I would air the place and make sure the fridge and freezer are stocked up.' He held up the coffee jug and offered to refill her cup.

She nodded. 'Thanks.' She studied him. 'Are you not going to suggest to your father that you stay with him, at least for a while?'

'And risk a third world war? I don't think so.' He spread marmalade onto his toast. 'Besides, I have my own place, Mill House, and it will be easier to supervise the work on my next renovation from there.'

'Your next renovation? Does that mean you've bought another property?' She raised a brow. 'Do I know the place?'

'The old barn next to the mill. I've been doing a two-storey conversion. There's a stable block there, too, and I'm planning to turn it into some kind of business unit. There's a lot of land with the prospect of development.'

She frowned. 'I heard something about that. There was talk around the village when the for-sale sign was taken down and I know a lot of work has been going on there. I think a lot of people are worried about what kind of business will be started up.'

'And when they find out that I'm the one who has bought the land and property, they'll have even more to say on that score, I expect.' His mouth slanted. 'It doesn't bother me. I'll listen to what they have to say and I'll try to address their concerns, but at the end of the day I have planning permission and that gives me the right to do what I want.'

'Don't you always do that anyway?' She put down her knife and fork. 'What kind of business are you planning? Another shop unit, like the bakery and tea shop?'

'I'm not sure yet. There are certain limitations, given the natural surroundings, but I'm thinking something agricultural. A farm shop, maybe. There's a lot of land attached to the barn and outbuildings.'

'That'll be interesting…in more ways than one.' She gave him a thoughtful glance, and he chuckled.

'You want to see me get my comeuppance, don't you? I can see the headlines now in the village paper: *Woodsley ne'er do well comes unstuck with his latest project. Villagers in outcry over plans to turn place of natural beauty into business hot spot. Traffic jams predicted as outsiders pour in from all around the county.*'

'You may well scoff, but perhaps you need to rethink your approach…more softly-softly might work better than bull at a gate. People are more likely to respond to quiet reasoning.'

'Try telling that to my father.'

She sipped her coffee, watching his expression change to one of sad resignation. 'I know he objected to you restoring Mill House and bringing back the water mill into working order, but you went ahead anyway, so you could hardly say that you lost out.'

'That wasn't what the argument was about.' His lips compressed, as though he was dredging up a painful memory. 'He didn't care that it had been my grand-mother's home for years. To him, it was a waste of time and energy to do any work on it. To me, it was the chance for my gran to stay in the house where she had lived with my grandfather for most of her married life. It was the opportunity for her to live in comfort for the remainder of her years.' He frowned. 'I would do it again, without a second thought, if I was presented with the same choice.'

She gave him a gentle smile. 'If it's any consola-tion, I think you did the right thing. Your grandmother was so happy to be able to stay in the house. I know it must have been hard for you, because it was common knowledge your father put obstacles in your way. I'm not sure exactly what he did, but I know it meant you delayed going to medical school, and you carried out the renovations in spite of him.'

He stood up and started to clear away the breakfast dishes. 'He didn't want me to go to medical school. He said I would never see it through, that it would be one of those fly-by-night ideas that would disappear in a matter of months.'

His mouth twisted. 'Of course, he was set on me going into finance like him, and when I chose not to go to university to study economics and accounting, he held back the money from my trust fund. He had the power to release some of it when I was eighteen, and again when I was twenty-one, but he refused to do it. It was a kind of blackmail, but I called his bluff. And once he'd stated his position, he couldn't back down. Or wouldn't.'

'So how did you find the money to do the work on Mill House?' She put down her coffee cup and began to help him stack the crockery in the dishwasher.

'I took a job with a computer company in town. There was training on the job, and soon I was earning quite a good salary. I saved as much as I could and put it to use doing the renovations. I did most of the work myself, with help and advice from experts, so in the end it didn't cost too much. And then I had the idea of starting up the bakery next door and selling the products in the teashop. It all worked out pretty well.'

'And that funded your medical studies?'

'That's right. It meant that I started a few years later than I would have liked, much the same as Callum did with his studies, but I managed it in the end, so it all ended well.'

'Except that you never made things up with your father.'

He shrugged. 'I suppose it was a matter of pride with him. I'd gone against him, and he had difficulty coming to terms with that. Even though I qualified as a doctor, it wasn't the profession he would have chosen for me. And I couldn't forgive him for his attitude towards my gran. He liked Gran well enough, but he had tunnel vision and he couldn't see why she wanted to stay in that house. It wasn't a profitable option, he said. It was pure folly to cling on to it, he thought, and he said it was silly sentiment. He had no time for that.'

He closed the door of the dishwasher and began to set the controls.

It was a battle of wills that went on and on between them, Jasmine conceded as she started to straighten the chairs. The final straw, she recalled, had come when Ben had gone away with Anna. Perhaps Stuart had mourned the fact that his son was finally leaving the village. The fact that he was taking Anna with him was one last hurdle he hadn't been able to overcome.

It was also the stumbling block that had tripped Jasmine. How could she even think of trying to get closer to Ben when Anna was still part of his life?

CHAPTER FIVE

'How does it feel to be coming back to Woodsley Bridge?' Jasmine sent Ben a sideways glance as he drove along the country lane leading towards the village. 'I always love to see it as we approach along this road. From the top of the hill the whole place is laid out before you...all those hills and dales and lovely white-painted houses mixed in with stone built cottages... And then there's the sea, shimmering in the distance.'

'It's a pretty place, I'll give you that, even more so when the sun's shining, as it is now.'

She nodded agreement. 'The snow's just about gone from the rooftops, and the sky's such a lovely blue. It's exhilarating. I love it here. The view never fails to take my breath away.' She turned to him. 'But you didn't tell me how you feel about it. Are you having mixed feelings about coming back to the Lake District after all this time?'

He hesitated for a moment. 'I think I am. On the one hand it's good to see the place, but on the other I'm not so sure I'll be welcomed with open arms in some quarters...my father, your brother, the villagers who object to me buying up the land next to the mill.'

She understood how he felt. 'It was never going to be easy, but at least you've taken the first step. Will you be dropping in on your father?'

'Yes. I have to. In fact, I'll probably make that my first call—get it over and done with and see how the land lies after that. I rang him to say that I would be stopping by.'

'How did he react to that?'

He grimaced. 'It's hard to tell. He's not exactly welcoming me with open arms—I'm certainly not the prodigal son redeeming myself in his eyes.' He shot her a quick glance. 'He was fairly noncommittal, I suppose… though I did tell him I'd heard he was ill and wanted to check that he was all right.'

'That must have pleased him, surely—the fact that you cared enough to come back and find out?'

'Probably not. He said he was okay and he didn't need people fussing over him. Then again, he was always a man who preferred to keep himself to himself. I doubt he's going to change very much at this late stage.' He turned the car into the village and headed down a winding road. 'I'm not certain where you want me to take you…would you like me to drop you off at your place, or would you prefer to go straight to your parents' house?'

His smile was crooked. 'I'm assuming you don't want to come back with me to Mill House, of course. If you did, it would be great if we could spend some more time together.'

She smiled. 'Now, there's a dilemma. I'd love to hang around with you for a bit longer, and I'd like to see the house again some time—it's such a beautiful old place—but I really don't think it would be a good idea to do either of those things right now. Besides, my mother's expecting me to go straight to their house. So…I'd like to head right to to my mother's, if that's all right with you?'

'That's fine. No problem.'

'Thanks. We generally do a stack of baking this time of year and finish the day with decorating the tree. I think she's expecting Callum to drop by later on, too.'

'Ah.' His expression sobered. 'Then I expect you have quite a bit of catching up to do. I know he finished his university course about eighteen months ago…I saw the announcement of his honours degree in horticulture in your local paper. I have it sent over so that I can keep up with what's going on. But then I heard he'd taken a job with one of the National Trust gardens so I don't suppose you see an awful lot of him these days?'

She frowned. 'How did you hear that—about his job, I mean?'

'Anna mentioned it. She still has friends in the village who pass her snippets of news from time to time.'

'Oh, I see.' She nodded. 'Yes, he's away quite a bit. He comes back sometimes for the weekend, and of course at holiday times. The rest of the time he stays at his flat down in Essex.'

'Another man with itchy feet, then?' He sent her a considering glance. 'Anna was never sure that Callum would stay in the village, even when he qualified, and she was right, wasn't she? And maybe it was the fact that he was planning to go off to university that sparked her decision to break off with him—don't you think that's a strong possibility?'

'That's not what Callum thought, or most of the village, by all accounts. All anyone could see was that you and she were growing closer, and Millie Rossiter, the postie, saw you with your arms around her on more than one occasion.' She gave him a long look. 'So, no, I don't think that was it at all. I think she went off with you because she fell for you, big time. And we were left to pick up the pieces when Callum's world collapsed around him.'

His mouth made a rueful quirk. 'Well, I'm sorry about that. But Anna made her own decision to leave. I was heading for Cheshire to take up a new job, and she wanted to come with me.'

She gave him a sceptical look. 'There's really no point in you trying to tell me that you had nothing to do with it. I'm siding with the rest of the villagers on this one.'

He smiled wryly. 'Yes, I thought you might.' He drove by the village green, through the small shopping centre that was the hub of community life and, after a while, turned into a leafy lane bordered by a scattering of houses. They stopped at Jasmine's cottage to drop off her case and then headed west towards the park.

Her parents lived in a large house at the end of the park road. Ben cut the engine and slid out from the driver's seat, going to stand in front of the house, looking around.

Jasmine joined him. She loved this house. It was where she and her brother had grown up, cherished by the love of both parents, and she wondered how Ben must feel, having missed out on all that. His father had always been a solitary man for the most part, immersing himself in his work, not sure how to deal with the infant son who turned to him for love and wanted so much more of his attention than he was able to give.

She looked at the rambling building, the front walls covered with neatly trimmed ivy. The front garden had a perfect, bowling-green lawn, her father's pride and joy, though now it was dotted here and there with clumps of melting snow. There were shrubs all around, firethorn, glowing with bright red berries, and berberis, showing off its rich, bronze leaves. Yellow wallflowers peeped out from the borders.

The house was solidly built from local stone. The ground-floor rooms were used for the most part as a surgery and waiting room, but the large lounge and kitchen were kept separate from them. Upstairs, there were three bedrooms, a bathroom and a study.

Her mother must have seen them arrive, because she opened the door to them now and welcomed Jasmine with a hug. 'Thank goodness you made it home,' she said. 'I was afraid you'd be stuck in the snow for days.'

'I probably would have been, if it hadn't been for Ben.' Jasmine turned and waved Ben forward to meet her mother. 'He rescued me from the snowdrift and when I told him I needed to get back here to decorate the tree, he offered to drive me home.'

'Well, thank you for that, Ben,' her mother said, giving him a quick, but faintly cautious smile. Her green eyes were a little troubled, and she took a moment to brush back a lock of chestnut hair, tucking it behind her ear. Jasmine guessed she was debating how best to handle the situation. 'Would you like to come in and have a drink of something to warm you up?'

'No, thanks all the same, Helen. It's good of you to offer, but I have to go over to the manor, and then I've some arrangements to make at Mill House.'

'Oh, I see. Some other time, then, perhaps?' Jasmine wasn't sure whether she detected a hint of relief in her mother's acknowledging smile. She liked Ben well enough, she guessed, but Callum would be horrified to know that his parents had welcomed him into their house, and her mother had to be conscious of that.

'Thanks again for bringing me home, Ben,' Jasmine told him, and he nodded.

She watched as he walked to his car. He wouldn't have missed her mother's hesitation, but wasn't one to let his feelings show. His stride was confident, his back straight, but she couldn't help wondering how he would fare with his father. She wished she could be at his side to lend him moral support…but, then, Ben didn't need anyone's help. He was his own man. He did what he felt to be right, no matter what the circumstances, and meeting his father after all this time was just one more challenge he had to face.

'I wasn't sure what time you would get here,' her mother said, 'so I started on the baking. I'm doing mince pies for the freezer and I've made a start on the Christmas pudding. Do you want to help? You could make your lovely fruit loaf, if you like. You know how much we love to have it for tea on Christmas Day. I have everything you need…flour, yeast, fruit, spices, and so on.'

She walked along the hallway to the kitchen, and Jasmine followed. 'I just have to put the covers on the Christmas pudding,' her mother added, 'and then it's all set to go in the pan of water. I'd better get moving—it has to cook for eight hours…' She rolled her eyes. 'I shall have to set the timer to remind me to keep topping up the water.'

'I thought I could smell delicious things coming from the kitchen.' Jasmine smiled. She loved her mother's Christmas traditions, the baking sessions where she would prepare everything possible ahead of the big day.

'I've made a pot of tea, and there's pizza and salad for lunch later on. Your father's off on his rounds, so he won't be back for a while.' Her mother was already bringing out cups and saucers, and Jasmine went to wash her hands at the sink. Then she put on an apron and readied herself to start cooking.

'So what does Ben have to say for himself?' her mother asked as they carefully kneaded dough. 'Apart from the fact that he's planning on coming home? Is he still with Anna?'

Jasmine made a face. 'I'm not sure exactly what the situation is. I'm certain he's still seeing her, and she stays at his place sometimes, but I don't think it's a full-on relationship any more. She has a little boy, four years old, and I think he feels that he has to take care of them.'

'Good heavens.' Her mother's eyes widened and she stopped what she was doing, lifting her hands away from the dough. 'I suppose the child must be his?' She frowned. 'He has to be, given that they've been away from here for five years. That's going to be a bitter blow for Callum, isn't it?'

'What's going to be a bitter blow for me?' The male voice startled both women, and they turned to see Callum walk into the kitchen. He must have let himself in by the front door, and now he dropped a couple of holdalls onto the floor and went to put his arms around his mother. Tall and strong bodied, his embrace engulfed her. 'It's good to see you again, Mum,' he said, his grey eyes filled with affection. 'You too, Jass,' he added, coming to give her a quick hug.

'We weren't expecting you till later,' Helen said, wiping her hands on a tea towel.

'I know, but I've worked the weekend, filling in for a colleague, and the boss gave me the nod to finish early. I have time off until Christmas now, so I've brought a big case.'

'And a load of washing, too, by the looks of things.' His mother smiled as she noted one of the bulging bags.

He gave a sheepish grin. 'So what's this thing I'm not going to like?' he asked, checking the teapot to see if it was hot and then reaching for a cup. 'Have you gone and let my room out to a stranger while I've been away? Don't tell me you're casting your only son out onto the street?'

'Oh, now, there's an idea.' Helen put on a thoughtful expression. 'Letting your room out…that could turn out to be quite a lucrative proposition, couldn't it? Why didn't I think of that?' Her mouth twitched at the corners.

Callum made a wry face, and turned to Jasmine. 'Are you going to tell me what's going on? What's happening?' He swallowed his tea like a man escaping from a desert.

'We were just saying that Ben Radcliffe's coming back to live in the village,' she told him. She wasn't sure how wise it would be to mention Anna in the same breath, let alone tell him about her son. 'He'll be living at Mill House and working with the rescue services.'

Callum's face became shuttered. 'How do you know that?'

She sent him a quick, appraising look. It was difficult to know how he would react after all this time, but the signs so far weren't good. 'We met up on the last day of my course, and then he helped me out when my car was stuck in a snowdrift. He told me he plans to work here for a couple of months, based at Wellbeck Hospital.'

'I see.' He put down his cup and seemed to be waiting for the information to sink in. After a moment or two, he said flatly, 'At least I'm forewarned. I should be able to steer clear of him.'

He pulled out a chair and sat down at the table. 'Is there any news of Anna? How's she doing? I've heard bits and pieces over the years from her friends. She's kept up with the baking, so I'm told. And they say she's still with Ben…or, at least, still close to him.'

Jasmine looked to her mother for help. What was she to say? Anna's friends had obviously kept quiet about the child. Her mother looked apprehensive, but lifted her hands in an expansive, resigned gesture that Jasmine took as a signal to go ahead.

'She's been running her own specialty catering business from home—making cakes, biscuits and the like.' She frowned. 'But there is something else you should know…she has a child, a little boy.'

Callum's swift intake of breath was audible. He was silent for a while, his dark head bent, and then he said in a taut voice, 'I suppose it was inevitable. He was always a charmer, that one, so why should Anna be the exception to the rule?'

Jasmine laid a gentle hand on his shoulder. 'I'm sorry, Callum. None of us would have wanted you to come home to this. Are you going to be all right?'

He straightened. 'Of course. I've had five years to get her out of my system, haven't I? I'll be fine.'

His glance roamed over his holdalls. 'Maybe I'll go and take these upstairs,' he suggested, looking towards their mother. 'Is it all right if I put the laundry in the wash bin? I'd quite like to have the blue shirt ready for tomorrow's Christmas dance, if that's okay? I thought I'd better make my presence felt, and give the local girls a run for their money.'

Helen gave a motherly smile. 'That's my boy, practical as ever. Of course it's all right. I'll put your things in the washer overnight.'

He stood up and gave her a quick kiss. 'Thanks, Mum. You're an angel.'

They watched as he left the room, and for a while neither of them spoke. They knew his words about the village Christmas dance were pure bravado, and it was clear he wanted to be alone for a while.

Jasmine kept her thoughts to herself and continued to knead the dough for a minute or two before shaping it into a crescent.

'I'd forgotten about the village social evening,' she said a moment or two later. 'I suppose everyone will be there.'

'Everyone except Stuart Radcliffe, I imagine. He rarely attends that sort of thing.' Her mother's gaze was far away. 'I can't help feeling sorry for that man, somehow. I know he seems austere in his attitude, and he can be brusque in the extreme sometimes, but how can we know what goes on inside his head? He must be a deeply troubled man, but he keeps it all locked up inside, and that can't be good for him, can it?'

'No, probably not.' Jasmine's thoughts swivelled to Ben. How was his meeting with his father going? And had he managed to find out anything more about his illness? Would he be able to do anything to help him?

By the following day, Sunday, the sun's rays had seen off the last of the snow. Everything in the garden looked newly washed and clean, and by the end of the day Jasmine looked about her cottage, pleased that everything in there was equally fresh and sparkling. Perhaps her feverish burst of house cleaning had to do with the fact that Ben was back home after all these years, and she needed a way of clearing him from her mind. The only way she knew how to do that was to keep busy.

At around half past six that evening, she was looking through her wardrobe, trying to decide what to wear for the dance. Something chic and sophisticated, perhaps, or should she go for floaty and feminine…or maybe a glitzy party dress? She couldn't decide, and as she was checking her closet once more, the doorbell rang downstairs.

She abandoned her search and went to answer the door. Ben stood on her porch, leaning negligently against the wooden post, eyeing the winter flowering jasmine that scrambled over the trellis around her door. Looking at him, her heart missed a beat. He was dressed in an immaculate dark grey suit, cut from fine-quality material, and his shirt was a soft dove-grey, enlivened by a silk tie in gentle tones of grey and blue. He looked truly impressive and her whole body responded to his presence with a surge of unbidden yearning.

'I was beginning to think you weren't going to answer,' he said, his tone dry. 'Did you realise it was me and decide to wait till I went away?' He studied her, a glimmer of amusement in his eyes. 'Obviously, I wasn't going to do that.'

She pulled herself together. 'I was trying to decide what to wear to the Christmas dance this evening,' she murmured, ushering him inside the cottage. She showed him into her small kitchen and switched on the coffee machine. 'You get girls wearing all sorts of outfits to these things, and I'm having trouble making up my mind.'

'You'd look good whatever you wear,' he murmured, his gaze lingering on her soft, feminine curves.

She tried not to respond to his flirtatious manner, but her pulse began to beat a little faster and, when she tried to speak, her voice sounded husky to her ears.

'Perhaps you'd like to sit down?' She waved him to a seat by the pine table. 'I expect you'd like a cup of coffee.' She set out cups and then asked casually, 'Are you planning on going to the dance?'

He nodded. 'I thought it might be a good opportunity to speak to one or two business contacts. I need to clear up some issues over the building work I'm having done…and, besides, I have to attend because the vicar asked me to run the raffle. He collared me in the street yesterday and had me in a corner, so I really couldn't come up with an excuse. That was after he wrung a raffle donation out of me… I promised a couple of bottles of champagne from the cellar at the mill, along with an iced Christmas cake and a hamper. He seemed quite pleased overall.'

'I should imagine he would be, at that.'

'Anyway,' he said, 'I wondered if you'd like to go with me? I know it's a bit late to ask, but I've had a lot to sort out since I arrived back here. We could drive down there, if you like. It's a fair walk from here, and it looks as though it's going to be a cold night.' He paused, a frown crossing his brow. 'Unless, of course, you already have a date?'

'I don't. I was planning on being a wallflower at the back of the hall.'

He laughed. 'That would never happen. I've seen the way the local men eye you up. They must have asked and you refused.'

'Ah, well, I wasn't sure I'd be able to make it with my shift patterns. As it happens, though, I don't have to be back at work till Tuesday…at least by then I should have my car back.'

'So, will you come with me? Is it a date?'

'I… Yes, I'll come with you.' Her gaze was troubled. 'But let's not think of it as a date, shall we?' She ran her tongue over dry lips. 'You know, this isn't easy for me. I have to think about Callum. He'll be there, and I don't want to do anything that will cause him any grief.'

He gave her a look that was half cynical, half re-signed. 'Don't you think it's time Callum got over it and moved on? You can't live your life forever concerning yourself with what Callum thinks and feels. Shouldn't you be following your own instincts?'

She gave a short laugh. 'If I did that, I'd have taken to my heels whenever you came within shouting distance.

You don't have the best reputation in the world, Ben...a girl would have to be out of her mind to take your soft words to heart. And as to Callum, he's my brother, my family—but you wouldn't know about that kind of loyalty, would you? You never had a close family, so you don't understand about the ties that bind.' She shook her head, causing the chestnut waves to quiver. 'I don't blame you for that. I just think it's sad, that's all.' She poured the coffee and pushed a cup towards him.

He pressed a hand to his heart and put on a pained expression. 'I think I'm stung by all that you've just said. I may not have brothers and sisters, or any kind of close family unit, but that doesn't mean I don't understand what it is to care for someone. I loved my grandmother, and I miss her terribly. I was always fiercely loyal to her...she was like a mother to me. And even though my father and I have a difficult relationship, I do care about him. I just wish that I could find some way to break through the barriers he puts up.'

She sat down at the table and looked at him, her green eyes showing her concern. 'Did things not go well yesterday between you?'

'Not really.' He tested the heat of the coffee against his lips and sipped slowly. 'It's strange, isn't it, how much our parents' opinion matters? Even when we're grown men and women, successful in whatever we do, we need to know that we have that ultimate approval.'

He rested his cup on the saucer. 'I'm not going to get it, of course, because my father's pride demands that I follow his beliefs and traditions, and any deviation from that is taken as an insult.' He gave a negligent shrug. 'It doesn't really matter, because I've made my own way in life, and I can get by easily enough without him or his blessing, but it would have been good to break through that stubborn streak of his and find some way of reaching a new rapport.' He sighed. 'It's not to be, though.'

She frowned. 'I'm sorry. I hoped you and he might be able to patch things up. Perhaps his illness makes it more difficult for him to do that? People who are ill might tend to be tetchy or even unreasonable sometimes.'

'I doubt that's his problem, but you're right, he's not at all well, and it doesn't help.'

'How bad is it?'

He pulled in a deep breath. 'Bad enough. I think his high blood pressure is beginning to have an effect on his kidneys, and if he carries on the way he is, there could be some permanent damage. He's not taking his condition seriously enough, in my opinion. He says he missed his last monitoring session at the blood-pressure clinic, and he hasn't been back to his GP—your father—for a while. Apparently he doesn't have an appointment with the consultant for another three months, but I think he needs to go sooner.'

'I'm guessing he wouldn't let you examine him, so how do you know all this?'

'I noticed that his ankles were swollen, as well as his hands, and he seemed quite breathless, so there's probably a build-up of fluid on his lungs as well. He's taking ACE inhibitors to lower his blood pressure, along with beta blockers to regulate the heartbeat, but he needs to take a diuretic as well.' He grimaced. 'I tried to tell him that he needs to cut down on salt and eat a healthy diet, but I'm afraid my advice didn't go down too well.'

'You mean he didn't listen?'

He made a wry face. 'Oh, he listened. He just said that if he needed help he was perfectly capable of going to see his own doctor and he didn't need any input from me. In other words, mind my own business.'

'Oh, dear.' She could understand Ben's frustration. No matter what he said or did, there was no moving his father. He had taken up an inflexible stance, and Ben must feel as though he was banging his head against a wall. It was to his credit that he kept on trying. 'For what it's worth, I think you're doing the right thing by keeping the lines of communication open. I don't see how you can do any more, given the way he is.'

She was thoughtful for a moment. 'Would it be worth my asking my father to call him in to the surgery for a check-up…say that he's been going through his records and feels it's time for a routine examination, given his blood-pressure results and the fact that he missed his last appointment?'

He nodded. 'I'm sure that would be a great start. I know he respects your father. He might be able to get him to see sense.'

'I'll do that, then. He'll be at the dance tonight, so I'll try to find an opportunity to have a word with him about it.'

'Thanks.' His glance trailed over her. 'So, aren't we supposed to be there in about half an hour?'

She looked at the clock. 'Oh, heavens,' she said. 'Look at the time… And I'm still sitting here, when I should be getting ready.' She stood up and headed towards the door. Turning around, she said, 'Help yourself to more coffee. Read the paper. Just…just amuse yourself for half an hour or so, while I get ready.'

'Half an hour, when you're already perfection?' He raised a dark brow. 'Totally unnecessary but, yes, don't worry about me. I'll be fine down here.'

She shot off up the stairs and went back to checking her closet. Ben would be perfectly all right, hanging around downstairs, wouldn't he? If he hadn't turned up on her doorstep, she would be more than ready by now.

Some time later, she peered at her image in the mirror. Her dress was made of a soft, silky fabric, with thin shoulder straps and a bodice that was decorated with beads. The skirt swirled gently around her knees as she walked. She had brushed her hair until it gleamed, leaving it to fall over her shoulders, and she used a light touch with her make-up, adding soft colour to her cheeks.

Satisfied that she was ready at last, she picked up her bag and went downstairs.

'Wow.' Ben's eyes widened. He sat there, looking at her and not saying another word, as though he was utterly speechless, but at the same time his gaze wandered over her, taking in every detail of her appearance.

She waited, not knowing quite how to respond, and then he added softly, 'You take my breath away. You're stunning, Jassie, absolutely stunning.'

It gave her a warm feeling inside, knowing that he liked the way she looked, and that sense of well-being stayed with her all the way to the village hall where the dance was being held. Only then, as she walked through the door, did she wonder how she was going to deal with the issue of her brother.

The evening was already in full swing, with the local band playing popular music. The dance floor was

crowded, and at one side of the room people were helping themselves to a finger buffet. The hall was decorated
with glittering streamers of red and gold, and there were
garlands of holly and berries to either side of the platform where the band was performing.

'Perhaps we should go and look for Callum,' Ben
said, as though his mind was running along the same
groove as hers. 'That way, hopefully, your evening won't
be spoiled with worrying about his reaction.'

She nodded. 'He's over by the bar. I'll go and have a
word with him.' She had thought Ben might stay behind
and talk to one or two friends who were milling about
near the buffet table, but instead he came with her.

'How are things with you, Callum?' he asked, as they
approached. Ben went to stand next to her brother, and
ordered drinks from the barman, turning to Jasmine to
find out what she wanted.

Callum stiffened. 'I'd say I was fine until you came
along,' he said, his voice taut. 'What happened? Did
you decide to come back and wreak more havoc? From
what I've been hearing this evening, you're all set to
build a hotel on the land next to the mill. That hasn't
gone down well with the bed-and-breakfast proprietors
around here, I can tell you.'

Ben handed Jasmine a glass of red wine. 'Well, you'll
be able to tell your friends that I'm not planning on
building a hotel, so that's one worry out of the way, isn't
it?' He looked at Callum's empty glass. 'Can I buy you
a drink?'

Callum shook his head. 'No, thanks. I'll buy my
own.' He nodded towards the barman to fill up his glass
again. 'So where's Anna these days? Have you left her

and moved on to my sister?' He sent Jasmine a piercing glance so that she shifted uncomfortably and tried to look him in the eye without flinching.

'Not at all,' Ben said smoothly. 'Anna will be coming back to Woodsley shortly. She's going to be staying for a while…a couple of months, at least…so I imagine you and she will have a chance to become reacquainted.'

Jasmine gave a soft intake of breath. Anna was coming back here?

Callum's expression turned to a glower. 'I think I've said all that I want to say to you.' He looked at Jasmine. 'I hope you know what you're doing.'

'Ben helped me out a lot over the last couple of days,' she told him. 'I'm very grateful to him. It doesn't mean I'm planning on starting a full-blooded affair. Callum, you're my brother, and I love you, but you have to try to get over the past and think about the future. Anna played as much a part in your break-up as Ben did. And maybe you had a role to play, too.'

'And maybe you need to think a bit more carefully about who you're messing with. He's not some country boy who made an honest mistake. He's broken a lot of hearts around here and then casually walked away without looking back.'

'I doubt he was to blame on all counts. Anyway, I'm all grown up now, Callum. You don't need to watch out for me.' She said it convincingly enough, but his words had hit a little too close to home, and now she moved away from the bar, leaving her brother and Ben to continue their frosty exchange. 'I'm going to talk to friends for a while,' she murmured. She glanced at Ben.

'Why don't you go and talk to the people you wanted to see? I'll be over the other side of the room if you come looking for me.'

She didn't want to fall out with either of them. This was a Christmas dance, an annual event where villagers came in good spirits and looked forward to the coming festivities. It would have been good to find a little Christmas cheer coming her way, but it looked as though it wasn't to be.

She went to find her parents and talked to them for a while, sipping her wine and feeling its warmth creep through the whole of her body. It occurred to her that she ought to find something to eat before the alcohol had the better of her.

'I'll get my receptionist to give Stuart a ring,' her father said. 'It sounds as though he needs his medication updated.'

'Thanks, Dad. I appreciate it.'

After a while, friends came to join in the conversation, and Jasmine talked to them for a few minutes before going to help herself to hors d'oeuvres and a glass of mulled wine from a serving bowl on the buffet table. Then she joined her friends on the dance floor, moving in time to the beat of the music, letting the throbbing notes of the guitars and keyboard fill her soul.

Ben came in search of her when she was taking a break, talking to a young man who worked at the local garage. He slid an arm around her shoulders, a possessive, deliberate action, and clearly her companion took that as a hint to leave. He made a rueful face and went to find another girl to chat up.

'Sorry to leave you to your own devices for so long,' Ben said. 'I managed to iron out a few problems with

the local builders and the man from the planning department. No such luck with your brother, though. I hoped
I might be able to reason with him, but I had about
as much success as I did with my father. I'd say your
brother and I have reached a mutual stand-off. I don't
see any way the situation can be easily resolved, so we
may as well leave things alone for now.'

'You're probably right. Callum's been mulling things
over all this time, so he isn't going to change his attitude
overnight.'

'No, I suppose not.' He looked at her, his gaze moving
down to her strappy silver shoes. 'It would be a crime
not to give those a full outing, don't you think? Shall
we dance?' He laid a hand on the small of her back and
drew her onto the dance floor.

They joined the throng of people twisting and turning
and generally moving to the rhythm of the music in any
way they could, and the floor was so crowded that they
were frequently jostled together. Laughing, Ben caught
hold of her and held her close, pulling her gently to him.
'We could make our own special dance,' he murmured,
his voice rough edged. He lowered his head so that his
cheek softly grazed hers. 'Just the two of us, one that
lasts the whole night long.'

His words brought a swift surge of heat to race
through her entire body, and even as her hands discovered his hard rib cage, she knew that she ought to resist
him. She was powerless, though, unable and unwilling
to pull back from his tender embrace. He made her feel
that above all she was a sensual being, and her body
craved his touch.

And he was happy enough to oblige. His hand was lightly stroking the small of her back, drawing her ever nearer to him, so that her feminine curves were moulded to him and his thighs lightly brushed hers.

She was dizzy with sensation. The music throbbed in her head and all she wanted was for him to go on holding her like this for ever. She didn't even notice that he had carefully led her to a far corner of the room, where the lights were dim and they were shielded from prying eyes by a large Christmas tree.

It was only when she lifted her gaze to drink in his features in the soft light that she realised they were virtually alone in this little island of tranquillity. It was as though the outside world didn't exist. The people on the other side of the tree were oblivious to them and all that mattered was that she was here with him. His arms were around her and his hands were stroking her, smoothing over the curve of her hips, urging her ever closer to him.

The music pounded in her head, reaching a crescendo, an explosion of sound, and a brief moment of sanity intervened. 'I'm not sure how this fits in with your idea of good behaviour,' she said huskily. 'I have too much to lose, letting you work your magic on me, and you must know that I'm a little light-headed from the wine, or I wouldn't have let you get this far.'

He nuzzled her cheek with his lips, and murmured softly, 'There's no problem that I can see, Jassie. You only have to look up to see that.' He placed a curled finger lightly beneath her chin and tilted her head upwards.

A sprig of mistletoe hovered over them, the pale berries a stark contrast to the dark, green leaves. 'You see?'

he said, his voice a coaxing rumble against her cheek. 'Mistletoe is for lovers… And I'd love more than anything to fulfil its promise…to kiss you and make you mine, just for one moment.'

He didn't wait for her to answer and, if the truth were known, she couldn't have spoken at all right then. The mistletoe gleamed faintly above them, and she knew that what she wanted more than anything was for him to kiss her, a long, sweet and thorough kiss…and as if he had read her mind, that's exactly what he did. His lips lightly stroked hers, trailing fire where they touched, teasing them apart, and then he deepened the kiss, softly demanding, coaxing a response that she gave only too willingly.

Her fingers slid over his chest, gliding upwards to trace the line of his shoulders and his throat. She wanted him, she loved the feel of him, and the only thing that stood between them was the fact that they were in a room full of people.

That thought had a sobering effect on her. Cautiously, she eased her hands away from him and reluctantly drew back. 'This is the wrong place,' she whispered. 'The wrong time.'

'And the wrong man.' Her brother's clipped voice reached her through the haze of desire and alcohol. Slowly, she turned to face him, conscious that Ben had drawn back from her but still kept an arm around her waist.

'Callum,' she said shakily, 'what are you doing here? I mean, why are you saying this to me?' Her words were confused, and that was because her mind was struggling to take in what was going on.

'I'm warning you that you're playing with fire,' he said. 'You know how he manages to seduce every woman in sight. Haven't you learned anything? He has time on his hands and you just happen to be available.'

His glance flicked to Ben. 'I came to tell you that there's a phone call for you. Apparently, Anna's been trying to get in touch with you, but it seems you were too busy paying attention to my sister to answer your mobile. Or, who knows, maybe you switched it off so that you could concentrate better. She managed to get through to one of her friends instead. Apparently she needs you to call her urgently.'

Ben frowned. 'Thanks, Callum. Thanks for letting me know. I'll give her a call right now.'

Callum sent Jasmine a quick, appraising glance. 'I thought better of you. Are you going to throw away your integrity for the sake of a brief fling with the likes of him? I don't know you any more.'

Jasmine stared at him. Callum had every right to be annoyed with her. Wasn't he simply telling her what she already knew?

All at once she was distressed, conscious that she had let her brother down. She couldn't think what had possessed her. She knew that all the things he said were true, and yet once again she had allowed herself to be coaxed into Ben's arms. Would she never learn?

CHAPTER SIX

'I CAN'T stop more than five minutes, Mum, because I'm on my way to work, but I've brought the holly that you wanted... And there's a bottle of whisky for Dad, as a thank you for taking me to collect my car.' Jasmine placed a carrier bag on the kitchen worktop. 'There are some lovely red berries on the sprigs—I had to rescue them because the redwings and fieldfares were having themselves a feast and soon there would have been none left.'

Callum was eating breakfast at the table to one side of the room and she sent him a quick smile, but he merely glanced her way, stony faced, and said nothing.

It hurt that he ignored her, but she tried to tell herself that he would come around eventually. Okay, so she'd kissed Ben...was that really such a dreadful crime? She'd taken herself to task over this far more than Callum could ever have done. In part she could blame the alcohol, but for the rest...Ben had found his way into her heart and now she was torn in two.

'Thanks, Jasmine,' her mother said. 'I was hoping you would remember. I've always admired that lovely holly bush at the end of your garden. As to the whisky, you didn't need to do that—but I'm sure your father will appreciate it very much.'

She inspected the contents of the bag, and Jasmine added, 'There are some fir cones in there, too, that I picked up from the woods a while back. Do you have the gold and silver spray paint that you need?'

Her mother nodded. 'I do. I'll get on with making the Christmas wreath for the door just as soon as I can find a spare minute. With one thing and another, shopping, baking and so on, on top of working, it's all go just now.' She carefully emptied out the sprigs of holly and spread them on the worktop. 'I've enough here to make one for you, too, if you like.'

Jasmine nodded. 'I'd love that, thanks. It's a good thing you only work part-time nowadays, isn't it?' she commented with a smile. 'And maybe it's just as well that there aren't too many expectant mothers in the village due to give birth any time soon, otherwise you and Dad could be out delivering babies on Christmas Day.'

'That's true. But you can never tell with babies, can you? They often turn up off schedule and catch us all hopping.'

'And then everyone's glad to have you around to smooth the process along.' She studied her mother. 'You love your job, don't you?'

Helen nodded. 'There's something very satisfying about bringing babies into the world.' She glanced at Jasmine. 'I half expected you to go in for that line of work, but instead you chose A and E. For myself, I'm not sure I could cope with it long term.'

'No, it isn't to everyone's taste, I grant you. But my role's changing from today. The boss rang to confirm it—I'm to be on call with the rescue services, and it's been written into my contract that I go along as a first responder with the team. My only problem is that Ben is likely to be working with me, both at the hospital and with the rescue team. I'm just not quite sure how the land lies there. He's taken on a temporary job as locum registrar, but what happens after his two-month stint, I'm not sure. Perhaps he'll get wanderlust again. Quite how that will affect his work with the rescue services is anybody's guess.' And how would she feel if he decided to leave the village once more? She was foolhardy to even contemplate getting involved with Ben.

'Two months is the same length of time he said Anna would be staying in Woodsley,' Callum put in. His stare was hard and unflinching. 'Did you know that she'll be staying at Mill House for all that time?'

Jasmine ran the tip of her tongue over her lips. 'No, I didn't.' The fact that Anna would be living with Ben was definitely unsettling. It made her wonder if she really knew Ben at all. 'He doesn't tell me everything that's going on in his life. I still don't know what prompted Anna's call to him the other night. He left the village hall and went straight back to Cheshire.'

'Doesn't that tell you something about what's going on with him? How many men do you know who would drop everything to be at a woman's side?' He scowled. 'You're just an interlude to him, Jass...a pleasant way of passing the time.'

Jasmine pulled in a shuddery breath. 'I don't know about that. You may be right, but neither of us knows what really goes on in his mind, do we?'

'Maybe not, but I do know that Anna's going into hospital—Wellbeck. One of her friends told me that Anna had a message to say her appointment has been brought forward. She said that Ben will be bringing her over here today.' He frowned, giving Jasmine a cool look. 'Did you know about that? Do you know why she's going into hospital?'

Jasmine hesitated. 'I do…but I've been asked not to say anything. If you want to know any more about it, you'll have to go and see her at the hospital and ask her for yourself. That shouldn't be too hard, should it? I know you've tried to keep in touch with her from time to time, so it won't come as a surprise to her to know that you care. I'm sure the hospital will let you know what ward she's on and tell you about visiting times.' Wellbeck was probably the most sensible choice for her surgery, since her original consultant would be able to supervise her care…and that most likely had some part to play in Ben's decision to return home at this particular time.

He gritted his teeth. 'You're my sister. Isn't blood thicker than water? Aren't you supposed to side with me and confide in me?'

'You're my brother. Shouldn't you have trusted me to handle my own relationships and do what I think best?' she countered. 'Shouldn't you have tried to see things from my point of view? You and Anna aren't a couple any more. Why should I have to tread on eggshells because of what once went on between you? Five years have gone by and we've all changed in some way.'

Callum didn't answer. His mouth was clamped shut as he turned away from her, and he concentrated his attention on the morning paper. Jasmine clenched her fingers into small fists and tried to rid herself of her frustration. Then she glanced at her mother to see how she had been affected by their bickering.

'Perhaps you should get off to work,' her mother said. 'I hope it goes well for you. Are you going out with the rescue team today?'

'Only if there's a problem that the usual emergency services can't handle.' Jasmine picked up her bag and went to the door. 'I'll see you later,' she said, and then, after a moment's hesitation, called back, ''Bye, Callum.'

He stayed silent, and Jasmine went out to her car feeling tense and despondent.

She drove to the hospital and once she was there she tried to lose herself in her work. She was conscious that Ben might put in an appearance at any time, but she guessed he was helping Anna to settle in on her hospital ward.

Presumably the surgery had been advanced unexpectedly, and that must have upset Anna's arrangements. Who would be taking care of her little boy?

Jasmine tried to steer her mind away from such thoughts. She needed to pay full attention to her work, and in A and E everything was much as usual, except that the icy weather conditions in some parts had created havoc, and they had to deal with an unusual number of accidents due to falls.

Ben didn't arrive in the department until late afternoon and then it was to tell her that he'd just had a call out to Coniston Old Man, one of the local mountains.

'Yes, I heard about it,' she said. 'I'd like to come along, if I may—just for the experience. I've finished here for the day and handed over my workload, so I'm ready to go.'

He nodded. 'That's fine by me. I've spent most of the afternoon working on a patient who had a complicated chest injury, but thankfully he was out of the woods before I had to ask a colleague to take over.'

'A difficult case?'

'Yes. I had to open up his chest as an emergency procedure, but his condition deteriorated and he went into cardiac arrest. ' He was already walking with her to the exit doors. 'We managed to get him back, though.'

'I'm glad.' She smiled at him. 'You must be very relieved.' She picked up her jacket from the locker room. 'So how are we getting to the meeting point?'

'I'll drive. We'll park up at Coniston village and join up with the rest of the team. From there it will be a climb taking us up close to the summit. A man fell and broke his leg, I'm told, and so the sooner we get there, the better.'

'Let's hope that whoever's with him has thought to keep him warm. Hypothermia's one of the main hazards in these conditions, isn't it?'

'That's right.' They were already on their way out to the car park. Jasmine retrieved her mountain rescue kit from the boot of her car, and then went to sit beside Ben in the BMW.

He set the car in motion, and then glanced at her obliquely. 'I'm sorry I had to leave you so abruptly on Sunday evening.'

'That's all right,' she murmured. She didn't want to think about that evening and all the emotions it had stirred in her. 'I realise you didn't have much choice. Anna needed you, didn't she?'

He nodded. 'The surgery was brought forward because of a cancellation elsewhere, so she's being prepped for Theatre at this very moment.'

'What kind of surgery is she having?'

'An aortic valve replacement. Her own valve had only two cusps instead of three, and over the years it became more and more obstructed, so that her symptoms worsened. The cusps became stiff and calcified, so that blood couldn't circulate efficiently, and in the end she was increasingly breathless and started having chest pains. Pregnancy made things worse, and her heart rhythm became abnormal. That was when the cardiologist decided that she needed a replacement valve.' His expression was sombre. 'Anna was reluctant to go ahead with the surgery because she was afraid of what would happen to Kyle if anything went wrong.'

Jasmine felt a sudden rush of concern. 'Poor Anna. She must have been in a dreadful state. How is she bearing up?'

'Okay, I think. She's resigned to the inevitable, but I've managed to persuade her that I'll be looking after Kyle and she needn't have any worries on that score. I just want her to relax and concentrate on getting through the operation.'

Jasmine frowned. 'So where is Kyle now? Who's going to be taking care of him while you're working?'

'I've booked him in with a registered childminder in the village. If it wasn't so near Christmas he would have been at school, but the way things are, I didn't have much choice. It was a bit of a stressful situation for him, of course, because he doesn't know the woman, and he doesn't understand why his cosy little world has suddenly changed, but Carole Wainright seems to be really good with children, and her house has a warm and friendly atmosphere.'

Jasmine nodded. 'I know Carole. She's a lovely woman. I often see her collecting children from the village school. I'm sure she'll help him to settle, and there will be one or two other youngsters for him to play with.'

'I guess so. It's just difficult initially. We were hoping that we would have more time to explain things to him, but we hadn't expected the date of surgery to be brought forward.' Ben turned the car onto the road to Coniston village, and already Jasmine could see Coniston Old Man looming up ahead of them. The topmost slopes were covered in snow, but lower down it was still green and inviting to any would-be climbers.

Ben sent her another sideways glance. 'I was worried about Callum's attitude towards you the other night. Did you manage to smooth things over with him, or is he still upset?'

She made a wry face. 'He's still angry with me. I don't think that's going to change any time soon. I think the trouble is he still loves Anna. I know he's written to her occasionally and tried to talk to her on the phone, but although she was pleasant to him and wanted to know how he was getting on at university and so on, she's never given him any sign that she wants to get back with him.'

She saw Ben's brooding expression and added in a quiet voice, 'I realise you might not like the fact that they kept in touch, but I have to think of my brother in this. Anna was his childhood sweetheart, and it seems to be a love he's never fully recovered from.'

'He has only himself to blame. I'm sure if he'd paid her more attention in the first place she would never have left him. He was too busy making his career plans to think about what was going on in Anna's life.'

Her mouth made a cynical twist. 'Well, you were quick enough off the mark, stepping into the breach, weren't you? She was vulnerable, and you took advantage of that. You paid attention to her when Callum was getting all fired up about going off to university. If you had done the decent thing and backed off, they might still be together.'

His jaw set in a rigid line. 'But they aren't, and I don't see any point in going over old ground.' He swung the car into the car park and Jasmine looked around to see the rescue team assembling by the exit.

'We'll make our way towards the beck,' the leader said when they joined the group a moment or two later, 'and then aim for a brisk climb. It shouldn't be too difficult, but it gets pretty steep the higher you go, and it can be gruelling, so be prepared.'

As soon as the whole team had gathered, they set off. Jasmine looked around at the houses in the area, built with stone and slate from the mountain. It was a pretty village, and later, as they started their climb and came by a stone bridge, she paused for a moment to take in the full beauty of the area. She saw verdant slopes and rocky outcrops, along with tumbling waterfalls and fast-running streams. Here and there she spotted deer grazing, and occasionally a glimpse of a squirrel darting between the trees.

Higher up they came across old mine workings and disused tunnels, and in some places there were rusty remnants of copper mining.

'Just a little further and we should reach Low Water,' Ben said, coming alongside her. 'Our patient is just a short distance from there.'

'I hope he's doing all right,' she murmured. 'Having a broken leg up here must be pretty horrendous.'

'True. Let's hope there's nothing desperately serious to warrant an emergency evacuation, but if there is, we can at least make him more comfortable. The journey down here with a stretcher is going to be a tough one.'

He was right about that. The gradient up here was steep, and she was glad she wouldn't be the one carrying the man downhill.

Low Water was beautiful, a stretch of water that was half-frozen right now on the surface, and dark green-blue in colour.

They trekked on for a few more minutes, and at last they reached their destination. The injured man was in obvious pain, pale faced, his lips taking on a bluish tinge, and even though his companions had tried to shield him from the cold by wrapping him in water-proofs, he was chilled to the bone.

Ben quickly examined him, but it was clear from the way his leg was distorted and shorter than the other one that it was broken.

'I'll give you something for the pain, Simon,' Ben said, 'and we'll make you as comfortable as we can by splinting the leg. The bones need to be realigned, but we can't do that here. It will have to wait till you reach the hospital. They'll give you an anaesthetic and do it in Theatre.'

'Something for the pain sounds good,' Simon answered, his mouth making a taut line. He began to shiver, and the members of the rescue team came forward with blankets. Others started to ready the stretcher and casualty bag that would encase the patient to provide warmth and protection.

Ben gave Simon a painkilling injection and Jasmine checked his blood pressure and listened to his heart while the injection took effect.

'At least it isn't an open fracture, so that's one less thing to worry about,' Ben remarked.

He turned to Jasmine and said in a low voice, 'I'm worried about internal bleeding. His heart is racing, and his blood pressure's falling, so there's a distinct possibility that he could go into shock. I'm going to set up an intravenous line to try to counteract any blood loss, but I think we should contact the air ambulance to see if there's any chance they can get him to hospital quicker than we can. The longer we delay, the greater the danger of neurological damage.'

'I'll call them,' Jasmine said, and started to dial the number. 'The helicopter will be here in about ten minutes,' she told him a moment or two later. 'It'll have to be a winch rescue because there's no safe place to land.'

'Okay. Let's get him splinted and wrapped up.'

She helped Ben to put the splints in place, and when they were satisfied that they had done everything they could for the man medically, they started to prepare for the evacuation process.

They strapped Simon into a harness and made sure that he was secured safely to the stretcher. 'It seems like only the other day that we were going through this routine,' Ben said, throwing her a quick look.

She saw the glimmer of amusement in his eyes. 'I suppose I should be thankful it won't be me going up on the line,' she said softly, turning away from their patient so that he wouldn't hear. 'At least you won't be the one going up there with him...or will you?'

He shook his head. 'There will be a doctor on board the helicopter. He'll take over from here.'

Ben checked their patient once more. 'How are you holding up?' he asked. 'Are you a bit warmer now?'

Simon nodded. 'I'm much more comfortable, thanks. I'm really grateful to all of you for going to all this trouble to take care of me. I feel such a fool. I've been climbing for years and never done anything like this.'

Ben smiled. 'It happens to lots of people, believe me. That's why we have the rescue services.'

They heard the drone of the helicopter just a short time later, and within a minute or two a man descended on a line, to land just a foot away from the stretcher.

Jasmine stood back while Ben helped the winch man fasten the ropes in place and make sure that the stretcher was secure. A moment or two later he gave the signal to the pilot and the line was winched up.

As the helicopter moved away, heading in the direction of Wellbeck Hospital, the rescue team celebrated a job well done with flasks of coffee and hot chocolate. Someone even produced pasties that he handed around. 'Can't go without sustenance on these missions,' he said. He passed drinks and food to the patient's companions. 'Pity we couldn't give your friend anything to drink to warm him up, but it was obvious he was going to need an anaesthetic fairly soon.'

'I'm sure he'll be okay now,' Ben said. 'He'll be in a cast over Christmas, but on the whole I think he's been lucky. We made good time up the mountain.'

They lingered for a few minutes, taking time to refresh themselves before they started the descent down the mountain.

Jasmine looked around and took in the view from this vantage point. From here, she could see the long sweep of Coniston Water and, further afield, the blue waters of Morecambe Bay.

'It's lovely, isn't it?' Ben came to stand with her, taking in the scenery. 'That's what makes climbing such a worthwhile exercise. It's invigorating, it keeps you fit, and in the end you're rewarded with fantastic views over the whole of the region.'

'It is. I love this whole area. I don't think I could ever leave.' She turned to him. 'You don't have that same tug of emotion, though, do you? You and Callum were both content to move away.'

'I don't know about Callum, but for me, home has to be about people. I was happy in Woodsley while my grandmother was alive, but after she had passed on, there was no reason for me to stay. My father didn't show any sign of wanting me around, and so I went where the best career prospects took me. I expect Callum is doing the same thing, although he knows that your parents will welcome him back with open arms at any time.'

The team members readied themselves for the descent, and Jasmine prepared to join them. 'So when your two months here is finished, will you be moving on again?' she asked.

'I haven't made any specific plans as yet,' he said. 'I have to think about Anna and Kyle and make sure that all's well with them. And, of course, I'd like to make my peace with my father. It would be good if we could share at least one Christmas with a special father and son relationship.'

Jasmine stayed quiet. His thoughts first and foremost were with Anna and the boy, and surely that was how it should be? Anna was vulnerable right now and needed him, and as for Kyle…Ben was clearly taking his responsibilities seriously.

The descent down the mountain was tricky, especially where the incline was steepest. Ben helped her, giving her a supporting hand, making sure that she didn't slip or stumble. She was grateful to him for that, but his touch made her sorrowfully aware of what she was missing. She was conscious the whole time that he belonged to someone else, if not in a binding sense, at least morally and ethically.

When they finally arrived back in Coniston village, she said goodbye to the members of the rescue team and slid into the passenger seat of Ben's car. 'I suppose you're going to pick up Kyle from Carole's house now, are you?' she asked.

He shook his head. 'I thought I'd stop by the hospital and check up on Anna first. The theatre nurse texted me to say that the operation was proceeding as planned, so by the time we get back she should be in the recovery room. I'd like to be there when she wakes up, and I want to make sure that she's all right.'

'Of course.' She pressed her lips together briefly. 'When she's able to talk, would you ask her if it's all right if I visit her? She and I always got along well together and I'd like to see how she's doing.'

'I will.'

He studied her, his gaze lingering on her face, taking in the smooth line of her cheekbones, the fullness of her soft mouth. 'You know, when I get myself together over the next few days, I'll be starting work on the interior of the barn conversion. I could do with some advice on the furnishings and décor…and you're probably the ideal person to help me out with that. I've seen what you've done with the cottage, and you have a light, modern touch. Would you consider coming over to give me a hand with it?'

Jasmine's breath caught in her throat. On the surface, what he was asking was a simple favour, nothing untoward. But how could he know the dilemma he was thrusting onto her?

Working with him at the barn would bring her into close contact with him over a period of time…time when she should be doing her best to steer clear of him.

Knowing all this, why then did she hear herself saying softly, 'Yes, I could do that. I'd love to help out, in any way I can.'

CHAPTER SEVEN

JASMINE placed her hands at the back of her hips and slowly stretched, easing the stiffness in her spine. It had been a long day in A and E and her muscles were beginning to complain.

Looking around, though, at the main reception area and general thoroughfare, she was pleased with the festive appearance of the place. Staff had been busy, hanging glittering red and gold foil decorations here and there, and equally cheerful garlands festooned the reception desk. People might be feeling at a low ebb when they entered the department, but their mood was invariably lighter when they left. Of course, that was partly down to the care and attention they received from the medical staff. Everyone here was dedicated to the job.

'It looks as though you've had a tough day,' Ben commented, coming to stand by the desk alongside her. 'Have you had a break lately?'

'Not for several hours. It's been non-stop in here, with nasty infections, strokes, fractures...you name it, we've seen it.' She grimaced, and then added, 'And talking of fractures, I checked up on Simon, who we sent here yesterday by air ambulance. I thought you'd like to know he's doing well, apparently. He's uncomfortable, obviously, but his fracture was reduced under anaesthetic, and now his leg's in a cast and the surgeon is thinking of discharging him sometime tomorrow.'

'That's great news. I was worried the situation might be worse, with internal bleeding causing problems.'

She nodded. 'Getting him here quickly helped tremendously, but I think they're keeping him in hospital for an extra day just to make sure he's making a proper recovery, but so far it's looking good.'

Ben smiled. 'I'm glad you thought to find out about him. I was planning on ringing Admissions myself, but I've been kept busy all day with several nasty traffic accident cases. At least all the injured are safe now, thankfully.'

She could see he was relieved about that. He looked weary, too, with lines of tiredness around his eyes that she hadn't noticed before, and her heart went out to him. He worked hard, she'd discovered. Even in the short time he'd been at this hospital, he'd impressed the staff with his dedication to the job and his care and attention towards the patients.

'Are you going off duty now?' She guessed from the work rota that he was on the same shift pattern as her.

'Yes. Carole will be dropping off Kyle at the hospital any minute now, and we're going up to see his mother in Intensive Care. She's going off to do some Christmas shopping afterwards, so she said it was no bother to bring him in.'

He sent her a quick glance. 'Would you like to come with me to see Anna? You'll be free in a few minutes, won't you? Unless, of course, you had other plans?'

'I'd love to come with you if she's up to having visitors. Did you mention to Anna I'd like to see her?'

'I did. She was pleased. Actually, she's doing really well. She had minimally invasive surgery, which means the surgeon made a smaller incision and she should experience less pain as a result. It's cosmetically better too, of course.'

'I'm glad things have worked out all right. I've been thinking about her all day.'

He nodded. 'Me, too.'

Just then there was a minor commotion at the main door, and a harassed Carole Wainright came into the emergency unit, towing a very fractious young boy. Her blonde hair was slightly tousled and there was faint look of tension in her demeanour.

'Don't want to come here,' the child said vehemently, his whole body stiff and resistant. 'Don't want to wait for Daddy-Ben. He'll be ages. He always takes a long time. I want to see my mum now.' He scowled. 'You can take me there. You maked me wait all day and I don't want to wait any more.'

The boy's chin jutted belligerently as though daring her to cross him, and the usually serene Carole gave a smile that was held in place by sheer willpower.

'Look, he's over there and he's ready now, see.' She shot Ben a look as if to say, *Please make it true, I'm about at the end of my tether.*

Ben moved forward to greet them. 'Hi, soldier,' he said, stooping to pick up the child and hold him securely in his arms. The boy glowered at him, and Jasmine couldn't help noticing that his features were very similar to Anna's, with that troubled, vulnerable look that she sometimes had. His neatly cut hair was a touch lighter than Ben's, but his eyes were that same shade of blue, with maybe a hint of grey.

'We're going to see your mother now, Kyle,' Ben said, soothingly. 'But you need to calm down, because she's very poorly and you must be on your best behaviour. Can you do that for me?'

Kyle nodded reluctantly, his mouth still truculent, as though the slightest thing might cause him to change his mind.

Ben turned his attention to Carole. 'Thanks for bringing him in, Carole. I really appreciate it. As to the rest...' his gaze flicked to the top of the boy's head '...I know what you've been going through. You're a saint, you know that, don't you?'

'I'm beginning to believe it.' Carole laughed. 'We tried out all sorts of toys and activities today to see if anything would help to rid him of his frustrations.' She winced. 'Do you know...he really liked the drum kit?'

Ben laughed. 'I can imagine how that must have cheered you up no end. Go off and enjoy your shopping, Carole. I've heard it's lovely in town now with the Christmas lights and the Salvation Army singing carols.'

'The stores are open till late, too, so that's a big relief. I've left my husband watching my two girls, so I can shop in peace.'

Carole left, and Jasmine tried to introduce herself to Kyle. 'Hi, there,' she said in a cheerful tone. 'I'm Jasmine. I'm a friend of your mother, so we thought it would be nice if I went along with you and your daddy to see her.'

Kyle scrunched up his face as though he was trying to decide if that was a good or bad thing. In the end he gave up thinking about it and instead turned to look at Ben. 'You can put me down now,' he said. 'I'm not a baby. I'm four years old.'

Ben lifted his dark brows. 'Well, I do beg your pardon. How could I have forgotten that?' He gently lowered the boy to the floor. 'So, have you been having a good time at Carole's house?'

'No,' Kyle answered crossly. 'Her soppy girls kept telling me what to do…and they kept trying to take the drum off me. And then when I played the recorder instead, they tried to grab that. So I took their dollies and hid them where they couldn't find them and they *cried* and *cried*.' He rolled his eyes. 'And then they ran off shouting for Carole. And then I got into trouble when it wasn't my fault.' He was glowering again, and Jasmine hid a smile.

'Girls can be like that,' she said. 'They don't really understand how boys like to play, do they?'

He looked at her with a glimmer of interest. 'No.' Then he turned back to Ben. 'You said you'd take me to see my mum. You're not going to do any more work, are you? You always have to work, but I want to see her now.'

'Okay.' Ben nodded. 'Come on. Best foot forward.'

Puzzled, Kyle looked down at his feet. 'Which one is that?'

Ben gave it some thought, then pointed to the child's right foot. 'You can start with that one today, and maybe try the other one tomorrow.'

'Okay.'

They took the lift to the upper floor where Anna was being cared for in the intensive care unit. Jasmine glanced at Ben and said quietly, 'He calls you Daddy-Ben. That's unusual, isn't it? How did that come about?'

His mouth tilted at the corners. 'The first word he ever learned was *da-da*, and he would say it all the time. Any man who came by would be *da-da*. And then he listened to what was going on around him and would hear people calling me by my name, so after a while it sort of stuck. I became Daddy-Ben.'

By now they were approaching the unit, and Ben's attention swivelled back to the child.

'Your mother is in that room over there,' he said, pointing to a door ahead of them and looking down at Kyle as he and the boy walked, hand in hand, along the corridor. 'It might seem a little scary to you in there at first, so before we go in there I want you to explain to you what you'll see.'

Kyle nodded. 'Mummy will be in bed.'

'Yes, that's true, but there will be some pads on your mother's chest, with wires attached to them. They're connected to monitors to show how fast her heart is beating and to let the doctors know if her breathing is as it should be. There will be small tubes fitted just inside her nose to help her to breathe properly and perhaps another one to make her tummy more comfortable.' He studied the child. 'Are you okay with that so far?'

'Yes,' Kyle said on a doubtful note. His expression was solemn. 'Mummy's very poorly, isn't she?'

'She's doing all right, Kyle. She's had an operation to make her better, but it will be quite a long time before she's properly well again.'

'But she will get better?'

'Yes. If she gets plenty of rest, and everybody helps to look after her, she'll get better. But for now, as well as the wires, she has tubes coming from her chest, and from her arm, to make sure that she's comfortable and not in any pain.'

The enormity of the situation seemed to dawn on the boy at that moment, and it threatened to overwhelm him. He swallowed hard and his face crumpled a little as though he was about to cry. More than anything, Jasmine wanted to put her arms about him and hold him close, but she hesitated. She was a stranger to him and perhaps it wouldn't be right.

She needn't have worried, though. Ben drew the boy to him and wrapped an arm around his shoulders in a comforting gesture.

'I know it might seem as though your mother is helpless, Kyle,' he said, 'but, in fact, she isn't. She's really looking forward to seeing you, and she wants to know that you're settling in all right with Carole in the daytime when I'm at work. That way she can rest more easily. And the more she rests, the sooner she'll get better.' He placed a hand under the boy's chin and gently tilted his face so that he could look into his eyes. 'Do you understand?'

Kyle sniffed and rubbed his tears away. 'Yes.'

'That's my boy. I think you're very brave.' He held his hand once more. 'Okay, then. If you're ready, we'll go in.'

Ben pushed open the door, and Kyle stepped cautiously into the ward, casting a wary look around, as though afraid of what he might see. Then he appeared to brace himself, and he walked slowly over to his mother's bedside.

He stayed there, silently watching Anna sleep, his gaze wandering fearfully over the myriad tubes, wires and monitors that surrounded her, his eyes widening. The monitors beeped and flashed, and Kyle pulled in a deep, shuddery breath. He said nothing, but stood very still, as though waiting for something.

At last, Anna's eyes fluttered open. 'Kyle, my little treasure,' she whispered, and her face lit up in a smile.

Then he moved, very gently reaching out to take her hand, and he bent his head towards her so that his cheek rested in the crook of her shoulder.

Watching him, Jasmine was suddenly immensely proud of this little boy. It seemed as though he was wise beyond his years, and even though he was upset and afraid, he had hidden all that from his mother.

She glanced at Ben. 'It was good that you spoke to him before we came in here,' she said in a low voice. 'Otherwise it would have been very scary for him. It's an awful lot for a young child to take in.'

He nodded and went to stand next to Kyle. He leaned over and kissed Anna on the forehead and on the cheek, and all at once Jasmine felt as though she was an intruder, as though she didn't belong here.

She hung back for a while, letting Ben and the boy have these precious moments with Anna, and just as she was thinking of retreating altogether, Ben turned around and beckoned her forward.

'You've a special visitor,' he told Anna. 'She's been worried about you. We've all been worried about you.'

Anna's eyes reflected her contentment as she saw Jasmine standing there. 'I'm so glad you came,' she said softly, her voice thready as a result of her weakened condition. 'It's been such a long time.'

Jasmine gave her a quick smile. 'Yes, it has. I never expected to see you like this, though. How are you bearing up?'

'All right.' Anna's hand rested on Kyle's head, lightly stroking his hair. 'Better now that the operation's over and done with.'

'I can imagine. From here on, you should start to get your strength back, and hopefully life should be a lot easier for you. I'd no idea what you must have been going through.'

Anna's mouth made a small curve. 'That's what Callum said.' She spoke softly, as though everything was a bit of an effort, and Jasmine was afraid that she was becoming overtired.

'He's been here to see you?'

Anna nodded. 'I think he was shocked. It was a lot for him to take in.' She pressed her lips together. 'Of course, I was still a bit groggy from the anaesthetic yesterday. Tell him it's not as bad as it seems, will you?'

'I will.'

They stayed for a while longer, but it was clear that Anna's energy reserves were failing, and Ben very gently persuaded Kyle to relinquish his hold on his mother. 'We have to go now,' he said, 'so that your mother can get some sleep.'

Kyle tried to cling on, unwilling to move from Anna's bedside, but Anna said quietly, 'Do you know what I'd like, Kyle?'

The boy shook his head, his eyes wide and his expression solemn.

'I'd like to come home to a lovely Christmas tree. One that is fresh from the woods and smells of pine.' She smiled. 'I wonder if you and Daddy-Ben could find one like that for me?'

Kyle looked up at Ben, his gaze questioning, and Ben nodded. 'We could go out to the woods on Saturday and pick one out, if you like.'

The child nodded vigorously. 'Yes,' he said. 'A great big, enormous tree—this big.' He spread his arms wide open to show how wide it would be, and then looked up at the ceiling. 'And it will go right up to there.'

Ben chuckled. 'I can see we're going to have fun finding just the right one.'

They left Anna a few minutes later and headed out to the car park. Ben walked with Jasmine to her car, holding Kyle's hand so that the boy didn't dash out into the road.

'Would you like to come with us to pick out the tree?' he asked, holding open the car door for her so that she could slide into the driver's seat. 'Between the three of us, we should manage to find one that's exactly right.'

The invitation startled her, but she was pleased to be included in the outing. 'I'd like that,' she said. She looked at Kyle, who was kicking up remnants of snow from the grass verge. 'Is that all right with you?'

The boy's shoulders moved in a negligent gesture. 'Yeah, sure.'

She looked back at Ben, a smile hovering on her lips. 'I guess that's settled, then.'

She started the car's engine and waved goodbye to them, conscious of Ben's thoughtful gaze as she drove out of the car park a short time later.

It had been strange seeing him with Anna, watching his gentleness with her, the way he kissed her with such deep affection. What exactly was his relationship with her? It seemed as though they shared a loving bond, and even though Ben said their relationship was not quite the same as it once had been, he had made arrangements for Anna to stay with him at his house.

Where did that leave her, with Ben trying to steal kisses? She couldn't work out what was going on in his head. His involvement with Anna made everything even more bewildering.

And what about Kyle? He certainly seemed to love the boy in the way that a father would love his son. His whole attitude to the child was considerate and caring. She frowned. None of this made any sense and she was thoroughly confused. What was he doing, making plans to be with her while Anna lay ill in bed?

Perhaps his invitation for her to join them on Saturday had been a spur-of-the-moment thing. Maybe he wasn't thinking logically, but instead was following his instincts. Whatever the reasoning behind the suggestion, she realised that she was looking forward to spending time with him.

It snowed again over the next couple of days, and by the time Ben arrived with Kyle to pick her up at lunchtime on Saturday, the whole landscape was covered in a blanket of white. Kyle was dressed in a warm coat and trousers, with a woolly hat and Wellington boots, and he took great delight in making footprints in the virgin snow.

'I hope you're ready for this,' Ben commented, glancing at Jasmine as they settled themselves in his car. 'Kyle's in fine form today. The tree has to be exactly right, and he's intent on examining every single one in the forest from the sound of things.'

Jasmine laughed. 'So we're in for the long haul. I'll bear that in mind.'

'Carole says there's a playground at the forest,' Kyle put in eagerly, 'where you can climb on fallen down trees and swing on ropes and things. I want to do that. And I want to crawl through the tunnels. She says there are little dens and things what you can play in.' He drummed his fingers on his knees in expectation and looked out of the window to see how far they had gone along the road. 'Will we soon be there?'

'It takes about half an hour. Sit back and see if you can spot any birds' nests high up in the trees as we go along,' Ben suggested. 'There won't be any birds in them, this time of year, but you should be able to see the nests now that the branches are bare.'

Kyle began to stare intently at the passing scenery and for a while peace reigned.

'I've never been out to this forest,' Jasmine said when they finally turned into the car park. 'It sounds as though everything's geared up here for a family day out.'

'That's the general idea, I think.' He locked up the car and they set off along the path, with Kyle keeping a lookout for the playground.

'There it is,' he said, after a minute or two, giving a joyful whoop. 'I'm going over there now.' He raced away, as fast as he could go with his boots making in-roads in the deep snow, leaving Jasmine and Ben to follow at their own pace.

'I don't suppose he can come to any harm around here,' Ben commented, scanning the playground. All the activities were woodland based, a children's para-dise, with climbing frames and wooden structures to be explored. 'Shall we go and sit on the bench and watch him for a while?'

'Good idea.'

They cleared the snow off a nearby bench and sat together, following Kyle's progress as he embarked on his adventure.

'Have you been to see Anna recently?' Jasmine asked. 'They moved her from Intensive Care on Thursday, so that was a good sign. I've been trying to go and visit her every day, but the times vary, according to when I can get a break from work.'

'Yes, same here. I dropped by the hospital with Kyle this morning. She looks much stronger, and with a bit of luck they'll be sending her home on Monday.' He smiled. 'At least that will give me time to get the tree installed and decorated. I think it was a good idea of Anna's to give Kyle something to focus on but, then, she always knew how to handle him.'

'You don't seem to do too badly yourself.' Jasmine gazed at him, taking in his strong features, the firm angle of his jaw, his beautifully moulded mouth. He was incredibly good looking, but there was more to him than that, much more. He was also a good and capable man, one who shouldered his responsibilities, who made his own way in life and took in his stride the knocks along the way. This was a man she could love, a man she could share her life with.

Shocked by a sudden rush of longing, she dragged her gaze away.

'Are you okay?' he asked. 'Are you cold?' He put his arm around her as though to protect her from the bleak winter, and she relished that warm and comforting touch.

'I'm all right,' she said. She tried to gather her thoughts and send them somewhere where it was safe to venture. 'I expect you have your hands full these days, with work in A and E, the rescue services and looking after Kyle. I don't suppose you've had time to do any work on the barn conversion?'

He kept his arm around her, and she tried to tell herself that she shouldn't read anything into that. He was just being thoughtful and making sure that she was all right.

'It's still going along well enough. The oak floors have been laid, and the walls have been painted in very pale colours, so all that remains now is to choose the décor. Maybe you'd like to come over tomorrow afternoon and help me do that? I can't really do it this evening because Kyle goes to bed early, but tomorrow he'll be able to bring his toys along with him and he can play while we talk.'

'Sounds good to me.'

'Then we're on. It's a date…sort of.' He laughed, looking into her eyes, his mouth curving in amusement.

'Are we going to get the tree?' Kyle appeared by his side and tapped him on the knee to drag his attention away from Jasmine.

Ben took a moment to pull his thoughts back on track. 'Oh, you've finished playing, have you?'

Kyle nodded.

'We'd better make a move, then.' Ben let his arm slide from Jasmine's shoulders, and instantly her feeling of well-being disappeared. He got to his feet. 'Straight along the path,' he told him. 'No wandering off. We don't want to lose you and have to send the dogs out, do we?'

'Big dogs, like huskies?' Kyle appeared to find that notion interesting.

'Bigger, probably. There's a lot of forest to search if anyone goes missing. So you'd better stay close.'

They inspected all the trees along the way, but Kyle wasn't satisfied with any of them.

'Too small,' he said, or, 'The shape's all wrong,' or, 'Some of the branches are wonky.'

They came across a small stream, its crystal-clear waters bubbling over rocks, with ancient trees lining its route. Kyle stepped into it gingerly, testing his footing, and then laughed gleefully as the water splashed around his feet. 'It's washed all the snow off my boots,' he said.

'So it has.' Ben let him play for a little while longer and then flicked a glance towards the fir trees. 'We'd better sort something out soon,' he said, 'or your mother will be coming home to an empty corner where she expects a beautiful display.'

'You know, Kyle, there are some beautiful Scots pines over there, just along that other path,' Jasmine said. 'They're a lovely blue-green colour, and the needles are usually soft, so they won't prickle when you put the baubles in place. And they smell lovely, too. How about looking at one of those?'

'Okay.' Kyle was happy to oblige and they turned off in that direction, following a winding path.

'I like this one,' he said, when they came upon the cluster of trees. He had picked out the tallest one around. He went up to it, standing close to the lower branches. Then he looked up and giggled as the pine needles tickled his face. 'I can't see the top,' he said. 'It's gone right up into the sky.'

'That's the one, is it? It looks magnificent,' Ben told him. 'I think you made a good choice there.' He gave a satisfied nod. 'It smells wonderful, too, just as Jassie said. I'll tell the forestry man that's the one we want.'

He was about to step back onto the path when a snowball hit him squarely in the neck and stopped him in the tracks. 'Who…? What…?' Ben looked around for the culprit, and then his gaze settled on Kyle, who was giggling fit to burst the zip on his coat. Another snowball splattered on Ben's shoulder, and then another one flew in quick succession to disintegrate on Jasmine's jacket.

'Right,' they said in chorus. 'Where is he? Let's get him.'

Kyle darted behind the tree as Ben and Jasmine scrambled to gather up snow, and after that it was a free-for-all, with snowballs flying in all directions. They were all laughing, squealing and shaking themselves down as the snow melted and left icy runnels here and there.

Jasmine cleared ice water from her face and neck and spluttered, gasping with the cold, while Ben chased Kyle and swooped on him, gathering him up into his arms. 'Enough, monster,' he said. 'Now we'll have to go to the café to warm up.'

Kyle nodded in excitement. 'Can I have a toasted sandwich? And some pop?'

'I think we can run to that.' Ben looked him in the eye. 'If I put you down, do you promise not to throw any more snowballs?'

Kyle looked as though that might be a trifle more difficult than he could manage.

'We're talking ham and cheese melt, here,' Ben reminded him. 'Think about it. Toasted sandwich, snowball…which one's going to win?'

'Ham and cheese,' Kyle conceded, and Ben carefully lowered him to the ground.

'Okay. I'll order the food and settle you and Jassie at a table and then I'll go and arrange for someone to cut the tree.'

The café was a cheerful place, bright and warm, with clean pine tables and chairs and greenery all around to add a natural touch to the surroundings. Jasmine and Kyle chose a table by the window where they could look out at the paved terrace with its wooden benches and seats and, beyond that, the beginnings of the forest.

Jasmine ordered soup, and it arrived just as Ben returned from talking to the woodcutter.

'Mmm…that smells good,' he said, sniffing appreciatively. 'They make it themselves, you know, in the kitchens, from fresh ingredients that they grow on the land here…carrots, turnips, leeks, potatoes. It's the kind of thing I had in mind for the stable block—a chance to sell off fresh produce. Maybe fruit from the orchard, for a start. There are some really old varieties of apple trees on the land, as well as plums and pears.'

Jasmine dipped her spoon into the steaming hot soup. 'That sounds the sort of thing that Callum would like... though he'd want his mainstay to be the sale of plants. He had a vision of running an open garden, showing people various ways of landscaping and offering them the chance to buy whatever they need on site. It's an ambitious project, and I suppose it would take a fair bit of money for him to get started. I know he's been saving hard, and he's talking of getting a loan from the bank to start his own business.' She savoured the taste of the soup. 'Of course, the banks aren't so keen to lend these days.'

'That's true.'

He sat down as the waitress brought his meal, lasagne with chips on the side. 'I'm ready for this,' he said, tucking in. Kyle was eating his toasted sandwich, swinging his legs under the table and looking around at the display on the wall showing a map of the forest and its attractions.

'I've been amazed at how well you've done these last few years,' Jasmine said, giving Ben a quick glance. 'Considering that you had so much opposition from your father in the beginning. You said that he held back your trust fund, so much of what you did, buying up property and so on, must have been done on your own merit.'

He swallowed a forkful of pasta. 'I suppose I succeeded *because* of my father. He used to manage my grandmother's investments and would have sold Mill House if I hadn't stepped in. She was beginning to be confused as she went into old age, but I managed to gain power of attorney over her interests and stopped him from selling up. From then on, I was on my own. He couldn't forgive me for interfering, but I knew I had to make things work, for her sake.'

'So it gave you a taste for developing property?'

'That's right. And it's good to have an interest outside medicine. It helps to give your mind something to work on when things don't go the way you want them to. We'd all like things to go smoothly every time, but life isn't like that.'

'I know what you mean.' She finished off her soup, and the waitress brought a meat pasty to the table. Jasmine accepted it with a smile. 'Thanks.'

She studied Ben's brooding features. 'Have you had any more luck with getting your father on your side?'

He shook his head. 'I went to see him again the other day, but his attitude was cool. I wanted to find out what arrangements he'd made for Christmas, and I was planning on inviting him over to Mill House for the day, but I didn't get the chance. It was as though by being there I was reminding him of things he didn't want to think about.'

She frowned. 'Like what?'

'It was just a feeling I had. At one point I was looking at the grandfather clock in the study and I said I remembered the casing used to stick sometimes. He just changed after that. Where he'd been guarded and stilted before, he became positively cool. I guessed he wanted me to leave.'

'Was there something special about the clock, something significant, perhaps?'

He frowned, deep in thought. 'Not that I recall. When I was very small, I used to open the glass door and put my toy soldiers inside, so that they could hide from the enemy. I was always being told that it would interfere with the workings of the clock, but as far as I know, it didn't stop me.'

Jasmine smiled. 'I expect it was difficult for your father, coping with a small boy after your mother died.'

He nodded. 'I suppose so.' He looked across the table at Kyle, who was off in a dream world of his own, his toasted sandwich held to his mouth as though someone had pressed the pause button on the video. 'Who knows what he had to contend with?'

He gave his attention back to his lasagne, and then added, 'He did tell me that your father had arranged an appointment for him at the surgery and he was planning on keeping it, so that's a positive result.'

'I'm glad.' Jasmine finished off her pasty and wiped her hands on a serviette. 'You know, perhaps the only way to win your father round is to keep batting at the door. Maybe you could take him a hamper from the Mill Bakery and I could add some mince pies and a bottle of my father's elderberry wine—or does he only like the sort you have in your cellar?'

'I'm sure he'd appreciate a bottle of elderberry. Something that a person has taken the time and trouble to make themselves has to be special, doesn't it?' He laid a hand on hers. 'That's a great idea, Jassie. Perhaps we could go over to the manor together—say tomorrow, before we go over to the barn?'

She nodded, but then a thought crossed her mind. 'Does he know about Kyle?'

He shook his head. 'No, but he will after tomorrow, won't he? He knows that Anna is in hospital, but I still have to break it to him that she'll be staying with me afterwards.'

'It's tough, isn't it, dealing with fractious relatives?' Her mouth made a downward turn. 'I've never really experienced it until now. My family's always been close knit, and whenever there's a problem, we rally round one another.'

His eyes narrowed slightly. 'You're thinking of Callum?'

She nodded.

'He'll come round, eventually. For as long as I've known you, I've envied the way your family hangs together. I think of how it will be at your house on Christmas Day, with your mother presiding over the Christmas dinner and your father carving the turkey. Your aunt and uncle and cousins will be there, and I expect you'll all be wearing paper hats from the Christmas crackers and reading out the corny jokes and falling about laughing. I envy you that, Jassie.'

He looked into her eyes. 'It's something I've never experienced, and somehow I think that being with you would make it all the more special.'

She felt his fingers curl around hers, and with that simple touch he, filled her heart with pure joy. He wanted to be with her. He had said it. What more could she ask?

And then she remembered that Anna would be spending Christmas with him, and Kyle would be opening his toys in front of the fire at Mill House on Christmas Day, and the brief joy that had seared her soul quickly turned to ashes.

CHAPTER EIGHT

'Is HE coming back soon?' Kyle was watching the kitchen door, willing it to open. He'd been doing that for the last half-hour, and Jasmine decided it was time to distract him. She started to gather together the ingredients for a baking session.

'I'm not sure how long Ben will be,' she told him. 'He had to go out with the mountain rescue team to find someone who has been hurt. I expect he'll call us as soon as he's on his way back.'

Kyle was clearly not happy with that answer. 'But we were going to the big house and he was going to show me the secret hiding place. Why can't he come back now?'

'Because helping people who are injured is his job. Just imagine that you had hurt your knee, Kyle.' Jasmine finished setting out flour, sugar and spices on the kitchen table. 'If it was a really bad pain, you'd want somebody to help you and take the pain away, wouldn't you?'

He nodded solemnly.

'Well, the man on the mountainside banged his knee when he slipped and fell, and it's very swollen and hurts a lot, so Ben has gone to help make him better. As soon as the man is safely in hospital, Ben will come back here and we'll all go off to the manor house as we planned.'

She added butter to the assembled items and then let her glance sweep over the kitchen table. 'In the meantime,' she said, 'we've all the ingredients here that we need to make cookies—and I have all these lovely Christmas cookie cutters. Look, there's an angel…and a Christmas tree…'

'And a Christmas stocking…and a bell.' Kyle laughed gleefully. 'Can I cut some, Jassie…please? I'd like to do that.'

'Of course you can. And afterwards, when they're cooked, we'll ice them and put little silver balls on some of them.'

'Yes-s-s!' Kyle's excitement was growing by the minute, but he stopped and stood very still as someone knocked on the kitchen door.

'Jassie?' The door opened a notch and Callum peered into the room. 'Is it all right if I come in?'

'Of course.' Callum was the last person she expected, and seeing him now made her more than a little uneasy. They hadn't spoken properly since the other day when he had been upset about her seeing Ben, and now she wondered if he was about to go on where they had left off. With Kyle listening in, that would make life difficult. 'Come in,' she said, 'but perhaps you could make yourself useful and put the kettle on. I'm parched and I've no time to stop. We're about to have a serious cookie-making session here.' She sent him a swift glance, trying to gauge his mood. Maybe he wanted to declare a truce.

Callum did as she suggested, and then came to sit down at the table. He looked curiously at Kyle. The little boy was lifting up each one of the cookie cutters, examining them carefully in turn.

'This one's my favouritest,' Kyle said, holding up the star for him to see. 'This goes over the stable, see?' He laid them out on the table, placing the star over the stable, and putting the angel next to both. 'And then we can have a tree over there.' He looked at Jasmine. 'Have you got any green icing? And we need white for the angel, yellow for the stable and silver for the star.'

Callum smiled. 'I think we have a budding artist here. He knows exactly what he wants, doesn't he?'

Jasmine nodded. 'He does.' She was busy making dough, but at the same time she was anxious to know what had prompted Callum's visit. Perhaps he just wanted to talk about Anna.

'I heard you'd been over to the hospital to see Anna,' she said. 'It must have come as a shock to learn that she'd had such a difficult time of it.' She glanced at Kyle to see if he was taking any notice of what they were saying, but he was engrossed in rolling out the dough, concentrating hard, his tongue peeping out from between his lips.

'Yes, I've been to see her several times. I was stunned. I had no idea that she had a heart problem,' he answered softly. 'I don't understand why she didn't tell me when we were together.'

Jasmine shot him a quick glance. 'Perhaps she didn't know how. Sometimes these congenital defects are missed, especially if they don't give any problems early on. Trouble can set in later, though, and sometimes the defect can be repaired. In Anna's case they decided that wasn't possible, and a new valve was the best option. It should give her a much better quality of life.'

'Maybe.' Callum frowned. 'But you could have told me all this before. You knew. Why did it have to stay secret?'

Jasmine paused, laying down her rolling pin. 'I didn't know myself until recently, when Ben told me. He said Anna didn't want anyone to know.'

'I still don't get it.' The lines in Callum's brow furrowed deeper. 'For her condition to get this bad, it must have been coming on for some time, so she probably knew way back when she left Woodsley. Why would she not say anything? And then to go and get pregnant, knowing that she had a problem that could become worse as a result seems like madness to me.'

Jasmine was thoughtful for a moment or two. 'Unless, of course, she only found out about the illness when she became pregnant. That could account for a lot of things. She was often breathless and sometimes complained of dizziness, but as far as I know she never went to see a doctor about it. Perhaps everything changed when she became pregnant.'

Callum mulled that over for a while. 'That makes a kind of sense. I suppose you could be right.' A look of melancholy crossed over his face. 'All I know is that when she left just after New Year, I was devastated. I couldn't understand what was happening. I knew she had been seeing more and more of Ben, but I wasn't expecting her to leave with him. I don't think I ever really got over the shock.'

'I know.' She said the words softly, on a ragged sigh. 'I always thought you and she were made for each other, but perhaps the thought of you going away to university was too much for her. After all, you weren't eighteen, you were twenty-one, and she might have expected you to have bypassed that kind of extensive education.'

He winced. 'Well, you know how it was. I was never as clear thinking as you. I couldn't make up my mind what I wanted to do, so I tried working at all kinds of different jobs. Then I discovered horticulture and realised it was something I could do for the rest of my life, even go into business for myself, but I needed to get the best qualifications possible. I suppose that must have come as a shock to Anna.'

Jasmine nodded. 'It could be what pushed her into leaving. You and she had always been a couple, but she probably thought the relationship wouldn't stand the strain of you being away at university. And then I guess people started to talk. Village life can be very closed in, with everybody knowing everything about everyone else. It could have been too much for her. She always used to join in with village activities, and I thought she was content here, but perhaps she needed a bit of space. Maybe that's why she turned to Ben, and when he said he was leaving she realised she could go with him and put everything behind her.'

'Yes, that's possible, but I still think we could have made a go of it if he hadn't started cosying up to her.' He contemplated that for a moment or two, frowning, but then he seemed to brace himself. 'Anyway, I'm glad she came through the surgery all right. It must have been a scary prospect for her.' He pressed his lips together. 'When I went to see her this morning, she was talking about going to the village carol-singing event on the green next Friday, but I don't think that will be a good idea, do you? She said Ben had to go because he was supposed to be helping out with the refreshment stall. The vicar roped him in, she said.' He grinned. 'She said he thinks the vicar's making him do penance for all his youthful misdeeds.'

Jasmine chuckled. 'More than likely.' She handed Kyle a cutter and showed him how to press it down into the dough. 'But you're right, it's probably best if she keeps away from crowds for the time being. Now that she's had a new heart valve fitted, she'll have to guard against infections. It's probably even more important at this stage, when she's fresh from surgery.'

'Hmm. That's what I thought.' He was silent for a moment or two. 'Maybe I'll suggest to her that she comes over to Mum's house instead. I don't know what Ben had in mind, but I can't imagine she'll want to be alone at Mill House. I know Mum and Dad are planning on going out for the evening to take part in the festivities, but I doubt they'll mind her coming over. And I'm sure we can find a bed for Kyle in the spare room, so that he can sleep over.'

She glanced at him from under her lashes. 'That sounds like a good idea, if she'll agree. I doubt she'd be up to standing around for long, anyway.' Knowing Ben, he would have made plans to do his stint at the refreshment stall and then he would return home instead of staying to enjoy the events.

'Yes, she said she was still feeling a little groggy. The anaesthetic can stay in your system for quite a while, can't it? And, of course, she's still healing.'

'That's true.'

He looked at Kyle's efforts with the cookie shapes. 'You've done really well there, lad. They'll be great when they've been baked in the oven.'

Kyle gave him a beaming smile. 'You have to press them down really hard, like this…else they don't cut properly.' He demonstrated, using the flat of his hand to press down on the cutter. 'You can make some, if you like,' he added generously. His face became instantly stern. 'But you have to wash your hands or you're not allowed.'

'Oh, I see. I'd better do that, then, hadn't I? And maybe I should make the tea, as well.'

They were on their second pot of tea an hour later when Ben returned from his rescue mission. 'Callum,' he said, nodding towards him. 'It's good to see you again. Are you home for the holidays?'

'I'm off for Christmas and New Year,' Callum answered, his manner remote. 'I suppose it's possible you could be working over the holiday period, isn't it? I know Jass has managed to get both days off this year.'

Jasmine gave a wry smile. 'Only because I've worked every one for the last several years,' she said. 'I thought it was time I had the option of staying home, and Mum particularly wanted me to help out this year. We have relatives coming over and there's a lot of work to do.'

'I'm off on Christmas Day,' Ben murmured. He turned as Kyle tugged on his shirt. 'What is it, Kyle?'

'Come and see the cookies I made.' Kyle dragged him over to the side of the room where the cookies were spread out on the worktops on baking trays, iced and gleaming, making a colourful array.

'They look super-scrumptious, don't they?' Ben exclaimed. His mouth curved. 'Good enough to eat,

I'd say.' His hand swooped over the trays as though making a selection, and Kyle stopped him, pulling on his shirtsleeve.

'We saved you some. Over here, see…an angel and a star. I made them.'

'They're just perfect, aren't they?' Ben bit a corner off the star and savoured the taste. 'Mmm…delicious. Best I've ever tasted.'

Kyle's eyes glowed with pleasure, and his whole body seemed to puff up with pride. 'I've saved some for Mummy as well…the very prettiest angel with silver on her wings, and a star with lots and lots of silver balls.'

'She'll love them,' Ben said. 'She'll think they're the best cookies she ever had.'

Kyle's face was one big smile. Then he said in an accommodating tone, 'Callum made some as well, but his icing went a bit wrong. We had to put silver balls to hide the bits where it went too thick, and some of the icing got a bit squashy where he pressed them in…but he did all right, really.'

Callum tried to keep a straight face. 'Cooking never was my strong point,' he said. 'Give me a plant and I can make it grow and thrive, but baking I leave to those who do it best…like Jass and your mum.'

Jasmine chuckled. 'Still, you're right about the plants. I envy you your green fingers.'

Kyle peered closely at Callum's hands. 'They're not green,' he said. 'Only a bit when he used the green icing.' He frowned. Grown-ups were clearly a little odd.

Callum smiled, and stood up. 'I have to go,' he said. He lightly ruffled Kyle's hair and added, 'Thanks for helping me with the cookies. You were great.' Then he gave Jasmine a quick hug. 'See you later, Jass.'

He nodded towards Ben, almost as an afterthought, a cool, superficial nod, as though he was only doing it because the rules of good manners demanded it of him. Then he closed the door behind him.

'He still hasn't changed his opinion of me, has he?' Ben commented. 'His feelings for Anna must be stronger than anyone could have imagined.'

'Yes, they are.'

Jasmine prepared a basket with cookies, mince pies and a bottle of elderberry wine. 'I take it your father is expecting us?' she murmured.

He nodded. 'I told him you and your mother wanted him to have some goodies for Christmas in return for all the sound financial advice he's given your father over the year. I think he would have liked to say don't bother, but I didn't give him the option. I said it was a done deal, and then I rang him to let him know that we'll be late.'

'Good.' She glanced at the bottle of wine. 'Will he be all right drinking this if he has hypertension? Perhaps I should exchange it for another gift?'

'I doubt he'll drink it all in one go,' Ben remarked. 'I don't suppose a small amount will do him much harm.'

'Are we going, then?' Kyle asked, coming to stand between them. With the baking out of the way, his impatience was growing, and Jasmine could see trouble brewing if they didn't soon make a move.

'Right away,' Ben said.

'Best foot forward.' Kyle looked down at his feet and started with his left foot.

Jasmine gave a wry smile. 'You're going to have to put him right on that one,' she told Ben. 'He's a very astute little boy, and he takes in everything you tell him, like a sponge.'

Ben laughed. 'I will.'

They arrived at the manor house some half an hour later, but by then Kyle was a trifle subdued. The long, sweeping drive had left him in awe of the place to begin with, and now, standing in front of the glorious eighteenth-century house, with its Georgian façade, his eyes grew wide. 'Does your daddy live here all by himself?' he asked, sending a swift glance towards Ben, who nodded.

Kyle frowned but said nothing more, and Jasmine said softly, 'The house seems more beautiful every time I see it. Given its age, you wouldn't expect that, would you?'

'Perhaps not, but a good deal of love and care has gone into it over the years. Parts of it date back to the sixteenth and seventeenth centuries, but the majority of the building is eighteenth century.'

Stuart Radcliffe opened the door to them. He was a tall, distinguished-looking man, a smattering of silver threaded through his once dark hair. Now, though, he appeared uncomfortable, as though visitors were the last thing he wanted, but he put on an expression of welcome for Jasmine, and then looked down at the child.

'You must be Kyle,' he said. 'I've heard all about you from Dr Brett…Jasmine's father.' The look he gave Ben was a clear reproof, as if his son had made a glaring omission. 'Come in, all of you. We'll go into the drawing room.'

'Are we going to draw?' Kyle asked, picking up on the word. 'Do you have crayons and pencils? I like to draw pictures.'

'Um…no…not exactly…' Stuart looked perplexed. 'It's just a name…for when people used to withdraw to another room after dinner.'

Kyle was puzzled. 'We don't do that. We generally stay in the kitchen, or I go to play in my bedroom.'

'Yes, well…um…' Stuart's voice tailed off. He led the way along the hall and showed them into a large room dominated by a grand fireplace, finished with an ornate Chippendale mantelpiece.

The furnishings in here were sumptuous, with comfortable settees and chairs, and there were floor-to-ceiling windows giving views over the beautifully maintained gardens.

'Please, sit down.' He waved them to a sofa, and then glanced distractedly around. 'I hear the boy's mother's in hospital,' he said, glancing towards Kyle, who was giving the room a systematic survey.

'That's right,' Ben said. 'She'd been ill for some time, but Wellbeck Hospital seemed the best place for her to have the operation. The cardiology department here has always monitored her condition, and I think she wanted to come back to her roots for such a major operation. Wellbeck has a good track record for heart surgery.'

'So I've heard.' Stuart frowned, looking uncomfortable once more, and Jasmine thought now might be the appropriate time to offer her gift.

'My mother sent you mince pies, and the elderberry wine is from my father,' she told him. 'He was really pleased with the advice you gave him about putting the surgery onto a better financial footing. And the cookies are courtesy of Kyle and me. We had a baking session this morning. Very messy, a lot of flour and icing sugar all over the place, but we had a great time making them.'

'I… Thank you…' Stuart's reaction wasn't quite what she'd expected. He seemed a little taken aback, at a loss for words, and she couldn't fathom what was going through his head.

'Are you all right?' she asked. 'I can exchange the wine for something else, if you'd rather?'

'No…no…not at all.' He pulled in a steadying breath. 'It just struck me that I have such a large kitchen here, with all the modern, high-tech equipment installed, and it's hardly ever used.' His eyes were troubled. 'Not for something as exciting as cookie making, anyway.' He seemed sad all at once, and Jasmine felt a strong pull of emotion towards him. Ben's father was not what he seemed. She was sure there were layers beneath that surface that, as yet, no one had uncovered.

Ben went to offer him the hamper he had brought with him, but Kyle stalled him, asking Stuart what was uppermost in his mind.

'Don't you have any pencils at all?' He tugged on Stuart's trouser leg and his chin jutted as he tried to gain his attention. 'My mummy always finds things for me to do, so's I don't get bored.' He looked into Stuart's eyes. ''Cos it isn't very good if I'm bored, you know. I get up to things, Mummy says.'

Ben stifled a chuckle, and Stuart was startled into paying the boy some heed. 'Ah…' he said. 'Well, then… uh…perhaps I can find you a pencil or two, and some paper.' He stood up and looked about him distractedly. 'Yes, let me see.'

He went over to the bureau to one side of the room and rummaged through various drawers.

Coming back to Kyle a moment or two later, he said, 'Here we are. Will this do?' He handed the boy several sheets of white paper, along with a couple of graphite pencils. 'You can sit over there at the table.'

Kyle peered up at him. 'Thank you.' He gave him a sympathetic smile. 'You don't know much about children, do you?' he said, showing a wise head on young shoulders. 'But it's all right. My mummy says we have to be kind to old people who don't understand about us. Noise hurts their ears, she says, and they don't like lots of running about.' He pondered that for a second or two. 'Which is a shame 'cos I love running and jumping and making lots of noise.'

Ben put his hand over his mouth to hide a grin, while Jasmine tried not to laugh out loud and turned her response into a cough instead. Stuart, on the other hand, was more confounded than ever.

'I…uh… I don't know about that, Kyle. I only had the one son, Ben, and as I recall he didn't run about or make a lot of noise.'

'That's because you packed me off to my grandmother whenever you had the chance,' Ben said in a flat tone. 'And then when I was eight years old, you tried sending me off to boarding school.' He smiled wryly. 'Not that it worked. I made such a nuisance of myself that they sent me home.'

'And cost me a packet in school fees into the bargain,' Stuart responded, his mouth taut. 'How could I cope with a young boy with more energy than a dynamo? I had a very high-powered job in the finance industry. There was no time for babysitting.'

'No, there wasn't,' Ben said. 'I noticed.'

'Perhaps you should show your father the hamper you brought him?' Jasmine put in hastily. The two men were building up to a confrontation and that was the very opposite of what they had set out to do.

Ben obliged, backing down.

'Thank you,' Stuart said, looking at the basket that was brimful of produce from the Mill Bakery. There was a Christmas cake, beautifully iced, with frost-covered fir trees and small sugar figurines depicting children dressed up in winter clothes playing in the snow. Ben had added jars of preserves, made from the autumn crops of fruits, and there was a large, honey-glazed ham.

'I know you like the hams that we sell at the bakery,' Ben said. 'And I've added a couple of jars of home-made chutney to go with it.'

'Thank you. I appreciate this.' Stuart's manner was restrained, and Jasmine sighed inwardly, despairing of the two of them ever becoming fully reconciled.

Kyle stepped into the breach. 'I made you a picture,' he said, waving a piece of paper under Stuart's nose.

'Oh.' Stuart looked at the pencil drawing, as though undecided which way round it should go, until Ben leaned across and turned it the right way up. 'Oh, I see. Thank you.' He still looked faintly bewildered, unsure about the precise nature of the picture.

Kyle gave a disgruntled sigh. 'It's a big house, see, like this one, and there's a secret room inside it, where people could hide from the bad people that came to get them, or p'r'aps they put their treasure in there.' He jabbed a finger at the picture. 'That's a boy, hiding.'

Stuart's face cleared. 'Oh, I see it now. Ben's been telling you about the priest hole, has he?'

Ben nodded. 'He said he would show it to me.'

'Yes, we can do that. It's at the back of the house, through the library.' Stuart glanced at Jasmine. 'You've never seen it, have you? I mean, you've been to the house on occasion over the years, but you haven't seen the secret passage or the hidden room?'

She shook her head. 'No, I haven't. I'd love to look at it, though.'

He led the way through the house to the library, a wonderful, oak-panelled room with a magnificent inglenook fireplace and bookshelves lined with leather-bound volumes. There were chairs upholstered in fine fabrics and a beautiful, burnished wood desk to one side.

Stuart paused by one of the bookcases and then waved Kyle over to him. 'Just bend down and reach your hand into the gap behind the bookcase,' he said. 'Now press your finger quite hard into the carved wooden flower pattern on the panelling.'

Kyle did as he was told, and a moment later there was a soft click and a section of the panelling moved inwards.

'Wow,' Kyle said, his eyes lighting up. 'That's cool!'

'There's only room for two at a time in there,' Stuart murmured. He looked at Ben. 'Perhaps you should go first and help him down the steps. Show him the secret passage, and then help Jasmine to find her way. I'll stay here and wait for you to come back. I don't seem to be able to manage stairs quite so well these days.'

'Because of your blood pressure?' Ben was immediately concerned.

'Yes. But Dr Brett is going to see me about that to-morrow. I spoke to him on the phone and he said something about diuretics to take away the excess fluid…and a diet plan to make sure I'm not overloaded with salt and so on.'

'Good.' He looked at his father. 'Perhaps you should sit and wait for us. We could be gone for a while if Kyle takes to exploring.'

'I'll do that. Take your time.'

Ben led the way down the stone-carved steps into the priest's hole, and Jasmine followed Kyle. It was eerie down there, with cold stone walls and a room barely big enough to move around in. There was another door at one end, again with a hidden catch, opening up into a secret passageway.

'Where does this come out?' Kyle asked. 'Is it another secret room?'

'You'll see,' Ben murmured. 'Just keep going until you come to the door at the end.'

'This one?' A few minutes later Kyle felt around the edges of the door, frowning as he looked for a way to open it. Then he ran his fingers along a small groove, and the door obligingly sprang open. He stepped out into a stonebuilt folly, with mullioned windows that let in the light of the afternoon sun.

Kyle's mouth dropped open. 'We're in a little house!' he exclaimed in delight. Going to a second door, he looked outside and said excitedly, 'We're in a garden… only there are walls all around.'

'That's because it's a sunken garden,' Ben explained. 'People may not know it's here because it's surrounded by hedges and shrubs that hide the wall from prying eyes, for the most part.'

'Wow! I love it!' Kyle went off to explore, his boots leaving footprints in the snow.

He disappeared behind a bank of shrubs, and Ben said quietly, 'He'll be all right. He won't be able to go far from here unless he finds the gate, and that's always locked.'

Jasmine looked around and smiled. 'What a great childhood it would have been, to explore that secret passage and this lovely little folly.' She glanced at him. 'It's a pity you didn't have brothers and sisters to keep you company.'

He gave a soft laugh. 'Just as well that I didn't. My father could barely cope with me.'

'True.' She gave a small shiver as the shock of cold air seeped into her bones, and he was instantly concerned.

'Are you cold? Come back inside the folly and I'll keep you warm.' He wrapped his arms around her, drawing her against him and gently rubbing warmth into her body with the gentle sweep of his hands. 'Thanks for coming with me today to see my father,' he murmured. 'I wasn't looking forward to making the visit on my own, but with you around he seems much more mellow.'

'I think he was a bit nonplussed by young Kyle,' she murmured, resting her cheek against his chest. She felt the steady beating of his heart and felt totally at peace with the world, as if this was where she was meant to be. His hand came to rest at the nape of her neck, lightly stroking the silk of her hair. 'It must be difficult for him,' she said. 'He's not used to children, and yet now he has to come to terms with the fact that he'll be around from now on. Kyle's part of your life, so he has to have a place in his.'

'I suppose he…' Ben broke off as Kyle came back into the folly.

'Why are you holding Jasmine?' Kyle asked, giving them a curious look.

'She was feeling cold.' Ben's glance wandered over him. 'You're covered in snow, so I guess you've had a good time out there.'

'Yes…I built a snowman. Come and see.'

Ben gave Jasmine one last squeeze, before reluctantly releasing her. 'Onward and upward,' he said. 'We'll have you back in the warm in a minute or two.'

'I'm fine now, thanks,' she said, but the truth was she wasn't fine at all. It had been a mistake to stay in his arms for even a few seconds, because it stirred up all kinds of yearnings inside her, and he could answer none of them. She loved Ben, but he had a unique bond with Anna and Kyle, and she didn't see where she fitted in. She was an outsider, looking in.

CHAPTER NINE

'Do you have the test results back on Mr Farnham?' Ben asked, coming to join Jasmine at the main desk in A and E.

'I do.' She handed him the lab report. 'There's a ninety per cent blockage of the blood vessel, so I've called the neurosurgeon for a consultation.'

'Good.' He gave a satisfied nod. 'I expect he'll want to operate straight away.'

He leaned back against the desk, idly scanning through various reports while Jasmine added her signature to the patients' charts she was working on. 'Thanks for helping me out with choosing the furnishings for the barn the other day. It didn't seem as though we had much time after we were late going to the manor house, but I do appreciate your input. You've a real eye for textiles.'

'It was my pleasure. I thought what you'd done at the barn was wonderful. Very clean lines, so modern looking. It's wonderful.'

'Yes, I'm pleased with it myself. It's all coming along well.'

She went on signing charts. 'How is Anna coping now that she's out of hospital?' she asked after a minute or two. 'Has she settled in all right at Mill House?'

He looked up from the report he had been studying. 'I think she's doing okay…the best we can expect…though she's not really up to coping with a boisterous four-year-old just yet. I've arranged for Molly from the village to be with her during the day, to keep an eye on her and to look after Kyle while I'm at work. I would have left him with Carole, as before, but Anna wanted him to be at home with her. It's understandable, I suppose.'

'Yes.' Jasmine sent him a brief look from under her lashes. He cared a great deal for Anna, that was plain to see, and it went without saying that he thought the world of Kyle. She said softly, 'I heard that she wanted to go to the carol singing on the green tomorrow. Do you think she'll be up to it?'

He shook his head. 'I don't think it's a good idea, and we talked it through. It was mostly for Kyle's benefit that she wanted to do it. I told her I would take him there and keep an eye on him. Then I'll drop him back with her when I have to man the refreshment stall later on. She seemed happy enough with that compromise.'

He put the reports to one side. 'I left her looking over the plans for the interior of the barn conversion. She seemed to like the ideas you came up with…especially the textiles and the furniture. So all that's left to work on now is the kitchen. I gave her some brochures to sift through, and as soon as she decides on the units I can go ahead and order. One way or another it should all start to come together fairly soon. I'm hoping that it will all be finished not too long after Christmas.'

'Are you having Christmas at Mill House? I wondered if things might have improved enough with you and your father for him to invite you to the manor.'

His mouth turned down at the corners. 'That's not going to happen…though I have invited him to come and spend the holiday with us. He hasn't given me an answer yet.'

'I'm sorry.' Her gaze was sympathetic. 'Maybe he'll come round, given a little more time.'

'As though five years wasn't enough?' He gave a short laugh. 'To be honest, I've given up on the idea of spending Christmas together like a complete family. It isn't going to happen.'

'No, maybe not.' She laid a hand on his arm in a gesture of sympathy, and he responded by gently squeezing her hand. That simple action was enough to stir up all kinds of emotions in her. His warmth enveloped her, made her long for what she couldn't have, and above all she was saddened. She would be with her own family at Christmas, something she always cherished, and yet she would have given anything to have Ben with her on that day. She was wishing for the impossible, of course. His priorities were marked out. He would be with Anna and Kyle, and somehow that seemed to be the only proper option.

'We have a patient coming in by ambulance,' the triage nurse said, hurrying over to them and shattering Jasmine's thoughts. 'He should be here in about ten minutes. It's a young boy, Mitchell, about three years old, wandered off and fell into an icy pond close to his home. His father pulled him out of the water, but he didn't appear to be breathing.'

Ben sucked in his breath. 'Are there any life signs?'

'Yes, but his pulse is barely discernible.' She looked anxious. 'His body temperature is twenty degrees C. He appeared lifeless, but the paramedics have started him on oxygen therapy and rewarming.'

'Good.' Ben was tense. 'Let's get everything set up to receive him. We'll need to check arterial blood gases, do a series of chest X-rays over the next few hours and set up a twelve-lead electrocardiogram.' He frowned. 'Jassie, I want you to set up an intravenous line and initiate cardio-respiratory monitoring. I'll intubate him and get him ready for extracorporeal membrane oxygenation and warming.'

Jasmine hurried away to prepare for the little boy's arrival. This was the kind of event every medical professional dreaded. There was no guarantee that they could pull him through. They might simply be too late.

Even so, the staff would work as a team to do whatever was possible to save him. They would circulate the child's blood through an oxygenating system that would gradually raise his temperature and ensure that adequate oxygen went to all the tissues of his body.

It was a desperately worrying situation, and when the child was brought in just a few minutes later, Jasmine was overwhelmed by compassion for him. He was just a baby, really. He was deathly pale, unresponsive and his life signs barely registered on the monitors. Her heart went out to his parents, who were white faced and distraught with grief.

Once they had put all the lifesaving measures in process, Ben began to explain the procedure to them, taking time to ensure that they knew what to expect. 'It will take some time for his temperature to come up to anything near normal,' he said. 'It could take several hours.'

'And will he be all right then? Will he recover?' It was a desperate plea.

'We're doing everything we can for him. Our aim is to get him to breathe on his own, but with near-drowning the outcome is not always straightforward. There could be complications, which we have to deal with as they occur.'

Jasmine knew he was trying not to give them false hope, yet he wanted to reassure them at the same time. For her part, she made the boy her prime focus for the rest of her shift, monitoring his condition continuously, praying for even some slight improvement.

Ben came to find her later that day. 'You're still here? Shouldn't you have gone home a couple of hours ago?'

She looked at him wearily. 'I was hoping there would be some change in him. He's so pale, so still. It's heartbreaking, seeing him this way.'

He laid an arm around her shoulders. 'I know. I keep imagining how I would feel if it was Kyle lying there. It makes me shudder to think of it.' He let his gaze run over her. 'But you really should go home, you know. You've been on your feet for hours and you look washed out. There's nothing more you can do for him. Everything's in hand, and the nurses will let us know as soon as there's any change.'

She shook her head. 'I can't go home. I know they say we shouldn't get too involved with our patients, but this little boy wrings my heart to shreds. I'm going to stay here until I see that he's on the mend.'

Gently, he ran the backs of his fingers across her cheek and tucked back a lock of silky, chestnut hair that had escaped from its silver clip. 'I always knew you would make a good doctor,' he said softly. 'It makes me glad I came back here, knowing that you're around. You care about people, and you never give up on anyone, do you? I've seen how you are with other patients. But it isn't just here, at work, where it shows. You care about everyone.' He gave a wry smile. 'You stood by me all those years ago when people were ready to condemn me, even your own brother. I don't think I showed it at the time, but I appreciated how you went out on a limb for me.'

She gave a weary smile. 'I don't recall anyone listening. I wanted them to know that there are two sides to every story…that you had a messed-up childhood that was bound to turn you into a rebel. And as for Anna, who are we to judge what goes on in other people's relationships?' She didn't tell him that she'd grieved when he'd left and, besides, he would have found the notion incredible. After all, she had always kept her distance from him, hadn't she? It would have been all too easy to be sucked into his charismatic whirlpool.

'But people do.' His fingers were threading lightly through her hair, a caress soft as a whisper, and she doubted he was even aware of what he was doing. His touch sent delicate ripples of pleasure to eddy along her nerve endings, and heat surged in her cheeks. 'I thought by coming back here, I could begin to put things right, but I'm not sure that I'm succeeding very well. My father is as obstinate as ever, and the business people in the village are holding meetings to protest about the barn and stable conversion. They're a bit late, that's all I can say.'

She glanced up at him. 'They're just worried that whatever you have planned will put them out of business. You can hardly blame them for that.'

'True…but I don't have a strict plan of action as yet, and whatever I do will have to go before the planning committee. I don't see why they're concerned but, then, it's probably a hangover from the old days. Whatever Radcliffe does is bound to be bad news.'

'Are they likely to make you think twice about staying? I mean, what will you do when your two months here come to an end?'

He frowned. 'I'm not sure yet. I've been offered a post back in Cheshire, so that's something I'll have to consider.'

Jasmine felt her throat close up. Of course, Anna would be happy to go back there, wouldn't she? Kyle had his roots there, and Anna had built up a business. Why had she even imagined that Ben might want to stay here in his home village? He had never been one for settling down.

She straightened, moving away from that absently caressing hand. It stopped her from thinking straight, and she had to hang on to her common sense right now. Falling for Ben had been a bad move. There was no future in it, and she should have stuck to her original plan…avoid him like the plague.

'A job offer has to be good news, doesn't it? At least it means you have one option already in the bag.' She looked at the little boy lying motionless on the bed. 'I think I'll go and take a break in the staff lounge for a while. You're right. I've been on my feet for too long.'

'I'll let you know if anything happens.'

'Thanks.'

She stayed in the lounge for some time, sitting in one of the armchairs and sipping coffee. The hot liquid was reviving, and it helped to clear her head. She would concentrate solely on her patients from now on and avoid getting any further entangled with Ben. Just being around him was disturbing to her peace of mind.

The nurse called her back to the treatment room just half an hour later. 'Mitchell's showing signs of pulmonary oedema,' she said, her tone urgent.

Jasmine was instantly on her feet. 'I'll come right away.'

She checked the child's X-rays and oxygen saturation level. 'His lungs are filling with fluid,' she told the nurse. 'We'll start him on diuretics right away. Let Ben know what's happening, will you?'

'I will. He had to go and deal with another emergency, but I'll get a message to him right away.' She looked at the boy. 'Poor little chap. I wouldn't like to be the parent going through this agony. It's bad enough dealing with it from our side of the bed.'

'That's true.' Jasmine went back to the staffroom and as the night wore on she curled up on the sofa in there. She must have slept for a while, but when she woke in the early hours of the morning, she discovered that someone had thoughtfully laid a blanket over her. From the other side of the room there was a satisfying aroma of freshly made coffee, and as she struggled to sit up she saw that Ben was coming towards her, a steaming mug in each hand.

'I saw that you were beginning to stir,' he said, 'so I thought you might like this.' He handed her a mug and then sat down beside her on the sofa.

'Is there any news?' Jasmine couldn't hide her anxiety.

'His temperature's almost back to normal. We'll take him off the extracorporeal membrane oxygenation in a while and continue with normal warming measures.'

'And the fluid in his lungs?'

'We're still working on that. It'll take a while to clear. I shan't be happy until I see some signs that he's able to cope on his own.'

'No, of course not. How are his parents managing?'

'Reasonably well, I think, given what they're going through. He's warmer, but there's still no colour in his face.'

She sent him a quick glance as she sipped her coffee. 'Shouldn't you have gone off duty hours ago?'

He gave a sheepish grin. 'Like you, I couldn't go home knowing that a child was in such a dire condition.'

'Will Anna cope on her own?'

He nodded. 'I rang to check. Molly saw Kyle off to bed and then stayed for a while until he dropped off to sleep. Anna was watching TV earlier, but I'm sure she'll be tucked up in bed by now.'

They drank their coffee slowly, neither of them wanting to move just then. The hospital was quiet in these early hours. Even the flow of emergency admissions had slowed up. It was strange sitting here in the half-light, with Ben by her side. She felt the brush of his thigh against hers and struggled as the heat of that contact sizzled through her entire body. She swallowed more coffee. She would not let it faze her.

'Shall we go and check on Mitchell?' Ben suggested a few minutes later. 'Let's hope there's some good news.'

'Yes.' She rinsed the mugs at the sink and then followed him out of the door.

With Mitchell's body temperature back to normal, Ben set about removing the ECMO. Jasmine checked the monitors to make sure that all was as it should be, and then she gazed down at the small child.

'Is he going to be all right?' his mother asked, her eyes reddened with the strain of keeping watch over him.

'We can't be sure how things will turn out at this stage,' Jasmine said, 'but the monitors aren't showing anything that we didn't expect. We just have to make sure that his lungs are cleared of fluid, and we're waiting for some kind of response from him. Why don't you try holding his hand and talking to him for a while? You might manage to get a reaction.'

The woman did as she'd suggested, and Jasmine turned away to write up Mitchell's charts. Ben adjusted the dose of diuretic, and for the next hour everything was quiet in the room, except for the boy's mother's soft voice, telling him about the Christmas presents waiting for him back home and how his sister was waiting for him to play with her on the karaoke machine.

The child coughed and seemed to stir, and in an instant Ben was at his bedside. 'I'm going to remove the tube from his throat,' he said, after a while, 'and we'll see how he manages on his own.'

'Will there be any damage to his brain?' his father asked worriedly, anxiety rapidly overcoming relief. He turned to Jasmine. 'I mean, he was under the water for several minutes. Is he going to remember who we are… or even be able to live a normal life after what's happened to him?'

'Hopefully, he'll be fine. Very cold water causes a reflex that protects the brain and organs from a lack of oxygen, so we'll hope for the best.'

With the tube removed from his throat, Mitchell coughed again and began to whimper, making soft mumbling sounds that Jasmine couldn't interpret.

'He's saying it's his turn on the karaoke,' his mother said, a broken sob in her voice but her mouth creasing into a smile. 'He and his sister are always arguing about it.' She stroked her son's hand and wept silently, the torment of the last fifteen hours breaking like a dam with her child's recovery.

Jasmine's gaze tangled with Ben's. The relief was overwhelming, and what she wanted most of all right then was to hug him and celebrate. Perhaps he had the same idea because he nodded towards the door, and they left the parents alone with their son for a while.

Out in the corridor, he wrapped his arms around her and kissed her tenderly on the forehead. 'That was a good result,' he said, his voice rough around the edges. 'I'm glad we were both here to see it.'

'It was the best,' she murmured, loving the way he held her close in his embrace. 'The very best.'

Slowly, carefully, he released her with a sigh and drew back. 'I wish we were somewhere else,' he said, 'somewhere where I could hold you without fear of someone coming along.'

His comment brought her to her senses with a small jolt. 'There's the rub,' she whispered. 'There's always someone waiting in the wings. Life just doesn't turn out the way we want it to, does it?'

He looked at her oddly, but if he understood what she was saying, he didn't respond. 'You should go home and get some rest while you can,' he said. 'You still have another shift to do tomorrow, and then there will be the Christmas festivities waiting for you.'

'And for you. Maybe you should take your own advice.'

They went back into the treatment room to check on Mitchell once more. He appeared to be sleeping peacefully, and the monitors showed nothing untoward. 'We'll keep him on the diuretics for a while,' Ben told the boy's parents, 'and we'll continue with oxygen by mask, but everything seems to be going along reasonably well, so I'm hopeful that he's out of the woods now. I'm going to hand over to my colleague, and I'll see you both again tomorrow.'

Jasmine said her own goodbyes, and then headed out to the car park. As he had said, she had a full day ahead of her tomorrow—or rather today. And the carol singing was something she never missed. It wouldn't do for her to be looking peaky. Her parents would be there, along with her friends and most of the people from the village. She'd even heard that her father had encouraged Stuart Radcliffe to come along. Her father and Stuart seemed to have built up some kind of rapport, because apparently Ben's father had accepted an invitation to come to the house for drinks on Christmas Day afternoon.

The hours flew by once she managed to get some sleep. Refreshed, she went back to the hospital to start her shift and check on Mitchell once more. He was making a brilliant recovery, and after that she felt as though she was walking on air.

By the evening, she was wrapped up in warm clothes, a winter coat, scarf and hat, and leather boots to keep out the cold. Everyone gathered on the village green for the lighting-up ceremony, and on a signal from the vicar, the huge tree and all the surrounding streets became a blaze of colour. Then the carol singing began in earnest.

Ben held Kyle in his arms so that he could see what was going on, and the boy gazed around in wonder at the shimmering tree and the myriad stars that made up the street decorations. 'Mummy would like those,' Kyle said.

'She'll be able to see them soon,' Ben promised. 'When she's feeling a bit stronger.'

'That's what Callum said.' Kyle frowned. 'He took her to his house…his dad's house. I don't know why we couldn't stay at the mill.'

'I'm with you on that one, lad,' Ben murmured. 'But it was your mother's choice. She thought it would be a good thing to do.'

Kyle hunched his shoulders and looked around once more, taking in the sights and sounds all around him—the funfair that had been set up in the village square, the candyfloss stalls and the mobile unit selling beef burgers and bacon butties. He sniffed the air appreciatively.

Jasmine looked at Ben. 'Are you not comfortable with the fact that she's staying at my parents' house this evening?'

'I think it was a mistake to move her. It was disruptive and unnecessary when both she and Kyle were settled at my house.'

'But Callum wanted to keep her company, and perhaps he wouldn't have felt right doing that at the mill. And as you say, it was Anna's choice. She had the option to stay but she chose to go with Callum. Is that what bothers you…that she's with my brother? Are you jealous?'

'Do I have anything to be jealous of?' He raised a dark brow.

'I'm not sure. Callum has never stopped loving Anna, and since she's come back to Woodsley he's been trying to see her whenever possible. If you don't like that, perhaps you are jealous.'

'Or it could be that I don't want her to be hurt. She's vulnerable. She's been through a lot these last few years.'

The carol singing came to an end a few minutes later, and the crowd dispersed. People cheerfully made their way towards the funfair or the bric-a-brac stalls. The atmosphere was good humoured, full of laughter and the joy of the Christmas season.

'What do you want to do first?' Ben asked Kyle, carefully lowering him to the ground. 'The funfair or the stalls?'

'The rides.' The answer was emphatic, and Kyle tugged eagerly at Ben's hand, impatient to get under way. 'I want to go on the horses that go up and down.'

'Okay, that's what we'll do, then.' He glanced at Jasmine. 'Luckily, Molly offered to look after the refreshment stall for the first half of the evening, so we should have plenty of time to fit everything in.'

'I could always watch him for you when you have to go and take over,' she volunteered, but he shook his head. 'It'll be his bedtime by then, anyway, but thanks for that.'

She went with them to the carousel and stood to one side, watching as the boy tried out as many of the rides as possible. Ben chatted with the vicar while keeping an eye on Kyle, and after a while she realised that Stuart Radcliffe had also come along to watch.

She sent him a quick smile. 'I wasn't expecting to see you here tonight,' she said. 'It's good that you were able to come along.'

'Your father persuaded me that it was the right thing to do,' Stuart answered, with the air of a man who felt somehow out of place. 'He said the fresh air would do me good, and it was time I mixed in a bit more with village life.' His expression was rueful. 'He seems to think I'm in danger of becoming a recluse, and that will never do.'

Jasmine chuckled. 'My father was always one for straight talking...but I'm glad you took his advice.' She glanced at Kyle, who was holding on to the steering-wheel of a racing car, making brumming sounds as though he was on a real racetrack. 'It must be great for you to see your grandson enjoying himself.'

He didn't answer, and she added softly, 'I know all this must have come as a great shock to you, but at least Ben has done the right thing and brought him back here.'

He pulled in a shuddery breath. 'I'm not convinced that any of my son's actions are quite what they seem to the outside world.' He turned to her. 'He never introduced Kyle to me as my grandson, and even though everyone around here thinks that's so, I'm not sure of it. Kyle is a delightful child, and much as I would love to know that the boy is my own flesh and blood, I'm afraid I don't think that's possible. I don't believe that Ben is the boy's father.'

It was Jasmine's turn to suck in a shocked breath. 'You don't?'

He shook his head. 'Over the years, Ben and I have had our differences of opinion—sometimes quite forceful differences, as you probably know. I always thought he was a rebel, a stubborn, obstinate and wilful boy who grew into a stubborn, obstinate and wilful man.' He frowned. 'But over the last few months I've begun to realise that one thing above all marks him out among men. He's strong willed and determined, and he always goes straight for what he believes to be right, no matter whether anyone thinks otherwise. I just don't believe he's the kind of person who would get a girl pregnant and not insist on marrying her. I would stake my life on it. He has too much honour to consider any other course of action.'

Jasmine's mind was in a whirl. Could Stuart be right in what he was saying? She was struggling to take it all in, and it felt very much as though all the breath had left her body.

She took a moment or two to get herself together, then she said in a quiet voice, 'It sounds as though you have a lot of respect for your son.'

He nodded. 'I think I do. It's as though I've been blind for all these years, locked in my own preconceived ideas and beliefs, and now I'm beginning to see how things really are.'

She lightly touched his arm. 'Perhaps you should tell him how you feel?'

He didn't answer, and she guessed he was turning things over in his mind. She went back to watching the child on the carousel. Was Stuart right? Was it possible Kyle wasn't Ben's son after all?

CHAPTER TEN

'THAT was a delicious Christmas dinner, Mum.' Jasmine leaned back in her chair, full to the brim with turkey and stuffed bacon rolls, roast potatoes and all the trimmings. 'Everything was perfect.'

'Thank you. I'm glad you enjoyed it.' Her mother smiled. 'I hope you've saved some room for Christmas pudding.'

Jasmine ran a hand over her stomach. 'Maybe in a while, when this lot's gone down.'

Callum added his appreciation, and their uncle, aunt and cousins echoed what he'd said. Her father sat and surveyed the table, a contented smile on his face. There were sparkly table decorations as a centrepiece, gold-sprayed pine cones and red and gold poinsettia providing a glorious splash of colour. And throughout there were the remnants of Christmas crackers, their motifs chuckled over and discarded, and small trinkets abandoned along with an assortment of paper hats.

They all helped clear the table, and Jasmine began to load the dishwasher. It had been a wonderful Christmas Day so far, with the church bells waking her in the morning, and when she had drawn back the curtains it had been to look out onto gently falling snow. Soft flakes had drifted on the air and begun to slowly cover everything in their path with a coat of white.

Only one thing was missing. The day would have been perfect if Ben was there. But, of course, he was at Mill House, with Anna and Kyle, and there was probably no chance that she would be able to see him at all today. Going to visit him would seem like an intrusion, and yet it was what she wanted most of all.

They sat down at the table once more for Christmas pudding, brought to the table in a haze of pale blue flame and served with brandy cream. Jasmine ate a small portion and thought about all the patients in hospital who would be eating their own Christmas dinners, hopefully in the company of family and friends who had come to visit.

Mitchell was still recovering and was well enough to sit up now. He had been chatting to his parents when she'd checked that morning. Santa had done a round of the wards, giving gifts to all the children unfortunate enough to be in hospital, and the adults had been rewarded with impromptu entertainment and a string of hilarious jokes from the senior house officer on duty.

A couple of hours later, Jasmine and her family said goodbye to the relatives who had come to visit, and the house settled down to a comparatively quiet time. The TV was on, the Queen's traditional speech had been broadcast to all and sundry and there were films showing on most channels. Her father was dozing in his armchair by the fire.

Then the doorbell rang, and Jasmine guessed it was Stuart Radcliffe coming to join them for drinks as her father had suggested. She laid a hand on her father's

shoulder and gently shook him awake. 'I think this must
be Stuart come to visit,' she said. 'Are you ready to go
and say hello to him?'

'Ah, yes. I'll be glad if he could make it. He's come
out of his shell a lot over these last few weeks. Let's go
and make him welcome.'

Only it wasn't just Stuart who was waiting at the door.
Anna and Kyle were with him, and, to Jasmine's great
joy, Ben was there, too.

'I'm so glad you came over,' she told him, giving him
a hug. He looked fantastic, wearing dark chinos and a
dark blue shirt beneath a winter overcoat that was open
to flap loosely around his legs. 'I was wondering how
your Christmas was going.'

'It's been really good so far,' he said with a smile.
'My father decided to accept my invitation, so that was
great. It feels like a new beginning somehow.'

'That's wonderful.' She showed him into the living
room, and her father added his greetings, inviting them
to sit down.

'I'm glad you could all drop by,' he said. 'I did suggest that Stuart bring you along with him, but I wasn't
sure whether you would want to do that, especially if
you were full up with all the Christmas food—not to
mention that Kyle must be eager to play with the toys
Santa brought him.'

He looked at Kyle. 'I see you've brought a couple of
toys with you. Did Santa bring you some nice things?'

Kyle nodded vigorously. 'I had a red fire engine and
a racing track so the cars go round and round.' He demonstrated with his hands, making whirring noises as
though he was on the circuit. 'And there was a robot
that walks and talks, and a remote control car. And lots

of things.' He waved his fire engine under everyone's noses and followed up with a box kite that was decorated like a bird in flight. 'Ben gave me the fire engine and Callum bought me the kite. Mummy says we might go and fly it later on today if we have time.'

'Well, it's stopped snowing, and there's a bit of a wind starting up, so you might be all right to do that. I dare say the snow will keep the darkness at bay for a while.' Callum was smiling as he looked at the boy. 'I'm glad you're pleased with all your presents.' He sat down with Anna and the boy on the settee, inspecting the kite to see how many brightly coloured trailers it had, while Jasmine's father went to fetch drinks for everyone.

Stuart was talking to their mother, and Jasmine excused herself to go and get ice from the freezer.

'Do you need any help?' Ben asked, following her into the kitchen.

'Thanks,' she said. 'Perhaps you could tip the cubes into the ice bucket for me. I always have trouble getting them out.'

He obliged, giving the tray a sharp tap with his hand, and the ice cascaded into the container.

She gave him a rueful look. 'Whenever I do that, they scatter all over the place.'

They went back into the living room. Kyle was still talking to Callum about the kite. 'You have to go up a hill and let it catch the wind,' he said, 'and if it's a good kite, it will go way up in the air, like this.' He stretched his hand out to the ceiling.

'It sounds as though you've flown a kite before,' Callum said, and Kyle nodded.

'I had one for my birthday, but it got tangled up in a tree and it broke. I cried, 'cos I really liked that kite.'

Callum gave him a thoughtful glance. 'When is your birthday, Kyle? Do you know?'

'June. I don't know the date, but Mummy said the sun was shining and it was really hot.'

Callum looked at Anna. 'So he's actually four and a half years old?'

'Yes.' It came out as a whisper, and as soon as she had said it, she stood up and went over to the window, looking out over the snow-laden garden.

Jasmine gazed at her brother. He must surely be putting two and two together and coming up with the fact that Anna had been pregnant before she'd left Woodsley Bridge. Was it possible that Kyle was Callum's son?

She glanced at Ben, who was helping to hand out drinks. His gaze meshed with hers, a faint smile curving his lips. 'Seems like now would be a good time for flying a kite,' he murmured, handing a glass to Callum. 'Anna's much stronger now, and I expect she would be able to manage the short walk to Brier's Field, if you take things slowly. It isn't hilly, but the wind blows across the meadow and Kyle would have a great time, I'm sure.'

'Good idea,' Callum said. He was staring at Anna. 'Maybe we could go as soon as we finish our drinks?'

Anna nodded cautiously. She looked towards Jasmine's parents. 'I feel perhaps it would be rude to leave so soon, when you've been kind enough to invite us over.'

'Heavens, girl, you don't need to worry about that,' Jasmine's mother said. 'You young things need to get out, and it's a shame not to catch what's left of the light. You go off and enjoy yourselves.'

Her father echoed that. 'Sounds as though you two have a good deal to talk about, anyway,' he said, in his usual straightforward manner, and Jasmine inwardly groaned. Tact wasn't his strong point.

Ben leaned towards her. 'Maybe you and I could take a walk over to the mill in a while?' he suggested in an undertone. 'It appears to me that Anna and Callum aren't the only people who have things they need to clear up between them.'

'I think you're right,' she said softly. 'Even your father guessed that everything wasn't as it seemed.'

He gave her a crooked smile. 'It just goes to show there are times when he can be surprisingly astute.'

They gave it a decent interval before they left, chatting with Stuart and Jasmine's parents for a while. 'We're going to take a walk over to Mill House,' Ben said at last. 'Perhaps we'll see you all later?'

'Of course.' Her mother saw them to the door. 'Don't worry about Stuart, he seems content to be with us.' She pulled in a quick breath. 'My word, this is turning out to be a day of happenings and new beginnings. Not at all what I expected, but absolutely wonderful.' She gave them both a beaming smile, and Jasmine wondered how much her mother knew of what went on in her heart…a lot more than she said, obviously.

It was a short walk to the mill. Jasmine's boots crunched in the snow, and she looked around her, marvelling at the sheer white light that was reflected from the ground. There were icicles hanging from the branches of the trees, cobwebs frozen and outlined in the hedgerows and the crystalline sparkle of snow overall. It was beautiful.

'I love it here,' she said, as they approached Ben's house. A cheerful light welcomed them in the porch, and there was a lovely old-world look about the place. It was perfect, with a thick blanket of snow on the roof and latticed windows like jewels in the fading light. 'I don't know how you could even think of leaving. And as to the house, you've put so much effort into it, and yet you've hardly lived here. Surely you'll miss it?'

He opened the front door and ushered her inside. 'A lot of what I decide to do will depend pretty much on what you have to say,' he murmured. He helped her off with her coat and then led the way into the sitting room.

As in his other properties, there were exposed beams about the place, polished wood floors, and in the sitting room a grand, open fireplace, where logs crackled and spat, sending a golden glow into the room. 'Sit down, and I'll get you a drink,' he said, indicating a luxuriously upholstered sofa. 'Would you like something alcoholic, or coffee, maybe?'

'Coffee, I think. I've had a tad too much alcohol already today. Any more and I might not be in control of my actions.'

'Well, there's something I'd like to see,' he said with a laugh. 'Perhaps I should make you a liqueur coffee?'

She sighed. 'Ah, now you've found my weak spot. I'm more than tempted. I can't resist.' She stood up. 'I'll come and help you make them.'

The kitchen was similarly old-worldly, a delightful combination of oak units, exposed beams and an island bar where they could sit and drink their coffee and look out over the back garden. Darkness was falling now, and Ben drew the curtains, so it felt as though they were cocooned in this tranquil oasis of calm.

'I think Callum will have realised by now that Kyle is his son, don't you?' Ben asked, coming to stand beside her as she was perched on the barstool.

'I imagine so…unless you and Anna were deeply involved some three months before you left the village?'

He gazed at her. 'You must know that isn't true. Anna and I have never been involved in that way. She was ill, she was vulnerable and she didn't know what to do for the best, so she turned to me. I told her to tell Callum that she was pregnant, but she wouldn't. She said he was going away and, anyway, what would he want with a girl who had a defective heart? It would put a blight on his life, she said.'

He pressed his lips together. 'Of course, I told her she was wrong and that he would stand by her, but she wouldn't hear of it. She thought he would stay with her out of pity and duty, and she didn't want that. So she decided to leave, and I've been keeping an eye on her ever since. She made me promise that I wouldn't say anything to anyone, because she didn't want Callum to find out.'

Jasmine sipped her coffee. 'I suppose I should have known when you didn't give me a straight answer, but you seemed so fond of Anna and Kyle, and I was sure there was more going on between you. She was even living with you from time to time, and then you brought her here, to the mill. That confused me.'

He slid his arms around her. 'What should I have done? I could hardly leave her to fend for herself. She needed support through the operation and afterwards, and I was determined to give her that. Afterwards, though, I told her she had to tell Callum the truth. He already half suspected anyway, and it's been clear all along that he had never got over their break-up.'

'I'm not sure she's ready to tell him, even now. She looked mortified when he started asking about Kyle's birthday.'

He smiled. 'I think she was perturbed more because he said it in front of everyone. Callum's a bit like your father in that respect—he says things as he sees them and thinks about it afterwards.'

She laughed. 'I hope they manage to sort things out, anyway.'

'They'd better.' Ben was frowning now. 'I've had to keep my feelings on hold for what seems like ages, all because Anna refused to let me speak up. But not any more.' He looked her in the eyes. 'You have to know that I'm in love with you, Jassie.'

She stared at him, her eyes widening. 'Are you? Really?'

'Really. I think I've always been half in love with you from when you were a teenager, but there wasn't a thing I could do about it back then. Our lives were taking separate paths, and you were just starting out on your medical career. Then when you came back into my life, I just knew I had to make you mine.'

He ran his hand over her face, lightly caressing her cheek, drawing her towards him with infinite care until their lips met in a tender, blissfully satisfying kiss. 'You can't imagine how hard it has been for me,' he said gruffly. 'I've wanted you so much. It was like torture to have you distance yourself from me. And yet I felt sure that you wanted me just as much as I wanted you. Am I right, Jassie?'

'Yes, you're right,' she whispered, sliding down from the barstool and moving into his embrace. 'I love you, Ben. It feels as though I've loved you for ever.'

He groaned raggedly and kissed her again, his hunger building, his body moving against hers as though he would possess her, body and soul. His hands stroked her, gliding over her curves and tugging her into the warmth of his thighs. 'I've waited for this moment for so long,' he said huskily. 'I love you, Jassie. I want to marry you. Will you marry me? Will you be my wife?'

'I will.' Her heart was running over with happiness. 'Oh, yes. Please.'

They stayed locked in each other's arms for what seemed like an eternity. The outside world ceased to exist, and all either of them wanted was to be melded together as one for the foreseeable future.

'We'll be married in the village church and invite everyone we know,' Ben said softly against her cheek.

'That means the entire village, then,' she said with a laugh. 'Still, I dare say we'll manage to fit them all in somehow.'

He gently nuzzled the silky skin of her throat. 'And we'll live here, at Mill House, and bring up our children in this beautiful countryside.'

'That sounds absolutely wonderful to me.' She gazed up at him. 'But what about the job in Cheshire? How does that fit into things?'

'It doesn't. I've been talking to the consultant at Wellbeck, and they're looking for another registrar. I've been told the job's mine, if I want it.'

She smiled happily. 'And you do want it, don't you?'

'Oh, yes, definitely, I do. Life is going to be just perfect, Jassie. I love you, and we'll be man and wife just as soon as the arrangements can be made.' He hugged her tight. 'Sooner rather than later…or I might just blow a fuse.'

She snuggled against him, resting her cheek against his chest. 'That would never do.' She was thoughtful for a moment, and then said, 'I expect there will be another wedding fairly soon, if things go well for Callum and Anna.'

'I'm sure they will. They love one another, and it looks as though nothing will stop Callum from winning her back. His only problem is that he's working away… though I dare say I could offer to lease him the barn and stable block at a low enough price so that he could set up business in the village. The set-up is ideal for horticulture and landscaping, and if he plays his cards right, people will come from all over to buy specialty produce. In time, he could buy the place, if he wanted.'

She cupped his face in her hands. 'Now I know why it is that I want to marry you,' she said. 'You're simply the best man in the whole world.'

He laughed and scooped her up in his arms once more. 'Goes without saying,' he murmured. Then he lowered his head towards her, claiming her lips once more, and Jasmine snuggled into his embrace. This was where she belonged. Everything was perfect.

OFFICER,
SURGEON...
GENTLEMAN!

BY
JANICE LYNN

MILLS
BOON

First published in Great Britain 2010
Harlequin Mills & Boon Limited,
Eton House, 18-24 Paradise Road, Richmond, Surrey TW9 1SR

© Janice Lynn 2010

ISBN: 978 0 263 87921 6

Harlequin Mills & Boon policy is to use papers that are natural, renewable and recyclable products and made from wood grown in sustainable forests. The logging and manufacturing process conform to the legal environmental regulations of the country of origin.

Printed and bound in Spain
by Litografia Rosés, S.A., Barcelona

Janice Lynn has a Masters in Nursing from Vanderbilt University, and works as a nurse practitioner in a family practice. She lives in the southern United States with her husband, their four children, their Jack Russell—appropriately named Trouble—and a lot of unnamed dust bunnies that have moved in since she started her writing career. To find out more about Janice and her writing, visit www.janicelynn.net

Recent titles by the same author:

DR DI ANGELO'S BABY BOMBSHELL
PLAYBOY SURGEON, TOP-NOTCH DAD
THE PLAYBOY DOCTOR CLAIMS HIS BRIDE
SURGEON BOSS, SURPRISE DAD

Dedication:

*To Dr. Tamara Worlton Kindelan for inspiring my muse
by just being herself, for her patience and generosity
in answering my questions. To Teresa Rose Owens
for her fabulous military knowledge.
And to Terri Garey, my wig-wearing,
fairy-winged partner in crime (aka cover model-
stalking RT roomie), who believed I could and should
write this story. You rock, ladies!*

*Any and all mistakes regarding military life
are mine alone. Please forgive.*

Dear Reader

Ever met someone and been fascinated by their life? That happened to me at the 2009 *RT Book Reviews* Booklovers' Convention. I met a fascinating lady who worked as a ship surgeon on an aircraft carrier and my muse jumped into warp-drive, creating the Stockton family.

The Stocktons are true-blue military, serving their country with honour and pride. How can loner Dr Cole Stanley *not* want to be a part of their tightly knit family? Unfortunately, he met the wrong Stockton daughter first, and didn't realise until almost too late. Now he's a man on an impossible mission: to win Amelia's love.

I hope you enjoy Cole and Amelia's story. I love to hear from readers. Please e-mail me at Janice@janicelynn.net, or visit me at www.janicelynn.net to find out my latest news.

Janice

CHAPTER ONE

WHAT was *he* doing here?

Dr Amelia Stockton's head spun at the sight of the uniformed naval officer crossing the sick bay of the USS *Benjamin Franklin*.

No way was Dr Cole Stanley really walking towards her.

And if that was Cole with the senior medical officer, well, she couldn't consider what his presence on board her ship implied, what that would mean to her hard-won peace of mind.

"Wow, Dr Stockton," Tracy whispered under her breath, nudging Amelia's arm. "Is that the new ship's surgeon? If so, sign me up for an elective procedure stat. Yum."

Amelia didn't turn to look at the petite blonde nurse, neither did she answer. She couldn't even if she wanted to. Along with her spinning head, now her throat had swelled shut.

Cole really was on board her ship.

She'd known the aircraft carrier's new surgeon would be arriving today. But Dr Evans's replacement was supposed to be Dr Gerald Lewis, not Cole Stanley, military surgeon and heartbreaker extraordinaire. Just because she hadn't seen him for two years, it didn't mean she hadn't instantly recognized that confident swagger, those piercing blue eyes, the crazy tune of her heart that had only ever played for him.

What was he doing here and why were her lungs crying for air?

From the overwhelming need to hit him for how he'd walked out on her and her family. That's why her head spun, her throat swelled, and she couldn't breathe. Her body functions hadn't gone haywire because of Cole himself, just what he'd done. Really.

Certainly, her fluttery heart had nothing to do with the last time she'd seen him, the things they'd said, done. Dear sweet heavens above, the last time she'd set eyes on Cole he'd kissed her until her lungs had felt just like they did this very moment.

"Dr Stanley, welcome aboard, sir." A corpsman saluted Cole, as did the physician's assistant, acknowledging Cole's higher military rank. "It's good to see you again."

"You, too, Richard. It's been a while."

He spoke with that voice. The one that haunted her sleep, her dreams. Nightmares, not dreams.

He shook both men's hands, said something about the naval hospital he and Richard had worked at together, but Amelia's ears roared, blocking out the details.

Cole. Was. On. Her. Ship.

No!

Oblivious to the turmoil he was creating in Amelia's safe, tight-knit world, in her mind and entire body—just as he'd always done—he acknowledged Tracy.

The nurse practically fell over herself batting her lashes and blushing up a storm. Puh-leeze. Tracy could do so much better. Any woman could. Sure, Cole came in an eye-catching package—and how!—but so did most poisonous snakes.

Cole Stanley was a low-down, belly-crawling snake of the worst kind. Yes, Amelia had once thought he'd hung the moon and walked on water, but her eyes had been opened.

Lastly, he turned to her, acknowledging her salute. He hesitated only the slightest of seconds, making her wonder if perhaps she'd been wrong, if perhaps he did know how his being there affected her, that perhaps he was equally as affected by seeing her after all this time.

"Dr Stockton." His gaze sought hers, searching, but for what she wasn't sure. Did he expect her to welcome him? Not after what he'd done to her, *to her sister*, surely?

Still, her heart sped up and stalled all at once when their gazes tangled for the first time in two years. Memories from the past assailed her. Memories of her and Cole, laughing, working, devouring pizza while he quizzed her, caring for patients together during residency. Memories of Clara, Cole and herself spending hour after hour together back during Cole and her sister's last year at medical school. They'd been two years ahead of her.

Clara.

Amelia sank her teeth into the soft flesh of her lower lip, welcoming the pain, the metallic tang of blood.

A tentative smile cut dimples into Cole's cheeks. "It's been a while since our paths have crossed, too."

Not long enough. Not nearly long enough. *Oh, Cole, what are you doing here?*

His eyes were still bluer than the sea. His light brown hair still streaked with gold, as if the sun hadn't been able to resist reaching out and touching him. Clara had called him Dr Delicious. Amelia and Josie had agreed when they'd met Cole. After all was said and done, though, they'd dubbed him Dr Disastrous.

Cole was here. On board her ship. In the middle of the Pacific Ocean. Tainting her first real deployment.

Oh, yeah, Dr Disastrous fit and she suspected she was headed for the biggest disaster of her life. The *Titanic* of disasters. Especially since she wavered between wanting to punch his handsome face and...she wasn't sure what the other emotion battling for pole position was, but either way she didn't like the uneasy fluttering in her chest.

"You know him?" Tracy asked from beside her, nudging her again, much to Cole's obvious amusement. "You never said anything about knowing Dr Evans's replacement."

Taking a deep breath and reminding herself she was a lieutenant in the United States Navy, the middle daughter of Admiral John Stockton and a force to be reckoned with under any set of circumstances, Amelia shifted her gaze to her nurse.

"Dr Stanley graduated from Uniformed Services University of the Health Sciences with my oldest sister, Clara, two years ahead of me." She kept her face stoic, kept her tone even, emotionless. "With the last names so close, they were constantly thrown together and became acquainted. I met him during that time."

"Oh," Tracy said, her curious gaze going back and forth between them. "I see. Thrown together. Acquainted."

Cole's eyes flashed, hinting at the fire that burned beneath the surface, at the fact he'd known he'd be seeing her even if she hadn't known of his arrival.

"How is Clara?"

Despite the tight rein she always held on her emotions, Amelia's eyes narrowed. How could he ask that question? She wanted to scream, wanted to rip out his hair and kick him in the solar plexus. He'd been her big brother, her friend, her biggest crush, *her sister's fiancé.*

And then he'd walked away.

"She's fine." *Not really, but I'd never let you know how you hurt her, how you hurt me!* Oh, God, why was breathing so difficult? "She's serving as a flight surgeon with an air wing unit in the Middle East and has been commissioned there for about three months."

He studied her much as she scanned a blood smear beneath her microscope, looking at each individual cell, searching for anything outside the norm. "I'd heard that."

Did you hear how she went a little crazy after you left her? How she volunteered for the most dangerous assignments? How I've wondered if I played a role in my sister's unhappiness and have had to live with that guilt?

"Josie and Robert? Are they well?"

As if he really cared how her vivacious younger sister and daredevil brother were. Oh, please. Why was he making the conversation between them so personal when the crew watched? Did he know that if they were alone she'd give him a piece of her mind? That she'd tell him where he could go and she'd happily buy him a one-way ticket? Her family had taken him in as one of their own and all he'd left them with was fragmented relationships and hearts.

She despised Cole for what he'd done to her family.

Except that he was her superior officer and as such she had to pay him respect, whether she felt one iota of it or not.

Life could be so unfair.

"Robert is serving on board the USS *George Washington* as the senior medical officer and Josie is doing field training exercises at a combat support hospital. She earned her nursing degree. They're both fine. They're Stocktons."

His smile deepened at her last comment. It was a given all four Stockton children would succeed in life and medicine. Even when jerks like Cole came along and pulled the rug out from under their feet.

After her experience with Cole, Amelia had vowed never to give her heart to any man. Never did she want to feel the pain her devastated sister still hadn't recovered from.

Just look at how *much* she had been hurt, too, and she had simply had a hero-worship crush on Cole, not been in love with him. *Thank goodness.*

When a Stockton gave their heart, they gave it forever.

"I'm glad to hear they're doing well," Cole said, pulling Amelia back to the present, moving closer to where she and Tracy stood.

Although she couldn't possibly really smell him, she'd swear her nostrils filled with the musky scent of his

FREE BOOKS OFFER

To get you started, we'll send you
2 FREE books and a FREE gift

There's no catch, everything is **FREE**

Accepting your 2 **FREE** books and **FREE** mystery gift
places you under no obligation to buy anything.

Be part of the Mills & Boon® Book Club™ and receive your favourite
Series books up to 2 months before they are in the shops and delivered
straight to your door. Plus, enjoy a wide range of **EXCLUSIVE** benefits!

- Best new women's fiction – delivered right to
  your door with FREE P&P
- Avoid disappointment – get your books up to
  2 months before they are in the shops
- No contract – no obligation to buy

We hope that after receiving your free books you'll
want to remain a member. But the choice is yours.
So why not give us a go? You'll be glad you did!

Visit **millsandboon.co.uk** to stay up to date
with offers and to sign-up for our newsletter

2 **FREE** books
and a
FREE gift

MZJIA

Mrs/Miss/Ms/Mr	Initials

BLOCK CAPITALS PLEASE

Surname _____

Address _____

_____

Postcode _____

Email _____

MILLS & BOON®

The Mills & Boon® Book Club™ – Here's how it works:

Accepting your free books places you under no obligation to buy anything. You may keep the books and gift and return the despatch note marked "cancel". If we do not hear from you about a month later we'll send you 3 brand new books including two 2-in-1 titles priced at £5.30* each and a single title priced at £3.30*. That is the complete price - there is no extra charge for post and packaging. You may cancel at any time, otherwise we will send you 5 stories a month which you may purchase or return to us – the choice is yours.

*Terms and prices subject to change without notice.

NO STAMP NEEDED!

MILLS & BOON®
Book Club

FREE BOOK OFFER
FREEPOST NAT 10298
RICHMOND
TW9 1BR

NO STAMP
NECESSARY
IF POSTED IN
THE U.K. OR N.I.

skin, a scent once so familiar to her that, again, she was swamped by unwanted memories of when he'd starred in a daily role in her life.

"Your parents must be proud."

Amelia didn't answer. All four Stockton children had been raised to never show weakness to the enemy. Clara had put on a good front when Cole had dumped her, but privately her overachieving sister hadn't been able to "Suck it up and move on," as their father advised in any given situation. If she had, she'd have moved on, dated. Clara hadn't. There'd been no one since Cole. Amelia's heart ached at the enormity of her sister's pain, and her role in it. At her own pain. All at the mercy of this man's careless hand.

The others in the sick ward eyed them as if observing a ping-pong match. Cole's gaze bore into Amelia, waiting, but for what she didn't have a clue. For her to melt under his intense blue laser vision? For her to tense to the point she cracked into a thousand pieces?

Ha, he could wait until hell froze over.

She'd had enough.

"We've patients to see," she reminded the crew. "A full schedule this morning." She turned to the corpsman who eyed Cole with a bit of hero-worship. She recalled the look well. "Richard, since you and Dr Stanley are acquainted, why don't you show him the surgery suite? I'm sure it's similar to ones he's worked from in the past, but he'll want to familiarize himself with his new workstation and our equipment before getting started in the morning."

Cole's gaze lingered on her, but Amelia refused to meet his eyes again. Later, no doubt, they'd talk. Not that she wanted to talk to him. But how would they avoid doing so when they'd be forced to work together for the length of their deployment?

How would she deal with him at such close quarters? Although there were five thousand crew members aboard the aircraft carrier when the air wing was on board, she wouldn't be able to keep from interacting with Cole. Not in the medical ward.

What were the odds of being stuck in the middle of the Pacific Ocean with the last man on earth she'd ever wanted to see again?

And yet, even with that thought, she couldn't deny that she'd always known their paths would cross again.

How could it not when they'd left so much unfinished business between them?

Amelia Stockton in the flesh shamed Cole's memory of John Stockton's middle daughter. How had he forgotten how her melted-chocolate eyes sparkled with intelligence? How her high cheekbones accented her heart-shaped face? How her dark hair beckoned his fingers to free the upswept locks? How just being near her turned his insides outward?

No, he hadn't forgotten that. Neither had he forgotten how fiercely loyal the Stockton siblings were, how they'd been trained to be soldier tough from the time they'd worn diapers. Although Amelia's father had been civil when their paths had crossed recently, Cole suspected the majority of the Stocktons despised him.

All but Clara.

Then again, his former fiancée was the only one who knew the truth of what had transpired between them.

Cole stepped into the privacy of the surgical suite just off the sick ward, wondering if he'd really known what he was getting himself into when he'd finagled the assignment on board the USS *Benjamin Franklin*. He'd thought he had, but now, after seeing Amelia again, he had to wonder at his logic. Had he made a horrible miscalculation?

"I thought that went surprisingly well, considering."

He glanced at the corpsman serving as his guide. "Considering?"

Had word already gotten out? The military community, especially the military medical community, was small, but surely his and Clara's wedding fiasco hadn't been such a hot topic that two years later folks were still talking about it?

"Considering you obviously upset Dr Stockton in a former life."

"Obviously," Cole muttered, knowing exactly what he'd done that had upset the lovely Dr Stockton and wishing circumstances had been different, that their relationship hadn't taken the disastrous course it had. Tagging along with him and Clara, frequently working beside him during residency, she'd been like the kid sister he'd never had. Only, his feelings for his fiancée's little sister had developed into something much more intense than those of a big brother.

Something so intense that no matter how he'd tried fighting those feelings, how long he'd denied them, he'd had to face facts. He had been engaged to the wrong Stockton daughter. He'd wanted Amelia. Deep down, all-consuming, wanted her with a passion he'd never felt before or since.

"She's usually even-keeled," Richard continued, looking intrigued. He crossed his arms, leaning against the bulkhead. "I've never seen her lose her cool, or even come close as she almost did when you walked into the sick bay. Honestly, I didn't think anyone could rattle her infamous Stockton stoicism. What happened?"

"Between Dr Stockton and I? Nothing." Cole took in his shipmate's "yeah, right" expression and clarified. Better to get his version of the truth out before the rumor mill started something nasty that would add fire to Amelia's hatred toward him.

"I was engaged to her older sister. It didn't work out."

Didn't work out. Such an understatement, but what had happened between Clara and himself wasn't his secret to tell. He'd promised he'd never reveal that she'd been the one to call off their wedding. Yes, only because she'd beaten him to it, but she had spoken up before he had. She'd also sworn him to secrecy. Cole hadn't told a soul. Not even Amelia when he'd gone to her that night, desperately wanting to explain, to beg her to forgive him.

"You were engaged to Clara Stockton?" Richard whistled, looking impressed. "How come I never knew that?"

Cole shrugged.

"I met her, when I was inland. She was stationed nearby and joined several of us for drinks." He whistled again. "She's a looker."

"Yes," he agreed. Clara was a beautiful woman. On the day they'd met, she'd charmed him with her smile, her intelligence, her inherent toughness that was so in contradiction of her beauty-queen looks. She'd had a passion for medicine that matched his own and had professed to want the same things out of life. For the first time, he'd connected—really connected—with a woman.

For the first time, he'd felt a part of a family.

A wonderful, admirable family that would take on the world to protect each other.

Or to keep from disappointing each other.

Cole had longed for such a family his whole life. To be a part of something so strong.

He and Clara had studied together, worked together, laughed together. On the occasions they'd visited with her family, the Stocktons had welcomed him into their ranks with open arms. During their second year, asking her to marry him had seemed the logical thing to do. Becoming a real, permanent part of the Stockton family had seemed the most desirable thing he could imagine. He'd loved the time spent with them. With Clara. And Amelia.

Especially Amelia, he'd realized too late.

All the Stockton children were close, but Clara and Amelia shared a special bond, more best friends than sisters. Cole had spent as much if not more time with Amelia than he had Clara after Amelia had started medical school. Had gone from treating her as a kid sister to looking at her and seeing a woman who inspired fantasies.

"What happened?" Richard prompted when Cole stayed lost in his thoughts too long.

Cole inwardly sighed, but kept his shoulders square. He'd known coming aboard this ship would open old wounds. Wasn't that one of the reasons he'd come? To open those wounds so they could finally properly heal? "Clara and I realized we'd made a mistake in becoming engaged and broke things off. I've not seen her since."

Because Clara had completely changed her life plans and signed up to serve as a flight surgeon, going to helicopter flight school rather than a military hospital or aircraft carrier medical unit. They e-mailed on the rare occasion, but even that had grown further and further apart.

Richard's brows rose. "That would have been, what? Two? Three years ago?"

"Yes." Two long and torturous years where a single weekend had forever changed the course of his life. Two long and torturous years in which he'd tried to forget the Stocktons. Yet here he was, seeking out the Stockton he couldn't forget. He glanced around the surgical suite, taking in the neutral tones of the room. Dull gray bulkheads and metal cabinets of sturdy construction. "Tell me, where are the laparoscopic instruments? I'll put together a laparoscopic appendectomy set to my preferences. Then I want to go through and make sure the staples match the handles and check out the rest of the equipment so I don't run into any surprises mid-procedure."

Accurately sensing Cole's desire to change the subject, the corpsman explained the day-to-day basics in the surgical ward.

Not much different from what he'd expected, even better equipped than some of the sites he'd worked at prior to being deployed. Yet he couldn't recall his palms sweating and his heart racing at any other new assignment.

He knew the reason why.

The same reason he'd finagled his assignment on board this ship when doing so could cost him everything.

Amelia Stockton.

CHAPTER TWO

LATER that morning, Amelia grimaced at the oozing wound on Corporal Wright's left inner thigh. "How long has the area looked like this?"

He shrugged his brawny shoulders. "Yesterday the spot was a little red. Today it looks like I got shot and the place festered all to hell."

The abscess looked nothing like a real gunshot wound, but she didn't bother explaining that to the eighteen-year-old. She hoped he never had reason to learn otherwise.

She turned to the cabinet that contained the appropriate supplies, pulled out a bottle of one percent Xylocaine, and drew up a syringe full of the numbing agent. "Are you allergic to any medicines?"

"I'm not allergic to anything." He shook his head, eyeing the syringe with pale-faced dread but trying not to show his dislike of needles. "What are you planning to do, Doc?"

"I'm going to open the area, drain the abscess, then pack the wound with special sterile packing gauze that will stay in the opened area for a few days."

The corporal swallowed, his gaze lingering on the syringe. "Will it hurt?"

Amelia could laugh at the irony of his question. The men she dealt with had been through so much with their training, could endure great hardships, yet wave a needle and syringe in front of the biggest, baddest of the lot and he just might turn green in the face.

"Just a stick and some burn when the numbing agent is injected. After the medication, you shouldn't feel a thing," she explained.

She swabbed the area with an antiseptic solution then stuck the needle bevel up into the raised red area, numbing the overlying skin. Once she'd finished injecting the area, she dropped the used syringe into a sharps container then smiled at her still-pale patient.

"While the numbing agent is taking effect, my nurse, Tracy, is going to set up a surgical tray so I can open the area and drain the abscess. I'll be back in a few minutes, and we'll get this taken care of."

Tossing her protective gloves into the appropriate waste receptacle, she left the small exam area and went into the room that served as the medical office.

Her gaze went to the computer on her desk and she winced.

Unless her sister was out in the field, she'd have an e-mail from Clara. She didn't want to tell her sister that her runaway groom was on board, that for the next few months Amelia would be working alongside him, spending more time with him than she'd like.

Than she'd like?

She didn't want to spend any time with Cole.

None. Never again.

If she'd never met the blasted man that would have been just fine.

Better than fine.

Her life would have been better. Less haunted by twinkling blue eyes and a sexily timbered voice that belonged to a man she'd once idolized. How could fate have been so cruel as to assign him to serve on the same ship?

"Need help?"

She spun, coming face-to-face with the source of her agitation. "Not from you."

His brow arched.

"Sir," she added, in deference to his higher rank.

Cole's gaze narrowed. "That's not what I was getting at."

"No? Not tossing around your weight, sir?"

"No." He said the word slowly, studying her.

Hello, she was not a bug under a magnifying glass and could he please just go jump overboard? Anything, just so long as she didn't have to look at him, didn't have to remember.

Her fingers clenched into tight fists. "Then what were you getting at, Dr Stanley?"

He crammed his hands into his pants pockets. "I suppose asking you to call me Cole would be useless?"

"You suppose correctly, sir."

Her eyes had to be tiny slits of disdain because she was holding back none of her anger, none of her frustration. However, she desperately held back all of her hurt, all of the pain she'd felt at his sudden absence from her life two years ago when he'd been such an integral part of her very being for the majority of her university days. God, how she'd hurt, ached to her very core.

"Amelia."

"I did not give you permission to call me Amelia." She did not want to hear her name on his lips. Memories of another time, another place, of him whispering her name echoed through her mind, twisting her insides with feelings she'd denied for so long, feelings she didn't want. Not then. Certainly not now.

"Actually, you did," he reminded her, his gaze not leaving hers, pinning her beneath intense blue. "Just because time has passed, it doesn't mean I've forgotten."

That she understood. Two years certainly hadn't been enough time for her to forget a single thing about Cole. Sometimes she wondered if forever would be long enough or if she was doomed to spend eternity remembering every detail about the man looking so intently at her.

"We were friends once." The color of his eyes darkened to a deep blue. "Good friends."

Gritting her teeth, forcing her breathing to remain even, calm, she busied herself picking up a stack of papers from her desk and thumbing through them, reminding herself that she'd likely be thrown in the brig if she didn't get her emotions under control. How could he say that after…after…?

"Well, I have forgotten," she lied for pure self-preservation. "We were never friends. You're just some joker who had a laugh at my sister's and my expense and walked away from my family without a backward glance."

"Amelia," he began, then sighed, glanced over his shoulders down the narrow corridor leading off the sick ward to the office. When his gaze met hers next, steely determination had settled in. "We need to talk."

She crossed her arms, glared. He wasn't going to intimidate her if that's what he was trying to do. "Was the surgical suite not to your satisfaction?"

"I haven't been satisfied in years, Amelia."

"Call me Dr Stockton." She emphasized each word. "And I fail to see what your lack of satisfaction has to do with me."

"Don't you?" he asked softly, laughing with more than a hint of irony.

"Go away." She didn't look at him. She couldn't. How dared he bring *that* up, that crazy night, weeks after the non-wedding, when he'd come to see her and she'd eventually sent him packing? Besides, if he was trying to tell her he hadn't been with anyone for two years, she'd never believe him. Not in a million years. Which meant he was trying to play her for a fool. Again. She touched the desk, running her fingers over the smooth surface, collecting her wits before glancing up. "I never wanted to see you again."

"You made that obvious."

"Yet here you stand," she needlessly pointed out, riffling through papers as if she was bored with their conversation. Truth was, she needed to get away from him, needed to breathe. She couldn't breathe with Cole standing so close, with him eyeing her with such intensity.

"Unless orders come stating otherwise, I'm here for the full deployment. Dr Lewis has been assigned landside."

Six months. That was the usual duration of a surgeon on board a ship. Anything longer than that and their surgical skills might become rusty. Their usual days consisted of elective procedures such as vasectomies or ingrown toenail extractions, with the occasional gallbladder and appendix removal thrown in for good measure. Usually nothing as intense as working in a hospital setting like Cole must be used to.

"Good for you." She kept her tone level but, as she had for much of the day, inside she screamed. Loud and fierce and full of frustration.

Six months she was stuck working with him. Six whole months. Fine. She could do anything for six months. She was a Stockton.

"Which means we need to work through your anger for me."

She glanced up, met his gaze. "There's nothing to work through."

"You don't hate me?" He didn't look convinced. "Because I'm picking up pretty strong vibes that you'd like to dump me overboard."

He was picking up on that, was he? Good, maybe he'd take the hint.

"You don't rate that much of my thoughts." Liar, liar, pants on fire, but she couldn't admit that she'd thought of him often during the past two years.

Way too often.

"You've forgiven me?" He looked skeptical.

"For breaking my sister's heart and making a mockery of her the night before her wedding?" she asked, laughing cynically. *For making me look at you with stars in my eyes and breaking my heart right along with Clara's? Never.* "One thing you should know about us Stocktons, we're a loyal bunch. We look after our own and don't take kindly to anyone who messes with our family."

"I remember. You have an exceptional family." He smiled as if from fond memories. "Your father is one of the greatest men I've ever met."

"Yes, he is." No one was more dependable or loyal than her father and Amelia loved him with her whole heart. He deserved her love because a finer man had never lived. John Stockton ruled with an iron fist and expected everyone to jump to his tune. Everyone did, all the Stockton children included. "He thinks you're a piece of no-good trash."

Cole flinched, but she felt no pleasure that her barb had hit home. She should be pleased, should want him to feel as much pain and remorse as humanly possible for the cruel way he'd treated her family.

Yet all she felt was the desire to be far away from him, to actually still be in her bunk, fast asleep, to wake up and find Cole's presence on board to be a horrible nightmare rather than her current reality.

Tiring of whatever game he played, she took a deep breath. "What is it you want, Dr Stanley?"

You, Cole thought, reeling at how forcefully the thought hit him.

He had always wanted Amelia.

For two years she'd haunted him, showing up in his thoughts, featuring in his dreams. Knowing that at their last meeting she'd professed to hate him until the day he died, well, Cole had tried to forget her.

After all, even if she didn't hate his guts, it wasn't as if they could have a relationship. He'd been less than twenty-four hours from getting married to her sister and her family thought he was a heel.

Perhaps he was. Because when he'd watched Maid of Honor Amelia walk down the aisle during his wedding rehearsal, he'd wished he was marrying her, not Clara. For months, he'd tried to tell himself he was only have pre-wedding jitters, that he was being a fool, but when their eyes had met, his heart had gone into a mimicry of atrial fibrillation, fluttering like crazy and making him feel light-headed.

When the rehearsal had ended he'd gone outdoors, had had to have a moment to himself, to breathe, to process his thoughts, to figure out how he was going to tell Clara that he couldn't marry her, that he loved her, but not in the way he should, not with passion.

Amelia had followed him.

"Cole? Are you okay?"

He'd wanted to touch her. To pull her to him and let her heat warm him. He'd closed his eyes, fisted his fingers and nodded.

When he'd opened his eyes, she'd moved closer.

"Go back inside, Amelia."

But she hadn't. She'd lifted her hand, run her fingers across his cheek, slowly, tenderly. He'd trembled. Trembled like a schoolboy being touched by a goddess.

"Tell me what just happened," she'd prompted, her palm caressing his face.

Cole swallowed, reminding himself that he had to break things off with Clara, that as much as he wanted this moment, he couldn't grab it. Not until he'd told Clara the truth. That he couldn't marry her.

"We had the wedding rehearsal."

She studied him with those adorable chocolate eyes he loved to see dance with laughter. They weren't laughing now. No, they were staring up at him with great emotion shining in their depths. Emotion for him. "Are you having second thoughts about tomorrow, Cole?"

God, she was fearless, plunged ahead into dark waters without the slightest hesitation, knowing it was her God-given right as a Stockton to conquer the world.

"We shouldn't be having this conversation." *Not yet.*

"Why not?"

Had she moved closer or had he? Either way, mere millimeters separated their mouths. Her warm breath brushed his lips and need, hot and heavy, consumed him.

Need that he was tired of denying, tired of fighting.

"Because of this." He'd foolishly closed the minuscule distance, devoured her mouth with his, held on to her as if she were his only lifeline.

In that moment, she was the heat that warmed the cold numbness in his veins. Time had stopped and all that existed was the two of them.

Unfortunately, the moment ended all too quickly. Ended when Amelia pulled back, stared up at him with wonder and shock in her eyes. "Cole?"

"That shouldn't have happened." Not before he had the chance to break things off with Clara. "I need to talk to your sister."

He'd stepped back, determined to go find Clara, to put a stop to the events unfolding, then paused at the horrified look on Amelia's face.

"But, Cole, I..." She hesitated. "You..." Her fingers closed on his biceps, clamping down as if for support. "You can't, Cole. You kissed me. *Me.*"

"Amelia." He raked his fingers through his hair, searching for the right words to tell her that somewhere along the line he'd fallen for her, but had denied his feelings even to himself for far too long. "This is complicated." Such an understatement. "Wait for me. Let me talk to Clara and wait for me."

Her lower lip disappeared into her mouth. "Are you getting married tomorrow, Cole? Tell me."

"No, I'm not getting married tomorrow." He'd tipped her chin toward him, pressed another kiss to her up-turned lips. "Promise me that you'll wait. I'll explain everything."

Because he'd had to talk to Clara first, to put a stop to their wedding, to be free to tell Amelia that it was her smile that warmed his soul.

Only, when he found Clara, she was crying, something he'd never seen her do. Never seen any Stockton do. He was hit with horrendous guilt, thinking she'd seen him and Amelia, had overheard what he'd said. She hadn't.

Instead, she'd had similar realizations to his own and didn't want to get married any more than he did. It seemed they'd both been hanging on to something that hadn't existed, something neither of them had wanted, but each hadn't wanted to hurt the other because they truly did love one another—just not in the way a man and woman should love the person they were going to marry.

He hadn't been able to refuse her one request, to leave immediately without explaining to anyone why they'd decided to call the wedding off. But that one request had cost him more than Clara could imagine.

"I'm busy," Amelia practically growled, making Cole refocus on the present, on the fact he stood on the USS *Benjamin Franklin* wanting to finish what he and

Amelia had started years ago, wanting the fulfillment of the promises in her eyes when she'd looked at him that night. "So if there's something you want..."

He itched to reach out, to brush his fingers over her sleeked-back hair, to loosen the long silky strands from the tight bun at the base of her head. He wanted to know if she'd thought of him during the time since they'd last seen each other, if she remembered all the hours they'd spent together as friends, if she remembered the passion of their kisses.

"I want to put the past behind us." He couldn't have spoken truer words had he searched the Holy Scriptures.

"Fine, you want to put the past behind us." Her melted-chocolate eyes narrowed with growing irritation. "But why would I want to do that? Why would I even care?"

Because not a day has gone by since I last saw you that you haven't crossed my mind. For two years he'd waited, hoping she'd forgive him, hoping time would heal the rift, but she hadn't forgiven him and he'd gotten tired of waiting.

He'd done what he'd said he wouldn't do, what she'd asked him not to do before she'd kicked him out of her dorm. He'd come for her. This time, he wouldn't let her push him away. Not when there were unresolved feelings between them. One way or another, they would deal with the chemistry between them.

"We're going to be working closely together for the next few months, Amelia."

Her upper lip rose in an almost snarl at his use of her first name. He should call her Dr Stockton, but changing how he thought of her wasn't going to be easy.

"If we don't come to some sort of understanding, it'll affect our jobs," he told her honestly, knowing they did have to come to an understanding until they dealt with the past and appealing to her professionalism. "Neither of us wants that."

"You're the ship's surgeon. I'm the general medical officer. You stay in your surgical suite, and I'll stay in my sick ward." Her gaze burned into him, searing him with her hatred.

Hatred he deserved in her eyes.

"Our paths don't have to meet often," she continued. "When they do, we'll pretend we don't see each other. No big deal."

He raked his fingers through his hair. He didn't want to pretend he didn't see her.

He wanted to see her. Lots of her. *All of her.*

Every delectable inch of her. Right here. Right now.

Wrong. He couldn't do that even if she begged him to. He couldn't kill his career. Sexual relations were strictly forbidden aboard ship and most often punished with a dishonorable discharge.

Hadn't he wanted time for him and Amelia to get to know each other outside the parameters of their former relationship? Hadn't he wanted time to win her trust before they acted on the physical chemistry? Wasn't that why he was here? He needed to focus on the here and now. On work. On building bridges with Amelia, not getting her into bed.

"I'll expect to consult with you on cases, *Dr Stockton*. I'll expect to help when the sick ward is busy, and I'm not in surgery. Don't be naïve in thinking we can easily avoid each other," he warned. "Our paths are going to meet often."

He'd see to it.

Her lips pursed in displeasure. "As I said, we'll just pretend not to see each other."

Frustration surged through him.

"No." Hell, no. Seeing Amelia was why he was here.

Her brow quirked upward. "No?"

"Under the senior medical officer, I'll be next in command in the medical division," he pointed out. "I won't have the GMO pretending not to see me. How would that look?"

"Who cares?"

"I care." Cole's comment stemmed from professionalism as much as personal desire.

"Afraid it might hurt your precious career?"

His career? Yes, suddenly he was afraid that being here, with her, might hurt his career. They needed forced time together, but just being near her again made reason fly out the door.

"I did mention that our not working as a cohesive team could hurt our careers," he reminded her. "Mine and yours. But I'm more afraid not working together will compromise our patients' health and the working environment of our colleagues."

True, but not the whole truth.

Her full lips compressed into a defensive bow. "I would never purposely compromise one of my patients or my crew."

"If you're unwilling to discuss cases with me because of the past, you might make the wrong choice regarding whether or not a person needs a surgical consult."

"Were you not listening? I just said that I wouldn't compromise my patients' health. If a patient needs a surgical consult, I'll send him or her to you." Her gaze narrowed, nonverbally telling him where he could go and that she'd love to shove him down the elevator shaft to take him there. "Got it?"

"Amelia—" At her glare, he sighed. "Dr Stockton," he began again, wishing he knew what to say to mend the bridges he'd had to burn. He hadn't had a choice.

"For whatever it's worth." He kept his voice steady, held her gaze even though looking away would have been easier than seeing the contempt burning in her brown eyes. "I'm sorry about what happened with Clara. I never meant to hurt her."

Amelia's pupils dilated and she failed to hide the pain that flashed across her face.

Pain that he'd caused.

Almost immediately a frigid glare replaced her hurt.

"And what you did to me?" she asked, studying him with eyes he wanted nothing more than to lose himself in. She would likely never forgive him, never let her guard down. "Are you sorry for that, too, Dr Stanley?"

"More than I can say."

Maybe, just maybe, a six-month stint with her would give him the chance to put right a few wrongs from his past.

CHAPTER THREE

"Wow, you're really working up a sweat today," Suzie, one of the two on board dentists and Amelia's bunk mate, commented when she climbed onto the elliptical machine next to Amelia.

"You've no idea," she mumbled, knowing she'd already beaten her best time on the exercise equipment by several minutes, yet still she pushed on. Faster and faster, drops of moisture running down her face, between her breasts, causing her sports bra to stick to her like a damp second skin.

Truth was, even if she weren't on a stationary machine, all her efforts would be for naught.

Some things couldn't be run away from.

Like Cole.

From the time she could walk, Amelia had faced life head-on. With one exception. Cole. Until the night before her sister's wedding. As the maid of honor, she'd walked up the aisle toward him and been filled with longing. Longing she'd had no right to feel. Longing that had almost stopped her in mid-step.

She'd always been a bit in love with her sister's perfect fiancé, had always hoped to meet a man like Cole someday. But during the rehearsal, when their eyes had met, she'd seen something she'd only caught glimmers of previously.

She'd seen matching attraction. Cole had wanted her. And not in a way a soon-to-be married man should want another woman, especially his bride-to-be's little sister. He'd looked at her the way some dark, secret, forbidden part of her had always wanted him to look at her. He'd looked at her as if she were the most desirable woman in the world and he couldn't believe he was lucky enough to stand in her presence, to see her walking down the aisle toward him.

Which was ridiculous.

She wasn't his bride-to-be, wasn't desirable. But even now she could recall the way he'd stared at her, and the way her heart had pounded in response to his burning blue gaze.

"Um, Amelia." Suzie interrupted her thoughts. "You want to talk about whatever's eating you before that machine starts smoking?"

Amelia slowed her pace a few notches, dragged air into her protesting lungs and shrugged. Her bunk mate would prise the truth out of her eventually. By being up-front, perhaps she'd waylay her friend's naturally suspicious nature and avoid questions she didn't have answers to. "My sister's ex-fiancé is the new surgeon. I don't like him."

Two simple sentences that held a world of complexity and heartache.

Suzie programmed her stair machine to her preferred workout routine. "Ouch. That sucks." Her gaze flickered past Amelia to the workout area entrance. "Is he really, really drop-dead gorgeous?"

Amelia glared. "What do you mean, is he drop-dead gorgeous? What does it matter what he looks like? He's a creep who broke my sister's heart."

Who broke my heart.

"Never mind. He is or you'd have said so." Her friend's lips curled into a smile that flashed pearly whites that would make all her dental professors proud, her gaze still focused beyond Amelia toward the entranceway. "Besides, I see for myself, and I agree. He is really, really drop-dead gorgeous. Amazing eyes and that body—oh, my. Somebody should slap a warning label on that man's forehead because just looking at him may send me into cardiac arrest."

Amelia battled to keep from looking toward the door. Cole was there? In the workout room? Why? Well, she knew why. A man didn't have a body like his without being active.

"I might not have guessed it was him except he's new. No way would I not have noticed if Tall, Dark and Yummy had ever been in this room before." Suzie gave a smug smile, gliding back and forth on her elliptical machine with practiced ease. "Plus, he walked in, scanned the room and paused when his gaze settled on my very own Little Miss Sunshine."

Cole was looking at her? Why? Ready for round two? Or was it three? Please don't let him be looking, because even after two years and a million attempts to compartmentalize what had happened between them, she still felt ill prepared on how to deal with Cole. Was he still looking? She was not going to check. She wasn't. She didn't even want to.

Much.

And then only to glare.

"He's still looking, by the way." Suzie's voice held a teasing quality. "Just in case you were wondering."

The heat spreading across her cheeks had nothing to do with her friend's knowing snicker. Overdoing it on the elliptical was why her face burned. Really.

"Don't stare," she ordered in the sternest tone she could manage, trying to keep her pace on the stair machine casual rather than returning to her frantic break-neck speed on a new wave of adrenaline. Why the heck had she pushed herself to the point her limbs were water? To the point her black gym clothes clung to her body? To the point her face was on fire? "He might think we're talking about him."

"Honey," Suzie said, her eyes still eating Cole up, "he's used to women talking about him. Has to be. That is one fine specimen of man. Looking at him makes my tongue want to wag and I'm not ashamed to say so."

"Hello. The man broke my sister's heart into a billion pieces," Amelia reminded her, not mentioning her own billion-pieced heart.

Suzie's gaze reluctantly returned to Amelia. "What happened? Give me the gory details so I can look beyond his lip-smacking exterior to the disgusting bastard filling."

The gory details? That might be a bit of a problem. Amelia didn't know the specifics. Even in the midst of a crying jag, Clara hadn't offered the whole story. Afraid of what her sister might say as to the reasons Cole had called off the wedding, Amelia hadn't pushed for the full details.

"They were engaged to be married. Following their rehearsal, he decided he didn't want to be married after all and left." How could her words sound so calm? So just stating the facts? She was talking about an event that had forever changed her sister's life. He'd made Clara weak. Her, too. "Clara was devastated."

Amelia had been, too. And guilty. Had her questioning him on the way he'd looked at her when she'd walked up the aisle, their amazing kiss that shouldn't have happened, played a role in Cole calling off his wedding? Of course it had. She'd unwittingly sabotaged her sister's happiness. Oh, yeah, she'd lived with guilt.

"I see why." As if she couldn't resist, Suzie's eyes shifted toward where Cole warmed up by stretching his long limbs.

Amelia's traitorous gaze played follow the leader to Cole, not content to only see him in her peripheral vision.

He wore gray cotton gym shorts that loosely hung to mid-thigh, riding up to reveal well-defined quads when he touched the tips of his tennis shoes. A white cotton T-shirt with "NAVY" emblazoned across the front caressed his thick chest. He straightened, reached high over his head, his shirt hem riding up to reveal a sliver of toned abdomen.

Suzie sighed with great appreciation. "If I'd thought I was going to spend the rest of my life curled up in bed next to that and suddenly found out I wasn't, I'd be devastated, too."

"Be serious," Amelia snapped, wanting to physically drag her friend's eyeballs away from Cole, practically having to do the same to keep her own gaze from bouncing around like an overeager puppy wanting another glimpse of tanned flesh. Did he know they were talking about him? "There's more to a man than the way he looks."

"Yeah, but when a man looks like he does, a girl can forgive a lot of flaws." Suzie sighed, moving her arms back and forth in motion with the handlebars, her workout making her sound slightly breathless.

Or maybe it was Cole making her friend breathless.

"I can't forgive his flaws." Amelia refused to be so superficial. She'd once been fooled by his in-your-face male magnetism and charm. Never again would a man weaken her that way.

"Yeah." Her friend nodded in agreement. "But you're made of fortified Stockton steel and only have an Achilles' heel for stray kittens."

"Stray kittens?" Amelia scowled. "I do not."

"Sure, you don't," Suzie teased, knowing Amelia well enough, unfortunately, to push her buttons. "If you lived inland you'd have a yard full of fuzz-balls, and you know it."

Would she? Amelia rarely thought of what her life would be like if she weren't in the military. Not that she'd ever considered doing anything other than military medicine. She hadn't. It's what their family did. Her father had been a surgeon with the navy, her mother an air force nurse.

"I don't even like cats," she protested half under her breath. She'd actually never had a pet to know if she'd like a cat or not. Growing up in a military family where they'd lived either on base or with whatever relative could look after them while their parents served their country, they'd moved too often to accumulate pets. Or close friends. Was that why she'd latched onto Cole? Had treasured their friendship so much?

"Don't look now, but something else you don't like is headed this way." Suzie slid a sly look her way. "Or should I say someone?"

Before she could stop, Amelia glanced toward where Cole had been stretching. Her gaze collided with his vivid blue eyes. His lips curved upward in an amiable, hopeful smile and her breath caught in a way no exercise equipment could ever induce.

In a way that was pure Cole Stanley breathless.

She almost agreed with Suzie. A woman could forgive a multitude of sins when a man looked like Cole. It would be easy to get caught in his charm, in the warmth of his smile, the intensity of his azure eyes, the lure of his friendly demeanor. He wasn't her friend, though.

In that moment, Amelia hated Cole. Hated him for hurting her family, hated him for whatever it was that seeing him did to her insides, hated him for turning her brain to mush by merely slanting his gorgeous mouth upwards.

She ignored the little voice warning that she protested too much, that hate was a strong emotion and she should be careful: the opposite of hate was love.

That was one emotion she could never feel for Cole.

Great. Cole sighed in frustration at Amelia's narrow-eyed rejection of his smiled peace offering. Right back to square one.

For just a millisecond when their gazes had met, before the anger had slid into place, he'd glimpsed the same curiosity that burned in his soul. A curiosity that made him long to open Pandora's box and dive into the unknown depths of whatever mysteries lay between them.

He cursed that her anger had quickly bubbled to the surface and drowned out all other emotions. Amelia hated him for what she believed he'd done to Clara and she wasn't going to forgive him any time soon. If ever.

Damn it. He wanted her forgiveness. Now. Yesterday. *Two years ago.*

Patience had never been one of his virtues, but surely he didn't expect her to welcome him on his first day aboard ship?

No, Amelia Stockton was like a wild mustang. To gain her trust would require endurance, fortitude, strength of mind, diligence.

Why Amelia? Why Clara's sister? He'd asked himself why a thousand times. More. But he never came up with a satisfying answer.

Satisfying. A wry smile twitched at his lips. He hadn't lied when he'd told Amelia he hadn't been satisfied in years.

He hadn't. Amelia had bewitched him and he simply didn't want anyone other than her. No doubt that played into his current level of frustration, but sex for the sake of sex had been a poor substitute. After a few failed attempts to forget Amelia, he hadn't been willing to settle for that.

He still wasn't, which explained the insanity of his request to serve on the USS *Benjamin Franklin*.

Amelia's glossy dark hair was swept back in a ponytail, swishing to and fro with each movement of her tight body. Her legs pumped the elliptical machine back and forth, her arms making a rapid ski motion while she stared straight ahead as if she couldn't see him, as if he no longer existed. Was that what she'd done? Written him out of her life as if they'd never shared kisses that had set his insides aflame?

Cole bit back an appreciative groan. He wasn't the type who ogled women at the gym. Usually. Today, he was thankful his gym shorts were loose. Otherwise he'd find himself in an embarrassing predicament. She was hot—and not just because sweat glistened on her skin, dampened her hair.

He wanted to step into her fire and go up in smoke. Rich, deep, *satisfied* smoke.

"Ame—Dr Stockton," he recalled just in time, climbing onto the elliptical on the opposite side of her, reminding himself to take baby steps, not to push too much too soon or his hopes for the future would be what went up in smoke.

Without glancing toward him, a scowl was her only response.

Cole reminded himself not to jump the gun. Eventually, Amelia would come around, would see that he was the same old Cole who had once been such an integral part of her life. He hoped. He desperately wanted that position back. But this time he didn't want her to see him as her sister's fiancé and he sure didn't want her feeling like his baby sister.

Not that he believed she'd kissed him that way. No, Amelia had wanted him the way a woman wanted a man when the chemistry is crackling.

They'd crackled.

"Hi," a pretty Asian woman on Amelia's right called, leaning forward. "Amelia was just telling me you're the new surgeon." The woman ignored the I'm-going-to-kill-you glare coming her way from Amelia and gave him a welcoming nod without missing a beat on her machine. "I'm Suzie Long, one of the two dentists. Welcome aboard."

Grateful for a friendly face in enemy territory, he flashed a smile. "Nice to meet you, Suzie. Or should I say Dr Long?"

Blowing out an exasperated huff, Amelia muttered something unintelligible under her breath.

"Unless I'm telling you to open wide," the petite woman flirted, giving him a friendly smile, "it's Suzie."

Liking her, Cole laughed. "I'll keep that in mind."

In between them, Amelia stopped exercising, waited for inertia to catch up with her machine. The moment the movement stilled enough for safe dismount, she climbed off. Without a word to him and only a glare at the woman she'd been chatting with until he'd joined them, she walked off. Picking up a gym bag, she took out a sports bottle and took a long drink.

Cole tried not to watch. But he did. When it came to Amelia he couldn't help but watch. His throat grew dry, withering him with thirst. A thirst he desperately wanted to quench, but which only her lips could quell.

Medical school had trained him to do without sleep. The navy had trained him to do without basic life necessities. Neither had prepared him for denying his need for Amelia.

"You're so barking up the wrong tree," the dentist advised, following his gaze to where Amelia tightened the lid and dropped the water bottle back into her bag. "Not meaning to be blunt, but she can't stand you."

"I know." He sighed. "She has reason."

"She told me."

Cole cut his gaze to her. "She told you?"

"About her sister and you? Yep."

That surprised him.

Apparently reading his mind, the woman went on. "I doubt she's told anyone else you were a runaway groom, though. Shame on you for that, by the way!" Her smile softened her reprimand. "Amelia and I are bunk mates."

Runaway groom? He cringed at the description. Yes, he supposed that's how Amelia saw him. He glanced toward the woman two machines down. "You're Amelia's bunk mate? That's good to know."

Her expression was positively wicked. "In case you ever want to visit?"

"In case I ever want to visit," he repeated, his gaze going back to where Amelia lifted a dumbbell from its rack. Her toned flesh flexed as she extended the weight, muscles shifting temptingly with her movements, making Cole think of other ways her muscles would shift with movement.

Snorting, Suzie's gaze followed his. "Yeah, right. She would have you court-martialed if you so much as made a pass at her. Even if she didn't think you were the scum stuck to the bottom of the boat, she wouldn't be interested in an on board romance. Her career means too much to her for that."

Not that on board sexual activities didn't occur, but one could lose everything if caught. Much better to take their time aboard ship to reestablish their friendship and earn her trust, as planned. Not destroy his career as well.

Besides, the only reason his request to serve aboard Amelia's ship had been granted was that they both valued their careers enough not to put them as risk. Of that, he had no doubt. When they were at port call, off ship, well, all was fair in lust and war, but Cole hadn't pointed that out.

Suzie eyed him expectantly, waiting for his comeback, waiting for him to tell her what she wanted to know. What she already knew because she could see his interest in Amelia as plain as the nose on his face.

If he played his cards right, she might just be on his side. An ally behind enemy lines. Something he hadn't counted on. Not beyond the person who'd helped him get on board.

A slow smile spread across his face. "What I want to know is whether or not you think I'm the scum on the bottom of the boat, too?"

Obviously pleased by his response, the woman laughed. "I think you're far worse than the scum on the bottom of the boat, but I'm pretty sure I'm going to like you, anyway."

His gaze went back again to where Amelia curled a free weight, her muscles flexing beneath her sleek skin.

"At least that'll be one person in your room who likes me."

But if the way Amelia kept casting surreptitious glances toward him was anything to go on, she felt the chemistry between them that hadn't let up with time and distance.

He understood she was confused. Understood her dislike of him. Understood she was going to combat the underlying attraction between them.

Cole was ready for the fight of his lifetime and when all was said and done, he'd win Amelia's forgiveness. The stakes were too high not to win.

CHAPTER FOUR

COLE had been on board the USS *Benjamin Franklin* for two weeks and had fallen into a routine. He scheduled procedures early morning, finished in the surgery suite on most days by ten, and then hung out in the sick ward "helping" until all patients had been examined.

Amelia could do without his kind of help.

His kind of help distracted her.

Made her feel as if she were in need of a doctor herself.

Tachycardia, shortness of breath, dizziness, flushing, mental cloudiness, thick tongue, tingling breasts.

Pathetic. Absolutely pathetic that he was having such an effect on her body. Her breasts did not tingle. It was more like an itch. And not the kind she needed scratched. At least, not that kind of scratching. No, it was more the allergic-to-jerks, stay-away-from-me type of itch. A reaction one had when something was harmful to their health. *Yeah, right.*

"I heard Dr Carter—" the other medical doctor on board "—wasn't feeling well and you're by yourself. Need my help?"

Think of the devil and there he was, looking way too handsome in his scrubs. His stethoscope dangled around his neck and he looked the picture of good health. Not like he'd barely slept for the past two weeks because of a disturbing presence from his past. Irritated that she was the one looking like the walking dead, she gritted her teeth.

"No." What she needed was him off her ship so she could get back to her regularly scheduled life program.

"Fine." His smile never faltered.

No matter how many times she cut him off, he just kept smiling, kept being nice, kept coming back for more. He was driving her crazy, making her remember too many of the reasons she'd fallen under his spell to begin with.

"I'll see who's in triage and take care of whoever I can."

During his short time on board, Cole had gained the respect of the medical crew by jumping in to help wherever needed. He triaged patients, took blood pressures, gave shots, whatever.

Not only had he gained the crew's respect, he'd gained their friendship. Everyone liked him. Except Amelia.

"Hey, Dr Stockton, is it okay if Dr Stanley uses bay two? He's going to repack an abscess."

Cole stepped back into the sick bay, holding a triage sheet. Having heard Richard's question, he glanced at her, seemingly waiting for her approval. As if what she said made any difference whatsoever. Along with Richard and the rest of the crew, the senior medical officer thought Cole was the greatest thing since butter on toast.

Amelia had thought the same once upon a time. During medical school she'd idolized him, had viewed

Cole as the perfect man. Funny, generous, intelligent, handsome, charming, compassionate. Had she not loved Clara so much she might have resented her sister's perfect life. Beautiful inside and out, Clara had held Cole's heart from nearly the moment they'd met. Only, in the end, Cole had kissed Amelia and walked away from both women.

"If that's okay?" he added to the corporal's request.

"Fine." She turned away, knowing she was unnecessarily brusque yet unable to bring herself to show any grace. If she gave Cole an inch, he'd take a foot. She had to keep her distance for her own peace of mind, from loyalty to her sister.

Clara, whom she hadn't been able to tell that Cole was on her ship despite their e-mails. Clara, who had volunteered for yet another crazy assignment. Clara, whose notes sounded so unlike the woman she'd once been while engaged to Cole.

Oh! She despised what he'd done to her big sister and she clung to that like a drowning woman clutching a life preserver.

"There's a positive strep throat in bay one," Tracy said, snagging Amelia's thoughts back to where she was washing her hands.

She'd scrubbed so hard she was surprised to still see skin.

Drying her hands, she nodded at the nurse. "Thanks."

Tracy's face twisted in thought then she pulled Amelia aside. Under her breath, she quickly spoke. "I wouldn't say this if I wasn't your friend, but the whole crew has picked up on your…not *hostility* but a definite lack of friendliness toward Dr Stanley."

"And?" Amelia fought to keep her face emotionless. As she'd told Cole on that first day, she wouldn't let her animosity toward him interfere with the care of her patients. In her mind, she'd stuck to that. She may not like him, but she was doing her best to be professional. She'd even set up several patients to see him during his stint thus far. Obviously, however, she hadn't done such a great job of hiding her feelings from the crew, which truly did affect both their jobs.

Tracy looked uncertain about going on. "You're one of the fairest people I know, Amelia. Always level-headed and logical. Kind, too. Yet, with Cole, you're... prickly."

"Prickly?" She wanted to laugh. "Prickly" was as good a word as any to define how she felt about being forced to work with Cole. Just call her Cactus Woman. "It's true I do my best to avoid the man, but I am professional when our paths cross." Usually. "He's the one who keeps invading my workspace." And her workout space, her dining hall space, her dreams.

"Invading your space?" Tracy frowned, and chided gently, "You're lucky he's such a caring doctor. Not all would spend their free time seeing more patients so he can lighten someone else's workload. Maybe you should give the guy a break."

Okay, Tracy had a point. Cole did go above and beyond his workload and try to make the sick ward run more smoothly. He was an excellent, caring doctor. And, no, she really hadn't rolled out the welcome mat, but surely no one thought she should? As gossip always did, word had gotten out.

"All I ask is that he stay out of my personal space, take care of his patients, allow me to take care of my patients, and beyond that, it's really irrelevant if I like him. Every crew member doesn't have to like every other crew member. Actually, to expect that is idyllic and naïve," Amelia pointed out, knowing she was being too defensive. "He isn't someone I can like because of the past, but I can tolerate him for the time we serve on board together."

"So he used to be engaged to your sister? So what?" Tracy shrugged in frustration. "If he didn't love her, he did her a favor by ending things before the wedding."

Anger bubbled deep in Amelia's belly. "A favor? You think he did my sister a favor by breaking their engagement?" she fumed, clenching and unclenching her hands at her sides.

She wanted to scream that he'd waited until the night before their wedding to bestow his *favor*. That her family had arranged to all be home, that their friends had all been there, that Clara had been left to tell everyone the wedding was off because, after getting cold feet, he'd left. Left! Deserting Clara to face the music alone. Deserting *her*, letting her wait hopelessly for him, telling her by his actions all she'd needed to know, leaving her with mountains of guilt.

As much as she'd like to point out what a cad Cole really was, Amelia couldn't bear to make Clara's humiliation public. Nor her own, particularly not in the medical ward where she might be overheard by other crew members and perhaps even Cole.

"See, this is what I mean. Look at you. Your face is red, your voice is low, and your words are erupting from between gritted teeth." Tracy gave her a concerned look. "Before Dr Stanley arrived, we all thought you were one cool cookie and great to work with. Now…"

Now they all thought she'd turned into a witch.

One with pointed shoes and a wart on her nose.

Maybe she had. Cole obviously brought out the worst in her.

She'd had enough.

"Well, if you'll hand me my broom, I'll fly on over and see the strep throat in bay one."

"Amelia." Tracy clutched her shirtsleeve. "Please think about what I said. Whatever happened between Dr Stanley and your sister is in the past. Maybe he did make mistakes but whatever happened, he's a great guy now and genuinely seems to want your forgiveness. Let the past go."

Let the past go.

As if it was that simple.

As if it weren't her right as next of kin to nail the jerk who'd hurt and humiliated her family, and crushed her heart.

As if it wasn't in her best interest now to protect that heart at all costs by keeping distance between herself and Cole.

The object of her animosity stepped out of bay two, peeled off a pair of disposable gloves and dropped them into a waste receptacle.

He glanced up, met her gaze with his cerulean one and gave her a smile. The same smile he flashed every chance he got, regardless of who saw. One that said, *Forgive me*. One that said, *I'm sorry*. One that said, *Remember me. The me you adored. The me you kissed as if we were long-lost lovers*. One that said he hadn't forgotten two years ago, and he wanted her still.

Maybe that was why she couldn't forgive him.

Maybe that was why she clung to her anger so fiercely.

Because if she quit hating Cole for what he'd done to Clara, to her, if she forgave him, she'd have to confront what she saw in his eyes.

Cole wanted her.

A fact that left her uncomfortable in her own skin.

Worse, if she stopped clinging to her anger at Cole, she'd have to face her own feelings—what she'd been feeling when their gazes had met and how her world had stood still during a wedding rehearsal meant to forever link him to another woman.

But if those were her reasons for disliking Cole, what did that say about her? That she was a coward? Not worthy of the crew's respect?

Amelia was no coward.

After all, she was a Stockton.

She turned back to her nurse. "You know, Tracy, I owe you and everyone an apology. I have been walking around with a chip on my shoulder where Dr Stanley is concerned. If that has affected my job performance or my interaction with the crew, I'm sorry."

Looking relieved, Tracy smiled. "It's okay, Amelia. We were just a bit worried as it's so unlike you." Tracy gave her a kind look. "Does your sister have any idea of how loyal you are? How lucky she is to have you for a sister?"

Loyal? Amelia didn't feel loyal. She felt like a traitor. She had betrayed her sister in the worst possible way.

That was why Cole had contacted her after the break-up. Why he'd come to see her that night a few weeks later. After he'd stood her up! Wait for me, he'd said, and then he'd left. Without a word. Had he really thought she'd talk to him? Had he really thought she'd just let him move from one Stockton sister to the next without batting an eyelash of protest at him showing up on her doorstep, saying he couldn't get her out of his mind and wanted a relationship with her?

He wanted a relationship with her now.

He hadn't spoken the words out loud, but when he looked at her, the message blazed in his eyes.

But whatever chance they'd had disappeared the moment he'd left her waiting, the moment he'd walked away and left Clara to deal with everything on her own. Maybe, under the circumstances, they'd never even had a real chance.

Still, regardless of what Cole wanted or even what she wanted, she had a job to do, a responsibility to her crew, and Amelia took her responsibilities seriously.

"You're right. It is time I let the past go." She intentionally said the words loud enough for the others to hear.

Cole's eyes widened, then narrowed.

She arched a brow in challenge at him, a slow smile curving her lips. Somehow his distrust made swallowing her pride, facing her fears where he was concerned, a little easier. She'd do what was right for her crew, what they needed to see from her for the overall good.

As her father would say, sometimes a man—or woman—had to prove their worth by taking one for the team.

For the next few months, Amelia would take one for the team and pray she didn't live to regret her decision.

* * *

A bad feeling crawled up Cole's neck. One of those that warned something wasn't right.

Amelia walked toward him. Of her own free will. No gun to head necessary.

"How did Corporal Wright's abscess look? Healing well?"

Had she really just spoken to him of her own accord? Smiled at him with her mega-wattage smile?

Something was definitely off-kilter.

Besides his equilibrium.

But who was he to look a gift horse in the mouth? Amelia was talking to him, smiling at him. The feeling was too good for him to do anything other than bask in her attention for however long the aberration lasted.

"The wound is draining more than the area should be with as much time as has passed." Had his voice croaked? "I want another culture to see if he's developed a secondary infection."

Her smile didn't miss a beat, perhaps even kicked up another few watts. "Any new symptoms?"

A stun gun blasted him, scrambling his thoughts. He forced himself to focus on his patient, on science, on anything but how Amelia's smile rerouted his circuitry.

"Increased redness and drainage. Nothing else."

"Good." She stared expectantly at him.

Cole had a flashback to a stolen moment between patients in the busy E.R. where they'd both been pulling residency hours. She'd looked tired, he'd cornered her, teased her, and she'd looked up at him with expectancy. And longing.

How had he missed that look at the time? How had he not realized what had been happening between them?

Because he'd definitely felt longing in return. Only he'd stuck a big fat brotherly label on everything to do with Amelia so he hadn't had to feel guilty at how his feelings for her had been growing.

"I haven't re-dressed the wound yet." Why did his tongue feel like a lead weight? "Do you want to look prior to seeing your next patient?"

"Thanks. I'd love to." With another smile, she nodded, as if she'd been waiting for the invitation. Just as she'd done when he'd been with a patient and she'd wanted to observe, only this time his head spun.

Maybe while she was in such an agreeable mood he should suggest a private talk in the office. One where he pushed her up against the wall and kissed her until they both had to come up for air.

Not that he could or would on board ship. Neither was he such a fool that he didn't realize she was up to something. She was. The question was what? And why? Because despite her butter-wouldn't-melt-in-her-mouth smile he had no illusions that he had a long way to go to win Amelia's forgiveness.

"Hey, Dr Stockton," the corpsman greeted her when Amelia stepped into the bay. The young man's eyes ate her up.

Quelling his dislike of another man checking her out, Cole admitted he didn't blame the guy. With her swept-back dark hair exposing the graceful lines of her neck, the luminous quality to her big brown eyes, the fullness of her naturally pink lips, Cole's eyes did some gobbling of their own when Amelia leaned in to examine Corporal Wright's thigh.

"Hmm," she mused, reaching for a pair of disposable gloves. "When I checked you last, the abscess looked better. When did the area start getting worse again?"

"Just last night, Doc. That's why I came back this morning rather than waiting until my follow-up appointment tomorrow." He flashed a flirty smile. "I remembered what you said about coming back sooner if there were any negative changes."

"Good job." Amelia smiled at the man, a real smile, inadvertently jump-starting Cole's heart as surely as if she'd hooked him up to a defibrillator and cranked the juice.

She used to smile at me like that. Only better.

Knowing he needed to do something before he succumbed to the errant electrical charges running rampant through his nervous system, Cole gloved up to swab the abscess again.

"Did you see the culture I'd previously done?" she asked, smiling sweetly. Sweetly? Cole didn't know whether to laugh or be afraid. Amelia was a lot of things, but *sweet* wasn't an adjective he'd use to describe her. Unless they were talking about her lips. She had tasted sweet.

"Yes," he answered, studying her, "but your notes say the area was healing well. That's obviously no longer true. I want a new culture."

She flashed her perfectly straight teeth. "Good idea."

Cole managed not to blink. Barely. Had she agreed with him without an argument? Something was definitely up. And not just his temperature and heart rate. He dabbed the swab in the center of the abscess, carefully inserted the tip into the auger filled tube and sealed the lid.

"You think something new is wrong?" the man lying back on the elevated exam table asked, watching as Amelia ungloved and opened a sterile drape, dropped gauze onto the field, poured a small cup of antiseptic solution and opened a package of sterilized scissors, needle holders and toothed tweezers.

"Possibly. That's what the culture will tell us." She opened a bottle of packing gauze and glanced toward Cole. "Do you want to irrigate the area or do you want me to do it?"

Cole hesitated only a millisecond. Despite her sugary sweetness of the past five minutes, Amelia was a take-charge, don't-put-me-in-the-backseat kind of woman. Even during her residency, she hadn't liked watching from the sidelines. If he wanted to win her trust he'd have to prove he could deal with her strength and independence, right along with her feigned sugary sweetness.

"You do it," he told her. "I'll assist."

The smile she gave him was so brilliant the sun could have come out in bay two. Definitely his body heated as if the sun had. He was on fire from the inside out.

She donned more gloves, cleaned and irrigated the wound, then packed a thin ribbon of sterile gauze into the opening, leaving the tip out for easier removal.

Watching her work, Cole handed her what she needed before she had to ask. When she was finished and had covered the area with a dressing, she glanced up at him, her eyes sparkling with something that bit deep into him.

"You make an excellent assistant, Cole."

Cole. She called him by his first name rather than Dr Stanley. Hearing his name on her lips made his knees wobble.

Whatever Amelia was up to, he was in trouble. Big trouble.

Because hearing his name on her lips brought back memories of the night he'd gone to her a few weeks after his breakup with Clara. Amelia had whispered his name right before he'd kissed her. As he'd kissed her.

As he'd pushed her back onto her dorm room bed, planning to make love to her.

Rubbing her fingers across Corporal Wright's bandage, Amelia wondered if she was laying her friendliness on too thick? She hadn't meant to be overly nice, but she'd be lying if she didn't admit to enjoying the perplexity in Cole's eyes.

Good. Let him wonder.

Not that he wouldn't figure it out. He'd once known her too well not to know what lengths she'd go to for her crew, for her patients. Still, she welcomed the respite. Carrying around her anger for him was starting to give her an ulcer. At least now she felt as if she was on the offensive.

She much preferred offensive strategies. Always had.

In the grand scheme of personal protection, being nice to Cole for the sake of the crew and their patients wasn't the greatest idea. But a girl had to do what a girl had to do for the greater good.

Besides, it wasn't as if she was going to fall right back into her crush for him. She'd seen what he was capable of. Had seen him bail out on Clara, had seen him walk away from her after a kiss that had singed her toes to the soles of her maid-of-honor high heels. Then walk away from her room after she'd kicked him out, despite her body screaming for him to stay.

Although he'd always seemed to long to be a part of her family, Cole had major commitment issues.

"It'll be a few days before I get the results of the culture back, but I'd like to see you again tomorrow," she told their patient. "Keep your appointment that's already scheduled, and I'll change the dressing."

"Yes, ma'am."

"I think we should change his antibiotic," Cole cut in. He told her the name of an antibiotic with better anaerobic coverage than the antibiotic Corporal Wright currently took.

"Okay, that sounds like a feasible plan." She shot the corpsman another smile. "Take the antibiotics exactly as prescribed and be sure to finish the entire prescription to prevent developing resistance."

"Yes, ma'am."

Cole gave his hand to the corpsman, helped him from the table. Amelia watched the man grimace at the pain that shot up his leg at weight-bearing. She hated it that he'd have to rest in the uncomfortable bunks where he'd have no privacy. As an officer, Amelia had the privilege of sharing a small room with only Suzie, but most of the crew shared large open berths where crew were stacked in so tightly they could barely roll over without bumping the cot above them.

"If you get worse today, make sure you let us know."

"Will do."

The corpsman left the bay and Amelia stared at Cole. He watched her with an inquisitive light in his eyes. One that saw a bit too clearly below the surface.

"What do you think is going on?" she asked, making great effort to keep her voice cordial, pleasant even.

"With Corporal Wright's leg or you?"

Good question. "With Corporal Wright's leg, of course."

"Most likely he has a secondary infection that's spreading into the tissue. If he doesn't respond to the new antibiotic, I'll consider excising the area."

"I doubt that'll be necessary."

"I hope not, but surgical excision would be preferable to him ending up with septicemia or gangrene."

"True." She sucked in a deep breath. "Do you want to stop by and see him with me tomorrow? That way you can decide if surgery should be arranged? You could schedule him if you feel that's the best treatment option."

Eyes narrowing, Cole nodded. "That would be great."

"I'll have Tracy see what time he's supposed to come in."

Amelia turned to step out of the bay, but Cole grabbed her arm. A thousand lightning bolts struck her at once, charring every brain cell to wispy bits of ash.

"About the other?"

"What other?" she gulped, although she knew exactly to what he referred.

"What's going on, Amelia? Did you suddenly decide I deserve forgiveness?"

Forgiveness? She wasn't touching that one.

"You wanted us to work in peace, right?" she challenged, biting her tongue to keep from correcting him on the use of her name. "I can manage being civil for five and a half months."

"Why the change of heart?" He studied her closely.

So closely Amelia wanted to squirm. She didn't. She held her chin up high and met his gaze head-on in a blatant dare. "Why do you think?"

"Amelia—"

"Hey, Dr Stockton, about that strep patient in bay one?" Tracy poked her head around the curtain, paused when she spotted Cole's hand wrapped around Amelia's upper arm and their low conversation. "Oh, sorry, I didn't mean to interrupt."

"No interruption," Amelia assured her, smiling appreciatively at her nurse. "I'm on my way to check the strep patient. Tell Richard to bring back the next patient, and, Tracy, could you let Dr Stanley know what time Corporal Wright will be by tomorrow for his follow-up? If he's not in surgery, he'll have a quick look at the patient."

CHAPTER FIVE

NEAR the end of Amelia's shift, a corpsman was brought in who'd slammed his fingers in a hatch during a training exercise.

Amazingly his X-ray didn't show any displaced breaks, only a hairline fracture of the proximal phalange of the index finger, which wouldn't require an off ship consult with an orthopedic.

After washing her hands and donning gloves, Amelia removed the bloody towel pressed over the man's hand. She didn't wince at the bleeding, macerated tissue. She'd been trained to see far worse than the man's sliced-open, deformed fingers.

"I hope the other guy looks worse," she teased, hoping to ease the strain from his face. An aircraft carrier with its ladders, hatches and catapults was a host of injuries waiting to happen. Unfortunately.

"Not even a scratch," the man responded, his eyes not leaving his injuries.

Where the heavy metal hatch had come across the top of his fingers, the skin was split in a deep gash. Amelia dabbed away blood with sterile gauze, seeing bone through the mangled flesh of his index and middle fingers. The cuts on his ring finger and pinky didn't appear to have reached the bone.

She turned to Tracy. "Set up two suture trays. I'm going to ask Dr Stanley to help with the two deeper wounds as they're more extensive."

Although her eyes widened, Tracy just nodded and went about setting up the trays.

Amelia explained what she was going to do to her patient then left the bay to find Cole. Technically, he should have left the medical ward hours ago. Instead, as he'd done each day since arriving, he'd hung around.

Now he stood across the sick ward, talking to Richard, Peyton, who was the ship's nurse anesthetist, and the physician assistant. As if sensing Amelia, he glanced up, met her gaze, and grinned. Why did her heart light up at his smile? She was just tolerating him to keep things running smoothly in her medical ward. She didn't like him, didn't enjoy being in his company, didn't even want him there.

But she'd been crazy about him once upon a time.

Crazy about him in the worst kind of way because she had liked him, had enjoyed being in his company, had wanted to spend as much time as possible with him because he'd made her smile, laugh, look at life in Technicolor.

She'd denied just how much the way he affected her had meant, had denied she'd cared more for him than she should have. On the night of the wedding rehearsal, she'd quit denying. And look how that had ended up—two Stockton hearts broken in one night. What a fool she'd been.

Even now, looking at him, unable to suppress the quivers low in her belly, she wondered if she was just as much a fool.

"I need your help," she said, shoving aside her self-preservation instincts.

Immediately, he stepped away from the men he'd been talking to. "I'm yours. All you have to do is ask."

She so wasn't touching his comment, but her imagination toyed with the double entendre. Had he intentionally sent her thoughts into a whirlwind?

"I have a hand injury that's going to require multiple sutures. Capillary refill is good in all fingers. Sensation is decreased. There's a hairline fracture in the index finger, but no other breaks. I was hoping you'd have a look. The index and middle fingers will require more extensive suturing."

"Sure." Cole followed her into the bay. While he washed his hands, he introduced himself to the injured corpsman. He examined the patient then turned to Amelia. "You're right about the first two fingers. I'll suture them."

She could do them, Amelia wanted to argue. But this wasn't about what she could and could not do. This was about proving to her crew that she wouldn't compromise them or their patients, that she could set aside her personal feelings because she was a professional, a Stockton.

"I was hoping you'd offer." And not because he really could do a better job on the man's fingers. She might be trying to make a point, but she didn't plan to beg Cole just to prove to her crew that she was a team player.

"Like I said…" his gaze sought hers "…I'm all yours."

Still not acknowledging his comment, she smiled at the pale man. "Dr Stanley is the ship's surgeon. He'll do an excellent job on those fingers while I sew the other two up so we get you put back together a little quicker."

With Tracy and Richard assisting and the man's fingers spread wide, Amelia and Cole worked from opposite sides of the exam table, slowly closing the man's wounds. Their workspace was tight due to the close proximity of the injuries, but just as they'd done earlier, done years ago, they worked well together, rarely encroaching on each other's space.

From time to time, Amelia would sense Cole glancing up, toward her, but for the most part their concentration centered directly on their patient and his well-being.

Amelia had asked Tracy to give the man something for pain prior to starting the closure. Between the narcotic and the local anesthetic at the injury site, the man seemed comfortable. Actually, Amelia was fairly positive near the end of the procedure that he'd fallen asleep.

She finished the less extensive lacerations on his pinky and ring fingers prior to Cole finishing the deeper wounds.

She turned to the nurse and Richard. "I'll assist Dr Stanley. If there are no more patients, you both can go ahead and sign out for the day. Thanks for all your assistance."

Sharing a stunned glance, Tracy and the corpsman left the bay to finish their day's duties.

"I'm glad you asked me to help," Cole told her when they were alone. "It was just like old times."

Old times when she'd been an eager resident and he'd allowed her to sit in on procedures to give her the experience.

"You'd have been here another hour at least if you hadn't."

"Saving time wasn't why I asked you to help."

"So why did you?" Pulling the ethilon thread through, Cole's gaze lifted to hers, his blue eyes twinkling with a teasing quality that made her almost giddy. "Because you knew I was a better seamstress?"

"No." Prior to seeing his handiwork on the man's lacerations she might have argued that these days she could out-suture him. She was good, but Cole was doing a great job of repairing the man's wounds. As much as she hated to admit it, she couldn't have done better. "That isn't why I asked, either."

Wondering why her insides shook when what he thought of her didn't matter. Neither should that twinkle in his eyes make her want to smile in return. She shouldn't want to smile at him, shouldn't feel lighter because he was teasing her.

But she did.

"Tracy told me I was treating you unfairly and should let go of the past."

"I see." Keeping his gaze trained on his handiwork, he looped the needle back through the sleeping corpsman's flesh. "How did you respond?"

He'd already seen her response. He knew she was going to set aside her aversion of him for the better of the crew. But he'd asked because he wanted her to tell him one on one that she was ready to let the past go, for them to develop an amicable working relationship.

Amelia wanted to dislike him all the more for it, but found she couldn't. Not when he seemed so genuinely pleased, as if she'd done him some great favor.

"She's right."

His hands stilled for a brief moment, shook ever so slightly.

Amelia hated the tremor that shook her own body in response. Why was she so in tune with Cole? Why did being here with him feel so right? And so very wrong?

"You were right," she admitted.

"About?"

Everything you said to me on the night you came to my dorm.

No, he hadn't been right about that.

There could be nothing between them. Not physically. Not emotionally. Not anything. Nothing except the need to work amicably together for the next few months.

So why had she just thought about that night again?

She took a deep breath. "The first day you were on board you told me we'd have to come to some type of peace or our past would affect our jobs."

He looped the needle through the patient's gaping flesh, pulled it the rest of the way through with the needle holders.

"Obviously, I wasn't as good at hiding my feelings toward you as I'd hoped. The crew thinks I don't like you for some reason." She said the last with a slight lilt to her voice, as if she couldn't fathom what had given them that idea. "I do think you're a great surgeon, for whatever that's worth." She nodded toward where he was closing the last wound. "And a fabulous seamstress.

I'm impressed with how neatly you were able to pull his lacerations on his index finger back together. I couldn't have done a better job."

He didn't look at her, just kept his gaze on his work. "My ability to outsew you makes me forgiven?"

"No," she denied, knowing he wouldn't buy it even if she lied. "I never said you were forgiven. I'm not sure I can forgive you. But for the duration of us working together, I'm willing to negotiate a peace treaty, so to speak."

He seemed to consider her offer. "For the benefit of our coworkers?"

"Hey." She tried to make light of it. "From time to time even sworn enemies have agreed to coexist for the greater good."

He pulled the thread back through and examined the now closed wound. Satisfied with his work, he wrapped the thread around the end of the needle holder several times, pulled the thread tight and tied off a knot. He then repeated the process several times, changing direction of the rotation of thread each time to strengthen the knot.

When he'd finished, Amelia handed him a pair of suture scissors. He cut the line, leaving only a few millimeters of thread above the knot, just enough to make removal easier.

"You're an interesting woman, Amelia Stockton. Generous to a fault." Generous to a fault? What was he saying? "But, for the record, you've never been my enemy. Neither have I been yours."

Amelia's breath caught.

Rather than look at her, Cole gently shook the dozing man's arm. "Paul? Wake up. We're finished closing the lacerations."

Slowly the man's eyes blinked open, adjusting bit by bit to his environment.

"It's okay that you aren't feeling much, if anything, in your fingers. Your hand is still numb from the anesthetic. I need you to make a fist then flatten your hand for me so I can check your range of motion."

The man did as asked.

"Excellent," Cole praised, taking hold of the needle holder and blocking Paul's vision of his hand. "I'm going to touch each of your fingers and without looking I need you to tell me when I'm touching you, if you can. Just like we did before we started to sew. Again, you still have anesthesia on board, so don't be alarmed if you don't feel anything yet." Cole grinned. "Actually, be grateful if the numbness lasts a while."

Sensation in the tip of Paul's pinky was normal, but there was still nothing in the other three lacerated fingers.

"It's not uncommon after an injury like this to have decreased sensation," Cole explained. "I didn't see any evidence of a lacerated nerve, but with the weight of the hatch crushing your fingers, it's possible."

Wincing, the man moved his fingers back and forth, studying the suture lines. "What if it isn't the anesthesia causing the numbness? Will I get the feeling back?"

"In most cases sensation will return on its own within a few days to weeks. However, we will need to keep a close watch on you," Cole told the pale, slightly dazed man. "I'm going to give you an antibiotic prophylaxis and something for pain, but you'll need to return to the sick ward tomorrow morning for a checkup."

Cole helped walk the man out of the bay.

Through the screen, Amelia heard him speak to a corpsman regarding getting the man safely to his berth. Cole was a thoughtful surgeon, caring of his patients. He always had been.

Trying to keep her thoughts off his comment about not being her enemy, she emptied the surgical trays, properly disposing of the sharps and contaminated materials used, saving everything that could be sterilized for future use. She was wiping down the metal tray when Cole stepped back behind the curtain.

"There aren't any more patients to be seen today," he informed her, leaning against the counter. His hair was tousled, his eyes intensely blue, his smile contagious.

God, he really was Dr Delicious.

No, no, Dr Disastrous. She had to remember that.

"Okay." Uncertain about her truce, she studied where her hands wiped the tray. Was she crazy to think she could be amicable to Cole after the way he'd hurt her sister? Or were her fears anything to do with her sister? Were her fears more wrapped up in the fact that her heart pounded against her rib cage like an out-of-control monster wanting out of its cage?

She glanced up, met his gaze, held her breath. Why did he affect her so crazily?

"Are you going to the gym?" He pushed off the counter, straightening to his full height of over six feet, making her feel small and feminine. "I'll see you there."

He hadn't had to wait for her answer. He knew she was. She always worked out after finishing in clinic. So did he, at exactly the same time. Actually, Cole seemed to be on the same wavelength with her on a lot of things. If she went for a walk on the "steel beach," so did he. If she went to the exercise room, so did he. When she arrived at the dining hall, so did he. The only time she'd had peace was while inside her room and calling being alone with her thoughts peaceful was stretching the truth to say the least.

There wasn't anything peaceful about closing her eyes and dreaming of the man gazing so intently at her.

Amelia was having a difficult time breathing, but not because of her workout routine. More like because of the man on the elliptical in front of her.

The very hot man wearing workout shorts and a form-fitting navy blue T-shirt that made his arms look ripped and hinted at abs worthy of a men's fitness magazine.

Not that she was looking at his abs.

No, she was facing his backside. His tight glutes, his sinewy thighs, his rock-hard calves, his—

"You're staring again," Suzie warned in a low voice so as not to be overheard in the semicrowded workout room.

Amelia shot a dirty look at her friend. "I'm looking straight ahead. Not staring."

"Sure, you're not staring. Neither am I." Her roommate snickered, waggling her eyebrows in Cole's direction.

The machine next to Amelia had been occupied by a captain when Cole had arrived. He'd taken a machine in front of Amelia and slightly to her right. Seriously, just looking straight ahead, she couldn't possibly not look at him unless she closed her eyes. And, really, who ever heard of exercising with your eyes closed?

"You have to admit," Suzie continued, obviously enjoying herself. "The view is mouthwatering."

Wiping her forearm across her sweaty face, Amelia rolled her eyes. "You have such a one-track mind."

Waggling her eyebrows again, Suzie laughed. "Absolutely. Tell me that isn't one fine specimen of man in front of us."

Amelia couldn't. Cole was one fine specimen of man.

If she'd met him for the first time on board the USS *Benjamin Franklin*, she'd have liked Cole. A lot. He was witty, helpful, generous, intelligent, charming, *sexy*.

If she'd just met Cole she'd be half in love with him.

Only she hadn't just met him. She'd met him years ago as her sister's fiancé. Clara had been deceived by Cole's false wonderfulness, too. What would her sister say if she knew Amelia was being suckered in by her ex-fiancé? That she'd been suckered in years ago and wondered if she'd truly ever gotten over her infatuation with him?

"You know, if I didn't know better, I'd think you were softening where he's concerned."

Amelia shot another glare at her bunkmate. "You'd be wrong if you thought that."

Okay, so she'd just been thinking she was being suckered in, but no way would she admit that out loud.

"Would I?" Suzie asked, her thin black brow arched high.

"Just because I have to work with him, it doesn't mean I like him." Or that she couldn't appreciate his positives.

Suzie and Amelia both turned back to stare ahead. At Cole.

His calves were taut as his legs worked up and down. Sweat dampened his T-shirt, causing the cotton material to cling to his back, his well-defined back that tapered from wide shoulders to a narrow waist to tight buttocks and strong thighs. Oh, *heaven*.

Amelia's tongue stuck to the roof of her mouth.

Okay, Cole was hotter than the Sahara Desert.

Way hotter.

She even found the sweat glistening on his skin and dampening his T-shirt oddly appealing. What was wrong with her? She did not find sweaty, overheated men appealing.

Amelia's machine beeped, indicating she'd hit peak speed.

"I heard you and he talked today," Suzie pressed, glancing toward the control panel on Amelia's elliptical and whistling.

"You heard that?" She tried to drag her gaze away from Cole. And failed. Which was okay, since she was only looking straight ahead, right? To not look at him she'd have to twist her head and that would be poor body mechanics.

Never let it be said a Stockton had poor body mechanics.

"Oh, yeah." Suzie laughed. "I heard that and more."

"More?" Amelia gulped, knowing she was the butt of ship gossip. *Great.* "What more?"

"You think everyone in Medical hasn't seen the way he looks at you? That they haven't noticed the way you watch him when you think they aren't paying attention?" Tsking, Suzie shook her head. "You should know better than to think you could get away with something like that."

"How does he look at me?"

Suzie's lips curled upwards. "Of everything I said, that's what caught your attention? That he looks at you?"

She shouldn't care, shouldn't be holding her breath, waiting. Should be more concerned that others had noticed. Yet…

"How does he look at me?" she stage-whispered, her gaze finally managing to shift from Cole to her bunkmate.

Suzie's black eyes bored into Amelia, her voice purred with envy. "Like he wants to dip you in chocolate and nibble his way to the center."

Amelia let that digest, fought to control the tiny spurts of anxiety. They were spurts of anxiety, not hope.

"Amelia?" Suzie questioned when she didn't respond.

"He doesn't want to do that to me," she denied, because she couldn't verbalize that Cole wanted her, that deep down she wanted him to want her. How could she want Cole to dip her in chocolate and nibble his way to her center? That would be wrong on so many counts. "That's crazy. Cole can't want me."

Because if he did, how would she deal with her own treacherous unresolved feelings?

"I wouldn't say that."

Both women jumped at Cole's voice.

When had he stepped off the machine? Walked over to them?

What did he mean, he wouldn't say that?

"You were listening to our private conversation?" Amelia snapped, her face flushing. Was he admitting to wanting her? If so, what did that mean? What did she want it to mean?

"If you didn't want me to listen, you shouldn't have been talking where I could hear." His gaze didn't leave hers. "Why can't I want you, Amelia? I told you I wanted you. Two years ago. Have you forgotten?"

This couldn't be happening. Shouldn't be happening. Why was Suzie smiling like the fool cat that ate the canary?

"You heard everything we said?"

"Not everything." His gaze went back and forth between the two women, his gaze settling back on Amelia. "But enough."

"Enough." He'd heard her question Suzie about how he looked at her. Her face burned in shame. *Oh, Clara, I'm sorry. I'll get whatever this hold he has over me under control.*

Amelia stopped moving on the machine, gave Suzie a dirty look, then walked toward the weights.

Cole followed her.

"I owe you an apology," she said stiffly when he stood next to her. "Suzie and I shouldn't have been discussing you."

"Maybe you haven't noticed, but I'm not complaining." The corner of his mouth lifted in a crooked smile and his eyes sparked with mischief. "You can discuss me anytime."

Amelia placed her hand on the weight rack, reluctantly met Cole's gaze.

She had to remember her sister, had to ignore the excited bubbles working their way through her like a pot of boiling water.

"What are we doing, Cole?"

His grin was contagious, but she pretended immunity.

"Working out?" he offered.

She sighed at his deliberate misunderstanding of what she'd asked. "I may have agreed to a truce for the sake of the crew, but that's as far as this goes."

His expression sobering, he nodded. "That truce is more than I expected, Amelia, but I'd be lying if I didn't admit to wanting more."

There went her heart rate again.

"What kind of more?" she dared ask, for the simple reason she couldn't not ask.

She knew what he was going to say, knew she wasn't prepared for his answer, knew she needed to put some distance between them right this very second.

Instead she stood still, her fingers curled around a dumbbell, waiting for him to say words she didn't want to hear, and yet she did want to hear them. Over and over.

And that made her weak, something she couldn't stand being, a failure in her own eyes. A failure to herself and to her family.

What would her family say if they knew she and Cole had kissed between the wedding rehearsal and the time he'd broken things off with Clara? What would Clara say?

Amelia couldn't bear to hurt her family, but she couldn't turn away from Cole. She stood her ground, waiting for words she hadn't heard in two years and yet had never been able to forget, had awakened in cold sweats hearing them echo through her dreams. Words she needed to hear again, even if for just one last time.

Clara, forgive me for what I'm feeling.

She held her breath, her lungs threatening to burst, her ears straining to hear his answer, wanting to believe he meant what he said and that he wasn't there because of some twisted reason to do with her sister.

"I want you."

CHAPTER SIX

AMELIA'S breath gushed out at the bombshell Cole dropped between them. "What do you mean, you want me?"

He stared down into Amelia's big brown eyes and thought her the most beautiful woman he'd ever seen. Yes, her hair was swept up in its usual ponytail and sweat glistened across her brow and ran down her neck, but she was beautiful.

Maybe because of the way those big brown eyes stared up at him. Maybe because of the way there was a growing acknowledgment that neither of them could stop what was happening between them, just as they hadn't been able to stop what had grown unbidden between them years ago.

A friendship that had developed into something much deeper.

"You know what I mean."

"Do I?" Her chin lifted, letting him know she wouldn't go down without a fight.

When would she figure out fighting with her was the last thing he wanted?

"I told you how I felt about you."

"The night you came to my dorm room and declared you'd fallen into lust with me despite the fact you'd been scheduled to walk down the aisle with my sister?"

He winced. Was that how she'd taken his confession that night? Lust? He wanted to deny the crude description, but she was right. He had felt an undeniable physical attraction to her, but lust didn't begin to cover the depth of his feelings.

"That isn't what I said."

"No?" Her brow arched and her chin raised another defensive notch. "That's distinctly how I remember your pitiful attempt to get into my bed that night."

"Pitiful?" A blast of wounded pride hit him. "It worked, didn't it?"

Her eyes narrowed with renewed anger and Cole instantly wished he could take back his biting words.

"You may have gotten into my bed." She spoke low, succinctly, coldly. "But I came to my senses before any real damage occurred."

Yes, she'd stopped him, told him she never wanted to see him again. Ever. She'd told him she hated him. She had hated him. Of that, Cole couldn't be mistaken. The look in her eyes when she'd ordered him out of her life had been murderous.

That look was what had kept him away from her for the past two years. What man wanted to put himself in the line of fire for sure rejection?

Yet wasn't that what he'd done by coming aboard her ship? By putting his career on the line to do so?

He couldn't explain that one even to himself.

He glanced around at the other crew working out. No one seemed to be paying them the slightest attention, except for Suzie, and even she was out of earshot as long as they kept their voices low. Still, their conversation wasn't meant for possible public consumption.

"This isn't the time or place for this discussion."

Seeming to recall where they were, Amelia took a measured breath, her chest rising and falling with re-membered anger. They'd made progress today, in the sick ward, but now she looked ready to rip her peace treaty to shreds and declare all-out war.

"I'm not sure we should ever have this particular conversation," she said between straight, gritted teeth.

"Make no mistake. This is one conversation that's long overdue and unavoidable." One they should have had years ago. "Eventually, we'll have to face what's between us. Past and present." But she wasn't ready to admit as much yet and he'd been a fool to try to push her into doing so. "It would be nice if we could forget everything we knew about each other and start over. Without the past clouding the way you view me."

"Short of a case of amnesia, I don't see that as a pos-sibility, do you?"

"You want me to hit you over the head and see if that works?" he offered, half-serious as if he thought that would erase the past, clear the slate. He wanted the opportunity to get to know Amelia, to explore the attraction between them.

"Just being near you is like constantly being hit over the head," she muttered, not looking at him.

"With good thoughts?"

"With thoughts of how much I'd like to hit you over the head."

He laughed.

"That wasn't supposed to be funny," she warned, but when her gaze met his, a smile twisted her lips.

Cole's body lit like a Fourth of July celebration. And just as quickly fizzled out when Amelia's expression tightened and she desperately began setting up boundaries again, terms to their peace treaty.

"Look, you were right about us having to set aside the past while working together. I've already admitted that. But that doesn't mean I want to be your friend or to recapture whatever was between us." She stared him straight in the eyes. "I don't. What happened in the past just needs to stay in the past."

Disappointment and frustration hit him. When he opened his mouth to say more, she shook her head at him.

"Whatever it is you want from me, Cole, it isn't going to happen."

"How do you know?" he pushed, obviously shocking her Stockton good sense. "How can you be so sure that what I want isn't going to happen?"

He wasn't sure about anything where she was concerned. Then again, he'd never had to work to gain a woman's good favor before. Women had always come to him, never mattered one way or the other.

Except Amelia.

"I just know," she stubbornly replied, dropping her free weight back onto the rack and glaring at him.

"Because you aren't willing to give me a chance?"

Looking totally exasperated, she faced him with her hands on her hips and her eyes full of fire. "A chance at what? What is it you want?"

"You."

She shook her head. "What kind of game are you playing?"

Is that what she thought? That he was playing with her? He wanted her, was honest enough to admit to that want, and she thought he was playing games? But what about her? Because for all her bluster, for all the hatred that blazed in her eyes, desire blazed just as strongly. She could deny it all she wanted, but Amelia wanted him every bit as much as he wanted her.

Glancing around the workout room, he noticed they'd started to attract some attention.

"Let's go somewhere we can talk in private, Amelia."

Looking as if she planned to run and never look back, she shook her head. "I agreed to a truce for professional reasons, Cole. Nothing more. If you have some sister fantasy or are just trying to use me to get to Clara, get over it. You are the last man I'd ever willingly become involved with. Understand?"

With that, she spun, swishing her ponytail at him, and walked away, leaving him to wonder why he couldn't have left well enough alone, biding his time and accepting the progress they'd made today instead of pushing for more.

But he knew.

The more time he spent with Amelia, the more he wanted her, the harder not pushing became.

He'd only been on board a few weeks. He had over five months to go. Five months of being with Amelia, of convincing her to give him a chance so he could work out the crazy hold she held over him.

Five months.

It seemed like no time at all.

It seemed like forever.

Why did Amelia think him being here had anything to do with Clara? All he wanted was for her to forget he and Clara had ever been engaged so Amelia could see the potential of him and her.

Sister fantasy indeed.

There wasn't room in his fantasies for anyone other than Amelia and hadn't been for years.

Six weeks into his deployment, Cole shined the light into a soldier's eyes, watching the reflexive size change in response. Perfect. He looked in ears, making note of bulging red tympanic membranes, checked nostrils that revealed swollen mucosa and purulent drainage. He checked a throat that was beefy red, raw.

Running his fingertips over the man's cervical lymph nodes, he felt swollen glands. "That sore?"

Wincing, the man nodded.

The soldier's submandibular, pre- and post-cervical and auricular nodes were all enlarged and tender.

The man's heart rate was increased, but that wasn't uncommon when febrile. Lungs sounded raspy with a soft inspiratory wheeze in both lower lobes. There was no abdominal tenderness, although the man had reported some digestive trouble over the past twenty-four hours.

"I'm going to start you on medication." Cole told him the names of the medicines and what each was for.

The man nodded his understanding.

"Unfortunately, you are infectious. I can't let you return to your berthing quarters."

Nodding, the man looked as if he'd expected as much. "I'll be sleeping in quarantine?"

"Yes." Cole let his nurse know the man would need to be put in quarantine, along with several others who were also suffering from the virus that had hit the ship. Keeping the virus from spreading to the rest of the crew was of paramount importance.

"There's an abdominal pain in bay one. Lieutenant Sanchez," Richard informed him. "Dr Stockton is in with her. She asked for a consult when you finished."

Amelia. With the viral outbreak, they'd been so busy they'd not had any more serious talks, only skimmed the surface, being cordial, being polite, only occasional unguarded glances hinting at what lay beneath.

"Knock, knock," Cole said, rounding the curtain to enter bay one and take in the scene before him.

Amelia looked fabulous in her khaki pants and navy knit shirt, the collar turned down at the base of her throat. Her hair was up in a ponytail and her eyes held compassion as she examined her patient.

A softly crying pretty Hispanic woman lay on the exam table, her arms crossed protectively over her ample chest.

Having been bent over the woman, stethoscope in her ears while listening to the woman's lower abdomen, Amelia glanced up, seeming surprised to see him. She straightened. "I'm sorry, Dr Stanley, but I don't need your help after all."

"You're sure?" Cole's brows drew together. She didn't want him to consult? Were they reverting back to that? He didn't buy it. Amelia was a wonderful doctor, one Cole trusted implicitly. Her professionalism and ethics wouldn't allow her to put a patient at risk for personal reasons. "It's no problem for me to have a quick look."

She shook her head, conveying with her eyes that she'd like him to leave without making a big deal of it. What was going on?

Making a quick decision, he shrugged. "If you need me, you know where to find me."

"Thanks." She waved him out and turned her attention back to her patient.

Half an hour later, he caught her coming out of the medical office. "Earlier, you released the abdominal pain without observation. False alarm?"

"Not really." She didn't meet his eyes, which sent up warning flags left and right.

"What was wrong?"

"I'd rather not discuss my patient."

He eyed her curiously.

"Look," she began, "it's not my place to tell you. There are a few things on this ship that are still private, believe it or not. I won't break patient confidentiality unnecessarily."

"How is consulting with me about an abdominal pain patient a breach of confidentiality?" he asked in frustration. "I'm the surgeon."

"Not all abdominal pains require a surgeon."

"This one didn't?"

"Obviously not or I would have gotten you to check her rather than asking you to leave."

"Obviously."

She hesitated a moment, her expression softening, reeling him in without even realizing that's what she was doing.

"Thanks for not making a scene in front of the patient. I was afraid you'd insist on checking her." She met his gaze. "I appreciate that you did the right thing, letting me do my job."

At her tentative smile, the ship shifted beneath his feet. "When is she coming back for follow-up?"

Again, a slight hesitation. "She'll come back if needed, but she's putting in for a reassignment."

A reassignment? "Sea life not for her?"

"Not everyone takes to ship life."

Which they would have discovered during the many training exercises prior to deployment. Interesting.

"She was suffering from seasickness?" he asked, wondering if Amelia would lie to him. Although he didn't know what had been bothering the woman, he did know seasickness wasn't a likely diagnosis.

"No, she's been aboard the ship for some time, but…" She paused, glanced at him and then shrugged. "Let's talk about something else. How are you holding up? Lots of viral patients?"

Cole studied her, admired her for protecting her patient, even though she should know she didn't have to protect the woman from him. Probably an STD, likely pelvic inflammatory disease or something similar, possibly even pregnancy, since Amelia was being so secretive.

"More than I'd like. If we can't get this quarantined, we're going to have an epidemic on our hands."

She ran her fingers through her ponytail then tightened the elastic band. "That's what I'm afraid of. I saw mostly viral patients during sick call this morning, too.

The senior medical officer has put out an advisory for everyone to come in at the first sign of symptoms so we can stop the spread."

Watching the play of light hit her shiny dark hair, wishing he could run his fingers through the silky gloss, could lean down and breathe in the scent of her shampoo, the scent of her, Cole gave a wry smile. "Which means the medical crew is going to be all the busier."

Returning his smile, she nodded. "Yes, sir. You sure you want to stick around for this?"

His gaze met hers, sent a thousand silent messages, asked a thousand questions, all of which Amelia didn't respond to. If only she'd tell him what was in her mind. Did her body heat up the way his did any time they were near each other? Did every sense become sharper, more alert, more aware, the way his did?

Of course, she didn't answer any of those questions and he couldn't voice them. Not yet. All he could do was smile at her and hope that with time whatever was between them would come to a head and free them both.

"There's nowhere I'd rather be than right here," he admitted, watching the color of her eyes darken to rich melted chocolate, watching her full pink lips part, and a short gust of air escape. "With you, Amelia. Nowhere else."

CHAPTER SEVEN

ONE day at a time, Amelia reminded herself later that day. One day at a time. That's how she'd deal with Cole. How she was dealing with him, and how she'd continue to deal with him.

So far she was six weeks down and twenty more to go. That was only one hundred and forty days, give or take a few pending either of their reassignments.

Not that she was counting.

Sighing, she glanced across the sick ward to where he stood, laughing at a joke the physician assistant had told. Tracy, Richard, Peyton and a couple of nurses and corpsmen stood with them. So did the senior medical officer. Despite the crazily busy day they'd had, they all looked relaxed, if a bit tired. They all looked toward Cole with respect and admiration, with friendship.

Cole belonged on board the USS *Benjamin Franklin* as much as if he'd been there from the day the ship had first sailed for training exercises.

As much as she hated to admit it, she'd grown to appreciate his presence in the sick ward, too.

They'd had another swamped sick call, which had run over into the scheduled appointments. A nasty upper respiratory virus was running rampant across the ship.

If Cole hadn't been there to help, following his surgery clinic, none of them would be anywhere near finished. They'd all had their hands full, mostly with viral patients but also with the usual plethora of cases as well.

Then there had been the young lieutenant who worked in the ship operations department and suffered from abdominal pain. Although the carrier intelligence center officer's diagnosis hadn't been anything out of the ordinary in the grand scheme of life occurrences, the diagnosis wasn't one Amelia commonly made. Actually, she hadn't diagnosed a pregnancy in months.

The woman hadn't wanted to put down that she thought she was pregnant, had begged Amelia to keep her secret until she'd figured out the course of action she wanted to take and for Amelia to please honor her wishes. The woman had likely had an on board affair with another officer and was fearful of both of them facing dishonorable discharge.

Regardless of her reasons, Amelia had hedged the best she could. Only she and the lab technician who'd performed the test knew the woman's real reason for visiting the sick ward.

She partially owed thanks to Cole for that. Had she realized the woman's true reasons for the visit she wouldn't have requested the consult, but she hadn't known prior to their private discussion.

Cole had deferred to her request. Would his predecessor have done so? She doubted it. Not only had the man who'd gone through the training exercises with the ship been higher ranked but Dr Evans had been full of arrogance as well. He'd have insisted on checking the woman.

Cole didn't pull rank. He listened, really listened. Just as he'd always listened to her. Whether in regard to a particular professor or a recount of her rounds, Cole had always had time to listen, to offer advice or guidance. He'd smile, offer a comforting word, a gentle pat of his hand across hers.

And she'd wanted more. Even in the earliest of days, she'd wanted Cole. Had been aware of everything about him. She'd denied her feelings, of course, even to herself. How could she not have when he'd belonged to Clara?

Even now, when she didn't want to like anything in regards to Cole, she was finding way too many things to like.

The way he smiled, the way he volunteered to help, the way he interacted with the crew, the way he threw himself one hundred percent into everything he did, the way he looked at her as if she were the only thing he saw.

Yesterday in the gym, while she and Suzie had put their time in on the elliptical, with him on the machine next to theirs, she'd found herself laughing at his corny jokes.

And when had he fallen into sitting with them in the dinner wardroom each night? When had she stopped resenting him for doing so? When had she started looking forward to the moment he joined their table, adding a flavor to the meals no cook could produce?

Remembering that she didn't like him was getting more and more difficult because, darn it, he was likeable.

More than likeable.

How could she like him when she was swamped with guilt? When each and every smile that passed between Cole and herself was a betrayal to her sister?

She ran her fingers through her hair, catching his gaze as he glanced up from the group he was talking to. He wore navy pants and shirt with the navy medical logo on the left breast. The color only intensified the blueness of his eyes, making her think of childhood days of playing beneath a cloudless sky. That's what Cole was. A sunny day. Only his sunshine was deceptive, more dangerous, threatening to burn her to ashes.

"Did you hear what Peyton said?" he asked, his smile lethal.

How was it possible for him to look so great when he should be dead on his feet? She must look like death warmed over. Yet he looked as if he could pull another clinic without batting an eyelash.

Amazed by his endless energy, she shook her head. "I think my ears are too tired to hear anything other than the call of my pillow."

Concern flickered in his eyes. "You okay? You're not coming down with the virus are you?"

She shook her head. "I'm just tired."

And disgusted with myself that I'm falling for your charms all over again even though I know better.

Analyzing every feature to the point she felt as if she should put her hands in front her face, he didn't look convinced. "You shouldn't have worked through lunch."

"I didn't do anything you didn't do," she reminded him.

Despite the fact that he didn't have to be there, Cole worked just as hard as the rest of them.

"I don't know about the rest of you, but I'm headed for a shower, then to grab something to eat." Tracy spoke, tossing her stethoscope down on the counter. "I'll see you guys in the morning. Let's pray this virus passes quickly and doesn't take hold of any of us."

Amelia nodded, as did the rest of the crew as they broke up, each heading their own way, until the sick ward became eerily quiet.

Only she and Cole remained.

Slowly, as if he had all the time in the world, Cole crossed the room to stand close. Too close.

Running her hand over her tight neck muscles, she held her ground, pretended like his nearness didn't make her nervous. "Thanks for your help today."

"You're welcome." His response was low, husky, a bit succinct for a man who seemed to search for things to talk to her about.

The only sound in the room was the lub-dub of Amelia's ticking heart. Ticking? Ha. More like ba-booming. That ba-boom was probably rocking the entire ship, causing tidal waves on far-away shores.

She stared at him, wondering at why he'd crossed the room, wondering at his silence, wondering at her foolishness for just standing there, waiting, for what?

Although they hadn't had another talk about the past, she could honestly say there hadn't been many awkward silences. Mostly because Cole always said something to fill any conversation void that arose. Something smart, witty, flirty, complimentary, *something*.

Now he didn't say anything. Not a word.

Standing with only a couple of feet between them, he just looked at her. Really, really looked at her.

Her whole body trembled and she knew something monumental was about to happen. She could see it in his eyes. Could feel it in the way his body called to hers.

After weeks of skimming the surface, of letting her pretend she was off the hook and that he'd go along with their truce and ignore the underlying currents, Cole wasn't planning to play nice.

"I'm sorry, Amelia."

She bit the inside of her lower lip, wishing he hadn't broken the silence, not with those words, words that penetrated deeper than any missile.

"What for? You were great today." Even as she said the words, she knew he wasn't talking about today. She knew exactly what he was talking about and she didn't want to discuss the past, wanted to keep her tone light and easygoing.

But Cole had obviously reached a breaking point.

"For kissing you, for leaving, for coming to your dorm that night, for hurting you and your family, for not being able to stay away from you even though it's what you said you wanted." He took a deep breath. "I'm sorry for every mistake I've made."

No, she didn't want to hear his apology, didn't want to feel the forgiveness welling in her heart.

Stocktons didn't forgive, they got even.

Yet that didn't feel right either.

"Why did you come?" she asked, needing to know what had driven him to show up at her dorm that crazy night so long ago when he'd obviously had no problems leaving her waiting on the night of his rehearsal. "Surely you didn't believe I'd welcome you? Not after what happened?"

"I couldn't not come." Stepping even closer, he grazed his knuckles across her cheek as if he also couldn't not touch her. "I tried to stay away, because I knew you wouldn't forgive me. That was a given." His fingers paused, tensing against her skin. "How could you? But I couldn't stay away."

Amelia fought leaning into his touch, fought the maelstrom of emotions swirling within her. She held his gaze, thinking him more dangerous to her well-being than any mission she might ever undertake. "Because?"

Of Clara? she wanted to ask, but couldn't. When he looked at her as if he wanted her so badly, surely he wasn't thinking of her sister?

"You were all I could think about, that I'd asked you to wait for me." His palm cupped her face, his gaze bore into hers. "You're still all I think about."

Bells blared in her head, warning *danger, danger*. But he hadn't said Clara, he'd said you, as in her. Not her sister. Her. Amelia.

Even as giddiness bubbled inside her, she had to stop him. Whether he was using her or not was irrelevant in the grand scheme of things. Cole had taken the cowardly way out, walking away. She could never respect that.

"Cole, don't do this."

Please don't do this.

But he didn't move away, only caressed her cheek as if she was the most precious thing he'd ever touched. "This? Is this what you don't want me to do? I can't deny it anymore, Amelia. I want to touch you. I've always wanted to touch you. You felt the heat between us as surely as I did."

"Don't say these things." *Don't touch me. I can't think when you do.*

"Why not?" His thumb brushed back and forth in a slow stroke across her tingling flesh, leaving a trail of fire that burned clear to her core. "They're true. I've never stopped thinking about you, wanting you. The moment I saw you again, I knew I was right to come here."

The blaring bells cleared enough for a new warning to pop into her head, one that told her she hadn't given Cole nearly enough credit for being the master strategist he so obviously was. She felt sucker punched.

"You being assigned on this ship, my ship, that wasn't a coincidence, was it?" If she hadn't been sure before, the truth shone in his eyes as clear as day, as clear as the message she was a fool was stamped on hers. "You purposely got yourself assigned to my ship."

Anger heightened her pitch.

He winced. "It's not like that."

"It's exactly like that. Unless you're denying you arranged this?" She spread out her arm to indicate his being in her sick ward.

"I'm not denying anything."

The way he looked at her made her wonder at just what else he wasn't denying. Surely much more than the reasons behind his arrival on her ship?

"How did you manage to pull off being assigned here? Getting this exact assignment couldn't have been easy. Getting Dr Evans transferred at the last minute, unless that was just a convenient coincidence, which I don't believe. Who owed you a favor? Or maybe it's you who now owes the favor?" She glared at him, battling with the knowledge that he'd gone to a lot of trouble to get assigned to her ship. Why? Even through her blaze of anger that one word shouted front and foremost. "Why? Because you wanted to sleep with me and I turned you down?"

"No."

"Odd," she continued. "For all your faults, I never pictured you as a suck-up, Cole, but you must have been to pull this off."

At least part of her accusations must have hit their target as he didn't say anything. Why had he gone to so much trouble? What had he hoped to gain?

Cole's lips clamped shut. He wouldn't tell her. No matter how many times she asked or how she insisted, he wouldn't tell her how he'd managed to achieve his presence aboard the USS *Benjamin Franklin*. But why not? Surely getting what he wanted was a prize worth bragging about?

Only he hadn't quite gotten what he wanted, had he?

But he'd been on the path. Seducing her into believing in his goodness, making her question what she thought she knew about him, seducing her into forgetting she thought he was a devil in disguise.

Disgusted that she'd let her guard down, that she'd let him in over the past few weeks, Amelia spun, heading toward the medical office, needing to be away from him in the hope of being able to think clearly, of being able to figure out what the truth of him actively pursuing an assignment on her ship implicated.

Why was he here? Doing this? Making her crazy? She wanted to scream over and over, wanted to grab his collar and shake him, make him tell her why he was doing this after he'd so easily walked away from her. Why was he torturing her so doggedly?

She'd just gotten inside the doorway, when Cole grasped her wrist and turned her toward him. Not roughly, but not gently.

"No, Amelia." He denied her escape, his eyes blue fire. "This time you're not running away. We're going to have this out."

What was he talking about? She hadn't run away from him. He'd been the one to ask her to wait for him and then he'd left. Always, Cole had been the one to run.

"There is nothing to have out. Nothing." She thrust her chin upward. "We're colleagues, working on an aircraft carrier together. As soon as this deployment is finished, our association ends."

"Our association will never end."

Amelia laughed. "Oh, please. Quit being melodramatic. You're acting as if we're star-crossed lovers."

His hold on her arm eased, his fingers feeling more a caress than a restraint when he asked, "Aren't we?"

Nervous tremors crept up her spine. "No. We've barely even kissed."

Kisses she'd relived a hundred times, a thousand times, but still only the kiss the night of the rehearsal dinner and the kiss in her dorm room.

When she'd told him to leave, that she'd waited for him that night and he'd left her, that his window of opportunity had closed, he'd grabbed her much as he just had, pulled her to him, cupped her face and kissed her until she couldn't breathe, until she couldn't tell where she ended and he began, until she'd wanted nothing more than to fall back into her bed with him.

They had fallen back into her bed.

Cole's long body had pressed her into the mattress, moving rhythmically over hers through their clothing, his hands caressing her everywhere at once, as if he'd waited a lifetime to touch her and couldn't quite believe he actually was. Even now she could remember the silky softness of his shiny brown hair, could remember the tangy taste of his mouth, the fervor of his lips on her throat, the hard pressure of his body covering hers.

Amelia gulped, willing the memory to permanently vanish.

"Barely kissed?" He stared into her eyes for long moments, watching, waiting, then his gaze dropped to her mouth. "That's a problem easily remedied."

His head bent, but just as the heat of his breath touched her lips, burned her with more unforgettable memories, she turned her head.

"No." She couldn't do this. Wouldn't do this.

She pulled free, moved away, turning her back to him, gulping air into her starved lungs. "Please leave."

"You don't want me to go."

She turned, forcing herself to laugh in a mocking way. His eyes were so blue they pierced her. His chest rose and fell in unsteady drags of air. She took all that in, but didn't allow herself to soften. To do so around Cole would be a grave mistake, one he'd pounce upon and devour all that she was.

"Don't tell me what I want," she spat at him in her coldest voice. "You have no idea."

Although maybe he did.

A part of her didn't want him to go. A part of her wanted him to expound on what he'd been telling her, wanted him to explain what had motivated him to show up at her dorm, to maneuver himself into working with her. Had sexual lust driven him to go against his better judgment and search out a woman he'd known would reject him? Did he really believe they were star-crossed lovers or had that only been a smooth line to throw her off balance?

"I know you want me as much as I want you," he countered, not moving from where he stood but looking like he had to force his muscles to remain still. "But you refuse to admit you want me because of loyalty to your sister."

No. She didn't want him.

Much.

"You don't know anything." At least she sounded brave, certain, as if she meant what she said. Inside she quaked. This man held the power to rip her world apart, the same way he had ripped it apart two years ago.

"Tell me I'm wrong, that you don't want me."

She wanted to, but couldn't lie to him. Couldn't lie to herself. Not a moment longer. She did want Cole. More than she'd ever wanted any man.

And it was wrong. Wrong. *Wrong*.

She swallowed the knot tightening her throat. "What I want doesn't matter."

He laughed wryly, without humor. "What you want matters more than anything. You matter. Tell me what you want."

She closed her eyes, praying for strength. "If what I want matters, you'll leave me alone, Cole, because I want you to go."

She heard his sigh, felt his frustration zinging from across the room. His tension wrapped around her like a cloak, willing her toward him, willing her to give in to her desires.

Just when she felt her strength waning, the sensation was gone. *Cole was gone.*

Wondering at her sense of loss when he'd done as she wanted, she opened her eyes to the empty room.

If she weren't a Stockton, tears would have prickled her eyes. But she was a Stockton and those weren't unshed tears blurring her vision because Cole had done exactly as she'd asked.

CHAPTER EIGHT

HEY, Sis. How are things? Still stationed in the Middle East? Life is busy. The ship was plagued with a virus, but things have calmed down. Only a few new cases this past week.

Amelia dropped her head into her hands.

Oh, God, she sounded like a polite stranger. Just as she'd been sounding in all correspondence with Clara since Cole had arrived on board. She'd told Josie a few weeks ago. She'd even told Robert. They'd both taken the news better than she'd expected but, then, she'd never told them she and Cole had kissed prior to Cole dumping their sister, had never told them about Cole coming to her dorm weeks later.

Just as she hadn't told Clara that her ex was aboard the USS *Benjamin Franklin*.

She had to tell her sister. Now. Today. In this very e-mail.

Pressing her finger on the backspace key, she deleted the entire note and started over.

I've been trying to figure out how to tell you, but Cole is on the USS Benjamin Franklin. He is a great surgeon and an asset to the ship, but working with him is difficult for me given the circumstances. I feel my loyalties are torn between you and what's best for my crew. I don't want to forgive him, Clara. I really don't want to, but he does have a way of getting under one's skin, doesn't he? I always cared about Cole, thought he was a wonderful man and doctor. It's so easy to forget how things ended when I'm spending so much time with him, when being with him reminds me of all the things I loved about him.

No, not loved. She deleted the word and typed *adored* instead.

How can I forget how he just abandoned you? Abandoned our family when we loved him as one of our own?

There was that word again. *Love.* They hadn't loved Cole. She hadn't loved him.

"About done?"

Reflexively hitting *Send* before he could read what she'd written, Amelia glanced up at the man standing in the doorway.

Oh, God, she'd just hit *Send*!

All the blood drained from her body to pool in the pit of her stomach.

Would she really have done so if Cole hadn't walked in?

How did he always manage to find her? Not that she was hiding, but he always turned up wherever she was. She'd resigned herself weeks ago to the fact that she wouldn't be able to avoid him. She wasn't even trying to avoid him anymore. What was the point? She was being pursued, stalked by a predator more deadly than any jungle cat.

One that slid on his belly and seduced with his mesmerizing eyes and silver tongue. Just like Eve in the Garden of Eden, Amelia was defenseless against his powers of temptation. Difficult for a Stockton to swallow, but one of their greatest traits was the ability to call an apple an apple and an orange an orange. Stocktons didn't lie, not even to themselves. Especially not to themselves.

She wanted Cole. Had from the beginning. Had he married her sister, she would never have acted on that want, but he hadn't married Clara. Instead, he'd come for her and was biding his time until she was willing to admit she'd been waiting for him to do just that for the past two years.

She'd done what he'd asked. She'd waited for him. Two damn years.

"I was e-mailing my sister," she said perversely, irritated with herself for her weakness.

He didn't physically react, just watched her. "Is everything okay?"

She snorted, too frustrated to hold back what she was truly thinking from him. "Nothing has been okay from the moment you arrived on this ship. No, longer. Nothing has been okay from the moment you walked away from your rehearsal dinner." A pause, as she dragged in an unsteady breath. "How could you have just left? How?"

A pause, a twitch of that perfect set of lips, then, "I'm not leaving you, Amelia. Not this time. I couldn't even if I wanted to."

She inhaled a breath meant to calm her frayed nerves. "Do you want to, Cole? Do you regret manipulating your way onto my ship?"

"No."

Why was she trying to pick a fight? For what purpose? She closed her eyes. "Was there something you needed?"

"Other than you in my bed?"

Amelia clamped her lips closed, her heart pounding at his directness. She should threaten him with sexual harassment, should walk over and slap his handsome face, should do so many things. But all she did was release her pent-up breath.

"Is that what all of this is about?" she asked in a calm voice. Too calm really. "Sex?"

He moved closer, regarded her with speculative eyes. "What do you want this to be about?"

"I don't want this at all, Cole. None of this." She put her hands up in front of her. "I don't want you here, period."

"But you do want me." He wasn't asking a question. He was stating a fact.

She swore softly under her breath in a way that would have her mother going for a bar of mouth-washing soap. "Yes, I want you, but to what purpose?"

"Mutual satisfaction?"

"What makes you so sure you can satisfy me?" she taunted.

His gaze raked over her face in a lazy caress, lowered down her throat, lower, until she'd swear he could see right through her clothes, her skin, to where sweat slicked her body.

"If you'd like proof…"

"No." She shook her head forcibly, moving away from the computer desk, away from where he stood. "I wouldn't like anything from you except to be left alone."

He laughed. "You're like a broken record, Amelia. Isn't it time you stop protesting so much?"

"Where you're concerned I'll never stop protesting."

"Then the next few months won't be dull, will they?"

How did he do that? Go from seductive devil to laughing like a good ole boy? As if he hadn't just had his proposition turned down flat?

"I thought I'd go up deck and get some fresh air," he said out of the blue, causing her to blink as if she'd missed part of their conversation. "I came to ask if you wanted to come with me."

"Have you heard a word I've said?" she asked incredulously.

"Have you heard a word I've said?" he retorted, arching a brow at her. "I'm not going away, Amelia. Neither am I leaving you. We've tried that, and guess what? Nothing's changed. We need to resolve the unfinished business between us."

"Unfinished business?" she scoffed, knowing she'd lost any offensive hold she'd had. "You mean sex?"

"More than just that but, yes, sex, too." He moved toward her and she got the distinct urge to take a step back. *Defensively.* "But you can rest assured, for the sake of our careers, I can wait until we're at port call." He flashed a smile that couldn't be called anything except bad. "For both our sakes, let's hope you're as disciplined."

Her jaw dropped. "You're a pig."

"I've been called worse."

Why did he keep smiling? Acting as if this was all one big joke? She wanted to hit him!

"Quit being so obtuse!" she chided, frustrated with his lackadaisical smile and attitude.

His lips twitched. "You want to grab a jacket before going up deck?"

Seething, she marched past him and headed up deck before she even realized that's where she was going.

Behind her Cole just laughed. A rich, deep-timbred sound that rocked through her soul.

She should have turned around, gone anywhere other than with him. But maybe fresh air would clear her befuddled brain.

Then again, perhaps only Cole could clear out the confusion he caused.

Thirty minutes later, Amelia and Cole looked out at the dark blue sea. Smoky gray clouds covered the sky and it looked as if it might rain later. They stood opposite an F-14 Tomcat fighter jet, providing them with a shield from prying eyes.

Somehow, he'd gotten her talking about her father. She was never quite sure how Cole did that, got her to talking about herself and her family when she'd had no intention of telling him a thing. He'd even gotten her to discussing her siblings' names.

"Your father is a great man, Amelia Earhart Stockton."

"I don't need you to know that about my father, but thanks." She rolled her eyes at her full name. Her parents had named all their children after individuals they'd admired from history. Well, except Josie. None of the Stockton siblings had ever quite understood why her parents had named their youngest after the lead singer of an all-girl band.

"Growing up with him as a father couldn't have been easy. I remember Clara saying he..." Cole's voice trailed off.

All righty, then, Amelia thought awkwardly.

"You told her I'm here?"

"Yes."

"What did she say?"

She couldn't tell him that she'd only told her sister earlier that very day in the e-mail she'd sent as he'd entered the room. Besides, why did he want to know what Clara had said? Why did he look so concerned?

She stared out over the horizon. "I'd rather not discuss my sister."

"Don't you think we should?"

She turned to him. "You're kidding, right?"

"Your sister is a wonderful woman."

La la la. Amelia mentally stuck her fingers in her ears. She didn't want to hear this. She didn't want to hear Cole extol Clara's virtues.

"But I should never have asked her to marry me," he continued.

La la la. She focused on where the sky met the sea, on the wind whipping at her clothes, her face, her hair, on the scent of the ocean.

"Clara was my closest friend, and I mixed that up with other feelings."

"It took you long enough to figure that out. You walked away on the night before your wedding," she pointed out, wincing inside. She hadn't meant to let him draw her into this conversation. She didn't want to have this conversation.

"I'm not going to make excuses for myself, Amelia. What I did was wrong."

"Oh, you're so sanctimonious. Do you want me to get on my knees and bow to your goodness?"

A tic jumped at his jaw. "Tell me you wanted me to marry your sister," he challenged, placing his hands on her upper arms, forcing her to face him. "Tell me you think I should have married her when kissing you that night far exceeded anything I'd ever felt."

"Don't say that."

He stared at her so intently she thrust her chin up.

"I couldn't marry Clara. Marrying Clara would have been the worst thing I could have done to her when I didn't love her the way she deserved to be loved."

"Do you want me to say you're forgiven? That you were a saint to walk away and break her heart?" She glared. "I'm not going to absolve you that way."

"I don't need your absolution," he informed her point-blank, his expression tight. "Clara forgave me years ago."

"Ha," she scoffed. "If you believe that you're a bigger fool than I thought."

He was close. So close. Despite the breeze she could feel the heat coming off him, could feel its pull, could feel the scorch of his fingers on her arms as if he branded her.

"Has anyone ever told you that you are the most stubborn female?"

She lifted her chin another notch, but focused on the slightly crooked slant of his nose rather than meet his eyes. "I'm not stubborn."

"And infuriating," he continued as if she hadn't spoken. "And beautiful. So damned beautiful you make me breathless. I want you, Amelia. More than I've ever wanted anything or anyone, I want *you*."

Shocked out of her anger, her gaze met his and she instantly realized she'd made a horrible tactical error.

Because the eyes truly were the windows to the soul and Cole had just seen how his words affected her.

His lips came down on hers. Hard.

Automatically, she bit him. Hard.

He swore against her mouth, but didn't step back, just kept on kissing her, willing to take whatever punishment she doled out. Only he gentled his lips against hers, swept his tongue into her mouth with slow thrusts, leaving himself vulnerable to any retribution she opted to wield against him.

She should bite him again.

She really should.

But he tasted so good, felt so good. She'd waited two long years to feel this good again. She leaned against him, her palms flattening against the width of his chest, and relaxed, giving free access to her mouth.

He held her, his hands pressing her tightly to him, his body hard against hers. But his kisses remained gentle, exploring, a mating dance meant to seduce her into bowing to his whims.

She hated him. And yet...she didn't.

He lifted his head, breathed raggedly against her mouth, stared into her eyes with a wildness in his she'd never witnessed. "You make me crazy, Amelia. Certifiably crazy."

Breathless, she strove for her usual cool. "You don't exactly do much for my intelligence either, Einstein."

He laughed softly, resting his forehead against hers. "That shouldn't have happened."

Something inside her plummeted at his words.

"Not here." He raked his fingers through his hair. "Not where someone could have seen us."

She bit the inside of her lower lip in relief, and frustration. He was right, but...

"Don't look at me like that, Amelia. I want you too much. At the moment I want to carry you off to the closest bunk and our careers be damned if it means I can have you."

"Oh." Was that pleasure curling in her belly? Why did his admission make her feel so...desirable? Wanton? Sexy?

"Yes, 'Oh,'" he mimicked, and gave her a look so intense she had to take a steadying breath. A look so full of desire and passion and pure unadulterated lust that she could only stare at him in wonder. "You're safe for now but, come port call, you're mine. No more games, no more pretenses, you are mine."

CHAPTER NINE

A TOTAL of three months had passed since Cole's arrival aboard the USS *Benjamin Franklin*. Currently, the aircraft carrier was docked at the Changi naval base in Singapore. Cole had spent the morning working with one of the ship's chaplains in humanitarian efforts in the city. He suspected Amelia had, too, but he hadn't seen her. Probably intentionally.

Since their kiss, she'd become wary, watching, studying him. The looks she'd stolen weren't hostile, more resigned. As if she'd accepted that eventually the sparks between them would ignite and burn them both.

You are mine. Where had that he-man statement come from? He wasn't the knock-them-out-drag-them-by-their-hair kind of man. Never had been. Then again, no woman had ever affected him the way Amelia did.

She really did make him a little crazy. Very crazy.

But all of that would change. Soon. Tonight?

Several of the crew had planned to meet up at a bar that was a regular hangout of military personnel in Singapore. The bar was just a few streets from the port and one of many that catered to the thousands of soldiers that made port call at the only Asian port deep channeled enough to accommodate an aircraft carrier.

Cole and a couple of the other medical crew who'd volunteered with the chaplain walked together at the end of their charity stint.

The streets were crowded, filled with exotic noises and smells. Fish markets, delicacies from street vendors, and Chinese, Malaysian and various ethnic restaurants tempted his nostrils. Modern skyscrapers gleamed high above the streets, glistening against the setting sun and providing a spectacular high-tech backdrop that spoke well of Singapore's prosperous world-class port.

Even without the upbeat rhythm of the city, an excitement filled the air. Physical excitement. Cole and Peyton had signed out as liberty buddies that morning and were checked into a hotel the ship had arranged. In separate rooms.

Inland, physical release was fair game and happened in excess. Thousands of young soldiers with money burning holes in their pockets and a few days to drink, party and be merry before returning to their life aboard ship.

With sexual relations forbidden on ship, port call often served as a sexual smorgasbord either between crew members or with locals.

Cole had never indulged in that particular aspect of port call. Drinking to excess and deafening his pals with poorly sung karaoke renditions, yes. Meaningless sex just didn't do it for him. Even before his assignment aboard the USS *Benjamin Franklin*, a long, long time had passed since he'd last been with a woman.

He'd been okay with that. Then. Now he could honestly say he was more sexually wound up than at any point during his life. But he had no plans to pick up a strange woman in a bar. Meaningless sex still didn't appeal. He planned to find Amelia and finally make good on his promise.

You are mine.

Amelia was going to be his.

If she wasn't at the bar, he wouldn't stay long, would go in search of her and he'd find her. She was checked into the same hotel as he was. All the medical staff were. Suzie was her liberty buddy and had no qualms in letting Cole know that their room was on the same floor as his, only a few doors down.

His sole purpose for the next two days was to spend as much time with Amelia as possible. Preferably in his bed.

When he and the group he was with entered the low-lit bar, Cole skimmed the crowd, taking in soldiers mixed in with locals. He recognized numerous USS *Benjamin Franklin* crew and nodded acknowledgment to several who called out to him, but he declined their offers to join them. He was on a mission.

"Who are you looking for?" Peyton asked, casting a sly glance Cole's way. "A particular female doctor perhaps?"

Cole didn't answer his colleague.

"It's no secret you've got the hots for her. You planning a little port call party for two?"

He scowled at his liberty buddy. "Watch what you say."

Peyton held up his hands. "No offense meant, man. I just figured she was who you were looking for. It's obvious there's something between the two of you."

Then Cole saw her. Every corpuscle in his body contracted into a tight ball.

She was his.

Her hair was down. Lying softly across her bare shoulders, the tips trailed between her shoulder blades. She wore an exotic sundress of reds, greens and golds that made her eyes shimmer like molten liquid. Never had her eyes seemed so erotic, so luminous. Possibly because of the makeup brushed across her lids, her cheeks, the gloss puckering her all too kissable lips, but he suspected the look had more to do with an internal beacon she emitted. One every ounce of testosterone within him responded to.

Sitting with a group of nurses, corpsman, Suzie and the ship's other medical officer, she had a brightly colored drink in front of her and a happy look on her face.

A little too happy a look.

She laughed at something someone said, leaned over and laid her head on Suzie's shoulder for a brief second in a very non-Amelia type gesture. Way too relaxed, way too touchy.

Cole frowned. How long had she been at the bar?

Her gaze lifted, clashed with his, sent conflicting signals that said *Come and get me if you think you're man enough* and *Go away, you're not wanted* at the exact same time. No woman had ever sent stronger mixed signals.

Cole chose to go with the first option. He was definitely man enough and he definitely wanted to come and get her. Still, he wouldn't rush. He'd found her. He'd take his time, savor the building sexual momentum and make his move when he was ready.

Of that, neither of them had any doubt. Was that why she drank? To lower her desperately clung-to guard? To have something to blame come morning light?

He didn't like the idea, but there was nothing he could do about it other than make sure she was sober by the time they got back to the hotel. No way would their first time be with her drunk. She'd come to him of her own free will.

Peyton and the others Cole had entered with joined Amelia's group, pushing up another table and chairs.

Amelia's lips parted and her gaze dared him to join them.

Shooting her a smile that revealed nothing and yet promised everything, he crossed to the bar, was greeted by more colleagues and ordered a beer.

He swapped stories with a friend he hadn't seen in over a year that was serving on a battleship in their battle group. He bought a beer for a crew member, turned down three offers to dance from women he didn't know and only occasionally glanced toward Amelia.

Each time he did, he found her watching him. And tonight, for the first time, she didn't bother to look away when he caught her.

Her big brown eyes boring into him, tracing over each feature as if trying to figure him out, to figure out why he hadn't tossed her over his shoulders and carried her back to his hotel room. If only she knew how desperately he wanted to do that, yet that same desperation was what held him back. He wouldn't lose control. To do that would just be foolish.

A captain, full of himself, presented himself to her, strutting like an inebriated peacock.

"Dance with me, pretty lady," he slurred, bowing in grand gesture and drawing a couple of chuckles from others at the table.

Amelia's gaze slid from Cole to the man. Slowly, she shook her head back and forth, declining his request.

He didn't leave, though, instead cajoling her to change her mind, flashing smiles and phony compliments. The room was too noisy for Cole to make out exactly what he said, but he'd have to be blind to miss Amelia's reaction to the flirting and her subsequent reconsideration of the man's request.

No.

Cole left his bar stool, cleared a straight path to Amelia's table, his gaze never leaving his quarry.

Distracted by the man, she hadn't noticed his approach, but her tablemates had. Suzie smiled, giving him a "what took you so long" look. Sitting to Amelia's right, Tracy elbowed her.

"Hey!" Amelia protested, glancing away from the captain to the nurse. "What was that for?"

Her brows lifted expressively, the woman gestured toward Cole. He didn't move, just stood, feet spread wide, arms at his sides, ready for whatever she threw at him.

"Oh." Her full lips rounded in surprise.

Or feigned surprise at any rate.

He'd just been had. She'd had no intention of dancing with the man, just of *making him* jealous, making him come to her. She'd played him.

"Cole," she purred, her eyes full of wicked delight.

"Yes. Cole." *Don't play games with me, Amelia. Not tonight. Not ever.* "Sorry I took so long," he said for the benefit of the captain unhappily observing his interruption and looking imbibed enough to mistakenly think he could stake a claim despite Cole's arrival. He shot the man a "she's mine, back off" glare, then returned his attention to Amelia. "I got caught up talking to an old friend, but I'm here now." He held out his hand to her. "Let's dance."

Amelia melted into Cole's arms, laying her cheek against the soft material of his cotton-blend shirt. He wore some funky button-down with jeans. Seeing him in civilian clothes should make her think of when they'd been in school. Perhaps it did. But rather than remember, she was assailed with new thoughts.

For years she'd blamed him for what had happened, never considering that perhaps Cole hadn't wanted the attraction between them any more than she had.

Perhaps he still didn't.

Maybe he was as trapped by the chemistry between them as she was. Not wanting the attraction, but unable to resist it. That she understood all too well. Hadn't she barely slept the past several nights, guilty with the knowledge she'd soon be at port call, would soon embrace her feelings for Cole?

Her arms draped loosely around his neck, toying at his nape. He'd had his hair cut at some point during the day, but the sun-streaked locks were just as soft as she remembered.

He smelled so good. Spice and soap and musky male. The scent of him intoxicated her more than the cocktails she'd been drinking in the hope of drowning out her guilt.

Sure, Clara's e-mails said she didn't want Amelia to hold the past against Cole, that Cole was a good man, that they'd just not been meant to be. Her sister was trying to make things easier, trying to lessen Amelia's burden. If only her sister knew.

Yet like a silly moth flitting into a light, she couldn't stop the events from unfolding, couldn't even try. Every instinct she had drew her to Cole, closer and closer until she'd burn.

His hands pressed against the bare skin of her back, his body swaying with hers to the music. "I like your dress."

"Thank you." She'd bought the multicolored dress earlier that day and liked the way the material clung to her body, almost making her appear to have curves. Had she worn the dress because the style made her feel feminine? Less of a soldier and more of a woman?

"I like what's in it better," he breathed close to her ear.

Puh-leeze. She may have been drinking, but she hadn't completely lost her senses. Not yet.

"Don't use cheesy lines on me."

"Why? Won't they work? Looked like the lines I interrupted were working quite effectively." The way his jaw worked when he said it belied the easy tone of his words.

"What's wrong, Cole? Jealous?"

"Of another man holding you?" he asked, tensing against her, his hands holding her a bit tighter, his jaw practically clenched. "Hell, yes."

"You don't own me, Cole. I can dance with whomever I please, whenever I please."

Some ground rules needed to be established. Like that no matter what happened between them, she was her own woman. She'd do as she pleased, when she pleased, and with whom she pleased. If he didn't like that, he could get over himself.

"I know," he agreed, looking smug and like he saw right through her, like he knew just why she protested and found it cute. Cute! "Which is why you're dancing with me, Amelia. You please me very much."

He'd twisted her words, which should infuriate her. Instead, warmth spread, settling low in her belly. "I do?"

"Don't play games," he warned in a low growl that sent shivers across her skin. "We're beyond games. You know you please me, that you're all I think about, kissing you, touching you, tasting you. I want you so much I ache."

The warmth erupted into all-out explosive heat at the intensity with which he spoke.

He was right. No more game playing.

Biting her lower lip, giving herself up to the inevitable, she met his gaze. "I ache, too."

"I know." He sighed, his palms flattening against her back, holding her against him. "I know you do. It's just the way things are between us. A constant, undeniable ache neither of us can fight."

"I'm tired of fighting, Cole. So tired." She rubbed her cheek against the strong wall of his chest, realizing that she *was* tired. Tired of having to be strong, tired of fighting what she was feeling, tired of the guilt, the frustration, the anger, the pain, the desire of wanting him, the wondering why he'd asked her to wait then left. She was tired of all of it and just wanted to lean on Cole, to soak in his confident strength, if only for a short while.

He kissed the top of her hair, breathed in her scent. "We both are, sweetheart. For the next two days, we don't have to fight anything, least of all each other."

Whatever resistance she might have been able to muster vanished. She gave herself over to the music playing between them, moving in beat to the tune, going wherever Cole led regardless of the consequences that were sure to follow.

Too bad that rather than leaving, he led her back to the table where their friends were, because escaping became almost impossible.

Where had the bottle of Jack Daniel's come from, anyway?

Peyton poured a measured amount into the glasses of everyone at the table. On a high from her dance with Cole, Amelia upended her shot glass and lifted it to the cheers of her tablemates.

They were drinking like the sailors they were.

Round after round, they drank, laughed, recounted tales of shared experiences, pranks pulled and personal blunders.

Amelia sat next to Cole, plastered to his side, their hands locked beneath the privacy of the table, although they probably weren't fooling a soul.

She laughed, shifted. Their hands slid across her lap. Cole tensed next to her with the awareness that his hand lay across her leg with only a thin scrap of silk between them. An awareness they both felt.

An awareness that was burning her up from the inside out, waiting, burning, building, growing hotter and hotter until she felt she was about to burst into uncontrollable flames.

Without letting go of her hand, he gently raked his fingers over the material, bunching the cloth higher, slowly exposing the flesh beneath. Other than a quick glance his way, she didn't externally acknowledge what he did, just carried on the conversation without skipping a beat, much as he did. Beneath the table, a whole different conversation was taking place.

One without words. One that didn't need words.

Cole's fingers did the talking, praising the toned lines of her thighs, telling her how much he wanted her, telling her all the things he planned to do to her before the sun came up.

They spoke volumes to each other, conveying all the things words couldn't.

Even when she was at the point of squirming in her seat, he didn't move to the damp juncture of her thighs. She wanted him. Desperately wanted him to touch her there. But he didn't. Just traced delicate lines along her inner thighs to almost the brink of where she craved him most.

Over and over he drew the path, circling, toying, rubbing over her skin in teasing little movements, his hand dragging hers along for each erotic stroke. His fingers touched her, but he also played her own fingers against her flesh, guiding each teasing touch. Each movement tugging her insides out until she reached the point she fully expected her skin to retract.

What was he doing? How could he stand it? Oh, God, she couldn't take much more without climbing into his lap.

Or dragging him under the table.

She glanced at him, her brow furrowing at how relaxed he looked, at how little he seemed affected by his tantalizing caresses. Her gaze settled on the rapid little beat pounding at his neck and she felt the beginnings of a smile.

Mr Hot Shot Doctor could act as if he were immune to what he was doing, but that jumping carotid pulse told a different story. One that emboldened Amelia.

Wiggling her hand free, she began an exploration of her own. One that involved her hand on his rock-hard thigh. Seconds later she discovered his thigh wasn't the only thing rock hard about his body. Had he just groaned or had she imagined that guttural sound?

No longer able to fake an interest in the conversation going on around them, she lifted her glass to her lips with her free hand and drank deeply. Her other hand remained on him. On the very male part of him that just touching had her panties going damp.

Through his pants, she cupped him, taking slow measure of his girth through the material. Impressive. Wow.

He swallowed, forgot what he was saying and laughed roughly. "Somebody pour me another drink. I need another."

"That's funny," Amelia said low next to him, quite enjoying herself. "I'd say you need something else entirely."

He turned to her and stopped. He swallowed. Hard.

"Never mind," he told no one in particular, his gaze not leaving Amelia's. "I've had enough anyway. I'm going to head back to the hotel. Anyone else ready to go?"

"Already? It's too early to turn in, man," Peyton denied, glancing at his watch. "The night is barely getting started."

A perverse part of Amelia wanted to deny Cole, to stay here and torture him, to make him beg her to come with him. But to do that would torture herself.

She'd been tortured two years too long already.

Although she liked the idea of Cole begging. Begging her to open her mouth to his kisses. Begging her to touch him. Begging her to strip off her clothes so he could—

"Amelia?"

She blinked, having missed whatever else had been said.

"Are you ready to go? You're looking a little flushed."

Oh, she was definitely feeling a little flushed. Otherwise she wouldn't be running her hands over the skirt of her dress, smoothing the material over her thighs and then sliding out of her chair. Her legs practically wobbled beneath her.

"Yes." She glanced around the table, but didn't meet any of her colleagues' eyes. "Thanks for a fun evening. I'm going to turn in so I'll be fresh for sightseeing tomorrow."

Not a single one of them were fooled by her and Cole's dialogue. She knew that. Cole knew that. They all knew that. Still, she smiled, waved goodbye and kept her head high.

Until she stumbled.

Cole caught her elbow, steadied her.

"Oh, to hell with this," he mumbled, wrapping his arm around her shoulder despite the fact they were still in the bar and in view of their friends and colleagues.

His arm felt too good to push away. Besides, now that she'd stood up she felt more than a little light-headed. She wasn't sure she could walk out of the bar without falling flat on her face if Cole let her go.

So she leaned against him, letting him guide her out of the bar and into a taxi. When the door closed, she turned to him, looking up, waiting for him to do what they'd been working toward all evening.

But he didn't.

Instead of kissing her, taking her back to that warm happy place she'd discovered on the deck of the USS *Benjamin Franklin* when he'd kissed her, he took her hands in his, clasped them tight and shook his head.

"Cole?" she asked, confused.

"I can't," he bit out between gritted teeth.

"You can't?" She blinked. Didn't he want to kiss her? Wasn't that why he'd rushed them out of the bar? Wasn't he going to take her back to her hotel room and fill this ache deep within her? Was he going to make her beg?

With the way she felt, she would.

"If I touch you, we'll end up making out in the back-seat of a taxi," he explained, his expression pained. "As much as I want to kiss you, I want more than desperate gropes in the backseat of a car."

"Desperate gropes in the backseat of a car aren't so bad," she muttered, both pleased and disappointed that he was restraining himself when she so desperately wanted to be kissed.

"It is when you want a lot more," he clarified, giving her a look that seared to her very core, a look that said once he started touching her, he wouldn't quit come hell or high water. "And have waited two years."

Gulping in anticipation, she leaned forward, getting the taxi driver's attention. "Could you drive faster, please?"

CHAPTER TEN

AMELIA woke with a bad taste in her mouth. A very bad taste.

Oh, God, had something crawled into her mouth and died?

Slowly she became aware of other body malfunctions. Like the steel drums playing inside her skull and the way her brain had swollen to three times its normal size. God, but she had a headache.

And what was that smell?

Not bad. Actually, quite wonderful. She breathed in deeper. Spicy. Musky. Yummy. Mmm, definitely male.

Male?

Amelia prised a heavy eyelid open and didn't know whether to wince or lick her lips.

Cole lay next to her, his bare chest easily qualifying as the most beautiful male flesh she'd ever laid eyes on. And not just her eyes were on him.

Oh, no, even in her sleep she'd reached out and touched him.

Her hand lay across his abdomen. Low on his abdomen. His flat, chiseled, hard abdomen that made her fingers tingle.

She licked her lips.

Then winced.

She jerked her hand back before she did something else. Like move lower to discover just what the sheet riding low on his narrow hips hid.

Or had she already discovered that?

Grimacing, she took stock of the fact she lay in a hotel room bed. She glanced around. His hotel room bed. She wore nothing but her underwear. Thank goodness she'd worn pretty matching blue silk numbers. But why did she still have them on?

Surely she hadn't taken time to get dressed afterwards?

Afterwards. Had she and Cole made love?

Maybe if her head didn't hurt so badly she could remember. Somewhere amidst the pounding was the knowledge she desperately needed to recall.

What did it say if they'd finally had sex and she couldn't even remember? That she was having to rack her brain in hopes of recapturing the moments?

It said she'd drunk way too much after night after night of not sleeping well from stress.

She'd known what was going to happen between them, known Cole would pursue her, would take what he wanted. What they both wanted. But she'd felt guilty knowing she and Cole would make love, that before the sun came up she'd have given herself fully to him and taken every morsel of affection he'd give to her.

She'd drunk her guilt away, but she had still wanted to remember!

She squeezed her eyes closed, willing the memories to come to her.

She thought back, remembered being in the cab, remembered walking through the elaborate hotel lobby, going up in the elevator. Cole had run the back of his hand along her neck, forcing every hair on her body to stand at attention. He'd leaned in, blown hot breath against her nape, his lips so close yet not actually touching her sensitized flesh.

Her nipples had puckered. Her knees had knocked. The elevator door had slid open. Cole's hand had moved low on her back. He'd guided her two doors down past her room into his own, pushed her inside and kissed her.

No, not kissed. He had *devoured* her mouth.

She remembered his lips on hers, remembered thinking he was the most marvelous kisser, him moving lower, kissing her throat, telling her how beautiful she was as his hands and mouth moved lower, and then… and then…nothing.

Opening her eyes, she glanced toward Cole, studied his sleeping perfection. From the top of his gorgeous head to where the narrow ribbon of hair disappeared under the sheet, he was perfection. Pure male perfection.

Had she had sex with that male perfection?

"Morning, beautiful."

Her gaze shot to his. Sleep gave the blue of his eyes a lazy hue, but she didn't mistake that hue for lack of complete awareness. After all, he knew what had happened between them.

Why was he *smiling*?

Panic rose up her throat. Disgust? Regret? Shame? She couldn't stand not knowing.

"What happened last night?"

He rolled onto his side, regarded her with an indulgent expression. "You don't remember?"

She wished she'd jumped up, brushed her teeth, combed her hair and washed her face before he'd awakened. This would be a lot easier if she didn't feel so grungy.

"Obviously sex with you isn't that memorable," she quipped, determined not to make a bigger fool of herself than she already had.

"Obviously," he surprised her by agreeing, laughter dancing in his eyes. "Only we didn't have sex."

Surprise number two.

"We didn't have sex?" Had her voice just squeaked? *They were practically naked in bed together.*

His lips twisted wryly. "When we have sex, I'd prefer you to be awake rather than asleep in my arms."

She'd slept in his arms?

"Yes."

Had she asked that out loud? Since he was grinning at her and he'd answered, she obviously had. Brilliant.

The corner of his mouth lifted higher. "You have the sexiest little snore when you're drunk."

"I wasn't drunk." She didn't even believe herself, neither did she want to tell him about her poor sleep habits as of late, so she added, "Much."

Scooting up on his pillow, he laughed.

"Okay, maybe I was a little tipsy." Dragging her gaze back from where the sheet had inched farther down on his hips, barely covering the very male part of him that she'd apparently not seen the night before. Her own state of undress became more of an issue and she tugged on the sheet, tucking the edges beneath her arms to hold the material snugly around her. "I should go."

The laughter in his gaze flickered and he let out a long sigh. "Are we back to that?"

She thought about what he was asking, what he was really wanting to know. Now that she wasn't under an alcoholic haze, was he once again the enemy?

She couldn't find the words to answer, didn't know how to answer. Could she get past what had happened? Had she already? Was that why she was with him? Because at some point over the past few weeks she'd stopped thinking of him as the bad guy and started seeing him as the attractive man she'd always been crazy about.

"Amelia." No longer looking amused, he raked his fingers through his short hair. "I'm not going to apologize for wanting you."

"I didn't ask you to apologize," she huffed, crossing her arms over her chest.

"But you regret being here with me? That we spent the night together?"

She tugged the sheet more tightly around her. "Nothing happened. You said so yourself."

"I didn't say that nothing happened." Two wonderfully sculpted shoulders shrugged. "Just that we didn't have sex."

"But—" She glared at him, feeling at a distinct disadvantage that she didn't remember what they'd done. Or not done. "What exactly happened?"

A smile once again pulled at the corner of his mouth. "One of the highlights was when you begged me to make love to you."

She gasped, wanting to call him a liar, to tell him he was remembering wrong.

"And?" Had he said no? She couldn't believe it. And if he had refused her, what were they doing in bed together?

"You stripped off your dress in the worst—and yet definitely the best," he added as if recalling a particular memory, "striptease I've ever been privileged to witness."

"Seen a lot of stripteases, have you?" she bit out, wondering how big a fool she'd been and vowing to never drink alcohol ever again. Never ever, *ever* again.

"Not really, but last night's was spectacular on many counts."

"But not so spectacular that we actually had sex."

Was she upset that the striptease she couldn't remember had been a dud? Pride. Had to be wounded pride.

"Make no mistake, Amelia, if you hadn't fallen asleep, I would have made love to you until you couldn't see straight." His gaze bored into hers, pinning her to the bed. "Until you couldn't do anything except whimper my name in ecstasy."

She'd have liked him to have made love to her like that. Over and over until her eyes rolled back in her head and she arched off the bed and...

"You have no idea how *frustrated* I was when I realized you weren't faking."

His all-too-real exasperation got to her and her spirits lifted a tad. They may not have had sex, but not from a lack of Cole having wanted to. Good.

"Most men don't want women to be faking in bed," she said, giving what she hoped was a sexy look of challenge. Something that might have been more effective if her hair wasn't wild about her head, and who knew what her smudged slept-in makeup looked like?

"Tell me about it." He snorted, taking measure of how she'd begun to relax. "Now what, Amelia? You didn't answer me. Do I need to buy a bottle of Jack Daniel's and ply you with whiskey to convince you to spend the day with me?"

Whether she'd meant to or not, she couldn't keep the smile from her face. Despite the way things had ended the night before, Cole wanted to spend the day with her. In bed?

"You'd better tell me what you want to convince me to do before I answer."

Good point. One Cole would think had a simple answer. But nothing about his relationship with this woman was simple and hadn't been from the moment they'd met.

Last night, she'd begged him to make love to her, to kiss her all over. Hell, he'd been on his way, his hands on her bare waist with her lying back on the bed. He'd been trailing kisses over her abdomen, tasting the salty goodness of her skin, working his way lower.

Then she'd snored.

Snored.

Even with as frustrated as he'd felt, he'd laughed out loud.

"Amelia?" he'd asked, moving to her side, trying to rouse her.

"Cole?" she'd muttered, rolling to her side and curling against him without ever opening her eyes.

"I'm here, babe." He'd wrapped his arms around her, knowing he wouldn't be making love to her. Not tonight. But soon.

Her face had nuzzled against him. "I waited for you, Cole. I waited and waited and you left. Please don't leave me again. I couldn't bear it."

Her sleepy request had pricked him, made him feel protective of her sleepy vulnerability, made him horribly guilty for past mistakes.

"I promise, Amelia. I won't leave you." He hadn't wanted to leave her that first time, but another promise, to Clara, had demanded he do just that.

He had held her all night, waking several times amazed to find her really with him, curled against his body spoon fashion.

Not the way he'd planned to spend his first night in bed with Amelia, but not bad. Holding her, waking to her chocolate eyes was quite nice.

The fact that her eyes begged him to push her back on the mattress and take the decision of how they'd spend the day out of her hands, to not give her a choice so she wouldn't have to feel guilty for her actions stole that nice feeling, though.

She didn't want to take responsibility for what happened between them.

Not last night. Not today. Possibly never.

Which meant nothing could happen between them.

Hell.

He wasn't a nice guy. It shouldn't matter what her reasons were. She wanted him, was giving him a come-hither look, was visually asking him to make love to her right at this moment.

He wanted to make love to her. Which made his rolling onto his back and staring up at the ceiling in frustration all the more crazy.

"I thought we could go sightseeing."

He didn't have to look to know she wore a surprised expression. She was stunned. He was feeling a little stunned, too. She'd been flirting with him, waiting for him to take advantage of the fact they were in bed together, practically naked, and that he could easily seduce her.

Her vulnerability when she'd asked him not to leave her flashed through his mind again. Amelia was too important to jump the gun. Yes, he wanted her, but he wanted her to want him just as much, for her to be willing to admit that she wanted him rather than feel guilty about their lovemaking. This time there could be no guilt, no bad blood between them. They'd make love because it was what they both wanted, no recriminations.

"There's an animal park not far from here," he rushed on, needing to step away from his making-love thoughts. "We could take a taxi over, spend the morning there, grab some lunch, then wander through Little India, check out the shops and eat dinner at whatever restaurant takes our fancy."

Mouth slightly slack, she stared at him as if she didn't know whether to hit him or kiss him. She did neither. She flopped back on the mattress, stared up at the ceiling along with him. The two of them must look a sight, both scantily clad, lying on their backs, staring up at a pristine white ceiling, frustration emanating from their bodies.

"Okay," she said slowly, not sounding sure of her voice. "I'll go to an animal park with you, and I've always wanted to check out Little India, so that would be good, too." Her lower lip pouted just a tad. "Maybe you won't put me to sleep again."

Did she have any idea how beautiful she was? How much he wanted to make love to her at this exact moment? But what was happening between them was too fragile to cloud the issues with sex. What issues he didn't want to cloud he wasn't sure, just that he'd made the right choice, however difficult, in delaying their mutual gratification.

It was simply a delay.

"If you go to sleep again," he threatened in his most menacing tone, "I'll toss you to the tigers and return to the ship alone."

"Hey." She reached out and punched his arm, then re-crossed her arms over her chest.

"Of course," he continued, unfazed, "that snore of yours might scare the stripes off them."

"I thought you said my snore was cute and little?" she shot back, without moving from where she lay, staring straight up. Her voice held a teasing quality that he could quite easily get addicted to.

He leaned over, but made no play to touch her, just moved into her line of vision, studying the way her hair lay about her head in tangles, how her makeup smudged beneath her eyes, how her lips pouted with the need to be kissed. A thousand sunsets couldn't compare to her beauty. "I called it sexy and little, but I might have exaggerated."

"You think?" She giggled and something shifted inside him and he wondered if he was too late, if perhaps issues were already so cloudy that eventually a storm would hit no matter how carefully he proceeded.

"I don't even want to think of all the ways I humiliated myself last night," she continued.

"Then don't. Last night doesn't matter. Today's a new day."

"You're right. It is a new day. Let's get started." With that, she darted from the bed, presenting him with the most delectable view of her bottom in tiny royal blue silk panties as she disappeared into the bathroom.

Later that day and for the dozenth time, Amelia wondered what was she doing and, just as she'd done each time, she shoved the thought aside.

She had the right to be with Cole. He was single. She was single. They were healthy, consenting adults going into this with their eyes wide open. The past didn't matter.

She didn't really buy her mental pep talk, but she deceived herself that she did. Otherwise she wouldn't be able to justify how her hand rested in Cole's as it had done most of the day. Neither would she be able to justify how they'd talked, laughed, enjoyed each other's company. Like lovers.

For crying out loud, she'd let him feed her bites of his lunch. The scrumptious pieces of fish they'd bought from a street vendor had practically melted in her mouth.

Just as she was melting in Cole's hands like butter in a hot frying pan and she was enjoying every sizzle.

"Come on," he urged, pulling her into a shop doorway.

She'd been too lost in her thoughts to pay attention to where they were, but looking around the luxurious, tranquil setting she knew.

His eyes sparkled with a happiness she hadn't seen in…years. Happiness like that they'd once always shared. Together. Because being together had made her happy and, looking back, she realized that being together had made Cole happy, too. He'd always smiled for her. A real, deep-down-from-the-heart smile.

No one's smile had ever lit up her world the way the man grinning at her did. In that moment just how much she'd missed him hit her. *Oh, Cole.*

"No one can come to Asia without getting a massage."

"Oh?" She arched a brow, intrigued by him having brought her there. "Is that in the travel guide?"

"Word for word. I memorized it when you went back to your room this morning to shower." He winked, talked to the Malaysian woman who greeted them, then handed Amelia over to her care. "Go with her. You'll be glad you did."

A massage was tempting, but not as tempting as the man whose hand she already missed. She hesitated only a moment. "What about you?"

"What about me?"

"Are you going to get a massage, too?"

His lips curved at the corners. "You think I need relaxing?"

"Actually, you look more relaxed than I recall seeing you in years."

His gaze tangled with hers, cocooning her in blue warmth. "Don't let the outside fool you. I'm so wound up on the inside I could snap in two."

Figuring he was referring to sexual tension, she grimaced, took a deep breath and told him the truth. "I really am sorry I fell asleep. I wanted to make love to you, Cole."

He studied her a moment then shook his head, surprising her yet again. "I can't believe I'm saying this, but I'm not sorry. We needed today, just you and me, spending time together, remembering what was good between us."

Yeah, maybe they had. But inebriated sex would have been easy to explain to her conscience. Tonight, when they made love, she wouldn't have anything to blame except the attraction between them. A terrifying thought.

Time for another mental shove. Clearing her thoughts, she lifted her chin in a play of deviance. "I'll only have a massage if you have one, too."

He laughed. "You're going to twist my arm?"

"If that's what it takes," she insisted, but knew the smile on her face disarmed her threat.

"Fine," he agreed, sounding more amused than anything. "We'll get a massage together."

He turned back to the woman who worked there, told her what he wanted, and she nodded her dark head.

A massage together? As in both of them on the table? How did that work? Instantly visions of her naked body lying on top of his flashed through her mind. Um, yes, that could work very nicely.

Cole took her hand and led her through a maze of exotic scents and colors, following the Malaysian woman into a room just for the two of them.

Twenty minutes later, Amelia was in heaven.

She lay on a massage table of sorts, a masseur rubbing and kneading every muscle in her body.

"I heard that moan," Cole said from opposite her, the head of his table a mere meter from hers with them lying in a straight line, feet outward. "You like?"

"I like," she admitted, wondering at herself for lying naked except the sheet covering her in a room with Cole also naked except for the thin cotton sheet covering his delectable backside. Not that she'd looked. Much. A young girl worked on him, sculpting his muscles between her nimble fingers in an almost exact mimic of how the young Chinese man rubbed Amelia.

They lay in silence except for the mood music playing in the background and the sounds of their breathing. Sweet incense burned in the four corners of the room. Peace, tranquility, happiness and love, they'd been told.

"I can't believe we've been naked in the same room twice and haven't slept together yet."

"I'll just bet." Amelia laughed at Cole's bemused comment. "Must be some kind of record for a man like you."

"Must be," he agreed, but only halfheartedly, his words slightly muffled from where he lay facedown on his massage table. "I'm not as active as you think."

Amelia laughed. "Don't tell me that, Cole. I heard about all the nurses you went through after you and Clara broke up."

"I was trying to forget." His admission was low, self-derisive, as if he had lots of regrets.

"My sister?"

His answer came out clearer than before. "You."

She lifted her head, saw that his was also raised, looking at her. She stared straight into his eyes, was pretty sure she was drowning in their blue depths. "Did it work?"

After a few moments, he said, "I'm here, aren't I?"

There was no justification for the satisfaction that filled her. None whatsoever. But satisfaction did fill her.

Cole had sought her because he'd wanted her. Other women hadn't done, hadn't satisfied him. Would she be able to?

"I'm not as experienced as you," she admitted. Lowering her head back into the face rest, she wondered how they could carry on a conversation with the two people giving them massages listening in. Maybe it was the anonymity of being halfway around the world. Maybe it was because the masseuse and masseur were foreign and it was easy to pretend they couldn't understand English, despite knowing that most everyone in Singapore spoke the language.

"I'm not some Casanova." He sounded a little irked. "I've been selective about who I've become involved with. There haven't been that many women in my life."

Closing her eyes, she tried to give herself over to the warm oils being massaged into her flesh. This was supposed to be relaxing. This was relaxing. Only the conversation made her feel tense, worried her. Why was she being so open with him? Why was she telling him the things she was?

"It's not that I'm a virgin." For instance, that was one of those things she really shouldn't have said out loud. She really hadn't needed to divulge that tidbit. "But a woman doesn't want to think she doesn't have enough experience to satisfy her man either."

"Are you calling me your man?" he asked slowly.

Heat burned her face, but to deny his question would be foolish. They'd slept together the night before. Literally slept together. Today they'd held hands, indulged in conversation and prolonged foreplay through long looks that revealed too much. Tonight, they'd make love.

"Is that okay?" She squeezed her eyes shut, holding her breath as she waited for his response. Praying he'd say the right thing.

"Yes, Amelia, that's more than okay." He lay there a moment then declared, "I'm going to buy a bale of whatever they're burning. Peace, tranquility, happiness and love."

"Do what?" Still smiling, Amelia craned her neck to glance at him. He lay with his chin propped up on his hands, watching her. The young woman kneaded his calf muscles.

He smiled at her. "Obviously, whatever we're breathing has made you mellow since you're talking out of your head."

She returned his smile. "Right or wrong, I do know what I'm saying."

More wrong than right, she knew, but wrong sure did feel right in regard to the man lying a few feet from her.

"I hope so, Amelia. I really hope so."

After that, they were silent for the remainder of their massages. No matter how wonderful the therapeutic oils and massage, she couldn't bring herself to completely relax. Not when her mind raced with events to come and not knowing quite how she would deal with the aftermath of those events.

Then again, how did one prepare for heartbreak?

And one was coming on as surely as she was a Stockton.

CHAPTER ELEVEN

AMELIA went to her room after she and Cole arrived back at the hotel. Suzie hadn't been there and it didn't look as if her bed had been slept in any more than Amelia's had. The damp towel hanging on the back of the bathroom door said her friend had returned and changed for the evening already, though.

Amelia showered, changed into a strapless dress she'd bought from a shop that afternoon and carefully put on makeup and styled her hair. She'd forgone a bra, her mostly flat chest not requiring much anyway, and slipped on a pair of barely there red silk panties that rested high on her hips.

"You look amazing," Cole greeted her when she opened her hotel room door following his knock.

"Thanks." She smiled, running her gaze over him. "You look pretty great yourself."

He did. At the same shop she'd bought her dress, she'd found a pirate shirt and teased him into buying it. She hadn't really expected him to wear the swirls of white material, but he was and he looked fabulous. All he was missing was a gold hoop in his ear and a sword. The shirt's material accentuated the width of his shoulders, the girth of his chest, the narrowness of his waist. Women would be lining up to walk the plank. She'd be at the front of the line.

"Let's just stay in."

Cole's suggestion echoed what was running through her mind. She might have grasped hold of his shirt and tugged him into her room if another hotel room door hadn't opened. Tracy stepped out into the hallway wearing a dynamite red dress.

"Hey," she called, immediately spotting them. "You two look great. We missed you today at the MRW tour out to the bird sanctuary and downtown."

"We decided to check out the city on our own."

Smiling, Tracy nodded at their clothes. "Looks like you found some good shops."

"A few."

Another door opened and Peyton stepped into the hallway, a blonde Amelia didn't recognize hanging on his arm. He invited them to a nearby bar. "We're all meeting at eight for drinking, dancing and lots of bad karaoke."

Cole's gaze met Amelia's. She saw longing to say no in his eyes, saw that he really did want to push her back into her hotel room and watch a repeat striptease, that the last thing he wanted was their colleagues as an audience to the emotions bouncing back and forth between them tonight because too much was happening between them for there to be witnesses.

But he said, "Sounds like fun. Are we walking or taking a cab?"

At the bar, Amelia limited herself to one drink, sipping slowly. Tonight, she wanted to be sober, to stay awake, to remember every detail of what happened between her and Cole. She laughed at all the right times, spoke at all the right times, but her mind danced ahead, to what the night would bring, to what making love with Cole would be like.

Heaven, she decided. Making love with him would be out of this world. Had to be since just thinking about making love with him had her on the brink of orgasm.

"You're not getting sleepy, are you?" Cole leaned in near her ear. His breath tickled, sending shivers over her flesh.

Lifting her glass and taking a small sip, she shook her head. "No way. I have plans for tonight."

"Oh?" He sounded intrigued, his breath warm, moist against her ear. "What kind of plans?"

"Ones involving being captured by a pirate and staying awake long into the night."

He glanced down at his shirt and frowned. "I'm no pirate, Amelia, and I won't capture you. Either you'll come to me of your own free will or nothing will happen. Not tonight. Not ever. That's how it has to be between us. No games. No lies. Just you and me together because it's what we both want."

Amelia blinked.

He'd pursued her. She'd just told him a fantasy. And he'd changed tactics? He wanted her to come to him? Did he want her to beg again, too? But knowing how she held a grudge for past actions, maybe he was right to insist on her being the one to initiate their physical relationship.

Actually, she knew he was.

She didn't like him for doing so, but she understood.

He was giving her no wiggle room to blame him for seducing her or to say that she hadn't wanted whatever happened between them.

No room for guilt afterwards. Either she made the conscious decision to make love with him or they didn't make love. The choice was hers.

Whether he meant to or not, he was seducing her, though.

With his eyes, his smiles, his little "accidental" touches. And then there was his leg rubbing against hers.

Unlike the night before, he hadn't attempted to push up her dress and touch her thigh, hadn't stroked her flesh into a tortured mass of nerves that cried for release. No, all he was doing was pressing his leg next to hers. That was enough to fry her brain cells.

"I will come to you, Cole. Tonight." Admitting as much wasn't easy, but with so many other issues between them, communication was of paramount importance. "But I'm not going to beg, do you hear?"

"I hear." Oblivious to the others at the table, he brushed a lock of hair off her cheek, tucking the strand behind her ear. "I'll be the one begging tonight, Amelia."

His husky promise caught her off guard, melted her to her seat.

"I want you, Cole." Heat flushed her cheeks. "I'm not going to make you beg."

"But I will," he whispered. "I'll beg for mercy, because you wield power over who I am and I want you that much. More."

His words sank in and she tried them on for size.

Maybe there was a reason they couldn't stay away from each other despite all the reasons they should. Maybe he'd fallen for her just as she'd fallen for him.

Even as she thought it, she knew she could never trust Cole, that at some point he'd walk away from her just as he'd done two years ago. But for the moment it was nice to bask in the glow of the magic of the promise in his eyes, in the fact that for now she was who he wanted, and they were together.

"I want to go back to the hotel," she admitted, not willing to wait another second. Afraid that if she did, reality would sink in and rob her of the warm feelings rushing through her.

His brow shot up. "Now?"

She nodded. "Let's go."

They said their goodbyes to their colleagues, most of whom were enthralled in a tale Richard was telling with great animation. Amelia didn't have a clue what he was talking about, didn't care. All that mattered was the burning desire in Cole's eyes.

Desire for her.

His palm pressed against her low back possessively, he led her across the dance floor toward the front of the bar so they could make their exit.

Unfortunately they were only halfway across the crowded room when a fight broke out.

Cole cursed, shaking his head in frustration. "What's Peyton done this time?"

Amelia's head whipped around to see the nurse anesthetist's fist smash into a man's face. She winced at the impact, at the way the man's head snapped back. Peyton reared back to hit him again. Others joined the fight, some in an attempt to break up the argument, others to get in hits of their own.

Amelia sighed. Fights weren't uncommon at port call. Actually, they were quite the norm. Several thousand soldiers barely out of their teens, some still in their teens, let loose with money in their pockets, too much pent-up testosterone and too much booze wasn't a good thing under the best of circumstances.

But Peyton wasn't a kid. He was a highly trained anesthetist and one of their own. Cole wouldn't leave him. Neither could she without making sure he was okay and not in need of medical attention once the fight ended. Plus, several of the men involved in the fight were USS *Benjamin Franklin* crewmen.

Warning her to step back, Cole bustled his way toward where a cluster of men scuffled. Knowing she could hold her own in any fight, she followed him. By the time they reached the group, the fight had broken up. A corpsman's face was bleeding from a cut on his cheek. Another's nose bled profusely. Peyton rubbed his knuckles. A few others would sport bruises of various shapes and sizes come morning, but no one seemed to have suffered any critical injuries. Getting a couple of towels and ice from a bartender, Amelia went to the bleeding soldiers.

"Here." She handed the towel to the one with the bleeding nose. "Pinch your nostrils tightly together."

Using her fingers and nose, she demonstrated the proper technique. When he looked as if he might lose his balance, she shoved a bar stool toward him. "Sit down, pinch your nose like I showed you and don't attempt to move until I tell you it's okay."

He did as ordered.

Cole was checking Peyton's hand so Amelia turned to the soldier with the cut on his face. The slash wasn't so deep or jagged that it required an emergency room visit, not really, but he would need a few stitches for the area to properly heal with minimal scarring.

Which meant she or Cole, probably both, would be heading back to the ship to attend to the injured crew's needs.

So much for their night of sexual excess.

A bus carried the somber group back to the ship. Although Cole's gaze met hers a time or two, they'd not talked more than to give a rundown of casualties.

On the bus, he sat with the soldier needing stitches and Amelia had ended up in a seat with Peyton, a plastic bag filled with melting ice plopped over his swollen hand.

"That's going to smart in the morning. Why did you hit that man, anyway?"

Peyton shrugged, not saying more. He didn't need to. The blonde she'd seen coming out of his room earlier now sat with the soldier whose nose had been broken by Peyton's punch. She oohed and aahed over the soldier like a mother hen. Had they had a lovers' spat and the woman had used Peyton? Or had Peyton taken advantage? Who knew?

"You should reset his nose without any pain-killers."

Amelia frowned at her friend. "You're just saying that because he got the girl."

"He can have the girl," Peyton scoffed. "I got the only thing I wanted from her this afternoon."

Amelia winced at his crudeness. "Men are so gross."

"Yeah? That wasn't the impression I got when you were looking at my boy earlier."

"Your boy?"

"You know who I'm talking about."

"You really should be quiet before you end up in another brawl, Peyton," she warned.

He laughed. "Talking about Cole get you hot and bothered?"

Half grinning, she narrowed her eyes. "Makes me fighting mad. Be quiet before it's your nose having to be reset without painkillers."

Amelia set the nasal bone back into place as best she could, and left the corpsman in a bay with the blonde watching over him.

A radiology technician had shot a few films of Peyton's hand and he had a non-displaced fracture of his middle metacarpal. He wouldn't need surgery, but he'd be sore for several days.

Cole was in bay two with the soldier with the cut face. He set up a suture tray.

"Here we are again," she teased when she scrubbed her hands and took over the task for him. "I'll finish setting this up. You scrub and get gloved."

Sending her a wry smile, he did as she asked, explaining to the man sitting on the table what he planned to do in step-by-step detail.

"I'm going to disinfect the cut and surrounding skin first. Then I'll numb the area with anesthetic. Once you're numb, I'm going to use skin glue to close the laceration."

"Glue?" the man questioned.

"It's special glue made for closing certain types of cuts. When used appropriately there's less scarring. Plus, there won't be a need for you to return to have sutures removed."

The soldier shrugged. "Ain't never had to return to no doctor to have stitches took out. Been doing it myself since I was a kid."

"Had a lot of accidents over the years?"

"A few," the man admitted, grinning. "A few fights, too."

When he was ready, Amelia held the edges of the wound perfectly closed while Cole ran the glue applicator over the area, creating a purplish clear coat over the cut and sealing the wound.

When they were finished, it was too late to return to the hotel.

"Not exactly the way we envisioned spending the night together," she mused when they stood outside her bunkroom door.

"We're starting a pattern here that I can't say I like," he teased, bringing her hand to his mouth and kissing each of her fingers.

"Agreed." She laughed, feeling like a kid on her first date.

"I wish I could stay with you tonight, Amelia." He squeezed her hand, held on tightly. "I would if I could."

"Maybe next time." But even as she said it, she wanted him to tell her to hell with rules, to hell with everything but them. Which was crazy. She didn't really want him to tell her that. They had too much to lose to risk if they were caught.

"Maybe."

She looked up into his eyes, wondering if he'd at least sneak a good-night kiss. But he straightened to his full height, gave a shake of his head.

"Good night, Amelia."

"Good night, Cole." Reluctantly, she watched him turn and go, disappointed and hoping they hadn't missed their window of opportunity forever.

Okay, so maybe covertly blowing a kiss at Cole when no one was looking wasn't exactly playing fair, or even mature, but Amelia couldn't resist it.

Since Singapore they'd walked a fine line between flirting and keeping enough distance to not end both their careers. With every day that passed it was getting a little more difficult to recall the reasons why her career mattered so much more than being with Cole.

Giving a wry shake of his head, he slyly winked back from across the sick ward. The flash of desire she'd seen in his eyes, the possessiveness, caused happiness to blossom inside her. Pure, deep-down happiness.

The only blight on her happiness was the fact that, despite the looks, the stolen touches, the fact they both wanted each other desperately, they'd played by the rules and hadn't slept together yet. Somehow.

Which was good, because if they had done there would be hell to pay. They couldn't, she knew they couldn't, but, oh, how she wanted to.

God, she wanted him, wasn't sure how much more she could stand.

"Dr Stanley," she said in her most professional voice, flashing her most innocent expression, "could I see you in the medical office for a few moments, please? I need your advice on the last patient I saw."

Another spark shone in those blue eyes. This one caused her stomach to somersault.

"I'll be right there, Dr Stockton."

He was, closing the door behind him because he'd known. Known she needed to touch him.

"We can't do this," he told her even as he pulled her to him.

"I know." She smiled against his mouth, flattening her palms against his chest, relishing the strength she found there. "I just needed to touch you."

"Amelia," he groaned. "You're killing me."

"I'm sorry." But she wasn't, and they both knew it. "I just look at you and have…" she stared at his mouth, bunched the material of his shirt beneath her fingers "…needs."

His lips twitched. "What kind of needs?"

"This kind." She tilted her pelvis against him, circled her arms around his neck. "The kind that makes me not be able to think about anything but how much I want you, Cole Stanley. How I ache with wanting you."

Another groan escaped him just as his mouth covered hers.

Amelia kissed him back, loving how he felt, how he tasted, how he poured every ounce of his being into kissing her.

"I want you so badly, Amelia."

She knew he did. She could feel just how badly digging into her belly.

"This is torture," he continued. "Being so close, wanting you, knowing you want me, too, and yet not being able to make love to you."

She knew just what he meant and nodded. "Sweet torture."

"There's nothing sweet about how I feel about you."

"How do you feel about me?" She hadn't meant her question to be a serious one, just a teasing one meant to elicit more comments about his sexual frustration and desire for her. Cole's answer was serious, though.

"Haven't you figured that out by now, Amelia?" He cupped her face. "You're all I think about, all I want. You are my everything."

"You're my everything, too, Cole." Unable to look away from the truth in his eyes, Amelia stroked her fingers across his precious face, worrying that she was so head over heels for Cole she'd never resurface if the ship tipped. "Now shut up and kiss me again before I go see my next patient."

He burst out laughing, hugged her tightly to him. "God, I love you."

When he kissed her, Amelia almost believed that he really meant it.

CHAPTER TWELVE

HAVING decided she wasn't going to sleep no matter how long she lay in bed, Amelia snuck out of her room, careful not to wake Suzie.

She'd go to the medical office, catch up on reports, check her e-mails, anything other than just lie in bed longing to be with Cole.

The weeks had passed by much more quickly than she would have liked. Weeks she spent every possible moment with Cole. Talking, laughing, stealing kisses, touches, sharing long looks, sharing longing for much more. By sheer determination, they'd held on to enough willpower to not go beyond kissing and hot touches.

Very quickly their deployment was coming to an end and they'd return to the naval base in San Diego. She'd likely go to work at a mainland hospital or perhaps even at a combat support hospital overseas. Who knew where Cole would end up?

Odds weren't that they'd be anywhere near each other. Possibly not even on the same continent.

Then what? Would their romance come to an end? Would they be able to steal a few days together at the base and finally make love before being reassigned?

Make love.

Because whether she'd wanted to or not, she'd fallen for Cole.

Okay, so if she was honest with herself, she'd admit she'd never stopped wanting him. He listened to her, took her needs into consideration, sometimes knowing what she needed more than she'd known herself.

Amelia paused in the medical office doorway, startled to see Cole at the desk. What was he doing?

Glancing past him to the lit computer screen, she could see his e-mail account opened. Ah, checking e-mails. The same as what she'd come to do.

Instead, she'd found the man she wanted. For all time.

Which scared her. How could she want Cole when he'd eventually leave her? But what if he didn't? What if he really did love her? He'd said he did that one night. Okay, so it had only been that once and it had come out on a laugh, but that hadn't stopped her heart from going thumpity-thump-thump.

Just as it was going thumpity-thump-thump right now. She hadn't counted on seeing him again tonight, hadn't counted on getting to steal more kisses.

God, she wanted more than just stolen kisses. She wanted hours and hours of Cole all to herself, no rules, no recriminations, no fear of dishonorable discharge.

But stolen kisses would do. For now. She smiled, planning to walk up behind him and cover his eyes with her hands and have him guess who. Maybe she'd just lean over and kiss his nape.

She noted the tension emanating off him.

He studied the screen, his shoulders a bit slumped, the angle of his head low.

Had he gotten bad news? His mother was the only family he'd ever talked about and she'd died when he'd been a teen. Suddenly worried that something was wrong and wanting to comfort him if needed, she stepped into the room.

"Hey, stranger," she said, smiling to hide the nervous flutters in her belly. "What's up?"

He straightened in his chair, taking on a stiff appearance, as if guilty of some dastardly deed. "Everything's fine."

He sounded distant, almost as if he didn't want her there. Something was definitely wrong. She stepped farther into the room, closed the heavy door behind her and moved into his line of sight so she could see his face.

"You're sure?" She dropped into a chair near his.

He leaned back in his chair, glanced toward the computer screen. "Nothing's wrong. Just have a few things on my mind."

She understood. She had a few things on her mind, too, all of which centered on him and how they were running out of time together. Soon they'd have to give whatever was between them a name, make decisions about whether or not they were going to see each other once their stint on the USS *Benjamin Franklin* ended.

"You seemed tense when I came in."

He scowled. "There's not anything wrong, Amelia. Go back to your room."

Right. Because he always sounded angry with her, always didn't look her in the eyes when he talked to her, always told her to go to her room.

Enough was enough. There was definitely something wrong and she had a pretty good idea what it was.

"You're shutting me out, aren't you?"

His jaw worked in a slow rotation and he raked his fingers through his hair. "I'm not shutting you out. Let it go. I'm really not up for this tonight."

She put her hands on her hips, not willing to walk away. "It feels as if you're shutting me out, and I don't like it."

What was wrong with him? She'd never seen him like this. So ragged. So rough. So raw.

"God, you just don't know what you do to me, do you?"

Her breath catching, she met his gaze, held it. "Tell me."

He laughed ironically. "You make me not care about anything except you, Amelia, about making love to you and holding you and being able to sleep with you in my arms."

Okay, not a bad start to their conversation so why did he look so upset? Angry almost?

"I'd say turnabout was fair play, wouldn't you? I care a lot about you, too, Cole. I want those same things, think about them when I'm lying in my bunk, unable to sleep because I want you there with me." She met his gaze. "Like tonight when I ached so badly to be near you that I had to escape out of my room."

His throat worked, his eyes closed and his fingers gripped the chair arm so tightly they blanched white. "I'm hanging by a thread here, Amelia. You should go."

He was pushing her away. As much as that hurt, she wouldn't let him push her away without giving her an explanation. "Why would I go?"

The blueness of his eyes threatened to engulf her. She fought to keep from glancing away.

"I want things I shouldn't want on board this ship." His words came out as a low growl.

Proverbial lights clicked on above Amelia's head. "I should stay away from you because of the ship rules? That's why you're telling me to go away?"

Looking tired, frustrated, he nodded. "We've both worked too hard to risk our careers for a night of passion."

He was trying to put distance between them to protect their careers. Admirable. Logical. She took a deep breath. "How about six nights of passion? That's what we have left."

His brow arched. "You think that would be enough?"

"You tell me. What's the past six months been about?"

He shrugged. "You. Me. Sex."

"Sex?" She laughed, hoping she didn't sound hysterical. No longer able to sit, she paced across the small room. "We've not had sex."

"You think I haven't noticed that?"

She twisted to glare at him. "It's our lack of sex that's the problem?"

He ran his fingers through his hair again. "Our lack of sex is a huge problem."

"Then why did you get assigned to the USS *Benjamin Franklin*, Cole? If not to sleep with me? You don't have to chase a woman halfway around the world to get laid, Cole. We both know that. Explain so I can understand why you came here and turned my world upside down."

Apparently unable to sit a moment longer either, he stood, his back to the desk. A tic jumped at the corner of his mouth. "You know why."

"We both know you could have had me months ago if sex was all you wanted." She hated admitting that, but it was true. Just a few touches and all protests would have gone up in smoke. "Tell me why you're here, Cole."

He didn't say anything, just stood seeming to consider his next words. She couldn't stand the silence. Not a moment longer.

"What made you pull favors and board my ship, Cole? Why did you pursue me and torture me by being everywhere I was? Was this all some sick joke to you? Mess with Clara's little sister's head and heart?"

Red splashed across his cheeks and his fingers clenched at his sides. "Why I'm here has nothing to do with Clara, and you know it."

"Do I?" But staring straight into those beautiful blue eyes, she did know. Cole cared about her. More than just wanting to get her into bed.

Despite the way her heart hammered in her chest, she pressed forward.

"I think you care more about me than you're willing to admit, Cole. I think that's why you're here, why you got assigned to the USS *Benjamin Franklin*—to be near me."

"God, you're direct."

He hadn't denied her claim. Oh, God, he hadn't denied what she'd said. He did care. She clung to that belief, clung to a lifetime of being taught to go after what she wanted and not let anything stand in her way. "I'm a Stockton."

"And Stocktons always get what they want?"

Had he read her mind? Laughing wryly, she shook her head. "Apparently not. If we did, I'd have made love to you every day and night since Singapore."

His gaze shifted from hers, then back. The pulse at his throat jumped wildly. Had her words brought him back to the night at the hotel, before she'd fallen asleep? Back to the following night when they'd been headed to the hotel to consummate the fire burning through them?

"You don't know what you're saying." He raked all his fingers through his hair, glanced toward the computer screen as if the monitor would give him the answers he needed. "You're better off that we haven't done anything."

"Do you really believe that? I don't." She took a few steps toward him. "What I do believe is that for the rest of my life I'm going to regret not making love to you while we have the chance." In her heart, she knew it was true. If she didn't seize the moment, if she was a coward and didn't embrace her feelings for Cole, she would always have regrets.

"This is crazy." He laughed, as if by doing so he was giving validation to his claim.

"It is crazy…" insanely, wonderfully crazy "…but it's true. We have one week left, Cole. Less."

"And?"

"I want to spend the remaining time with you."

"We've been spending time together." At her pointed look, he winced. "Amelia—"

"Don't Amelia me," she interrupted. "I know what I want." She leaned forward, cupped his face. "Kiss me, Cole."

His jaw tightened beneath her fingertips. "I can't kiss you. Not tonight. Not when we're both at our wit's end with need."

Part of her registered that he spoke sense, that she should heed his warning. But another, bigger part feared never knowing what it felt like to make love to him.

"You kissed me up on the steel beach prior to Singapore," she reminded him. "And a hundred times since."

"I shouldn't have. Anything that happens between us needs to wait until we're in San Diego. No more kisses until then, Amelia."

He made sense, yet she wasn't satisfied with his answer. Wasn't satisfied period.

"Who knows what's going to happen once we dock? We'll be given new assignments and may never see each other again." She couldn't imagine her life without seeing him and knew in her heart that she'd find a way to him, would ensure their paths crossed in the future. "Kiss me, Cole." When he didn't move, she sighed in frustration. "Fine, you just stand there and I'll do all the work myself."

She placed her lips against his. She half expected him to push her away, to tell her she was crazy again.

He didn't.

"What are you doing to me?" he groaned. He kissed her back, pulled her to him and wrapped his arms around her, cradling her next to him. "Don't you realize I've fought to keep from doing this for fear of what it would lead to? That I won't risk your career? Won't risk hurting you in any way? We can't do this. I can't do this. I'm not strong enough to kiss you and walk away, Amelia. Not tonight. I want more."

His anguished words were all it took for love to burst free in her chest, leaving no doubt in her mind exactly how she felt about him, leaving no doubt about exactly what she wanted. God bless him, he thought pulling away from her was the right thing to do.

It wasn't. Not by a long shot. Not for her. Not for him.

"I don't want you to walk away, Cole. I want you. I feel as if I've always wanted you." She sank against him, opened her heart and soul to his plundering.

With an agonized moan, he did plunder.

With his mouth, his teeth, his hands. Amelia plundered right back. She kissed him with all her heart, all her soul, with all the passion she'd felt for him for years. She touched his face, the strong lines of his neck, his broad shoulders, the sinewy contours of his back.

He touched her, too. With his hands. With his mouth. His lips were everywhere. Her throat, her clavicle, her breasts.

"Cole," she breathed, pulling him back to her mouth. "Oh, please."

She didn't want him to stop, ever.

She ran her hands down the front of his uniform, moved her hips against his hard groin.

She wanted him so much.

She hadn't planned this. She hadn't come looking for him, but now that she was kissing Cole, she didn't want to stop.

Not ever.

She tugged his shirt from his pants and slid her fingers under the material to the sculpted flesh.

At her touch, his stomach sucked in, his breath catching. "Amelia," he said on a warning note.

A warning she had no intention of heeding.

Her hands caressed his body, moved low, cupping him through his pants as his mouth ravaged hers in a conquering of spirits.

It wasn't enough, didn't satisfy the ache within her, and she fumbled for his zipper.

He broke the kiss, his head lifting as he stared down at her, his eyes a hazy, drugged blue. "Amelia?"

Worried that he meant to push her away, she kissed him, pressing as close as she could. She didn't want him to stop. She wanted him to love her. To really love her.

The way she loved him.

With all her heart and all her soul.

That's what she wanted from him. Everything.

"You're sure this is what you want?" he asked, his voice husky and raw.

For answer she parted the fly of his pants, shucking the material down just enough to run her hands greedily over him. "What do you think?"

"I think you're driving me crazy."

"Good, then we'll go together." She freed him, stroking her fingers along the length of him. "Love me, Cole. Please love me right now."

Even if just for this moment. Even if just for this short glimpse of time.

They'd both lost their minds, Cole thought. That could be the only explanation for Amelia coming to him.

Yes, he'd known she wanted him, just as he'd always wanted her. But to hear her openly admit how much she wanted him made him feel as if he could propel the USS *Benjamin Franklin* with the energy bursting free within him.

Her talented fingers closed around him, circling where he throbbed. He bit back a groan of unmitigated pleasure. A groan of sheer torture.

They couldn't do this.

"I don't have a condom, Amelia. We have to stop." While he still had enough wits to stop. He was close, so close to being beyond reason, beyond anything except the scent of her arousal, the feel of her desire enveloping them both in its seductive cocoon.

Looking dazed, she smiled at him, making him want to smash his mouth against hers in a savage kiss that would leave them breathless and clamoring for more.

"I'm on the birth control shot to stop my menstrual cycle." She named the brand. "I won't get pregnant, and I'm clean, if that's what you're worried about."

Although that was something he should have been worried about with as many diseases as were out there, that hadn't been what concerned him most. What worried him was his need for a barrier between their bodies, between his heart and hers. He definitely needed that.

And more.

Because she made him lose reason and he needed to stop this while he still could.

She blinked at him, her eyes soft melted-chocolate pools full of desire, her lips swollen from his kisses, her fingers circling him, not too tight, not too loose. Just right. Oh, hell.

"Are you?"

Was he what? He couldn't think with her hands on him.

"Yes." He wasn't sure if his response was in answer to her question or to her hands gliding along him.

"Good," she breathed against his mouth, kissing him.

Cole hadn't lost control during sex since…he couldn't remember ever having lost control. But if someone had forced him to describe what happened next, he'd have to say he'd lost control.

He certainly wasn't been under control when he jerked her pants down or when he flipped her around and pressed her against the wall. Control was nowhere in the building when, his hands holding hers above her head, he thrust into her wet softness.

There had been nothing controlled about the way he drove into her, letting go of her hands to rest his on either side of her head. Or in the way his mouth lowered to the curve of her neck, kissing, sucking, knowing he was leaving a mark and, despite the fact he'd never been one to leave marks on women, reveling in the fact Amelia would bear a sign of their passion. He wanted her marked as his. Forever.

Idiot.

When she convulsed against him, whimpering in pleasure, he lost it. Lost everything. Vision. Speech. Hearing. His *mind.*

He definitely lost that.

Black bursts blinded him. The taste of her throat muted him. Her pleasured cries deafened him. The quivers of her orgasm stole all semblance of sanity and he thrust hard, coming deep inside her, dropping his forehead to the top of her head.

Sweat soaked his skin, heat burned his body.

Shame burned his soul.

He'd taken Amelia like an animal in heat.

She turned, faced him, looked up at him with a smile on her contented face. "Wow," she whispered, wrapping her arms around his neck and kissing the corner of his mouth. "Wow. Wow. Wow."

Wow was right. It had been good. Great. But what he'd just done to her hadn't been making love. That had been sex.

Good old-fashioned up-against-the-wall sex for the sake of sating physical need. Amelia deserved so much better. He'd wanted to give her better. How could he have treated her this way? She'd never believe she meant more to him than just sex now.

He'd just used her and she was smiling at him as if he'd done her the greatest favor.

What had he done?

Someone knocked on the door. The handle moved. Amelia's smile disappeared, her eyes widening as she scrambled to restore her clothing. Cole did his pants up in record speed, trying not to look guilty as the door swung open.

Oh, hell. Someone could have walked in on them. To have been caught like teens would have been a horrible humiliation without the added issues of what getting caught on board ship would mean.

How could he have compromised Amelia this way? What was wrong with him?

"Hey," Peyton said, stepping into the room, then pausing, his astute eyes taking in where Amelia still stood next to the wall, Cole stood a few feet away. The room probably smelled of sex.

The nurse anesthetist paused, clearly deducing what had been going on as his gaze met Cole's. *What the hell?* his expression asked. *Have you lost your mind? You can be sent packing for this.*

Cole kept his expression blank, battling with a flurry of emotions. He couldn't put Peyton in the position of having to keep secrets. Neither could he put Amelia in the position of being dishonorably discharged. Hell, he'd already put her in that position. Had put his roommate in that position. *Idiot.*

"I, uh, came to…" Peyton paused, eyed where Cole stepped protectively in front of Amelia. "Actually, I forgot something. I'll just go take care of that." He gave Cole a meaningful look. "You coming?"

Cole tried not to wince at the question. "In a minute."

Peyton frowned. "You sure? Someone might get the wrong impression with you two shut up in here."

Or get the right impression.

"I need to close my e-mail account," Cole said, gesturing toward the computer screen. "I was checking my e-mails."

"Right, checking your e-mails," Peyton said, his forehead wrinkling. "You want me to wait for you?"

His friend was trying to save his rear end, to say that he'd be right on the other side of the door so nothing else could happen, so they wouldn't risk their careers for a few moments of pleasure.

Too late.

He glanced toward Amelia, took in her disheveled appearance, her kiss-bruised lips, the contentment yet appeal in her eyes. She didn't want him to go, not until they'd talked.

Need for reassurance shone in her chocolate depths and stupidly he wanted nothing more than to wrap his arms around her and give her that reassurance. To lift her into his arms, carry her to somewhere private and spend the night loving every inch of her body. The right way rather than against a wall.

They had to stay away from each other or a repeat would happen.

He couldn't allow a repeat.

Not when doing so would lead to Amelia hating him yet again.

If they got caught it would mean her career. In a heated moment, she might be willing to take that risk, but she'd grow to hate him if he dishonored her, destroyed her military career.

And his career right along with hers.

Where Amelia was concerned, he had a short fuse. Short? Knowing what being inside her felt like, he didn't have a fuse. He looked at her and wanted to self-detonate.

Which meant for both their sakes he had to establish distance between them right here and now before they destroyed their careers. Before he destroyed the way she felt about him beyond repair.

"Yes," he told Peyton, moving to the computer, "I think you'd better wait."

"Cole." Amelia moved toward him, but he held up his hand. She cast a cautious glance toward Peyton who in turn raised his brow at Cole.

"You mentioned you'd forgotten something?" Cole reminded his friend, knowing Amelia wouldn't let him just slink away like the fool he was. No, she'd make him confront what happened. Better if that happened without an audience.

Peyton's lips pursed. "I'll be just down the hallway."

He nodded his understanding. Peyton intended to play big brother and make sure Cole played by the rules. Where had his friend been twenty minutes ago when he'd needed a rush of sanity?

When Peyton stepped out of the room, Amelia took another step toward him, but Cole held up his hand to ward her off. The pain in her eyes sucker punched him.

But he had to do the right thing by Amelia. Even if he hadn't moments ago. Especially because he hadn't moments ago.

They'd almost been caught. Had it been someone other than Peyton they'd be in trouble already. He cared too much for her to do that to her. He shouldn't have put her in this position to begin with. But he couldn't resist her if she actively pursued him. Not when she was everything he wanted wrapped into the most amazing package. Saying to hell with rules and spending the next few days buried inside her was too tempting.

He'd do whatever was necessary to protect her, even if he was protecting her from him, from herself.

Unable to meet her eyes, he turned.

He never should have come on board. Never should have risked hurting her. What would her father say?

John Stockton had made him promise he wouldn't do anything to put Amelia at risk.

If discovered, the Admiral would have Cole's head on a platter.

But that wasn't the worst of it. No, the worst would be living with the guilt of knowing he'd hurt someone so precious to him. Again.

"That was too close," he began. "You need to stay away from me, Amelia. This can never happen again. It shouldn't have happened. I didn't want it to happen. Not like this."

She stared at him as if he'd lost his mind. "You're the one who pulled strings to get commissioned on my ship. You chased me until I couldn't deny what I felt for you any longer. Stay away from you?" Glaring, she snorted. "Is that what you told my sister when you broke her heart, too?"

"I didn't break her heart."

"You broke off the engagement. Of course you broke her heart."

Cole took a deep breath and told Amelia what he should have told her two years ago, but had felt honor bound not to. "I wasn't the one who broke things off."

Face tingling with disbelief, stomach roiling with nausea at the regret stamped on Cole's face, Amelia bit into her lower lip. "Clara called off the wedding?"

His shoulders sagged. With relief? Hurt?

She knew about hurt. She'd just had the best sexual experience of her life end in disaster. Yes, it could have been worse. Peyton could have walked in on them five minutes earlier. They could be facing charges for not abiding by the rules.

"Yes, she did."

Oh, God. Clara had called off their wedding? Not Cole? Amelia's brain tried to wrap around his words, around the implications, and couldn't.

"Why would she do that? She was devastated. She couldn't have been the one to call things off." Tears stung her eyes, but she'd die before she'd let a single drop fall. Dear sweet heaven. Clara broke things off with Cole? *Why would any sane woman not want to marry him?*

She must have seen their kiss. Must have been hurt by such a betrayal. Amelia's eyes stung. Why hadn't her sister said anything? Two years and Clara had never spoken of what she'd seen, had given Cole a glowing recommendation just a few weeks ago. Had her sister been giving her permission to love Cole?

"After you and I kissed," Cole began, "I went to find her, planning to confess, but she called off the wedding before I could say anything."

"Why didn't you say anything?" She wanted to hit him, hard. He hadn't been the one to break things off. Clara had. And he'd left. Left! "You asked me to wait for you and then you left me." She pushed against his chest, anger and hurt competing in her belly. "Why would you do that?"

"Clara asked me to leave."

He said it so matter-of-factly that she stared incredulously at him. "You couldn't have taken the time to talk to me? To tell me the truth?"

"No."

She let his answer digest. "What about when you came to my dorm? Why didn't you tell me then? If I'd known Clara had been the one to break things off..."

"What would knowing have changed, Amelia? Would you have welcomed me that night?"

Would she have? Probably not on the night he'd come to her dorm. She'd been too hurt by that point. "Had you come to me on the night of the rehearsal, had you told me everything then, I would have welcomed you."

"I couldn't tell you. Clara didn't want your father to know the truth." He glanced away, paused, then added, "For any of you to know the truth."

Amelia tried to ignore the fact that he'd let Clara's wants come between them, tried to understand, but she wasn't sure she did. "Why are you telling me now?"

"Clara released me from my promise."

Clara released him… Amelia's gaze landed on the computer screen, registered who the e-mail pulled up was from. A fist gripped her trachea and refused to let go. "You've been e-mailing my sister?"

Was that guilt on his face? Oh, she couldn't breathe, couldn't think, couldn't keep her hands from shaking.

"I hadn't talked to her in months, but she e-mailed me after port call in Singapore. We've been in contact since."

Cole hadn't left her sister. Cole hadn't called off his wedding. Clara had. Her brain cells fired in a million different directions. "Why did you just make love to me?"

"That wasn't making love, Amelia. That was sex, and it shouldn't have happened. Not with so much at stake."

Not making love. Sex. Shouldn't have happened. Her vision blurred. "Are you in love with my sister?"

He rubbed his hands across his face, looked torn, then his gaze lifted to hers and he took a deep breath. "I've always loved Clara. I always will love her, but that isn't what this is about, and you know it. This is about you and me and what's between us."

Amelia couldn't take any more, couldn't deal with all the emotions barreling through her. She'd given her heart to Cole, accepted that she loved him, had given her body to him freely, and he'd used her.

She felt dirty. Horribly, horribly dirty. Used. She was stupid. Very, very stupid. She'd been nothing more than an itch Cole had wanted to scratch. Part of her mind acknowledged that didn't make sense, that he'd gone to too much trouble for just sex, but heartache blinded her to reason.

She called him every vile name she could think of, balling her hands into fists and pounding them against his chest.

Rather than stop her, he took her abuse, letting her vent her anger until she realized she was accomplishing nothing. Her halfhearted hits didn't hurt Cole. Her rashly flung insults didn't pierce his cold heart. He didn't care. He'd gotten what he'd wanted from her.

"Clara dumped you and your damaged male pride demanded retribution. You knew how I felt about you and you used me, didn't you, Cole? Used me to get back at my sister."

He didn't deny her claim and great pain sliced through her, reminding her of all the reasons she'd vowed never to love in the first place.

CHAPTER THIRTEEN

THE USS *Benjamin Franklin* had come into home port in San Diego early that morning.

While taking inventory of the ship's remaining medical supplies, Amelia had mixed feelings on her first deployment coming to an end.

She'd barely seen Cole over the past week. He'd come to the office once, watched her, started to say something, then shaken his head and left. She'd wanted to follow him, to beg him to tell her whatever he'd been about to say, but what good would begging do?

Besides, she wouldn't beg for any man's love.

She couldn't even ask him to help out around the sick ward. Sick call had been slow. The fact they'd soon be home seemed to raise the crews' spirits and few needed their services.

Although she would have welcomed being busy to keep her thoughts from wandering, she also admitted she hadn't been thinking clearly. Probably from lack of sleep and a broken heart.

Why had she let Cole in? Why had she trusted him?

Wasn't that the crux of the matter? Even after the nasty ending to their lovemaking—she refused to call it sex despite him doing so—she didn't regret having made love with Cole, only its less-than-ideal conclusion.

Not that she'd expected claims of undying love and a proposal. Not from Cole.

Which left her wondering what exactly she had expected?

But even as she thought the question, she knew the answer.

She had expected his love.

Because she'd believed he loved her. That's why she hadn't hesitated to make love with him. That as crazy as it had been, he'd fallen in love with her years ago and had come to win her heart.

He'd had her heart from the beginning.

She hadn't known that's what she'd been feeling for him, but she hadn't been able to forget him, hadn't been able to not want him, no matter how much she'd tried.

Which put a dark and gloomy cloud over her future.

If she hadn't been able to forget Cole before, how was she supposed to move on with her life now, after what they'd shared over the past six months?

"You about done?" Suzie asked, crossing to where Amelia worked.

"About."

"I've finished everything I've got to do and plan to go ashore." Suzie eyed her worriedly, placed her hand on Amelia's arm and gave a gentle squeeze. "Call me tonight?"

Amelia hugged her friend goodbye. Who knew when they'd next be assigned to work together, if ever?

"You're going to your parents'?"

A sinking feeling settled into Amelia's stomach. How would she hide her heartache from her parents? They'd take one look at her and demand to know what was wrong.

"I am."

Plus, seeing her parents, being in their home, would envelop her with thoughts of her sister. Of Cole.

She loved him. Right or wrong. Smart or stupid. She loved him.

Who did Cole love? He'd cared enough for Clara to ask her to marry him and spend her life with him. He'd cared enough to keep her secret for two years.

He'd just *used her* for sex. Or to get back at Clara. Or whatever it was he'd done.

She should hate him.

So why didn't she?

It came to her in a blinding flash. Because she didn't believe him.

She didn't believe him.

Because he'd not been telling her the truth when he'd said they'd just had sex.

What they shared could never be just sex.

Why hadn't she realized at the time?

Because his words had been poison-tipped arrows and had hit their intended target—her faith in him. But why? Why would he lie to her about how he felt? Because of Clara? Because of his promise to her? She'd confronted her sister and heard the whole story, that Clara had asked Cole not to say anything, wanting freedom and not wanting to face her family's disappointment in her not marrying Cole since they all loved him so much. Clara had feared her father would march her down the aisle and tell her she'd thank him later.

Cole had gone along with her sister's wishes and left, left Amelia when he'd asked *her* to wait for him. Why? If he'd really cared, would he have agreed to just walk away?

Perhaps. If he'd been afraid of his feelings.

Perhaps. If he wasn't sure of how Amelia felt about him, if he wasn't sure if she could ever get past the fact that he'd once been engaged to her sister, if he'd felt as confused as she had.

"What?" Suzie asked, eyeing her oddly. "What?"

"I..." She shook her head, wiped her hands down her pants. "I've got to find Cole."

She needed to ask him why he'd come back that night to her dorm. To ask why he'd arranged his assignment on the USS *Benjamin Franklin*. To ask what he felt for her.

But she knew.

Cole cared for her. He had to. He wouldn't have gone to so much trouble otherwise. Did he love her? Hope bloomed deep in her soul. He just might.

Suzie winced. "That's not going to be as easy as you might think."

"Why not?" *Please, don't let him have already left the ship. Please, no.*

Please, don't let him have left me again.

Suzie hesitated, her olive skin wrinkling into a grimace. "He said his goodbyes this morning and was leaving immediately afterwards."

"Said his goodbyes?"

"He came by the dental office." Suzie looked stricken. "He didn't say goodbye to you? Really? He left without saying a word? After, well, everything?"

Amelia's heart shattered. She closed her eyes to hold the millions of pieces inside. Although Suzie didn't know about earlier in the week, she knew some of what had happened between her and Cole.

"Apparently so." Cole had left her. Again. Knowing they might never see each other, that she'd never forgive him for leaving her a second time, he'd left. If he'd really loved her, could he have done that? Could he really have just walked away without seeing her one last time?

Of course he could. Obviously without even a backward glance.

Very simply, she'd been mistaken. Cole hadn't loved her. Maybe he had feelings for her, but not enough. Not nearly enough.

She'd been such a naïve, love-sick fool.

"Oh, honey, I'm so sorry." Suzie wrapped her in another hug. "How could he just leave without saying goodbye? I can't believe he'd do that. I really thought he cared about you."

"Me, too." But they'd both been wrong because if Cole cared he wouldn't have left. Not without saying goodbye. Not knowing how that would devastate her and flash her back to the past.

Back to the first time he'd left her with a broken heart.

"Maybe he had his reasons," Suzie offered.

"I'm sure he did." But none that Amelia would ever want to hear. If she had to cut her heart from her chest, she was finished with Cole Stanley.

Finding Cole and Peyton's room empty didn't surprise her, only confirmed what she hadn't really wanted to believe.

Cole had left her without a word.

* * *

Amelia's parents lived a few miles outside the base. Amelia had been surprised her father hadn't come to see her off the ship. Her mother had picked her up from the naval port, claiming the need to stop by the grocery store prior to going home to pick up something for the Admiral, who'd been indisposed at home.

Amelia had wanted to protest, but had decided to be grateful that her mother seemed too distracted to notice her daughter's broken heart. She wanted to be home and curl up in the comfort of the familiar and pretend everything was going to be okay even when she felt as if things would never be okay again.

She knew she was being overly dramatic, that time healed all wounds. Even ones the size Cole had left in her chest. But right now it was hard to remember that.

"Amelia?"

She glanced toward her mother. The Californian sunshine shone in through the car windows as her mother drove towards the house, casting a glare across Sarah Stockton's face.

"I asked you what was wrong. You don't seem yourself."

Okay, so maybe her mother wasn't that distracted after all.

"It's good to be back on land, that's all." No way did she want to admit to her mother that she'd fallen in love with a man her family would think her crazy for trusting. After all, they had loved and welcomed him up to the point he'd walked away from the eldest Stockton daughter. He'd abandoned them all.

And now he'd abandoned Amelia a second time.

"You're sure? You look distraught."

Amelia nodded, asked about the hospital where her mother worked. Her mother should have retired years ago, but refused to hang up her nurse's cap, saying that as long as there was breath in her body she'd care for the ill.

Amelia was pretty sure her father felt exactly the same way, although apparently he'd gotten more and more wrapped up in military politics over the past few years and spent more and more time in D.C.

"I half expect him to announce we'll be moving, but he may be in for a surprise."

Startled, Amelia glanced toward her mother. "What do you mean?"

"I like San Diego and am tired of being uprooted. I plan to stay here regardless of his career plans."

"You're kidding!" Her mother never balked her father's wishes. Never in the history of mankind. Well, at least never that Amelia was aware of.

"No, dear, I'm not kidding." She reached across the bucket seat, patted Amelia on the knee. "No worries, darling. John won't take a job in Washington if it means leaving me behind."

"He won't?"

"Of course not, dear." Her mother smiled a knowing smile. "He'd miss me too much to ever do that. Besides, I have my ways of getting him to make the right decisions. Of course…" she winked "…he always thinks he's the one who came up with the right decision and I love him too much to ever point out otherwise."

With that, her mother considered the conversation over and returned her attention to the San Diego traffic.

Amelia stared in awe at the petite dynamo in the driver's seat. All these years she'd thought her mother had simply gone along with her father's wishes. In that moment, she'd seen her mother as the neck steering the head in whatever direction she wanted the Stockton family to go.

"Don't take this the wrong way, because there's no man I admire more, but I always thought Daddy a bit of a dictator."

Her mother laughed. "Are you kidding? Your father is a big pussycat."

"Only you would call Admiral John Stockton a pussycat."

Her mother blushed then laughed a sparkly little laugh that spoke of years of love. "You might be right on that, but he loves you children with all his heart. Perhaps he was a bit stern, but he wanted you to grow into strong individuals. Each of you has."

For the rest of the drive, Amelia was forced to re-evaluate every assumption she'd ever made about her parents' marriage. Sure, she'd never doubted her parents' love for each other, but she'd always believed her mother the victim of loving a man who was too militant to fully express that love.

Obviously her mother didn't see it that way. Her mother felt quite loved.

She was still marveling at her misconceptions when they arrived at a typical Californian-style home with stucco walls and a red tile roof. A white sedan sat in the driveway, as did her father's Humvee, his pride and joy.

A few days home would do her good. Amelia loved her family and missed the closeness her siblings and she had shared while growing up. All for one and one for all.

Her mother parked the car, turned off the ignition, jumped out and was grabbing bags of groceries from the backseat before Amelia finished soaking in the fact that she was home. At least, the closest thing she had to home.

If Amelia thought learning her mother led the family just as much as the Admiral did had surprised her, the sight that greeted her when she stepped onto her parents' patio stole ten years of her life.

Her father stood at a grill, flipping burgers, chatting to a man sitting on a wrought-iron swing a few meters away.

The most infuriating, frustrating, unbelievable man Amelia had ever met.

Cole.

Her gaze went back to her father. Why wasn't he screaming at Cole? Threatening to skewer him with a cooking utensil? Instead, he was chatting with him as if they were old buds. Where was the *Twilight Zone* music? Or maybe some camera crew was going to jump out and tell her she was on some hoax show? That she'd been had?

There had to be something, because everything about the scene was wrong.

So wrong she thought she might be physically ill.

Unless Cole had told the Admiral the truth about his and Clara's canceled wedding plans.

Was he seeking her father's forgiveness?

Had he known she was coming to her parents'?

Her legs wobbled and she grabbed hold of the frame of the sliding glass doors.

"Amelia?" Her father spotted her. "Don't stand there at attention, girl. Get over here and grab a plate. The burgers are cooked."

Would her legs even hold her up? Could she even put one foot in front of the other?

What was Cole doing at her parents' house?

Could she pretend nothing had happened between them for her parents' sake?

"Hello, Admiral." Just as she'd been doing since she'd been old enough to walk, she saluted the distinguished-looking silver-haired man who, even surprisingly wearing a kiss the cook apron, could never be mistaken for anyone other than a man who commanded authority.

He saluted her back. "Hand me that plate, then tell me all about your deployment, Lieutenant."

She couldn't keep her gaze from going to Cole. "Perhaps you've already heard?"

Her father's expression didn't change. Not that she'd expected it to. None of the Stockton four could ever get so much as an eyebrow rise out of their father. Not that they'd done much to push their father's buttons. High IQs ran in the family and they hadn't wanted to die at a young and tender age.

But even under John Stockton's eagle eye her brain cells all migrated toward Cole.

His blue gaze had settled onto her and she felt heat burning into her skin. He wore civilian clothes. A pair of khaki shorts and a T-shirt that showed off the shape of his chest and narrow waist. How dared he be in her parents' backyard looking so comfortable? So gorgeous? So...like he belonged?

Why hadn't she taken time to stop by the bathroom and wash her face? *Wait a minute.* What she looked like didn't matter. He had left her. Again.

"I asked you to tell me." Her father's shrewd eyes held hers. "Unless there's a reason you'd rather not?"

Her face flushed with embarrassment. Did he know what had transpired between her and Cole? She'd swear her father could see right through her, could read her mind. Hadn't he always been able to?

"No reason, sir," she said all the same, wondering if he'd call her on it.

He didn't, just flipped the burgers one by one onto the plate she held. "Good. Now tell me."

"The deployment was uneventful, sir."

"Uneventful?"

"I worked, learned a lot, got to visit Singapore and made new friends, but you already know all that, sir." *Oh, and I slept with my sister's ex-fiancé who is sitting in your backyard swing listening to every word I say. A man I happen to love and I'm not sure why he is here. Perhaps he came by to give me the opportunity to throttle him for once again breaking my heart?*

"Singapore? I was on board *Kitty Hawk* when she made port call there when the port first opened. But you already know that." Her father's eyes narrowed and again she was struck with the idea that he knew every single thing that had happened between her and Cole. But that was impossible. Cole wouldn't have told her father.

If Cole had, he wouldn't be breathing.

To further confound her, her father took the burger plate from her. "I'm going to take these in to your mother."

He was leaving her outside with Cole? Alone? Had he gone mad?

"I'll go with you."

He frowned. Being frowned at by her father was like being told you'd never eat ice cream again. A very bad thing.

"Or I could stay out here, sir," she amended, barely able to breathe. What was going on? Why had her father just maneuvered her into forced time alone with Cole?

"Good idea, Lieutenant." He nodded, motioning toward where Cole sat in the swing, observing their conversation. "For the record, I said yes."

Yes to what? she wanted to ask, but her father had already disappeared into the house, closing the sliding glass door, and if she didn't know better she'd swear she heard the sound of the lock clicking.

No way would her father, the great Admiral John Stockton, have just locked his middle daughter out of the house with a man her family despised. Or, at least, they had. Apparently things had changed.

"Are you going to say hello?"

Her gaze cut to where Cole had risen from the swing. "Oh, you mean the way you said goodbye?"

Oops. She hadn't meant to say that. She'd meant to be calm, cool and collected. Had meant to act as if it didn't matter that she loved him, had believed he loved her, and he'd walked away from her.

"There was something I needed to do first."

"Something you needed to do before saying goodbye to me? Gee, I see a pattern here."

He nodded, walked toward her. "There were a lot of things that needed to be settled prior to us saying goodbye, Amelia. Surely you realize that."

"Okay, now that we've established that ground-break-ing news..." she rolled her eyes, turned away from him because she couldn't bear looking at him a moment longer "...maybe you can tell me something I don't know."

"I love you."

Sure she'd heard wrong, Amelia spun toward him. "What did you say?"

Inhaling a deep breath, he raked his fingers through his hair, and held her gaze. "I love you, Amelia. That's something I'm not sure you know, although you should."

Every cell in her body turned into jumping beans on speed, threatening to burst free and causing complete chaos throughout her nervous system.

"I don't understand." Probably because her brain had turned to short-circuited mush. For a short while she'd believed he cared for her, but even then she hadn't dared to believe he really loved her. She'd hoped, but she'd never quite let herself believe his feelings ran that deep.

"I've been in love with you for years. I'm not sure the exact moment the way I felt about you changed, just that it did." Cole held his breath, watching every play of emotion cross Amelia's beautiful face. She didn't believe him.

Not that he blamed her. Why should she trust a man who she believed had abandoned her twice?

"You're saying you're in love with me?" She sounded ready to burst into laughter.

"I am. I do." He glanced around the backyard, hated it that they had no real privacy, knowing he had to tell her everything, that it was now or never. "Not quite seven months ago, I went to your father and asked for his permission to date you."

Her mouth dropped, her eyes staring at him incredulously. "You did what?"

"I told him that I deeply regretted what happened between Clara and me, but that I couldn't marry your sister. Not when it was you who took my breath away."

Had her eyes grown even wider? "You told him that?"

"And much more," he admitted. "Your father didn't trust me. But he's a fair man, and he did trust you. He arranged for me to be assigned to the USS *Benjamin Franklin*. What happened from there was up to us."

"My father helped you get assigned to my ship?" She picked up the metal spatula, waved it at him.

Hoping she wasn't planning to swat him, Cole nodded. When the Admiral had offered, he'd been floored, but he hadn't had to be asked twice. He'd jumped at the opportunity to spend six months with Amelia, to have six months to work through the feelings they'd once had for each other, that he'd still had for her.

"Let me get this straight. My father helped you sleep with me?"

Cole winced at Amelia's outrage. "That's not how I'd put it."

"How would you put it?" She pointed the tip of the spatula at him. "You were the one who said we were only about sex."

"You and I were never just about sex." He reached for the spatula, but she shook her head, waving the tool menacingly at him. Sighing, he dropped his hands to his sides, wanting to touch her, take her into his arms and tell her all the things in his heart. Could she ever forgive him? "I have never felt about any woman the way I feel about you, Amelia."

Her eyes darkened, closed, reopened with uncertainty in their shiny depths. "Once upon a time you could say the same thing about my sister."

"Clara and I were about friendship and mutual understanding of each other. We got along so well I just assumed the natural next step was marriage because I felt so comfortable with her."

She lowered the grilling tool. "Am I comfortable, too, Cole?"

"Comfortable?" He had to laugh at her question. "Amelia, you are more like a hot poker to my backside."

"Gee, thanks."

"I meant that in the nicest possible way."

"Because hot pokers to backsides have a nice way."

Her sarcasm wasn't lost on him, and he struggled to explain. "You push me to be more, to take chances, to see things in a different light. You make me want to move forward and walk planks that drop off into unknown seas just to experience them with you."

"I don't push you."

"Perhaps you don't realize the effect you have on me, the effect you've always had, but let me assure you, you have impacted my life in untold ways."

"Because I'm Clara's little sister?"

"Because you are you, Amelia Earhart Stockton, the woman I love with all my heart. Let me love you."

Dared Amelia believe him? God, she wanted to. So badly. But to what avail? She could never trust him.

Not with her heart. She'd constantly be waiting for the next time he'd leave and wasn't sure she could endure the pain of him abandoning her again.

"You're too late."

He winced, as if she'd struck him with the spatula she held. She dropped the tool onto the grill's side table.

"If you'd said something on the ship, perhaps I could believe you. Perhaps things could have worked. As is, there is too much bad blood between us, Cole."

"Because of Clara?"

"Because of what happened between us," she insisted. "Because of the fact you shut me out, ripped my heart to shreds on the night we made love when you insisted it was just sex, that all we were was sex."

"I had to protect you."

"Protect me? You broke my heart, Cole."

"If I hadn't put space between us, we'd have made love again."

"Had sex, and, yes, you're probably right, we probably would have."

"We might have been caught. I couldn't let you risk your career that way. Not for me. Not when you'd hate me if I cost you your career."

"I loved you, Cole."

"And now you don't?"

She bit her lip, not wanting to answer him.

"Because, like someone once said to me, I don't believe you."

"Don't toss my words back at me. This isn't a game, Cole."

"No, it's not. It's the story of the rest of our life."

Our life. As in singular. He said the words as if they had a life together, as one. They didn't. Did they?

"How can you be sure?" she demanded, tiring of the toll his words were taking on her heart.

He took her hand into his, placed her palm flat over his heart. "That's how I know."

His heart pounded against her palm, beating strong and fast. For her.

"I want to believe you, Cole. I really do."

"I know you do, sweetheart." He put his finger on her chin, tilted her face upwards to his. "Just give me the rest of your life to prove how much I love you."

The rest of her life. What was he saying?

"I asked your father for permission to date you, Amelia. That was six months ago. Earlier today I asked his permission to ask you to be my wife, to do everything within my means to convince you to spend the rest of your life letting me love and take care of you."

Amelia's vision blurred and she was pretty sure she swayed and that Cole caught her. Either way, his arms wrapped around her, holding her close, keeping her from collapsing onto the concrete patio.

"What did he say?" she croaked, wondering why she wasn't telling Cole there was no way she'd marry him. She didn't want to get married, had never wanted to get married. Except, on the weekend of Clara's wedding, she had wished it was her who'd been going to walk down the aisle to Cole, had wished it was her who'd be spending two weeks with him in a honeymoon suite.

Her father's parting words hit her.

"He said yes," she gasped.

"He said yes," Cole agreed. "But the more important question, Amelia, is what do you say?"

Holding her hand, Cole sank to one knee.

Amelia started shaking her head. "Don't do this, Cole. Please, don't."

He hesitated only a second then, looking up into her eyes, asked her to marry him. "Be my wife, Amelia. My life partner, friend and lover. Be the best part of me and let me spend all my days showing you how much I adore you."

"You adore me?" A crazy question at this point, but his word choice caught her off guard, seemed out of place for a man like Cole.

"I adore you, love you, want you." He squeezed her hand and she realized his trembled. "I need you, Amelia. For two years, I floundered, trying to convince myself I didn't, but I do. I need to know you're there, waiting for me, loving me in return. Maybe asking you to marry me is rushing things, but we've been apart too long already. I know how I feel about you and I know you're what I want for the rest of my life."

"Cole," she began, knowing she had to say no. She didn't want to get married. She didn't want to constantly worry that he'd leave her again someday. She needed her freedom.

But Cole's love was what freed her, gave her the power to be anything she wanted to be. And what she wanted to be more than anything else was his.

Because he was here, loved her, made her whole in a way no one else ever could. Because she'd rather be left by him a thousand times than live a single day without him. Because what she saw in his eyes assured her he'd never leave her, that for the rest of their lives he'd be by her side.

"I love you, Cole."

He pulled her hand to his face, rubbing the back of her fingers across his cheek. "You'll marry me? You trust me?"

Amelia didn't have to think about her answer. She dropped to her knees, cupped Cole's face and nodded. "With all my heart."

EPILOGUE

COLE smiled at the woman lying in his arms, knowing without doubt he was the happiest man alive.

"What are you thinking about?" Amelia asked, trailing her fingers along his throat, blasting him with a fresh shot of desire.

"What a lucky man your husband is."

"He is, isn't he?" Her lips curved in a delicious, contented smile. She stretched out beside him, contentment and happiness bright in her eyes. "Today was perfect, wasn't it?"

He rose, propping himself on his elbow to look at his wife. She lay against the cream-colored sheet of the San Diego hotel room they'd arranged for their wedding night. In the morning they'd fly out to New Zealand for two weeks of backpacking, kayaking, and just enjoying nature and each other. Not everyone's ideal honeymoon, but when they'd discussed places they wanted to go, exploring New Zealand had topped both of their lists.

"Not anywhere near as perfect as tonight will be," Cole promised. Their wedding had been perfect, but nothing compared to when the world receded and it was just the two of them, together, in love. That was perfection.

"Oh, really?" Amelia's brow arched provocatively, her eyes sparking with challenge. Damn, the woman was going to kill him. But what a way to go. "Because if you expect tonight to top my wedding today, you have your work cut out for you."

"A little hard work never scared me." He bent, nuzzled her neck, teased the lobe of her ear with the tip of his tongue. "I'm up to the challenge."

And would enjoy every moment of meeting that challenge.

"I don't know." She shifted on the bed, arching her naked body beneath the sheet, giving him better access to her throat. "Having the entire Stockton clan home is going to be pretty tough to top."

Topping that would never be an easy feat, but Cole wasn't worried. He had access to Top Secret insider information, such as the sensitive spot at Amelia's nape and the way she liked him to look into her eyes when they made love.

He couldn't get enough of her. The way she'd looked at him when their eyes had met when she'd stepped out of her parents' house to walk between the rows of guests in her parents' backyard. That look had taken his breath away.

Amelia had looked at him as if he was her entire world and Cole knew he'd been looking back at her exactly the same way. She was, and he'd take on the world to keep her safe, to keep her his, to love her all his days.

He breathed in her scent, loving her, wanting her despite them having made love not so long before, knowing she was his forever.

One breath at a time, one kiss at a time, one touch at a time, Cole put everything Amelia into his memory, discovering every nuance of her body, noting every delightful response, relishing her words of pleasure, her cries for more.

Rolling on top of her, Cole clasped their hands, and smiled down at his wife. "I hope you're enjoying your wedding night so far, Mrs. Stanley."

Amelia stared up at her husband, breathless with need. Did he have any idea what he did to her? How much she wanted and needed him? How happy he made her?

Today truly had been perfect. The California sunshine had been glorious. Her parents' backyard had been transformed into a lush wedding paradise complete with white chairs, white flowers trimmed with navy ribbon, a white lattice backdrop with ribbon and flowers entwined. Having wanted to keep the wedding small, they'd only had about thirty guests, but all the right people had been able to attend. Clara had been her maid of honor. Josie and Suzie bridesmaids. Robert had been Cole's best man, with Peyton and a schoolfriend of Cole's serving as groomsmen. Sarah Stockton had been a gorgeous mother of the bride and the Admiral had looked handsome decked out in his uniform as he'd given Amelia to Cole.

And Cole. No man had ever looked more gorgeous in his uniform. No man had ever given so much to a woman.

Not hiding the emotion rushing through her, Amelia held Cole's gaze, loving the feel of his body over hers, loving the adoration in his eyes.

"Just so long as you're mine…" she squeezed his hands, enthralled by the strength of his fingers laced with hers, of the strength in everything about this wonderful man "…every night is perfect, Cole."

"I'm always yours, Amelia. My heart, my love, all that I am I give to you and you alone. Forever."

And as he kissed her, made love to her, Amelia knew Cole's promise was true. Her husband was a man of his word.

Medical Romance™

THE MOST MAGICAL GIFT OF ALL
by Fiona Lowe

Dr Jack Armitage's trip is delayed when an unexpected gift is left on his doorstep…a little girl! His replacement Dr Sophie Norman didn't expect to be a stand-in mummy—but whilst ensuring this little girl has a magical Christmas to remember they find the most magical gift of all: a family.

CHRISTMAS MIRACLE: A FAMILY
by Dianne Drake

In the village of White Elk, Dr James Galbraith needs help from his ex, Nurse Fallon O'Gara. Fallon is only too happy to give it, but she's hiding a heartbreaking secret. As the snow flutters down Fallon finds safety in James's arms, and is finally ready to become mother and wife.

On sale from 5th November 2010
Don't miss out!

WE'VE GOT TWO MORE BEAUTIFUL
ROMANCES TO ENJOY THIS CHRISTMAS FROM

SARAH MORGAN

THE TWELVE NIGHTS OF CHRISTMAS

Mills & Boon® Modern™

This Christmas wicked
Rio Zacarelli cannot resist
innocent chambermaid Evie
Anderson! They have twelve
nights of endless pleasure,
but will it last once the
decorations come down?

On sale 15th October 2010

DR ZINETTI'S SNOWKISSED BRIDE

Mills & Boon® Medical™

Meg thought heartbreaker Dr Dino
Zinetti would never look twice at a
scruffy tomboy like her—but she's got
under Dino's skin! And this Christmas
it looks like he'll receive his very own
crash-course in love…

Enjoy double the romance! Part of
a 2-in-1 with Lynne Marshall's
THE CHRISTMAS BABY BUMP

On sale 5th November 2010

*Make sure you don't miss
out on the most romantic
stories of the season!*

MILLS & BOON®

are proud to present our...

Book of the Month

Proud Rancher, Precious Bundle
by Donna Alward
from Mills & Boon® Cherish™

Wyatt and Elli have already had a run-in. But when a
baby is left on his doorstep, Wyatt needs help.
Will romance between them flare as they
care for baby Darcy?

Mills & Boon® Cherish™
Available 1st October

Something to say about our Book of the Month?
Tell us what you think!

millsandboon.co.uk/community
facebook.com/romancehq
twitter.com/millsandboonuk

2 FREE BOOKS
AND A SURPRISE GIFT

We would like to take this opportunity to thank you for reading this
Mills & Boon® book by offering you the chance to take TWO more
specially selected books from the Medical™ series absolutely FREE!
We're also making this offer to introduce you to the benefits of the
Mills & Boon® Book Club™—

- **FREE home delivery**
- **FREE gifts and competitions**
- **FREE monthly Newsletter**
- **Exclusive Mills & Boon Book Club offers**
- **Books available before they're in the shops**

Accepting these FREE books and gift places you under no obligation to buy, you may cancel at any time, even after receiving your free
books. Simply complete your details below and return the entire page
to the address below. You don't even need a stamp!

YES Please send me 2 free Medical books and a surprise gift. I
understand that unless you hear from me, I will receive 5 superb new
stories every month including two 2-in-1 books priced at £5.30
each and a single book priced at £3.30, postage and packing free. I
am under no obligation to purchase any books and may cancel my
subscription at any time. The free books and gift will be mine to keep
in any case.

Ms/Mrs/Miss/Mr ———————— Initials ————————

Surname ————————————————————————
Address ————————————————————————

———————————————————— Postcode ————————
E-mail ————————————————————————

Send this whole page to: Mills & Boon Book Club, Free Book Offer,
FREEPOST NAT 10298, Richmond, TW9 1BR